C000224720

THE WIZARDRY OF JEWISH WOMEN

ENCHANTED AUSTRALIA BOOK 2

GILLIAN POLACK

Copyright (C) 2021 Gillian Polack

Layout design and Copyright (C) 2021 by Next Chapter

Published 2021 by Next Chapter

Edited by Stephen Ormsby

Cover art by CoverMint

Mass Market Paperback Edition

This book is a work of fiction. Names, characters, places, and incidents are the product of the author's imagination or are used fictitiously. Any resemblance to actual events, locales, or persons, living or dead, is purely coincidental.

All rights reserved. No part of this book may be reproduced or transmitted in any form or by any means, electronic or mechanical, including photocopying, recording, or by any information storage and retrieval system, without the author's permission.

*This book is dedicated to the National Council of Jewish
Women of Australia and to the late Helen Leonard. They
opened many worlds to me.
Some of those worlds peek into this book.*

CHAPTER ONE

1.

GHOSTS HAUNT. VAMPIRES APPEAR SOFTLY FROM DARK corners. Spirits look you in the eye and shock you into questioning your existence. Ideas stay wedged inside you, safe and happy.

Unless your name is Rhonda.

If your name is Rhonda, thoughts slide out of dark corners to drink your blood. If your name is Rhonda, ideas make you wish you were never born. If your name is Rhonda, the history that you study is the lives and futures of the people who listen to you.

If your name is Rhonda, then everything has consequences. Even thinking.

2.

Judith's life was turned inside out by a phone call.

"Hey, you." The voice was light, bright and very familiar. Her sister.

"Hi, you too. What're you ringing up about at this unholy hour?" *Perkiness ought to be canned and sold to tourists, not put on the phone at 7.30 a.m.*, thought Judith.

1

"I got a big delivery from Dad last night. Registered."

"From Dad?" Judith was impressed.

"He coughed up Great-Grandma's stuff. He sent it all to me."

"You could have rung me after work."

"Couldn't. Had to check with you about what you want from it. My friend Rhonda says she can drop the stuff off tonight. After work." There was a smile in Belinda's voice.

Judith decided, irrelevantly, that she would dye her hair green. *Saturday. Zoë will love it. Definitely green hair.*

"Besides, I can't ring later because I'm going on that bloody field trip."

"You're needed."

"I'm not needed for any reason apart from maybe advanced child minding. Make up your mind about what you want."

"I have no idea what Great-Grandma left. I have no idea why no one has touched it for fifty years. And I've no idea why Dad has sent it now. I have no mind to make up."

"Sorry." Belinda's tone was unrepentant. "There are two tea chests of papers, and a bunch of other things stacked in with them."

"What sort of papers are they? I assume you looked?" Judith's voice of many colours showed every feeling. At this moment it was harsh as sandpaper.

"You assume correctly." The grin was now audible. "One is recipes and household hints."

"That's yours, of course." Belinda only told Judith about it so Judith could say it was hers.

"The other chest is much more mixed."

"Send that one here, then. I can make the kids look."

"You're always giving your kids loads of things to do that you hate, because it's good for them."

"Too right." It was Judith's turn to be unrepentant. "I'm developing their characters."

"What are you going to do with your box of paper?"

"I'm not going to make a recipe CD," was Judith's firm comment. "One lunatic in the family is enough. I've often wondered why Mum never opened the boxes, and maybe there is a letter or something in there that'll explain."

"You should've asked," Belinda chided.

"I should've *asked*?" The words exploded out of Judith fast enough to splatter right down the phone line to Canberra. "You mean you *know* why Mum just left everything in the garage?"

"Of course I know." Now Belinda's tone was definitely older-sister-knows-all-family-secrets.

"Tell! The Bloody Enormous Family Secret, and my even bloodier sister has known it forever. Tell me!"

"Not forever, just since Mum was dying."

"Oh," and Judith was chastened. *Sometimes I hate me.*

"Grandma had problems with her mother," Belinda said. "Mum never knew what. But Mum was being loyal to her mother when she rejected her grandmother. Her papers got packed into tea chests to wait for us to become reasoning adults: we should have had it twenty years ago."

Judith wasn't a reasoning adult twenty years ago, she was a lovelorn fool. She stifled the memory.

"So there still is a family story that you don't know." Judith was determined there would be.

"Yes, there is, I suppose," Belinda admitted. Her thoughts took her a bit further, "You know, I think the family story might be Ada herself. I mean, what sort of person leaves such a strong intellectual legacy to her daughter, and all the cooking, and . . ."

"And is hated down two generations?" Judith had to

state the obvious. Her generous mouth scrunched in bitter memory.

"I'm not sure it was hate, that's the thing. Maybe it was fear. Maybe it was lack of understanding." Belinda sounded quite hesitant.

She wanted to *know*. Belinda's answer had really just stated what they could have worked out for themselves.

"Could it be the religion thing?"

"It's *not* the religion thing." Belinda said firmly.

"I suppose." Judith was dubious. She sighed. She realised she'd just accepted a box from Belinda because Belinda had the other box. Some things never changed.

———

Rhonda looked a bit familiar, but Judith couldn't place her. The long brown hair, the refusal to look her direct in the eye? Surely they had met? The way she bustled reminded Judith of herself, although Rhonda seemed so much less certain of everything. And this was the sum of her observations, for Rhonda was in and then out.

———

Belinda thought about family history all day and reported back with a quick email. All she could remember was that Great-Grandma had earned her own living successfully. She had come from a big Anglo-Jewish family, earned enough money to hire a chauffeur and everyone was jealous. Of the chauffeur, presumably. Then she married at the ripe age of thirty. Then she divorced. Somewhere along the way she paid her daughter's university fees.

That was all.

Why did she marry so late? Why did she only have the one daughter? Why on earth had she divorced? It seemed a hugely improbable thing to do in the early 1900s. It had been tough enough for Judith a century later.

Judith kept wondering. All the other great-grand-mothers had surnames. How was it that her mother's mother's mother was Great-Grandma? She was never Ada, always Great-Grandma. Great-Grandma loomed large. A colossal shadow.

Belinda emailed Judith the minute she got back from camp. She had decided to try calling Great-Grandma GG, to see if that changed her presence somehow. This was done purely with intent to irk.

It worked. "GG is such a stupid thing to call some-one," Judith emailed back. "I don't even call the Gover-nor-General that when I feel malicious. It always makes me think of the rhyme my kids have both said when they were young: what is a hungry horse? MT GG."

In one way Linnie is right — our minds are MT about GG. Damn, acronyms are catchy.

3.

The profession of history produces mundane beings that drink a great deal of coffee and talk far too much. Rhonda told herself this. Every day. She especially told herself this on days when the clouds bloomed like dull dreams, as they did on the way back home after her Sydney outing.

Technically, Rhonda heard voices. Rhonda would deny that.

Rhonda was in denial about everything she could define clearly enough to say, "I deny." She was in denial about her relationships and about the link between her history and whatever strange abysm of time it reached into. She was in denial about her social life and about her career prospects. She was even in denial about her looks, changing them and her clothing style and her hair whenever she had enough money for a do-over. She would deny her big toe if she could.

Rhonda was very good at denial. She admitted it, frequently. "I am like Pharaoh," she would say in an on-line discussion, "I am in de-Nile." The only thing she wasn't in denial about was being in denial.

4.

It's about time I told our story. Judith's and Belinda's. Belinda and I have many secrets. Some of these should never have been secrets.

It's my fault.

It never seems to be the right time to tell them. Zoë is only eleven after all, and her father is entirely okay. It's not his fault we're no longer married.

So. I'm convinced. I will bare all. Well, maybe not all, maybe just large chunks. I will bare those large chunks in this daring exposé. That reads like an adver-tisement for a King's Cross establishment.

You may be Nick. You may be Zoë. You may be someone who has found this on the internet. I don't know yet.

My life is a soap opera. A soap opera with magic. But however soap opera-ish it becomes, it's my life. And everything I write is true. That's a really important part of who I am. From my politics to the strange noises in my bathroom — they're all a part of my mun-dane existence.

_____

The next day, Judith opened her document. Secret Stuff, she called it.

Belinda is my big sister. My shorter big sister. Who

is a bloody natural blonde. Every time I see her I want to dye her hair mouse brown. She got the hair and the legs and the figure, and I got the men — did I say she is the one with all the luck? Except I got Nick and Zoë.

Zoë says to write nice things about her. She's peeking over my shoulder. I'm asking her what to say. She says, "Tell whoever how good I am at dancing."

She is wonderful at dancing. I made her a costume with lots of frills and she looks gorgeous in it, pink and gold and a giant smile, all twirling radiantly round the floor. She's also very good at school, when she remembers to do her homework. Which, for the girl-child reading over my shoulder, is NOW.

She's gone. Now I have to remember where I was up to. It was somewhere important.

5.

TVwhore: Baa baa meme sheep

TVwhore: MissTRie, I have a crazy little meme for you. Now is the hour. If you don't leave a comment I will leave one for you. Bwahahah. PS I am not guilty of cruel and exceptional torture. You don't have to ask anyone else — just me. My meme!! Me me me me

Meme: 4

1. Leave a comment, saying "me too".
2. I will respond with five questions.
3. You'll update your journal with my five questions, and your five answers.
4. *Who's your favourite comedian?* Voltaire. He *was* a comedian, right?
5. *If you could choose a new career, what would it be?* Underwear saleswoman. Just think of the perks!
6. *What is the one thing in the world that scares you*

most but you wish you could do? I wish I could stop lying. Ha ha. Really, though, I'm scared of trusting anyone too much.

7. *What's your favourite TV show?* The truth? I love watching talent shows. Any talent show. Even the ones that have been so obviously rigged you can predict the winner three days in advance.

8. *Describe your ideal man?* Blue eyes. I love big blue eyes — they give me a sense of a man who can gaze into infinity. Wiry. Intelligent. I need intelligent. Maybe even brilliant. A mad scientist, perhaps? Also, someone who shares everything. Funny — not too sober and serious — not someone who wants to change the world: I want to laugh. A charming and sharing and funny mad scientist with blue eyes?

––––––––––––

MissTRie was Rhonda's fan fiction name. She used it for the blog and for when she wanted to share stories. Her history-writing name was Dr Jane Smith. As Dr Jane, she wrote semi-serious articles for semi-serious people and had a developing reputation. Her field was mostly eighteenth century history, though she played around with Ancient Rome, with the nineteenth century and with almost anything literary, given half a chance.

Woman can't live on history articles alone. Woman wished she could. When the non-fiction wasn't paying, she took on temp work.

Every time she wrote an article she felt torn between a sense of relief that history was still permitted in her life and a sense of pain that pop history was not the stuff she ought to be doing. But there were consequences and causes. Rhonda was full of consequences and causes. Bloated with them. Mysteries, too. Mysteries and consequences and causes: Rhonda's daily existence.

Rhonda's July history article had possibilities. 'Possibilities' was such a glorious word; it opened up tempting futures. Dr Jane Smith with her own regular column. If the small piece attracted comment and if people enjoyed it, she was told, she would be asked for a set of ten articles. Rhonda pulled every bad joke she could out of the woodwork for her fun little article. She included extra one-liners, met her deadline, then waited anxiously for the result.

The editor pronounced by email, "Jane, this neat little piece works. I am tempted to try you on meatier stuff." Rhonda found herself discussing the contract for a series even before reader opinion started to emerge.

All Rhonda had to do, the editor said, was write about a particular book. She owned the book. She knew the subject. Rhonda went straight for an online chat binge to celebrate.

In the interstitial moment when her computer and the chat room were deciding if they liked each other, she checked all her online places. Most of her favourites were on another site, which collated feed so she didn't have to web surf. Rhonda the Geek. One of the two jokes she permitted herself on a regular basis. Only she knew she was Rhonda the Geek.

As she scanned the list for updates, Rhonda made a momentous decision. She felt very brave as she added a single current events source to her live feed. If it worked out, she could think about moving back into the real world. She hoped she could. She really, truly did. She didn't hope too hard though. When hope failed, life hurt.

Rhonda contemplated her daily reading thoughtfully and made a less momentous decision: the rest of her life would be literary and historical and fannish until she was certain that the last month was not a blip. Last month was the pattern card for all months. If it wasn't a blip, maybe she could watch TV news or, even more daringly, buy newspapers again. Newspapers would be good. Judy Horacek's mopey feminist cartoons. Return to civilisation.

Rhonda was so very happy to finally have history to write. There was something inside her that needed history. Geekdom was her hiding place: history was her reality. It was a vocation, pure love, intense almost beyond bearing.

She knew that life without studying the past was a mockery, because she had been living recently in that hollow world. Now the drought had broken: good pay, easy writing, and fun stuff to put together. What more could she ask for?

And it wasn't proper research. She was pretty positive that it was original research that prompted the rumblings. Being an historian, not just writing about history.

Her first article was a summary one, telling about the strangeness of history and the interesting man who had described some of the oddest strangeness for Europe. By the end of it, she felt she knew Charles Mackay personally. It was his style, she decided. She should make her next online persona a Mackay one.

That would be an incredibly stupid and mildly dangerous thing to do. Mackay could be linked to Dr Jane Smith and her learned and faintly witty articles. She banished the thought.

She emailed that first article to the journal editor and the journal editor changed a few words, said it was good, and committed to the series. Rhonda signed a contract. Great inner glee. More inner glee still because, in all that time, Rhonda didn't have a single daft dream. Only household dreams. No compulsions. Not a single 'must do' except for chocolate.

"And chocolate," Rhonda reasoned, "is not a compulsion — it is a necessity."

6.

Work that day was unexpected. Judith found herself composing an explanation of it in *Secret Stuff*.

"I'm not on diet!" Nick said, when dinner wasn't ready.

"I'm thinking of your future," Judith reassured him. She renamed her file *Secret: Women's Stuff.*

———

Here I need to note a nuisance, *Judith had written.*

He dropped into the gift shop to buy a present for a lady friend, and spent a long lunch flirting with the Boss and myself and every female who walked past. He's drop dead gorgeous. One of those Hugh Grant types; brown and sexy, with eyes that self-deprecate wistfully and give the lie to all the catty things that emerge from the mouth.

The Boss flirted. When her boyfriend dropped in for a cuppa and ran into our new client, the Boss developed a fit of the conniptions. Instead of getting rid of the guy, she pushed him my way. He and I teased each other enthusiastically for a little, then someone asked about amethyst crystals and I forgot him.

He came back today. He asked why I had given him the brush-off.

"I didn't give you the brush-off," I said. I was very

11

kind and very patient and very professional. "I had another customer."

His eyes took on an evil cast. I wondered if he was an axe murderer. I asked him. He laughed, bought something for a lady friend, and left.

7.

Rhonda's time online was innocently spent talking about knitting patterns with Starchild. Rhonda located Starchild a pattern for a knitted beanie that looked like a plucked chicken. Phased made jewellery and wasn't interested in knitting patterns, but she teased Starchild about the wearing of plucked chickens.

Rhonda felt meme-ish. "I have a meme," she posted, as MissTRie, "and I am tapping Starchild and Phased and TVwhore to answer it:

If you had to give each day a scent, what would it be and why? Here are mine:

Monday — rose geranium because it is my favourite

Tuesday — sassafras because sassafras reminds me of the US and Tuesday reminds me of the US

Wednesday — sandalwood because Wednesday leaves me hot and bothered and sandalwood is cooling

Thursday — petit grain because I feel eighteenth century on Thursdays and petit grain belongs in the eighteenth century

Friday — marjoram because it calms down those end-of-week stresses

Saturday — lavender because I like it

Sunday — frankincense so I can skip going to church."

TVwhore must have been online, because she answered almost immediately. "God, you're a tease, MissTRie. I can't think of seven scents. Yes I can. Dammit, why don't you ask the same things everyone else does? I can tell you my top movies? okay, here are my scents:

Monday — dung because I feel like dung on Monday mornings

Tuesday — formaldehyde or crushed ants because I feel stepped on every Tuesday

Wednesday — sweat because that's what I smell of

Thursday — shit because that's what I feel like

Friday — stale beer because that's what everyone round me has been drinking

Saturday — heavenly incense because I am not at work

Sunday — sleep, I smell sleep."

MissTRie: "TVwhore, do you know how mean you are?"

"Heh, yes. I am outstanding at it."

"Me! I want to do the meme!" Starchild had obviously just come online.

TVwhore: "You need permission?"

"Not from you :P"

"Don't poke your tongue out at me, dearie, the wind might change. And MissTRie, if you don't stop laughing I will do evil things."

"How did you know I was laughing? You are psychic."

"Just psychotic."

"Starchild's list of amazing scents:

Monday — fresh air (it has a smell, no?)

Tuesday — baby powder (a pink smell)

Wednesday — plastic shopping bags, melted in the sun (a messy smell)

Thursday — hot wool

Friday — roasting chicken

Saturday — something green. Saturday is my garden day so it has a green smell but I don't know green smells.

Sunday — lavender."

A while later Phased added her piece. "Sorry I missed you all. I have the same scent every day. I love old scents, like violets. TVwhore, I think I should send you some to cover up the dung and shit. MissTRie, do you have an oil burner?"

Rhonda forbore to say that it was her oil burner that had inspired the meme. The meme had energised her to write a new fanfic, letting her online friends into her private dreams about her current favourite TV show. Rhonda felt almost fairytale-ish. She had reached happy ever after, finally. Before her thirty-fifth birthday, at that.

Charles Mackay was obviously her good luck piece. She put away her small purse and replaced it with her old, giant handbag so that she could carry his book with her. Her private demons would be at bay. Forever.

8.

September came. A wet month. Full of green smells.

Rhonda was surprised to find that her life was still sane. Rain puddled down and she puddled round the house, eating macaroni cheese. No waking paradigm shifts and no weird vistas of the world. Rhonda could get up in the morning and yawn and be grumpy until she had her coffee. Normal. Boringly bloody normal.

She could even reread *Good Omens* without thinking how very lucky Agnes Nutter was. She still added rebelliously, *My filing systems are better.* Her filing systems *were* better. Many computer files, cross-referenced to the umpteenth degree were so much better than old card-index files. Rhonda the very smug Geek.

Rhonda went out and bought two dozen extra instant meals to celebrate. Rejoicing needed, after all, to be done with a certain flamboyance. Instant meals were a tool that Rhonda used to create and maintain her zone of normalcy. They reminded her that other people's lives were mundane. Like the essential oils reminded her that other people's lives had a weekly rhythm. She put 'rose geranium oil' on her shopping list — she got through more of that and of the lavender than all the other oils combined. Some days were longer than others.

The instant meals worked differently to the oils. Nothing to do with rhythm. The instant meals all tasted artificial. They had been recommended to her by two of her favourite beings on the planet, so they were emotionally sound. She never bought the gourmet ones. Cheap was part of the grand design. Normal. Boringly bloody normal. Boringly bloody entirely ecstatically normal.

Rhonda's September and October articles were both appropriately scented with frankincense, because she did them on the same day. They were parts one and two of a quick overview of the aspects of the book she would not be writing articles about.

The Crusades, for instance. The journal didn't want the Crusades as a separate piece, because they were planning an issue next year that would be entirely Crusading in theme. The editor hinted that she might ask Rhonda for a piece then, if any of their other authors fell through. She could do it, too. There was nothing to hide. Not a damn blasted thing. Her life was awesome.

9.

A few days later Judith rang Belinda. "Don't forget you're going to Melbourne next weekend for the high school reunion," she said.

"I forgot." Belinda sounded annoyed.

"I thought you had your airplane booked and your

ticket for the evening function and everything done months ago? I thought you always did everything way in advance." Judith's tone of voice was not nice.

"I do, and I have. I forgot all about it. I'm only just back from the excursion. Plus I hardly slept. Keeping an eye on the nocturnal activities of excursing kids is thankless *and* sleepless." Belinda's next thought was clueless and tactless and had obviously come out of her mouth without going by way of her brain. "You know, you can take all the tickets. I don't really want to go."

"No," was Judith's reply. She nearly put down the phone.

"No, I'm busy, or just no?" asked Belinda.

"Just no. I can't possibly go to the reunion. For one thing it's your year, not mine. You were entirely enthusiastic about it, just two months ago. And for another, I left Melbourne for a reason."

"Damn. I forgot he was in my year. How could I forget such a thing?"

Judith heard the worry lines. "Because he wasn't in class with you? Because he mostly acted like a normal human being when you were near?"

"I shouldn't go," Belinda thought aloud. "That's another reason not to go."

"Don't be stupid. He won't do anything. Just don't give my address out. Besides, he might not even turn up. Who knows what he's doing these days? Besides earning loads of money as an engineer."

"He ruined your life," Belinda said helplessly. "I don't want to see him."

So wear a blindfold, Judith thought. "Ring up one of your old friends — go in a group. Safety in numbers." She wanted Belinda to start living again. For fifteen years she had sublimated herself. Fifteen years. It was time.

"I just keep thinking about what you were like when

you ran from him. You were scared. So very scared . . ." Belinda's voice tapered. "I keep remembering how violent he was, and how no one would listen or believe what you were telling them. I remember Nick crying and crying and crying at my place, and both of us jumping at sounds."

"I was lucky to have you to run to, and that you protected me through the worst, and that you were prepared to move. I was lucky because of a whole heap of things you did for me. Other women aren't so lucky." Judith's hand was shaking. *Hands shake — it is one of their main functions in life — everyone knows this. Besides, Linnie can't see it.*

"Other women not being so lucky has nothing to do with this school reunion. Gods, I can be stupid."

"Well, no. I was so careful not to remind you, you know." Judith's grin was a bit twisted at her exceptional tact. And how wasted all this tact was proving. "Besides, I wouldn't have been a feminist for years and years probably, if I hadn't seen what was happening to other women when I was in the shelter. Just think what the world would have lost without me bugging everyone to let women have equality. And safety."

Damn. I should not have said 'safety'. Dangerous word; unsettling connotations. Please, Linnie, forget I said 'safety'. Please.

Judith tried again. "I help other women because I know how a woman can be hurt." She used her most sincere voice, the one she kept for people needing the most serious of convincing. "Also how little most people know about it or even care. Besides, I can't bear to think of you not going simply because of him."

"So you want me to go just to prove that he hasn't had any effect on our lives?"

"That's right," and Judith smiled. Nothing like a mild deception. She wanted Belinda to see her old friends,

17

and to spend time with Dad. "I'm not ready to be in his face yet — but you are. You're my big, strong sister. You can control young hooligans in the classroom; you can control him at a formal dinner."

"If you really want me to go, I'll go. But I *will* ring up some people and go in a group."

"That's good. I like that." Inside Judith did a little-girl leap and clapped her hands with glee.

"You want us to reclaim our lives, don't you?" Belinda asked this with her voice just very slightly quaking. "Sort of like reclaiming the night?"

"I do," Judith said. "But gently. We have complete and happy lives where we are now." *Another half-truth.* "But looking through Great-Grandma's things made me think that we've cut ourselves off from our past because of him. One bloody man."

She intentionally let some inner anger creep into her voice. *Gods, what a brilliant performer I am. I should have gone into TV soaps.* "We should have been able to spend more time with Mum when she was dying. We should be able to go to Melbourne and be tourists. And Dad should be talking to both of us. Both!"

"He wouldn't do anything, you know," Belinda said, "Not in public."

"I know this intellectually, and you know this intellectually, but neither of us knows it inside our gut." *Gods, this is tough.* "I'm not saying that you should do anything dangerous. I'm saying what I said when you got sent the information about the school reunion. I'm saying we have a right to renew old friendships, without being scared of one bloody bully. Who needs his brain rearranged. And his genitals. You're right — it wasn't as big to him as to us, and you'll be one hundred per cent safe."

"And you want me to soften things up and test the waters, because I'm less vulnerable."

"Dammit, Belinda."

"I'm right, aren't I?"

"Yes, you're absolutely correct. I want to reclaim our past."

"Then I'll go. I will enjoy myself. But don't expect to hear from me till I get back. Part of the problem is everyone around us underplaying that sort of thing, isn't it?" Belinda's voice was softened when she thought aloud. "It gets made tiny. Unimportant. Each time someone does that, we're smaller. Us. As if your life and maybe even Nick's life were never at risk."

"Now you're sounding like me." Odd. Their pain had made Belinda a closet feminist. "The trouble is not just domestic violence, though. It's women's stuff. And women's stuff is supposed to be petty and small and inconsequential. Even when it's the whole world."

Judith pulled herself up. *Occupational hazard,* she admitted, silently, *I do tend to sound like people's nightmares of a political lobbyist. I'm linguistically deformed.*

"Secret women's stuff," smiled Belinda. "Secret because most people don't want to know about it. Society doesn't want to face the canker in its midst."

"Or wants to blame us for the canker. I get that a lot — surely we're to blame if we get knifed or bashed up."

"So I'm a feminist and it's all your fault," Belinda mulled.

"You're a feminist and it's society's fault. And you should help me change society."

"No, I should not. I have my own garden to cultivate." Belinda was very pleased at her French joke.

Judith stuck out her tongue, since Belinda couldn't see.

"But I'll go to the school reunion for both of us."

That was something. Judith wished her sister would plant some politics along with the petunias. "Cautiously."

"Very cautiously." Then her tone of voice changed utterly, "I nearly forgot, how is your GG box going?"

"It's very much women's stuff. It is Ada's thoughts on all sorts of things, as far as I can tell. I can't make sense of it at all." Judith didn't want to talk about it. For once, she was not actually trying for secrets. *Secretive happens all by itself in my life. I bet I was a classified file in my previous existence; now that I'm a higher life form I just think like a classified file.*

"So now you're challenged, you want to make sense of it?"

"Yes. I'll report to you when I work out what she thought she was doing." *And stop reading my mind,* Judith added, internally. *My mind is private, damn your fourth toe.*

"I'll report to you when I come back from Melbourne. At least I don't have to read Hebrew to do my report."

"But I don't have to read Hebrew. That's the weird thing. Bunches of the stuff are in English. And I had a question for you — I'd completely forgotten."

"Yes?"

"Did GG's stuff include a scrapbook?"

"There's one of those late Victorian scrapbooks, with poems and pasted pictures. Is that what you mean?"

Silence. Judith's foot stopped in the middle of a tap and poised above the yellow lino. "It may be. I need to see it." Judith admired how she tempered her own enthusiasm.

"I was saving it with the other big things, for us to check over together. But I can post it to you if you want."

"I don't trust the post. We've had lots of stolen mail recently. When you get a few minutes, would you mind checking?"

"Wait a tick and I'll get it now and talk you through it. I put it on the bookshelf because it looks impressive."

"Show-off."

"Absolutely. Be right back."

10.

Rhonda was in a chatroom. She came in partway, identifying herself as M44M, which she did quite often. She knew quite a few of the people in a casual way, and they thought they knew her. To be strictly honest, they thought that they knew a married male age forty-four.

Sometimes she watched for a bit until she got things sorted out inside her head. She needed to make sure she didn't use British English or pure Strine when she was supposed to have an American voice, for instance. She wanted to watch and wait now, but this BB person wouldn't leave her be.

"How are you? I am glad to see a new person here. I am looking for new friends. I am thirteen and live in Milwaukee."

Bzz. You are the weakest link. This BB was a fake.

Then he started asking her questions. If he were a thirteen-year-old, maybe they would be normal questions. But he used English, not geekspeak. Whole words and correct spelling demonstrated adulthood. Rhonda wanted to fade at once, but in her supreme happiness and a certain stubbornness about maintaining it, she stayed on a little.

"I am a superhero," the false teen boasted. "Does anyone here have secret superpowers? Do you have secret powers, M44M?" BB asked.

"?" asked Rhonda, as M44M.

"The secret power I have is to spot people who tell lies. Talk and I will tell you if you are telling me lies."

"He is doing this to everyone," StayTuned messaged

privately. "Invent something. Kool sez he is govt. Checking chat rooms. Kool swore vengeance — hates being stalked."

"Stupid git," Rhonda said back. "Not you, Kool — BB." Kool had joined the private chat just in time to see the 'Stupid git.'

Just as well she hadn't fled one room and gone to another if he was checking a bunch of places. She would have looked guilty as hell. Courage was its own reward. "Know what he wants?"

"Kryptonite?" suggested Kool.

"LOL. Thanks." Rhonda said, and closed the private window. Laughing out loud was a good way of finishing conversations before they got anywhere. It was funny, in its way. Her personal kryptonite was idiots, like the one who was now saying, "I heard a rumour."

"Rumour?" asked Sekritmax.

"Someone comes on here and predicts the future. I want to test my power of truth on them."

"I wish," said Rhonda as M44M. "My wife would put a stop to it though."

"Why?" asked Kool.

"Against her religion."

"My wife sez that," answered Secritmax, "when I do anything she hates."

Everyone dutifully LOLed.

This was one of Rhonda's favourite chat rooms. People who dropped in mostly avoided txt. There wasn't much smut. Nice folks. It would be really sad if she had to drop it.

Maybe BB was just some kid who read comics. That's what she would have thought three years ago. Except there were too many BBs. Sometimes they asked about witchcraft, sometimes Nostradamus, sometimes they talked about prophecy, sometimes they dropped big hints about secret powers. Not all were as direct as BB. Rhonda hated it.

Anyway, she herself had had no incidents for three months now. She was very proud of this. There was nothing to hunt her down for. Not a damned thing. Life was joyous.

Not a soul had ever linked her history-writing to her incidents.

It would be a tough link to make. Publishing was an art, not a science, and it was the deadlines that brought out her inner demons, not the date the publication reached its audience. The nature of the industry she was in was a protection, and the nature of the net was a protection as well.

Just to be safe, every name she hid behind was an extra layer of protection. Rhonda felt safer with extra layers. Voices and layers and layers and voices. Protection.

She hated it. She hated it and herself quite vehemently every second she spent making coffee and every microsecond she spent crossing the floor and sitting down and coming back to the chat room. She hated her spider fascination with the web and that she watched BB and his questions as if she were a rabbit caught in headlights. She hated her mixed metaphors. Rhonda was so busy self-hating that she didn't make her de-Nile joke.

She drank her coffee slowly, the bitter taste reminding her of all she had that was worthy of sustained hate. Rhonda hated remembering ten years back, when her marriage had fallen to pieces because she couldn't tell her husband the simple truth. When she had lost everything.

All that wrongness.

She hated it that her friends were all hidden behind

the keyboard, with no real names or faces or family. She hated not having children. She hated.

The superhero writers and the superhero cartoonists and the superhero film makers never understood the creep and the under-skin crawl of being different. Not a single one of those writers and cartoonists and film makers. Not a one. There was no damn way she was going to stand up and correct them. Coming out of the dark would hurt more. Far more.

Rhonda hated herself most of all. Every time she let loose a vision, she hated herself. Every time she predicted the future, she hated herself. Every time she lost control over her mind and her fingers, she hated herself.

Then her thoughts went back to where they had been in her late twenties. Drugs. Each and every time, she thought about drugs. Suppressing instincts through partaking of forbidden fruits. She hadn't even enjoyed the fruits. Addiction was not part of who she was, because it was too much like being at the beck and call of that inner self she hated so virulently.

Still, drugs promised forgetfulness. That was the theory. They had done nothing good. No oblivion. No happiness. Not even respite. They had lost her the junior lecturing job.

Mind you, that last was a blessing in disguise, because those trawlers and seekers would have found her. University-based scholars are on display and their publications are known. So now she was drug free, and had been for years. And she was secret. And she was safe. Buried in her layers of protection. Secure.

She thought of BB with malice in her heart and decided that she had earned her safety. She told the chat room "Gotta go — the wife beckons," and left BB to his idiot questions: she had hung round in the background long enough so that it had looked like she had been listening. She could come back and play again in the electronic sandpit with all her little virtual playmates.

Thank God, Rhonda thought, after the bitterness had finally left her mouth, *Thank God for Great-Aunt Mabel.* If GAM had not seen Rhonda's marriage dissolve she would not have left Rhonda her house and an annuity. Great-Aunt Mabel had not known about the drugs. Or the weird at the centre of Rhonda's soul.

Or had she? Sometimes Rhonda worried about what GAM had known. Rhonda had never confided to her about the weird at the centre of her soul, but that might not have stopped her guessing.

Rhonda remembered when she held the letter from the lawyer. She had looked down at it in her hand, the soft rustle of the paper telling her it was real. Some dogged part of her had made her ring the lawyer to find out if it was a cruel practical joke.

GAM had left her enough that Rhonda would not starve. All she needed was temp work or those articles and she was fine. Not rich, but able to manage.

It had been like something out of a story, being left an inheritance just after her whole life had collapsed in a heap. Rhonda decided to swear off fiction forever in case she saw herself reflected inside. Then she repented. It was too much like swearing off life: she had already given up so many other things.

That was when she realised that she still hated. The hate wasn't just directed at BB and his questions. It wasn't just directed at that thing that lurked in her soul and came out of hiding to destroy her life just when it was convinced things were normal. Rhonda listened to her internal voice and realised that the voice of hate had become very strident. It was drowning out the real person.

There was no need. August and September had been good. Those articles meant she hadn't had to go to the temp agency and talk to Mr Ick. They had also meant she could write the history her soul craved without becoming the person she feared becoming, without falling into the snare of prophecy. Life was good, despite idiots.

It was so good in fact that she found the courage to talk about her history article on her history message board.

11.

"I'm back, with book." Belinda said this declaratively, a big announcement. "Why did you ask about it, anyway? I don't remember telling you that there were any books. Or did I?"

"I don't remember. I asked because on a bunch of pages there are notes, and some say to see the book." That was all Judith gave away — and even that was grudging.

"This book is so gorgeous." Belinda's voice oozed sensual joy. "Great-Grandma wrote a lovely clear copperplate. I'm going to scan it and do a colour printout for you, I think. Oh! The first and last sections are all the same sort of stuff, but the middle sections are different. It's a big book, brown and gold and black—"

"I don't need to know that," Judith complained. "Just the contents."

"Just the contents, then." *I could hear her bloody smile. Damn her gammy knee. She was 'Linnie' for that smile, not 'Belinda.'*

"It has some lovely die-cut things stuck all over." Judith was going to warn her off again, but Belinda said, "Ooh!"

"What is it?" Judith asked.

"Little snippets from newspapers," Linnie replied,

"And handwritten quotes, and I just found some die cuts of Egyptian gods. I was admiring them."

"Admire them in your own time. Tell me about the newspaper cuttings."

"There's a nice black and white picture of Victoria in early middle age." Belinda waxed very enthusiastic. "This book is a treasure."

"And it sounds as if Great-Grandma was a treasure of bad taste."

"You're wrong. All the sentiments in here are normal for the period. Very sickly, I admit. Patriotic and romantic and full of strained eloquence. But mainstream, very normal. I saw all the same things in the Victorian literature stuff I did whenever. It's a nicely presented book — gorgeous pictures, nothing crowded, all carefully placed for best effect — very good taste in fact, for its day."

————

Judith wrote this up, later: I had forgotten Lin's little excursus into Victoriana. It was a very long time ago, after all. A prior hobby. But now it was useful. Knowing how normal Great-Grandma was helped a lot. She was part of mainstream society in at least her scrapbook self. Well, the first section of her scrapbook self. Good taste and carefully placed for best effect.

"There's a poem about Victoria from Punch," said Belinda.

"Victoria again. Is she all the way through it?" This was supposed to be a rhetorical question; my voice indicated this fact undeniably.

"She isn't — this poem is to the State — not to the Queen." Belinda always answered my rhetorical questions.

"Oh," said I, the epitome of wit and intelligence.

"It's rather Gilbert and Sullivan. It has things like "Where Englishmen work well together/Under divine Italian weather" and "Australian waters shall not feel/The cleavage of a hostile keel." Do you want me to read the whole thing?"

"Gods, no," and I shuddered. This was not at all what I was expecting. My Great-Grandmother the bloody patriot. Or was that bloody Patriot? My ancestress the missile? Even thinking about Victoriana elicits bad jokes.

"Is it all like that?" I asked.

"Sentimental and sappy?"

"I meant mainstream, normal, fitting in. The good taste and the rest of it."

"Hang on a tick, let me look a bit more. She has some humorous things from newspapers too, listen: *Seeing is not always believing. There are many men whom you can see and yet not believe.*" A moment and then, "This is curious."

"What?"

"Lots and lots of anti-male stuff. That was one of a whole lot of quotes and extracts. I wonder if she did this before or after her divorce? Or even before she was married? It might say a lot about her."

"Can you tell by the dresses and things?"

"Bother it, Judith, why didn't I think of that?"

"'Cos I'm the clever sister," I needled. I wanted to see that book.

"It's nineteenth century. She must have made it either before she married or not too far into her marriage."

"You're certain?" This was puzzling.

"Pretty certain. Dress styles changed heaps, and there are even crinoline jokes here. So it can't be past the first decade of the twentieth century and most of it is not even nearly that."

"You're not making sense."

"I know," and she stopped a moment to recap. "The trouble is that the dress styles here are mixed — it looks as if GG shoved things in together. It's like she found a bunch of old postcards and cuttings and pictures, and pasted them all artistically in a nice book over a few weeks. Some of it is very 1880s, some of it early Edwardian. But it was put together at the same time."

"Huh?" By which I meant, of course, 'How do you come to that conclusion?'

"Everything's on the same pages. I mean, the earlier and later cuttings are all together. They don't seem to have been pasted in the scrapbook in date order."

"Um." My turn to think. "That's the first section — how about the last?"

"Much the same. Gorgeous pictures, nice layout. Mixed in date."

"Anti-male?"

"Mostly," Belinda admitted. "Except there's this strange poem that reads two ways. One way it's in praise of marriage, and the other way it's against marriage."

"Surely that's anti-male?"

"Not if it's misogynist."

"It's a press clipping?"

"No, it's exactly the same hand as all my recipes. She wrote it, all right. I think GG had a sick sense of humour."

"So do I," I said, wholeheartedly. "But what do you mean about the two ways of reading?"

"I mean if you read it line by line it says one thing and if you read it alternate lines it says the other. There are instructions to make sure you read it both ways."

"Strange woman, your ancestress," I commented.

"Yours too. Let me read you the first bit," was my sister's kindly answer.

That man must lead a happy life
Who is directed by a wife
Who's freed from matrimonial claims
Is sure to suffer for his pains.
Adam could find no solid peace
Till he beheld a woman's face
When Eve was given for a mate
Adam was in a happy state."

"And now the other way round," she was unstoppable, so I didn't even try. At least it was only two verses.

That man must lead a happy life
Who's freed from matrimonial claims
Who is directed by a wife
Is sure to suffer for his pains.
Adam could find no solid peace
When Eve was given for a mate
Till he beheld a woman's face
Adam was in a happy state."

"Isn't it lovely and horrid?" she enthused, sounding exactly like her niece. I bet Zoë would like it too, at that.

"Why on earth is it there?" I wondered.

"Maybe she was mocking herself? Maybe she was unhappy? Maybe she had a warped sense of what was clever? Just like you."

"Life is a mystery," I declared. "Maybe she put it in there to distract everyone from the anti-male stuff?"

Belinda laughed. "The only other thing in the end section is a note in her hand, but I can't read it. There's a lot of writing crammed very small."

"Damn," was my carefully considered reply. It took at least two seconds to find the exact phrase I needed.

"And double damn. I would love to know what that note says."

"I'll get back to you on it," she promised.

"Thanks. I doubt if any of the rest of what you have described is what I'm after," I was disappointed. "It doesn't match."

"What doesn't it match?"

"I can't make sense of it without the other half. It's kind of like one of those treasure maps from pirate stories."

Belinda knew something was up, because she didn't give me the middle section instantly. After a long pause she finally, finally, *finally* said, "Wait a second, let me tell you the middle section. Just in case it helps. It'll just take a moment to find it."

It was a long moment. I bet she had her finger in it the whole while, seeing how long she could keep me waiting.

"It's handwritten and hand drawn. No cut-outs of any sort, no newspaper articles." She was serious. A bit surprised.

"So it's different?" I asked.

"Very different. Firstly, there's a long, long list of dates." Finally. "It's headed 'Fumigation' and GG has two women's names — one against some dates and the other against all the later dates. There's a little picture of an eye next to Fumigation." Belinda's voice had taken on a querulous tone. "It has nothing in common with the other stuff."

"Go on." This might well be what I was after. I felt very proprietorial.

"There's a heading called seals, and a bunch of sketches?"

Yes! Maybe even Bingo!

"Can you scan me that page?" I tried to control my

voice, but a little excitement may have seeped out. "Soon?"

"Not until after Melbourne. There's no time."

"Dammit. I'll just have to wait. Is that all?"

Those pictures existed. Goody goody gum drops. I was so thrilled I was in danger of sounding like Zoë.

"Not at all. There's a diagram of a hand. I guess she was into palm reading?"

"Chiromancy." Here I was admitting things I hadn't known about until I had looked at Great-Grandma's papers and then done web research. I know what chiromancy is. Be impressed. Be very impressed. And yes, Nick made me see the Addams family movies about twenty times. With his own money. I wonder what he was trying to tell me?

"Is that what it is?" Belinda was teasing. I will never understand why she doesn't want to know everything instantly like a sane person.

"Since I have to wait forever for a copy, can you tell me quickly what the major lines are on the hand?"

"A week or so is not forever. Anyway, there's a life-line, a wisdom line, a table line and a line that's marked fate or health. Before you ask, there's no explanation, and I've never read a palm in my life."

"Damn, I'm going to have to look that up." This necessitated a writing pause.

Which gave my sister time to think. Which produced the inevitable question. "Why?"

"There's something funny about our ancient ancestress," I said.

"Not just her daughter hating her?" Belinda was politely inquiring. I would lay big bucks on her having seen the papers were not recipes and then saying 'for Judes' to herself.

"No. She might have been quite mad. Or she might

have been doing strange investigations. Or she was very gullible."

"So you're happy to have got that box."

"Oh yes. Exceedingly happy. This is terrific stuff. Very strange. Totally wacko. But fabulous." See, it all came tumbling out. Despite the bloody smug tone in my sister's voice.

"Do you want the other pages?" Innocence bloody personified.

"There's more?"

"Yes." Increasing amounts of smug.

"Then yes please." Very staccato. It was easier to say 'yes please' though, than to call her lots of names.

"There's a picture of a face with lots of lines."

"What does it say about the lines?" I thought it was the facial version of chiromancy. There was a version of it in the nineteenth century according to my sources. 'My sources.' Hah.

"Nothing, it refers to a page on physiognomy. I can't see it in the book."

So much for my future as Madame Judith, the fortune teller. Nick would be relieved. "Must be one of the loose ones then."

"Oh!" This was a huge excitement from her. Unexpected, but rather nice.

"What?"

"There's a nice diagram of the ten sefirot. I like that. I didn't know anyone in our family knew anything about Kabbalah."

My bubble burst. This was not as much fun as chiromancy.

Sefirot? Kabbalah? I knew the second word. It was something Jewish. Madonna studied it. Big deal. Lots of things were Jewish. "I'm not even sure what Kabbalah is." I said this with the grandest reluctance.

"It's a Jewish philosophical tradition. I would have

sworn that this sort of thing was not something our family might care about. I only know about it because it is a sort of craze here in the Jewish community right now. I'll find you a book on it, or an article."

"Your community thinks it's made up of popstars," I dismissed, airily. "You're certain it's Kabbalah? And what's a sefirot?" My self-esteem was being dented by this conversation. I would get even.

"The plural of a sefirah." Oh, but she was enjoying this. Little teacherly corrections gave it away. "Nothing else it could be," she continued. "But I can check it out. I do like this diagram, you know. The tree of life. I will check it with a friend who teaches basic Kabbalah, and find out how standard it is. I bet he would love to see it. And he knows how very secular I am, so he won't try to press me into doing anything more than social stuff. People think that any curiosity means instant syna-gogue attendance and keeping nicely kosher. Ultra-super frumness. Not even for you will I go that far."

"Can you do it without showing him the whole book?" And would she not ask tough questions? Please let her not ask tough questions.

"Of course I can. I can scan the page or copy it by hand. But why bother?"

"I don't know." I admitted. "Maybe I don't want us to admit to having descended from a lunatic?"

"Fine. I'll copy it out by hand and just ask if it is the usual diagram or not."

"Thanks. And you'll tell me what on earth a se-firthingie is at the same time?"

"Sure, can do," and I could hear the bloody smile in her voice.

"Is that all?"

"There's a bit more," she said. My emotions kept swinging from low to high — I wished they would stop — they were making me dizzy. "The next page has a hand of God. At least I think it's a hand of God because it says 'hand of G', a triangle with Hebrew letters in and a hexagram filled with Hebrew letters."

"Strange."

"It is. I can ask about it if you like."

"No, not yet. I might be able to match that up with some of her loose notes."

"You just like doing all the detective stuff yourself."

"That's it," and it was time for my voice to have a smile.

"I like this page," she commented to me, almost casually, "It has pictures of animals with Hebrew names. A worm coming out of a fissure in a rock labelled 'shamir', a unicorn-looking thing called a 'tachash' with the word 'kasher' beneath it — so I guess if you find your tachash and can get it killed properly by a certified kosher butcher, then you can eat it for dinner." She laughed at her own little joke. "And there are a few more."

"Another page I want," I sighed. I had no idea what it was about, but it sounded cool.

"Well, I'll just copy all this middle section. There's just one last page to it. After that the scrapbook goes back to what I told you it was before. Very Victorian and decorative and sumptuous. With that nice little rhyme."

"That nice rhyme indeed," I snorted. I hate it when I snort. "What's on that last page?"

"It's a picture of the ark where the Torah is kept," her sister replied, "It has six scrolls in it, and the doors are open. There are all sorts of nice pictures on either side of the Ark — several ritual candlesticks, branches that look like they come from palm trees, a ram's horn. All very Jewish. And above the ark there is a sun, a star and a moon."

"What does it mean?"

"Your guess is as good as mine," shrugged Belinda. "An embroidery pattern?"

"I want to sort it out." My voice resonated with deep sincerity. Truly it did.

"When I get more time I'll scan all the pages for you and either get them in the post or drive down and stay the weekend. But it'll take a few weeks."

Yes!! Lots of happy. While I wait for Lin to produce a photocopy, I've got other things to worry about. Not family. This government is hell on wheels at trying to ruin people's lives. I have two pieces of draft legislation to protest and a submission to write for an inquiry. Imagine how rich I would be if any of this was paid work!

"Thanks." And I did mean it. I was grateful. I just suddenly felt as if the world was burdening me too much. This happens from time to time. Either I get over it or I get sarcastic.

"Promise you will let me know what it is all about? I'm as curious about our mad ancestress as you are, you know."

"We don't know she was mad yet."

12.

Message boards, what wonders they were. Rhonda could be herself, and yet hidden. To her friends on the history message board she was Jane Smith, historian. The message board and the articles were her public self. They gave her back her dignity.

Rhonda spent a few hundred words waxing happy about how the weirdness of the nineteenth century produced people such as Charles Mackay, who could take the strangeness of our past and write a book about it. A good enough book to be in print one hundred and fifty years later.

One of her online friends asked where the articles were appearing and she told them, proudly and happily.

She celebrated by checking on what her fan fiction friends had been up to recently, and to see if Starchild had finished the chicken hat yet. Keeping Starchild in knitting patterns was more proof Rhonda was a real person. Also keeping Phased in bad jokes about men. She would never see anything that Starchild knitted, and she and Starchild would never exchange real names. But they knew each other and Rhonda the Geek was the supreme knitting pattern and bad joke finder. She could make her friends happy without compromising a thing.

Reality. The very best kind of reality.

CHAPTER TWO

1.

FIRST THERE WAS A SPECIAL DELIVERY. THAT GIFT SHOP
flirt had found Judith's full name and address by the
simple expedient of asking Judith's boss. He sent her a
huge cellophane bag full of Paddington truffles. With
no return address. Judith's breakfast was one cherry
truffle and one rum truffle and one big smile. She se-
creted the rest away for emergencies.

Then she remembered to check the mailbox. The
usual gumpf. Meeting notes. Invitations to meet Important People (for mythical feminists with free time).
A glossy government booklet with a request from June
to 'pull it to pieces and get back to me.' And a plain
yellow envelope.

Judith never opened plain yellow envelopes first.
Boredom should be delayed. When she finally ripped it
open, she sighed. It was full of pages torn out from old
school magazines. The Dark Side had struck again.
Linnie had been so much fun recently Judith had forgotten the Dark Side existed. She regretted pressuring
her sister to go to Melbourne.

All the pages contained Peter's photo. Peter with a

blackened eye and Peter with a knife pointing at his heart. Peter dripping red felt-tipped blood. Judith was willing to lay bets that Belinda's Evil Self had gone round the booklets of all her friends and ripped out that single page.

If Judith asked, Belinda would deny all knowledge. Judith consigned the pictures to the outside recycling bin and went upstairs to work.

2.

I didn't get any work done, *Judith admitted*. The sudden appearance of the Dark Side of the Lin spooked me. I ate three more truffles. My hands were on the computer keyboard, but nothing happened. I'd got as far as wondering if I should get the plumber in about the bathroom noises. Then the phone rang.

"Hey." How unBelinda. She wasn't happy. I just hoped like hell her evil had subsided.

"Hey. This is a strange hour to ring."

"I know, but I felt miserable and alone and you're the only person I can get out of bed to tell me how idiotic I am for being miserable."

I laughed. "I wasn't in bed, stupid. There is a government submission and I have to get my bit done tonight."

"Can you spare a bit of time for me?" The tone was pitiful.

"Yes, of course." I paused. "You do sound a bit disconsolate."

"Only a bit. And there's no good reason for it. Well, except that it's school holidays."

"I would have thought you would be happier when school is out."

"I am at first."

"But?"

"It's halfway through week two. Everyone's busy with their kids or away or doesn't have holidays. I'm so alone."

"And so self-pitying."

"Of course," Belinda was indignant. "What's the use of being lonely if you're not self-pitying?" Her tone moved from alive to wan. "I had a glass of wine and it didn't cheer me up."

"So you rang me."

"Isn't that what sisters are for?"

"That is exactly what sisters are for. Especially when deadlines are looming and I have to be up before seven to get to work."

"Sorry," Belinda's voice faded.

"Come off it. You know I don't sleep anyway. What's really wrong? It's the wrong time of the month to be PMT. And you don't normally ring up in the second week of holidays and tell me how impossibly servile you are."

"I'm not telling you how impossibly servile I am! And if I were, it wouldn't be servile. That's the wrong word entirely."

"You sound like someone bowed down by untold years of foul slavery. I know what you need."

"Don't tell me a boyfriend. I will go to the mountains and kill myself with exposure if you tell me a boyfriend."

"You need that too," I pretended to be very cheerful. "Especially the exposure." I needed to lay off the boyfriend thing for a while, especially given the advent of chocolate truffles. "But I'm thinking of something far more crucial."

"What?" Belinda was definitely suspicious.

"A dinner party."

"What?" This flummoxed her.

"How long is it since you organised a proper sit-down white-tablecloth three courses plus nibbles?"

"About the right length of time," Belinda's voice was tart. Bingo.

"Garbage."

"Okay, a dinner party." She was caving in quickly, hoping that the topic could be changed. All she wanted was a nice little weep.

Some nights just weren't fair. I could see her thinking this in my mind's eye. I could see Belinda doing a tiny private sulk and shedding a single tear, in protest at me being so much like a Girl Guide, all heartiness and practicality. Too bad. She rang *me*.

"Who are you going to invite?"

"People?" hazarded Belinda. "I'll make up a list," she promised, "when I have a menu sorted out. Since so many people can't eat so many things."

"Do it the other way. Work out who's coming, then devise a banquet."

"Garbage. The only real reason for a dinner party as far as I can see, is to try out some of GG's recipes."

"I hate that GG of yours. We need a proper name for her."

"You don't like GG?" Lin was amused.

"I do not. We could call her by her first name?" Note how restrained I was in refraining from using the 'f' word. If it had not been the particular word on the tip of my tongue, and if the escape had not been so narrow, maybe my reply would not have been quite so un-adorned. "Too disrespectful. Go back to Great-Grandma?"

"No." Belinda's negative was crystal clear. "I want to change the way we look at her. So we don't call her Great-Grandma."

"By cooking your friends her recipes?"

"I have a box full of family recipes that need trialling. I'm not going to waste an opportunity."

"And they all look edible?" I was dubious. Normal recipes seemed . . . unlikely.

Belinda laughed. "No, not at all. Some of them look foul. Some aren't recipes at all; they're notes for recipes and make no sense. I don't need to cook those. And I doubt a method of whitening felt hats would be suitable for a dinner party."

"So what are you going to cook for this dinner party?"

"I'll finish with stuffed monkeys, I think, and Madeira cake. They're both annotated as 'From Mother' so they go back to 1850. They should be interesting."

Interesting was not the word I would have used. Though Madeira cake sounded passable. Flanders and Swann passable, "Have some Madeira, m'dear," and all that.

"Stuffed monkeys?" Something to stir her about, since Madeira cake was unobjectionable.

"I think a kind of tart, with raisins and things."

"They sound the sort of food Nick would like." I said this to encourage her. Please note, I did not say this because I liked the thought of them myself.

"Because the name's lurid?"

"That, and because they sound like sweet stodge."

"I wish you liked desserts. I want someone to share all these recipes with." Belinda was playing with me now.

"Nick," I said as positively as I could. "I'll send him next holiday and he can taste-test everything."

"Just what I need during my break from teenage boys — a teenage boy living in."

"It'll be good for you." I was dismissive. "Damn,

that's my mobile — it's probably about this submission. Gotta go."

I left Lin to plan her menu.

3.

Mackay had written a bare few pages on the tulip mania in the seventeenth century, and Rhonda had to somehow translate that into two thousand words. He called it 'Tulipomania', which was the kind of pretentious word a nineteenth-century stuffed shirt might use to add gravitas. This swank naturally led her to think of words as a possible solution to her problem. Etymology might be the way to do it. It just might.

Rhonda rather liked the history of words. Except that Mackay's etymology for tulip was boring. According to him, it came from the Turkish word for turban. She could look it up and find out if he was right. She didn't want to. At this moment if someone gave her a black tulip worth a king's ransom, she would not bow down and worship: she would slice it up, fry it with garlic and onions, add a bit of meat and vegetable and turn it into a stew.

She sorted out her boredom by writing the article in breathily excited tone. Maybe the breathy excitement would infect her and turn her into a giggling idiot. A not-bored giggling idiot.

Her breathlessness included explaining how tulips were found in a rare plant collection and then marketed into mania. How they became the arbiter of good taste. How people would spend more money than any common sense allowed just to have a single bulb in their conservatory. Rhonda contemplated writing about the tulip being the original geek-toy.

You love something, she thought, *and it's not yours.* She wasn't thinking of tulips. She was thinking of the two children of her ex-husband, to whom she was Auntie Rhonda. They loved her and she loved them. Each moment she spent with them twisted a knife in the wound, for they weren't hers.

Rhonda returned to her article. Bad. Bad timing. Mackay pronounced just at that point, 'Many persons grow insensibly attached to that which gives them a great deal of trouble, as a mother often loves her sick and ever-ailing child better than her more healthy offspring.' Rhonda wished her power were to make people rot in hell. Mackay deserved it for that charming insight at that even more charming moment.

And the rumbling started.

Rhonda leaned both hands onto her keyboard and watched nonsense syllables spill out onto the screen. Safer than a historical article. Then she left the computer, made coffee and sat down to write the article by hand. Her malign mood didn't fade, but at least she wasn't going to send her computer up in smoke.

She extracted every negative she could about tulip madness from the book, and recounted them in fine style on paper. She wrote about the sailor who ate a bulb, thinking it was an onion. She used the anecdote as a lead-in to colourful details about seventeenth century trade. Rhonda used the sad case of an English traveller taken with a fit of science, who dissected someone's prize specimen, to add a few words about science in the period. Both of these digressions added to the word count. Rhonda included a nice moral sentence about how the scholar paid for his curiosity with a spell in debtor's prison. Scientific inquiry was insufficient to free him.

She was so tempted to do an aside on social conditions, but thought she might need that material for a later article. It was a pity. It fitted so much with the tail end of the tulip craze. When the bubble burst, too many were left with nothing in their hands but the dream of a flower.

Rhonda emailed the article to the editor, got a return receipt and sat back happy. All done. All safe. No more nonsense syllables necessary to derail a crisis.

Maybe the crisis was still to come? Rhonda sat waiting at her computer all night, waiting, waiting, waiting for her fingers to take over her brain and write what they would. While she was waiting she flitted from chat room to chat room, mentally shutting out obscene remarks and online imbeciles. She felt a bit of a rumble. Her brain started wondering what the modern tulip was. Her brain didn't come up with anything. Rhonda hoped that she was safe. That there was nothing to fear.

At four in the morning she sagged onto her keyboard again, this time in relief. Whatever had been possessing her had gone: she was free.

Her instant celebration was to insanely post her newest story to her fan fiction friends. She normally sat on her stories a bit and let them grow and develop. This time, though, she threw caution to the winds. She was in a mood for danger. No cogitation. No deep introspection.

Her tale was a charming murder mystery set aboard the Battlestar Galactica. One of her top-favourite science-fiction programs. The new Battlestar Galactica — she never wrote stories about the original series. In this she was a purist. Grissom from CSI (one of her favourite characters) was brought in to solve it. She loved Grissom: his intellect, his wry wit, and the fact that he was always, always alone. Even when he wasn't.

Bringing him into an alternate future where humans were looking for an almost-forgotten Earth was not, as all her fan fiction friends would say, canon: it changed the core of the story. Time warped. TV warped. Everything warped. Starbuck and Grissom belonged together, she reckoned, and toyed with the idea of tampering with canon even more.

This was what fiction by fans was all about, she thought drowsily, as she lay in bed, later. Bringing together all your wishes in one little story. Emotional satiety.

That night Rhonda didn't dream.

4.

We take it in turns to be down, Belinda and I. My depression was set off by another delivery from Prince Charming. I'm not used to pretty packages containing gourmet food. I'm especially not used to it on the weekend.

I should have been flattered. My friends would have said so, which is why I couldn't ring them. Goodlooking man the right age chasing me. What, in their minds, was to question? To question was the fact that I didn't even have a face to attach to the gourmet nuts. Just a memory that he was easy on the eye. He was a little burble of words in my mind.

This day of deep morbidity was a Sunday, so I grabbed the kids and we caught a bus into town and got off at Town Hall and walked to the Queen Victoria Building.

Zoë's favourite place in the whole world is the Queen Victoria Building. We start at the big statue out the front and then we progressively say hello to all our favourite bits and pieces. I have this vision of us doing it when we're very old and Nick has to help me with my zimmer frame.

We went to the top floor after we had met and greeted Victoria and told her she was even fatter and uglier than Zoë's third grade teacher. We have to spend enough time on the top level to see both clocks strike. It was easier when there was only one clock.

We worked hard at spending quality time with each and not letting Zoë get bored. Still fun, but with a kind of manic underlay. Maybe it was the manic underlay that cheered me up? Or maybe it was Zoë? Nick watched us. Big silent chuckles shook his whole body.

We walked round the shops until five minutes before the big clock struck, then we waited to get the best view. Handholding is an important part of the ritual. Especially when Drake gets knighted. Zoë squeals with fear: she thinks that Drake's head is going to come off.

She doesn't like Liz One. "A very mean queen," I'm told, each and every visit. My girl hides her eyes and peeks out between her fingers and squeals. So that morning I looked at the clock tableau and saw Elizabeth out for the kill, and waited for Zoë's reaction. It came, right on schedule. "A very mean queen."

After Elizabeth is Charles I. The head plonking down. Zoë kept muttering all the way through it that "she's horrible" and "it's horrible" and "I don't want him to die". And she was still talking about Elizabeth and Drake. When Charles' head rolled off, she simply nodded a little nod and waited for the next scene.

Her favourite bit (her pretend favourite — I personally think her real favourite is when she hides and squeals) is Henry VIII. She loves the wives and counts them, pretending to herself that one might forget to come out. And yes, she is almost a teenager and yes, she knows they are mechanical, but she loves that game. Every time she counts, one, two, three, four, five, six — all there. After this, she'll look for a tourist and talk to them very confidingly. She knows that Henry had the wives sequentially, and she fully understands divorce (at least, I hope so!). But she insists on telling tourists that he had all six wives at once and that he was a very greedy man. She sometimes continues that he ate too much and that he exploded.

That day, after she had counted the wives, I asked her why she says these things: she just looked at me pityingly. Nick immediately moved himself two paces away. "Mummy, you can be so silly sometimes," she told me. "All the wives are there, in the clock, and I don't want to confuse people." I wonder if she thinks all tourists are congenitally stupid, or only the ones who watch clocks?

After the old clock, we went to the crown jewels, because they were close. We chose our favourite crown as we do. We talked them over one by one. We try to find new things to say, but if I get too inventive I get scolded.

Zoë chose Queen Mary's crown (as usual) because it has a fairy princess feel. She says the fur has to go: fairy princesses don't wear fuzz. I felt a bit vicious (thunder had come from the wrong direction the night before, and it lurked at the back of my mind), so I chose the Prince of Wales' 1969 crown. The spiky bits look handy for hurting people. Possibly people who disrupt my emotional equilibrium by sending nuts.

Nick liked the death-crown. He chose the mace, to match it. We both plotted nasties until Zoë told us we were not funny and we had to stop.

After the crown jewels is the jade cart. Every time we see it we walk around it once then invent a new story about the lady and the attendant and the cart. Then comes the new clock. We call it the GAC because it's the Great Australian Clock and we make the worst jokes about it. Mostly they include words that rhyme with GAC. Sometimes these jokes are not related to toilets.

What on earth will I do when Zoë becomes a teenager? When Nick's wanderings take him further afield than the bookshop? I bet Zoë turns Goth. My little blonde incipient Goth.

We came back to a note in the letterbox. It was from Peter. That Peter. The man of my nightmares. It said, "I am not here to trouble you. Send me a photo of Nick, please? I want to show my wife." With a Melbourne address.

The first thing I did was spread my hand open and say "Hamesh". Nick looked at me blankly, Zoë curiously.

"What are you doing?" asked my son.

"Averting evil," I said, on automatic. This was something I had learned as a child. Like the thunder.

The note from Peter scared me. It had been hand delivered. Peter had stood outside our house. Looming. I took deep breaths so I would not show the kids how I really felt.

I was going to have to sit down with the two of them and tell them the truth. I'd put it off almost forever. As if normalcy came by, ignoring. I knew it didn't, and I'd still put off that talk. I'd run out of time.

Nick had the right to know his real father, but . . . Lots of buts.

Peter had stood there. Outside my nice, safe home.

This time I'm not going to run away.

He married. I hope his wife knew what she was doing. Or that he'd grown up. Gods, what if he hadn't? My mind edged round that thought in a fascinated way. Terrified, but fascinated. Was she being abused? Did she know about me?

Had Peter changed?

He'd stood there. Put a note in my letterbox.

I'm not going to run.

5.

The next day, Rhonda was happy. Happy as a skylark in space. Rhonda spent a whole day ignoring anything she was supposed to do and going 'ha ha, fooled you' to her inner prophet. She rang Belinda and arranged to meet her for lunch on the weekend. It was a delightful feeling on a delightful day at a delightful time of year. In fact, Rhonda realised, everything wasn't just delightful; it was *perfectly* delightful.

A day off. A day wandering around the house and doing a bit of this and a bit of that. A day of hopping in the car and window shopping. A day of sitting in a café eating black forest cake. A day of buying one pair of perfectly sublime shoes. Happy shoes, with four inches of dangerous heel.

With her new, elevated gaze, Rhonda realised something important. She had to take the threat of discovery seriously. She could not afford to be a cult figure or a tool of secret organisations or anything else. She could only afford to be herself.

Loftiness gave her the capacity to work on this from two directions. The first was to diminish her net profile for a bit. The second, and most important, was to watch and analyse.

———

In a chat room there are always silent people. Rhonda hated being one of them. She saw a chat room as a community, and wanted to do her part. For now, however, she was playing a waiting game and a watching game. She needed to know how many people were haunting her haunts and get some idea about who they were and what they were after. Rhonda logged in under several names, all new, all neutral. Rhonda took up a hunter's stance. Rhonda watched and waited.

A series of questions flitted through all her favourite places night after night. The hunters arrived about the time she normally came online and stayed until about an hour past her usual time. She looked at the files documenting her outpourings and the times corresponded. At least three groups or individuals had obviously come to the same conclusions about her working patterns.

The other possibility, Rhonda reflected, was that she was paranoid. She really wished she was paranoid.

After some reflection, Rhonda decided she was permitted annoyance. Her weird mind was its own punishment: she didn't need to be pursued around the clock as well. Except that, thank goodness, it wasn't around the clock. It was just at her favourite times of day for chat; the lonely times. She was suddenly isolated from real-time conversation with real people when she most needed it. Yes, Rhonda was most definitely annoyed.

Rhonda changed her working day. She moved her chat room sessions to much earlier in the Australian day, and used her evenings to log into her blog and talk with her fan fiction friends.

She changed her chat aliases. Her new ones sounded as if she had emerged from an alternate reality where sado-masochism was a common practice. She would probably regret this. She would probably have to invent a whole new set of aliases. She didn't care. Rhonda was spitting fire. She had spent so long building up a tolerable life, and now these . . . these . . . Rhonda-hunters were stealing it.

When she went online to check on her blog friends, Rhonda's mood shifted. There were only three reactions to her 'Grissom in Space' story that Rhonda felt she could handle. She didn't even look at posts by anyone other than those three.

She really had been stupid to send it out. Stupid. Stupid. Stupid. And she was going to be even more stupid any minute, because she was going to post her follow-up. Part Two of Grissom aboard the Battlestar Galactica, where Superman comes to help and gets mistaken for a Cylon and slash ensues.

Rhonda really loved this piece. The first part was so very serious and the whole thing ended up so very silly. By the end of it, her friends would have to go back and read the early bits and work out when Rhonda had started sending everything up.

Something in her wanted this to happen. She wanted her friends to know she was a walking, breathing lie. She wanted to do it gently, though, starting with a joke. She didn't know she wanted this until she was poised at the keyboard.

It wasn't as if she hadn't done humorous pieces before. Except that before she had made it very clear that she was making fun of canon and had warned everyone with big flashing signs. She had had a great deal of fun designing icons that warned people. She had made sure the tone of the story was clearly satirical. Lots of flags. 'There is bull in this story.'

This time there had been no flags. It was for real. Because it was for real, only three friends counted. Starchild, TVwhore, and Phased. She had no idea about their real identities and they had no idea about hers. She thought that Starchild and Phased lived in the US, and that TVwhore was from the UK. Unless someone volunteered something about themselves or threw a hissy fit about something going on in their mundane lives, you just didn't know what their mundane lives were. TVwhore's scent meme might have reflected a bitter reality, or she might be a London corporate executive, playing with tawdry. And so Rhonda felt safe there still. Her friends knew her, but they didn't know how she lived, or the blight on her existence.

All three had posted about her 'Grissom in Space'. TVwhore was sometimes too bright for comfort. She had said, "Can't wait for Part 2. Hee-hee." Rhonda had not said that this was part one, and the ending had not been a cliff-hanger. Phased had added, "Me neither, but mainly because this is a departure for you. I think I enjoyed it." Starchild simply loved it. Starchild adored anything that monkeyed with her reality. "Good story, well told," she posted. "Want love interest."

"Love interest is coming," Rhonda replied. She finished part two in a hurry, and then tacked it onto the end of part one. She got offline.

If she had not got offline, she would have been waiting for reactions. Which was stupid. She betted there would be flaming. So she got offline and caught up on housework. She had no other deadlines, and it was about time she cleaned that pigsty that was her kitchen.

By the time she went back to her blog, she was very tired of cleaning things.

"Sorry, MissTRie," Phased had posted. "I hated it. I normally like your work, but there was something not quite right. I can't quite put my finger on what it was, but I didn't like it."

"Loved it. Loved you. 'Specially loved Superman," TVwhore said, giving Rhonda a bit of relief. "Going to chase him into space. Now."

"I just couldn't finish this," Starchild posted. "I wanted a murder mystery and got gay love in space. I guess it isn't my sort of thing."

For some reason those short comments left Rhonda immeasurably depressed. Even TVwhore's was not right, somehow. Rhonda sighed at her mind for going round in circles. And then she sighed at the comments.

She wasn't a fiction writer anyway; she was an historian. Maybe she didn't know what she was doing, maybe she couldn't write. Maybe she had posted things that should never have been put online for the world to see because maybe they were private jokes. Maybe the freakiness of her life meant she entirely lacked judgement.

Rhonda went for a long, long walk to shake off the depression.

When she came back, Rhonda decided to spend five minutes checking out her history message board. Quite a few of her paid writing opportunities had come from being there. Rhonda used her Jane Smith name, and she kept her private life out of it entirely. Apart from that, though, she was herself, admitting openly to the doctorate and her field of research, answering questions where she could. Like today.

Someone anonymous was asking about the proscribed books in the Bibliothèque Nationale de France. Rhonda explained what they were and when they were set up and that she herself had consulted something entirely boring there. This led to two discussions, one (inevitably) on censorship and the other on how to get to look at books in places like that.

Rhonda wrote in the censorship discussion, "We self-censor all the time. Not a day goes by without us deciding what we say to someone else or silencing thoughts in ourselves we don't like. For me it is not at all surprising that a society like that in the French Enlightenment might have censorship. Sharp censorship. Acute censorship. Dangerous censorship."

Her post was largely ignored. This was a pity, because she loved her turn of phrase. It belonged to a Thursday and petit grain. Pity it was the tail end of

Tuesday and everything smelled faintly of forests. Maybe she should plagiarise herself and put the thoughts into an article sometime?

Most people were worried about what they weren't hearing and knowing than about access to forbidden books in the French Enlightenment. Rhonda consoled herself that there had been a black market and the books got round.

"Why," posted Cliostory — a regular who always attached history to modern happenings — "aren't we more worried about current censorship? I have seen reports of a whistleblower on the internet who manages to know the most amazing things about current events and what is about to happen. That means the information is there and we're being denied it. Why isn't it available? Why can't we all know what is going on in the world?"

ANON569 piped up with, "That guy is just making things up. Everyone has heard of him — he is the Scarlet Pumpernickel of the Net."

"You mean Scarlet Pimpernel," someone else suggested.

"No, I said Scarlet Pumpernickel and I meant it. There is no elegant Percy Blakeney, freeing doomed aristos. He's a nerd, making things up to draw attention to himself."

Cliostory argued against this. She pasted the full text of three of Rhonda's message board posts.

"Thank God, I don't post to anything that permanent these days," Rhonda thought. These were old, they had happened. All gone.

Cliostory proved this point by point, unintentionally. She demonstrated how George W. Bush had decimated the local emergency help and how, step by step, New Orleans had descended into a drowned pit because of it. Rhonda remembered Hurricane Katrina and the horror inside as her prophecy had come true, even to the number of corpses found floating and the number of people who died in the Superdome. She had blurted out a list of historic houses that would be saved. At every point she had been irrefutably correct. At each of those points, though, Cliostory assumed that this was insider knowledge. Thank God for rationalists.

Just to consolidate this thought, Rhonda posted information to the other side of the discussion, explaining which authorities to ask to get access to the French National Library's 'Hidden' section. Rhonda described the sort of backing letter that would help.

Someone immediately posted, "Can you do letters for us that will get us in?"

"I doubt it," Rhonda prevaricated. "You'd be better off with something with institutional letterhead. I am working from home for a little, so it would be wrong for me to write something from my university." 'Working at home for a little' was a phrase she used a lot. Everyone assumed a child or an elderly parent. One more lie in the barricade that protected her from the world.

While this was happening, TVwhore had posted messages to the fan fiction area. TVwhore suggested, "Meet in a chat room." Rhonda agreed. A few minutes later she was totally regretting having said yes. TVwhore had an unholy fascination with her.

"What's your day job?" she asked. "You say you write non-fiction, but what sort? Are you a journalist?"

Rhonda explained she was a freelance writer and used a variety of pseudonyms. "I keep my private self quite separate," she explained, "because otherwise my life gets too complicated."

"Ooh, undercover stuff. Exotic," TVwhore replied. "What other nicks do you have? Something for chat rooms like this, I would think." Too bright. Too inquisitive.

How to disconnect those ideas? How? How? Rhonda almost sprained her brain trying to think of something. In the end she opted for simple dissimulation. "I'm perfectly obvious and boring most of the time. Don't spoil my fun by looking too hard."

TVwhore desisted, and they talked about other things. Mainly books. Books were safe.

The next day the two met again in chat, very early in Rhonda's morning so that Phased and Starchild could join them. The four spent a happy hour discussing books. They were moving to TV shows, but Phased was worried about the differences between countries. "We could spoil things," she said.

Starchild pointed out that the group emulated real life.

"What do you mean?" Phased asked.

"The new Nostradamus. Telling us things before we ought to know."

"?" asked TVwhore.

Rhonda stared at the screen in horrified fascination. "There is this guy they claim predicts the future. He comes into chat rooms and spills the beans then leaves. Very mysterious."

"Oh," said TVwhore. "I thought it was something new. I'm a fan."

Rhonda had a cult following. How . . . cute. How utterly horrible. She decided it was time to say something. "Who can believe such tripe?"

"Oh, I don't believe it," answered TVwhore. "I just enjoy reading it."

"Me too," admitted Starchild. "It's like watching a TV show, except you never know what's going to happen."

"You know," Phased said, "it may be from TVland."

"?" typed Rhonda, intelligently.

"PR. In six months we'll all discover that a movie or show has been made and that Nostradamus Anonymous is a character."

"I don't buy it." TVwhore was stubborn. "It's more than that."

"Tell me that in six months when you can buy toys in all major retail outlets."

"Speaking of which," and Starchild changed the topic. "I need more knitting patterns."

"What for this time?" Rhonda was genuinely curious. Starchild had the most interesting knitting objectives of anyone she had ever met.

"I've decided that my collection of Shrek dolls needs costuming." Danger over.

"So you can write them a new fiction?"

"TVwhore, whatever gave you the idea I wrote Shrek stories? I stick to pure science-fiction."

"Except when you outfitted all your Shrek dolls in fur and wrote Caveman Shrek."

"It wasn't Caveman Shrek: it was Flintstones meet Shrek," suggested Rhonda.

"You would say that, MissTRIe," Phased said, "You have interesting juxtapositions."

"Juxtapositions is a nice word." Rhonda wondered if she was imagining wistfulness emanating from the computer screen. She wished she had been imagining the conversation about a modern Nostradamus. Her mind went lunatic for a moment; if Nostre and Damus meant 'our lady' then was Rhonda 'our lady of the puling fools'? The conversation babbled on the screen without her, as she let her mind drift.

A few minutes later she was hauled back into reality. "MissTRie will know," Rhonda read.

"MissTRIe will know what? Sorry, I went to get coffee."

"You can read what's on the screen," said TVwhore, sharply. What was it with her mind today, Rhonda wondered again, briefly? She could feel the emotions behind the screen words. She sighed. This wasn't her strange little talent manifesting, it was her even stranger little imagination.

"You know about history," Phased prompted.

"What do I know about history?" Rhonda asked.

"We want to know if Joan of Arc foretold the future, like Nostradamus," Starchild the ever-nice prompted.

"Nostradamus just wrote bad poetry in Middle French. Joan of Arc heard voices and went around in men's clothes, but she wasn't a prophet."

"Ooh, grumpy," TVwhore chided.

"Sorry. Too many distractions."

"It's the hubby," said Starchild. "Mine is hopelessly helpless, too."

"'Bye, folks. See you when I am less to bits."

As she logged off, Rhonda realised that this group of online friends still thought she was married. It was her own doing. She had mentioned Tony as her husband when she had first encountered them, as a way of protecting herself. It had been a half-lie. Rhonda found herself drawn into a whirlpool of self-recrimination. There didn't seem to be a single aspect of her life that she wasn't ambivalent about.

Rhonda decided that coffee was what was needed to bring sunshine back into her life. Whatever the question, Rhonda always knew that the answer was coffee. She hied to the nearest decent café and ordered the biggest coffee they provided. She had barely sipped her overlarge special when a tumult descended on her.

"Auntie!" cried half the tumult.

"Me first. I get first hug!" said the other. It was the children. Her children. Tony's and Lara's.

"What are you two doing here?" she asked.

"Hugging you," said Number One. Everyone else might call them Ben and Val, but between the three of them they were always Numbers One and Two.

"Having chocolate milkshakes," said Number Two. "If you move over, then I can sit next to you."

"I want to sit next to her," said Number One. "It's my turn. You sat next to her last time."

"You can both sit next to me, if we all squash up small," Rhonda said, grateful she had chosen a booth, not a table. She could just imagine the chairs noisily scraping if there had been a table. These children were incapable of doing anything quietly.

Soon Lara emerged from the toilets and Rhonda scolded her for leaving the children alone.

"They weren't alone," laughed Lara. "I decided to surprise you."

"Were you surprised? Were you surprised?" Number One was bouncy.

"Number One," Rhonda asked suspiciously, "Have you been drinking red cordial?"

"No. I spent my pocket money."

"What did you buy? Show."

When Lara and the children went in their own direction, Rhonda immediately missed the warmth of the pair. She missed Number One's confidential elbow on her knee, and Number Two's imperious tap on her forearm to make her listen properly.

Of all the hurts in her life, the biggest one was this: not having her own Number One and Number Two. She remembered that Tony had joked early in their marriage. "Tony and Rhonda need a link. Our first child will make it an alphabetical RST."

"So we're not naming her after your father?"

"No, we are naming him after someone called Simon."

"Who?"

"Anyone, just as long as he's called Simon."

But there had been no children.

When she turned her computer back on, she found she could not face work and she could not face friends. What else was there? She opened every single folder in her documents file, trying to find something to occupy her. In the end she found her fan fiction file and she sat for hours, reading every piece of bad fiction she had ever written. Reading it gave her the same bittersweet feel as her day.

6.

Rhonda's reading led her to writing.

As MissTRie words fell from her fingertips furiously: she read them as they formed before her eyes and nodded in savage agreement with each and every whimper. Rhonda pressed 'enter' before she could retract them.

The awful thing was that she knew that she made all of the mistakes she was describing on purpose. She hated herself for bad writing, even though she herself had designed the style carefully. The only online place she used her normal style was in the history forum, where she used her 'Jane Smith' persona, the same writing and thought she used in correspondence with editors. The mood she was in, though, she didn't care. She stared at the enter key in despair, wondering if anyone could hate themselves as much as she did.

There was relief in thinking that she should just leave the whole mess. Run away. Running away was always *such* a good solution, she reflected, as sarcastically as she knew how.

7.

That was one thing Judith was certain of. She was not going to run. She wasn't certain of anything else. Except that the kids were not going to be hurt. Zoë was going to be zippy and happy and buttonbright and pretend to scream at Drake and Elizabeth for just as long as she bloody well wanted to.

She felt so strongly about this, it looked like anger.

Judith stopped staring at that nasty piece of paper and walked slowly inside. It only took three tries to get the autodial to operate. Hands are supposed to shake, Judith explained to herself, but they can be a damn nuisance when they do.

8.

Folks, *wrote Rhonda*, I'm seriously thinking of giving up fanfic entirely. I read some of my stuff, and it pongs. I read 'Grissom meets Superman' back and it reeks. It stinks more than a rancid goat. More than a sewer. More than a politician.

In my next life I will be married to the word 'said'. I never use it. I have the most wonderful words to replace it and they make my prose scream with uglyfugly. I write 'She shrieked', 'he whimpered', 'he grimaced'. And they are all speaking. 'She said', 'he said', 'he said'. All purple. All putrid. All stinkers.

I hate private names for fiction, so I always write using a person's job. This is particularly foul when a husband looks across the table at his wife. This is a real example. I am posting it here so you can see I really, truly wrote this sentence.

"The accountant looked across at his wife and smiled fondly at the lawyer." It doesn't make much sense, does it? I thought I was being so clever. In non-fiction things are easier. You just don't get as close and personal in non-fiction. It could have been worse. It could have been "The cherubically fat accountant looked across at his charming wife and smiled fondly at the hot-shot lawyer."

Another sin of mine is that I like ellipses . . . a lot . . . all the time . . . even when I have nothing . . . to leave out of a phrase. Also capitals. When I began I put words like "shrieked" in capitals. Never "He said", but "He SHRIEKED". Sometimes even "He SHRIEKED loudly." I am better than that now — I use italics instead. I ought to retire from writing fanfic NOW.

I change points of view all the time. That's another thing I do that is really stupidly bad writing. I counted my shifts in a paragraph that really seemed strikingly strange and I changed three times. It FELT right (look, I'm back to upper case).

My top favourite switch is in a sentence. I must think it is really economical to have adjectives that prove that both characters are looking at things. My hero can admire my heroine's violet eyes in the same bloody phrase as my heroine admires my hero's noble brow.

I also like exploding myths about characters. You all know which stories I mean. I know it is fine for a heterosexual to suddenly turn gay if you write slash, but I don't write slash (mostly). I don't do Mary Sue's intentionally (okay, so I do *something* right — send me some flowers to celebrate. I keep myself at my computer typing stories instead of turning myself into the heroine in my stories — what a whacking great wonder I am.) I don't appear in my own fiction and take over the plot, but I will have crime fiction characters developing super powers.

I never notice how characters look on TV. Seriously. So brown hair and blue eyes gets written as brown eyes and fair hair. I need to *watch* my TV while I write fan fiction from it. And I can't watch and write, because I don't have a laptop, so I trust my stupendous memory, which would be just dandy if only I occasionally used my less than stupendous eyes. I swear I must never look at a TV screen. I must sort of go into glazed mode and accept what's on it, passively.

Oh! And I do the BIG thing that anyone writing science fiction isn't supposed to do. The BIG AWFUL thing. Except I can't really complain that I am a bad writer when I do this unless most of my favourite real writers are bad. You know, where you have a character sit someone down or walk them through a building and explain the whole background to the scene so that everyone knows where they are? Well, I do it. A lot.

And now you know.

This turned out to be the most popular piece of writing Rhonda had produced in her entire born existence. Answers poured in and just kept coming and coming and coming.

"Oh, sweetie. We all have to edit a bit."

"Your stuff is funny — I thought it was on purpose. Keep it up!"

"Dammit, MissTRie, YOU DON'T SCREAM IN CAPS ALL THE TIME. IF YOU DID, YOU WOULD LOOK LIKE THIS."

"I get sick of 'said' ... and ... I like ... ellipses .... A lot ..."

"Stay with us — don't leave me alone with all these crazies."

She worried that more people knew her through her fan fiction than she had realised. People who had never said a thing until now. As usual, she put her worries on hold: life was too short for the amount of fear her body ought to contain. Besides, MissTRie was not Rhonda.

"You guys just crack me up," Rhonda found herself replying. "I guess you would say I should stick with it and keep writing."

"Absolutely."

"If you dare drop us, we will send boxes of bad fanfic to your door . . . where did you live again?"

"Don't, sweetie. We loff you."

And Rhonda found herself in tears. TVwhore sent her a locked message on her own blog, giving her the most heartfelt support. She wrote, "Whatever you choose to do, MissTRie, I'm with you. The whole way."

Rhonda printed the messages and taped them to the inside of a bedroom cupboard. They would be her emotional sustenance when next she was in dire need.

She stood looking at that door for the longest time. She didn't want these friends to melt away in the harsh sunshine of reality. She liked them and their fun and their fiction and their frivol. She loved them and their big hearts.

CHAPTER THREE

1.

THE MINUTE JUDITH HEARD THAT HER FATHER HAD ASKED
Linnie for her address, she knew what had happened.

He's a good guy, Judith thought, *he just completely missed
what was happening around him. Peter went drinking with
him; Peter was a good bloke; Peter kicked and slashed and tried
to make my life impermanent. He loved me. He was an engineer. And all of these statements about Peter are equally true.*

Plus there was Nick. Dad had been nagging Belinda
to nag Judith about letting a poor child know his father.
He wouldn't tell Judith directly though, that would
have entailed speaking to his daughter.

It made Judith so weary to find this out. Deep in her
heart something hopeful had faded. This was one child
who might never speak to her father again. He could
have *asked.*

And the funny thing is, she kept remembering, savagely, *that I'd always planned that Nick would meet Peter.
They have their rights.*

*Nick knew that Peter and I had quarrelled big-time and I
didn't want to see him, but the minute he wanted to meet his*

66

father, he should let me know and I would arrange it. I was surprised at my courage when I said this to him, but say it I did. I repeat it from time to time.

Sometimes Judith caught Nick looking across the dinner table at her, his eyes large with compassion. Usually it was when Judith's fears twitched into the way she slammed down the potatoes or the way she sat on the edge of the chair. There was a pattern to it. Twitchy fears.

A political monologue. She was passionate about the needs of abused women and she never saw just how much her own children noticed. Those eyes would follow Judith's twitches and Nick would make her cups of tea until they quietened down.

Judith admitted to herself that she had her fears. Little fears. Insidious fears. Infections Peter left in her life. She thought perhaps Nick had guessed some. That's why she was shocked that her father still thought she was a liar.

He could have rung me, Judith thought. *He could have rung me and asked, "Are you stopping Nick from seeing his father?"*

2.

There was a person whose name Rhonda never spoke. She never even let it darken her mind.

Mr Ick glistened. He looked prosperous, faintly rotund, his eyes bright and watching. There was something about him that suggested strength. "Corrupt strength," Rhonda called it, in a poetic mood. There was also something that suggested he didn't know when to stop. He was the sort of guy that made any sensible woman run very fast in the other direction.

Despite this air, he had a wife and child. And despite

Rhonda's feelings, he was an unavoidable part of her existence.

He was her case manager. He found her useful temp employment when she needed it. *The agency should be more flexible*, she would think, rebelliously. But either the agency couldn't take a hint, or Mr Ick pulled strings, because whenever she went to look for work, there he was, larger than life and thrice as oily.

"Canberra is such a small town," she found herself explaining to Tony over the phone, "And he's really careful not to give me any reason to lodge a formal complaint. I need the temp jobs and he gets me them. I'm caught between a rock and a hard place."

"Can I do anything?"

"I don't think so, but I appreciate the offer. I've developed an amazing array of ways of saying 'no' when he asks me out."

"You need a social life."

"We've been through this and through this and through this. I'm stable and happy and can't ask any more of life than that. Besides, I have you and Lana and the kids. Oh, and there are my online friends. And your friend, Belinda, if it comes to that."

"You need a social life," Tony repeated.

"Quit it. I don't need broken record technique."

"No, you need a social life," and Tony broke down and laughed. "Okay, I'll stop. For now."

"You're so kind."

"I'm the kindest person in the world."

The sad thing was, Tony was indeed kind. Nice, kind, sensitive. And married to someone else. Rhonda was a failure. Mr Ick always did this to her. Got her thinking she was a failure.

Mr Ick proudly declared his own success. He told everyone about his wife and family. He showed off his boy's sports award. He compared her hips to his wife's.

She didn't know his first name and she didn't want to. She tried to forget his surname with every molecule of her being.

Last Christmas she had met his wife and son at the agency's annual gathering. The little wife knew all about Rhonda. She told Rhonda how her husband always said how Rhonda was undervalued. Rhonda squirmed. She also squirmed at the memory of Mr Ick 'accidentally' bumping into her and copping a feel.

What brought all this into her mind, and made it swirl round it incessantly as she drove into the city and parked the car, was that Rhonda was short of dosh until the journal paid for those articles. This meant paid work. Rhonda wished her special talent were to stop time. She didn't want to be in Ick's office in three minutes. She didn't want to be in his office ever.

The big glass doors showed her a tight and fearful face. This wouldn't do. Rhonda composed herself and put on a bright smile. Mr Ick would not know how scared he made her or how much she hated him. No matter how much he leered, no matter how many hints he gave, she would remain cool. The face she had put on hid everything. It was like her online aliases: he might have a name, but he would never have Rhonda.

3.

That little note in Judith's letterbox was a new ballgame.

All those years of secrecy, wasted. Well, not wasted. We had peace for a time. The devils inside still responded to the possibility of the devil outside finding me, of course. Invisible devils plaguing my life.

It led to questions that commanded answers. Did Judith need to go to the police? Carry a can of mace? Did she need to make sure Nick walked Zoë to school and herself to the train every day? Did she need to take any action at all, or was he a reformed character and a law-abiding citizen? Did he beat his wife?

Judith remembered her political self. Judith was no longer nineteen: she had friends. She had built a life and had instantly forgotten it when she had opened that note.

Judith started thinking about who could be trusted with this secret. One thing she had learned when life first went wrong is that you can't burden most friends with too much. *They tell you they can take it,* she thought, *but they can't.*

Lin set up spare beds so the family could join her if the worst happened. She had much more faith in the capacity of people than Judith, so she telephoned a friend and asked for help. The family had emergency beds at a friend's place by nightfall — not far from her place, but not anyone their father knew — in case he'd handed out more than one address.

They decided to go down to Canberra and visit Belinda next weekend, just to get away. In the meantime Judith had some Grim Tales to tell the children. And some phone calls to make.

She decided that Her Friend the Lawyer could post the picture of Nick (his father had a right to know what he looked like) and give whatever dire warnings were legally possible. She could enclose a letter from another friend. Judith had to sit down and write it for Shaz, instantly.

———

Just getting Shaz's name and title ('my friend the senator') on something would show Peter that I am not the girlchild he nearly killed. I hate asking my friends these things. Shaz was happy to do it. She wished that all women in trouble could be supported so easily. We put long-term backup for victims of abuse on our list of things to discuss at the next Women's Electoral Lobby meeting. It was highly improbable that I was the only one in this position. Besides, it made me feel better. Shaz agreed. She said, "Australia is going to the dogs, so it is about time we showed them that there are some bitches in the place."

That letter was still there. In fact, it was in my handbag, tempting me to throw the whole bag into a furnace somewhere. Peter's presence still haunted the gate. And I still had to tell the kids. Apart from this, life was normal. As long as I didn't think of Dad.

I told the kids that night. Zoë sat and cuddled me for ages. We had a tear-frenzy.

Zoë rang a friend and arranged her own safe house to run to if she should see him. Damn. She should not be scared. Or need a safe house. Not at eleven.

Nick told me he knew all about Peter already, and had told Zoë. But they'd never heard it from me, so they'd waited. They wanted to know what Peter looked like. And they wanted to take precautions. They have this wonderful streak of common sense and wisdom. Damn. I didn't mean to cry all over my keyboard.

4.

Rhonda sat down gingerly in the office chair. All the offices in the employment agency were dotted with child-cheerful splashes of colour, presumably to remind clients that any unhappiness was entirely their own fault.

"So," her nemesis said, as happy as the splashes of colour on the window frame, "You want some money for lipstick."

"I wanted two weeks work, or thereabouts," Rhonda said. "Preferably with research involved."

"There are other types of work you might consider," and the innocuous words were accompanied by a meaningful look.

"I have a doctorate," Rhonda fell back on the old, tired words. "I would like to use it."

The Sleazoid took the hint and actually opened up a file on the computer. "Three weeks temping at Parliament House, doing research for a politician suit you? Or does the party matter?"

"I don't care which party it is. If it's a research job, I will do it. Do I need any sort of clearance?"

"Not for this one," he replied, and then Rhonda saw the hated flickering lashes that made it look as if his eyes were glinting down at her. "Come to lunch with me and we'll discuss what jobs might be obtained with higher level clearances."

"I don't want any jobs that require a security clearance," said Rhonda. "I hate carrying other people's secrets."

"Most jobs with clearances aren't like that. We're talking your standard public service temping position." One thing she was always thankful for with this man was his basic honesty.

"Then why the clearance?"

He shrugged, "An 'in case'. The procedure really isn't tough. Come to lunch and I'll explain it."

Rhonda was torn between playing safe and finding out more. She chose to find out more. "When does the research job start?" she temporised.

"They said as soon as possible. I'll make the call after lunch and then you can be there tomorrow."

Mr Ick was playing his cards all correctly today. Rhonda sighed inside. There was nothing to cavil at in his manner and nothing really she could do. She agreed to lunch. He did tell her about security clearances during the meal.

She was listening and taking mental notes when she felt his hand moving gently on her thigh. "I have to go," she said, standing up, suddenly, "I didn't realise the time. Thank you for finding me the job." Rhonda was volcano-red inside. And there was nothing she could do until he had made that phone call. Nothing except leave.

She spent the afternoon in the Botanic Gardens. Her phone rang when she was quietly contemplating the coolness of the fern garden. It was the senator's office at Parliament House. Mr Ick had not said there was an interview involved. She offered to come over immediately. They asked if they could interview her now, over the phone, instead, "It's rather urgent."

"Not a problem," Rhonda put on her cheerful voice. The small interview world smelled green. At the end of the interview she was told, "You were our last interview. The decision will be made within the hour. Do you want us to ring back on this phone or on the landline?"

"This number, please," Rhonda said. She wasn't ready to go home. She rang Belinda to see if she was free and they could finally have that coffee.

An hour later she was outside the café under a giant umbrella, sipping coffee while looking over the lawn and the old gum trees, waiting for her friend. The Botanic Gardens had indeed redeemed her day. Her next day was also redeemed when she was told that she had the job.

She smiled at a giant eucalypt. Then she realised she had a Mackay article due in three days. Better do it now, she thought. Tomorrow, she had been told, she was working on long term ramifications of domestic violence. Tomorrow was a different Rhonda and she needed a different voice.

Today was the brightness of Belinda, full of information about her garden and her recipe collection.

5.

"Hee," Rhonda said to herself, as she read the Mackay account of the Mississippi Scheme. This article was going to be awesome. Then she collected herself.

"Writer's English, not netspeak," she said, out loud, to reorient her brain. Her reading was not interrupted by her hand heading for the warmth of the mug of coffee on her desk and by her mouth savouring the slightly bitter blend she was experimenting with. Drinking coffee always helped her focus.

Rhonda didn't like the Defoe quote at the top, but that was because she didn't like Defoe. He was a recognisable name — Robinson Crusoe and all that — so she should use it. Before she read too far then, she typed:

Some in clandestine companies combine;
Erect new stocks to trade beyond the line;
With air and empty names beguile the town,
And raise new credits first, then cry 'em down;
Divide the empty nothing into shares,
And set the crowd together by the ears.

Rhonda realised that she had the whole article. Defoe had said it all in six bloody lines. Mackay was just joining the dots. Well, sort of. Defoe had certainly summed up the insights she herself had about the Mississippi Scheme. Lunatic stuff, the whole lot of it.

As she contemplated those lines she felt a rumbling deep inside. She sincerely hoped it was hunger. She grabbed her coffee with one hand and took a warm swig while she opened the book with the other.

Keeping occupied might help to avoid arcane disturbances.

"Focus on the article," she instructed her conscious mind, hoping it would convey the message to her subconscious. "The article, Rhonda. The whole article. Nothing but the article." The rumbling subsided and Rhonda relaxed.

"John Law", she read for the umpteenth time and the name finally hit her conscious mind like a hammer. The Late Great John Law. How could she have forgotten? Rhonda realised that she had to explain John Law. Dates first. His social standing. His education. The importance of that whole financial stuff back then. She truly hated economic history, but in this case it was unavoidable. And maybe it took someone who truly hated it to write this article.

Rhonda refilled her mug, her feet treading her grump hard into the wooden floor with a series of small thumps. A part of Rhonda listened and wondered if the thumps would be harder if her grumpiness was bigger, or if she were fatter. She shook her head to shake the mood and got back to work.

As Mackay indicated, the Mississippi Scheme failed because human beings are . . . human beings. Good place to start. Human beings are just human beings, even the great John Law and the extremely exotic Regent of France. Explain this. Then explain Law. Then explain the rest.

And there was so much 'rest' to explain. She would have a very meaty article. Her writing would have to be tight; no space for fancy extrapolation and extended examples. Tight, convincing, dramatic.

She wanted to go into Law's background, but there were not enough words. She wanted to tell about how his early jobs allowed him to buy estates and act noble. Maybe he actually had become noble. If she was doing a proper research job she would check that one, but she wasn't doing a proper research job, she was simply writing a fun article for a few bucks. She was letting the side down with her sadly declining historical standards. One thing she'd learned early on, the academic's level of obsession with detail was pretty hard to sell commercially.

Mackay thought Law was a hit with women and a mathematical near-genius and said that men nicknamed him Jessamy John. But she didn't think the Mississippi Scheme was only about John Law, so she wrote herself a one-paragraph summary of the key points of Law's pre-scheme life, to be inserted at an appropriate point. She heard herself saying, "insert at an appropriate point" and followed that with a quiet "hee."

She then made a whole new pot of coffee, refreshed the sandalwood oil that was supposed to be fragrancing her surrounds and went into foolish mode. "He was now very young, very vain, good-looking, tolerably rich, and quite uncontrolled," Mackay had said. She put the article aside for a little and started listing the number of men she knew who fitted Mackay's description of Law. Her husband had been through that stage. Except that he had been comfortable instead of rich and only mildly uncontrolled. He had mellowed into a good bloke faster than most.

He'd grown up faster than most, too. That was her fault. At least they both survived those bad days. As friends. And Tony hadn't ever espoused the 'gay life' Law led.

Rhonda loved changes in language. A rampant heterosexual, leading a gay life. It appealed. It definitely appealed. And her humour was so low it was crawling at the bottom of the ocean.

An article on how she had destroyed her marriage was not what the editor ordered. She'd managed to down a lot of coffee and the room now smelled like a Chinese gift shop, but she hadn't done much work. She opened her Mackay again.

Law was a gambler and led a gay life. As part of his gay life he had unfortunately won a duel. What happened to Law after he won his duel? A series of expulsions, town after town after town. How curious that a man named Law should get himself into so much trouble with the law, Rhonda pondered. And how curious that his adulthood should be so closely linked to the decline of France. Well, not so much a coincidence, as a coincidence of interests: one of his close friends was that likewise gay Duc d'Orléans, who became the regent. Lucky Law.

And lucky Rhonda. Intrigue and politics and government decline. Financial problems and ingenious solutions. Dangerous and excitingly risky ingenious solutions. She wrote several hundred good words. Scandal broth was good drinking. It was also good scene setting, because it showed exactly how someone as unreliable as Law could be given such vast responsibilities. She couldn't pride herself on this amazing insight since Mackay got there first. He glamorised the financial bit though, and Rhonda had to do some quick research to work out exactly how Law's bank worked and why its major flaws didn't show themselves at once.

She was enjoying this. It was an aspect of history that she really hadn't tangled with properly and an approach to history she had never really appreciated.

She was halfway through the article before the words 'Mississippi' or 'Louisiana' came up, but she wasn't troubled by her delinquency. The article made sense; she had been building up to those magic words, merely. Law, it seemed, had established a company.

"Certain other companies," Rhonda wrote, "did not

make the fundamental error of allowing speculation on their stock before any worth in trade was proven." She wasn't even certain, to be honest, that the other big players were publicly owned, but delving into this would make her word count go over the limit (why was writing an article so much like writing an undergraduate essay?), so she left the subject alone.

She added some words on how speculation became political when more paper money was issued than the land held resources for and the coinage was forced into depreciation. Diocletianically. Was it Diocletian who did that, she wondered, or was she misremembering and did he stabilise it? And was Diocletianically even a word? Too bad, it was his period and it was her article, after all. She liked 'impunity' as a word, too, so she slipped that in for good measure.

She set the scene for dramatic downfall. Rhonda chronicled how Law's bank managed to get the tobacco monopoly and to refine gold and silver. All of this directed income, and that direction soon became the Royal Bank of France. Poor little Louis XV.

And so the Mississippi Scheme was set up as the French East India Company, to trade the wealth of the world and make France rich. Or make the Duc d'Orléans rich. Except that it was a company set up by a gambler with a talent in maths and by a regent with very particular ideas of the privileges of power. Everything was built on dividends and profits, and there wasn't much reality.

Rhonda loved saying that. Her life was so very unreal after all, and if it wasn't for GAM's dividends and profits, she would be sunk without trace, like many of those ships that sailed to the Spice Islands and to the Americas.

Stock traded at increasingly higher prices. A dream. It was all a dream. It was like the tulip craze except that paper speculation replaced bulbs. At least, Rhonda wrote, those bulbs would flower. The flowers might have been ruinously expensive, but they were tangible and pretty.

Rhonda was becoming very pleased with this article. It was as if she recognised parts of it.

Maybe she did. Maybe she had come across it as an undergraduate and had forgotten. One isn't born knowing things, after all. Not even cool columns and marble floors. And goodness knows where that thought came from. Rhonda found she was fretting the keyboard and making more typos than text. It was time for a coffee break. Or a break from coffee.

Rhonda sat on the couch for a few minutes, and had a choc-mint biscuit. The chocolate smoothed her palate and soothed her soul, and the clearness of the mint aftertaste helped her pretend the whole thing wasn't fattening. She had a second biscuit to test this theory.

She wasn't doing justice to the Scheme or to Mackay when it came down to it, but both deserved more than two thousand words. What she was doing was writing a damn good article. What she was also doing was filling the inner addict. This fix of history was what her soul craved. For every idea she wrote, she thought thirty others, and analysed the period and the places and the people. Happiness.

She even enjoyed describing why the stock crashed and how people were hurt. Rhonda did not forget to mention the six thousand souls who were theoretically conscripted to work in the 'gold mines' of New Orleans, to shore up the crashing stock, but many of whom were found in Paris a few weeks after their conscription. Had there ever been gold found near New Orleans?

Her own emotional stock market crash happened as she realised that if this were an academic article she would get to flesh out these by-ways and write a foot-note to her sources. Her life was full of corners that were cut and holes that ought to be filled. The whole Company scheme crashed, and with it many peoples' lives. So what? Hers had done that so many times. People got through. Somehow. Except those who didn't. Time for another break before finishing the piece.

Rhonda went online for a bit. She didn't go to a chat room. That would be tempting fate. She browsed a bit in online shops and dreamed of buying fine linen and elegant homewares. White tablecloths and silver can-dlesticks.

When her emotions were less roiling, she returned to Law. She wrote about rampant inflation and the cartloads of notes worth a loaf of bread. Rhonda won-dered if she wasn't writing about Germany before World War II. Cartloads of notes. Poor people taking the brunt of the policies of the rich and powerful.

Rhonda now wanted the article done with quickly. She could feel inside that there would be consequences when she finished.

Mackay lauded Law for refusing gains. He claimed that Law only bought land. Lots of land. Rhonda was not impressed with either man. She found herself writing — with the greatest of pleasure — how Law's land was confiscated. A powerful country was brought to its knees and all because everyone was addicted to paper money, unlimited amounts of paper money.

Perfect. Article finished. Time to move on. And if she went out to get milk, maybe she could avoid what was coming.

6.

Judith had one old photo she had not been able to throw out. Her children examined the Peter of many years ago from every angle possible and Nicholas the Computer Genius printed out versions of him with grey hair and beard and moustache. Then Nick found an up-to-date picture on the net.

Judith refused to look.

Zoë regarded it very intently, and then she asked Nick if he wanted to meet his father. He said, "Not right now. Maybe, someday." He looked worriedly at Judith.

His mother reassured him. It was his decision, and he wasn't going to lose love and support no matter what he decided. "Just as long as you don't decide we need to get back together," she said.

Zoë piped up with, "Nick wouldn't!" Nick laughed and hugged her.

And that was that. Judith hoped that was that.

———

Judith felt she had to explain in writing, to an invisible world that had not, as yet, read a single word of her deathless prose:

Nick sat me down midweek and explained to me, very carefully, that he'd thought it through. He had his blank face that meant he was agonised. Which meant I was agonised. I think both of us prefer the wild shouting. He said he needed more time before he met his father. The violence thing terrified him. It wasn't the same as his computer games: it was real.

What struck me most were his thoughts on how Peter's actions affected him. He explained he was scared he might be like his father. He just said this and retreated right into himself. This gave me a lot of extra worries.

Nick has never been violent. But now he's scared. Of himself. Of his potential for violence, of what his father might have left him, somewhere deep inside. He was obviously angry with Peter, but he just said what he said and wouldn't say more.

Then there was the other letter. Nick added himself to it. It was his idea. He said if there was an urgent need to get in touch — if his father got terminal cancer or something — he needed to know. He was like me, it gave him a foul feeling to get the letters directly. Shaz agreed to take letters for Nick.

At the same time Shaz also offered Nick work experience in her Canberra office. She's good. I'm glad she chose to give him that self-respect. He hid in his room the normal way and spoke in grunts. Shaz is a very good friend.

There was one more big thing we did. Or rather, I did, with Zoë's help. This was Zoë's turn for secrets. And we did it because Zoë was doing a good imitation of a very scared child, and that was just not on.

I told her Great-Grandma's box contained the family's magic. I told her I had no idea if any of it worked, but it might make us feel safer if we did a protection thing for the house. She lost some of her tension and instantly chipped in that we had to do one for Auntie Belinda, too. And for us.

We did the 'for us' bit first. I made us each protective amulets. My carving was miniscule, albeit scratchy. I made each amulet the same way I make my craft for the market. The words curved and spiralled from the outside in and were hard to read. I made them decorative intentionally; hard to read was a bonus.

Nick took one look at his and put it on his computer. He didn't know it was magic. I wasn't sure it was right to tell Nick. Poor Nick. But his computer is amulet protected.

Zoë and I did two other protections that day, feeling sneaky and magical. There was one against someone who wanted to kill you, which includes bending the little finger of the left hand and saying a charm.

The other spell was for guarding a house. We said our little rhyme over a cup of water and we poured it right round the outside of the house. Zoë wanted to do it near the fence, but we were worried about neighbours watching and couldn't work out what to do about the trees. All the plants under our eaves are in pots or are dead (don't ask what angst this causes my-sister-the-gardener) so we dripped water around every inch of the house proper. Well, except for our adjoining wall.

When we went to Canberra that Friday, Zoë and I did the same thing with Lin's house. This was funnier, because Zoë crept under and behind bushes and things to sprinkle the water — she adored squiggling every-where. I'm positive she was pretending to be a mouse when she went behind Linnie's prostanthera.

We had no idea if any of it would work, but Zoë walked lighter.

7.

In the chat room, Rhonda typed as if there was no to-morrow. She didn't know what she keyed in; she just knew that she had to get it out before she imploded.

"Cabals. Company mixed foully with company, where the law cannot see. On the outside competitors; on the inside, wells of corruption. Names that say great things, 'Joy' and 'Freedom' and 'Blessing', but reflect servitude and starvation. Doublespeak. Big Brother's Unbenevolent Rule. Workers' hours increase in proportion to their pay decreasing. Less is produced, just as more is claimed. Small companies are subsumed into the greater evil to remedy the deficit. Empty names. Empty morals. Empty companies.

Emptiness made public. The cabal is convinced that money will solve all, that cash injection equals redemption. The companies are floated on the stock exchange, all three companies. Claiming to be separate. Claiming to be sunrise. Claiming false honesty. America basks in putative profit. Citizens buy shares in Joy and Freedom and Blessing and condemn souls to servitude. Empty shares. Empty Joy. Empty Freedom. No Blessing.

The government promotes Joy and Freedom and Blessing. A government complicit in emptiness.

Private memoranda are written by the President and his chief advisor: they know how empty are the promises and how fraudulent the world of the promises. There is political gain for them. The country is ruled by Hollow Men. If the public finds out, the government will fall. Down will come Joy and Freedom and all."

"Who are you?" asked geeknerd.

Rhonda went silent. She knew she could just click and leave, but she also knew that if she didn't record what she had written, she would lose it.

Instead of re-reading and then typing it all up, she went straight to typing. She could find out what she'd written later. She wasn't sure she wanted to. Rhonda knew, though, that a record is a useful thing to have: the historian in her rearing its head.

She typed away furiously, getting down every word she could, paying attention out of the corner of her eye to the discussion about her outburst. The discussion that was gradually scrolling up and deleting her words of wisdom forever.

"M44M?" asked Kool. "Are you the same M44M who is normally here? You don't sound like him."

"M44M has been here before? Who are you, M44M?"

Geeknerd was persistent. None of her friends were helping. In fact, they were all busy telling geeknerd that she was a regular. Male. Forty-four. Married.

"Live in Ohio, don't you?" Kool said.

Rhonda kept an eye on the exchange, but refused to participate. Let them think what they liked. Hopefully they would keep leading themselves very far astray. Rhonda typed as quickly as she could, getting her words down before they scrolled off the top of the screen.

"M44M? Are you still there?" Kool messaged her privately.

"Not M44M," she messaged back. "Used his nick."

"You're M44M," said Kool. "He talks about politics a lot. You're on the same time. You even sound a bit like him. All those long words."

Rhonda remained totally silent. She watched in horrified fascination as Kool announced to all her erstwhile friends, to the great joy of geeknerd who was either a troll or someone investigating her, that M44M was really M44M. He gave the chat room the reasons he had given her privately and defied her to answer them. Kool was far too enamoured of honesty.

"So M44M is the New Nostradamus. We are in the presence of fame," someone commented. "We must bow and worship."

"We're in the midst of fraud," Kool said, and suddenly his betrayal had a reason. She couldn't blame him. She envied him his anger. "Chicanery. Leading innocents astray. This stuff is garbage."

Geeknerd spoke up. He was trying to convince her

85

he was on her side, perhaps. "He isn't a fraud. This is the voice of Nostradamus. He's for real."

The chat room became very excited and rather inarticulate as everyone jumped in to ask Rhonda questions. She could see no way to redeem herself. There was no explanation she could give that would bring this corner of her life back. She finished typing out what her fingers had keyed when divorced of her conscious will and she saved it and she exited the chat room.

Time to fade.

Step 1: clean the computer of all evidence of that alias. M44M no longer existed.

Step 2: change provider in case anyone traced back to her server. She rang up an ISP and arranged a new connection. This was the last time she could do this and get fast download: she'd run out of providers.

Step 3: Invent some new aliases. One new alias. More than one was too much of a mindstrain. Even that one was a bit dicey: 'penname' was the new Rhonda.

Step 4: have a nervous breakdown. A full phantasmagoric breakdown, with the assistance of alcohol.

Rhonda cast her mind back to the very merry afternoon when her friends at Syracuse found out how very uneducated she was.

"Never had a mixed drink?"

"I've had screwdrivers."

"Child's play. Not the real thing."

"I've had fluffy ducks."

"Oh God, where did you get served them?"

"At a disco."

In memory of all her long-unseen friends in the US, Rhonda decided that her breakdown would be accompanied by the drinks they had taught her to enjoy. And because she really needed to watch her health, she decided that Bloody Marys were the way to go. Each time she made one she would madly mutter, "Bloody, bloody, bloody, bloody."

Two days later she emerged from her binge, feeling a little ashamed. She logged into her blog and found that her friends had all posted fan fictions dedicated to her. She'd forgotten all about her fan fiction diatribe. And she'd forgotten her friends while they were so quiet. A little corner of Rhonda's soul was willing to admit that she was still alive.

"Mary Sue meets Grissom in Space", they called it. It was a chain story. Phased began it, then TVwhore had added, then Starchild, then other writers in the group had added their bits.

Rhonda printed all of them out and then read them over and over and over again. It was the kindest thing anyone had ever done for her and she told her friends this, repeatedly.

"Every MissTRie needs you lot and your bizarre senses of humour," she typed in her blog. "Every Miss-TRie in the world." As she typed, Rhonda resolved that she would hang onto this group of friends no matter what the world threw at her.

She had drawn her line in the sand.

CHAPTER FOUR

1.

ZOË GOT TO THE PHONE BEFORE JUDITH, WHICH WAS JUST
as well. "Hello, Auntie," she said, with joy. The room
lightened, so buttonlike bright was she. "You can't
speak to Mummy right now."

Judith raised her eyebrows.

"She's angry." A silence. "Oh, not at you. And it is
not that note or Nick or anything. We're all good. It's
the other people who ring. We had lots of phone calls
this week and everybody called her 'Mrs'. She got
madder than anything. It's fun. She said she's not going
to answer the phone for a week."

It's fun? My daughter thinks I'm a source of amusement?
If she weren't my one and only daughter I would damn her
pink scrunchie. It would fade and shred thread.

Another silence.

"I do," her daughter said proudly. "It's nice, too. Can
I sing it to you?"

This was not a good development. Judith edged out
of her chair and started moving to the door. But while
she was listening to Belinda, Zoë fixed her mother with
an Ancient Mariner eye.

"Auntie asks if she can talk once I've sung her my new silly. She says it's not important, but she wants to know all about you being mad."

Judith laughed and gave in. "Okay. I'll talk to her, but are you sure she wants you to sing?" Judith lived in hope.

"Mummy doesn't believe you want me to sing," Zoë reported back, aggrieved. "When I give the phone to her will you tell her it was your idea?"

Her smile regained all its brightness as she listened and nodded. Then Zoë sang. Of course she sang. At this moment, a steamroller could not stop her singing. Judith tried not to listen.

———

"Hi," said Belinda, and I suddenly realised that brightness was a family trait. Niece and aunt are a matched pair. I should hire them out to an electricity grid.

"Zoë said you were going to tell me something." I couldn't help it if my voice sounded suspicious. I was trapped in a sea of overwhelming family illumination.

"Firstly, I asked Zoë to sing to me. Zoë sings quite beautifully and I adore her song. It takes me right back to you pretending to being a Sontaran and wanting to kill me."

"I still want to kill you," I reassured her.

"I can't think why," my sister said, innocently, "when you're the one refusing to answer the phone."

"Just don't assume I'm married," I begged. "If anyone else calls me 'Mrs' this week, I'll go round the bend."

"You're already there. And it's happening to me, too. And I never was married, so it's even more of an insult."

"So why aren't you reacting to it?"

"Because I'm an ineffably nice person," my insufferably sugary sister informed me, infuriatingly sweetly. "Besides, I have it sorted out."

"How?"

"I put on my best teacher's voice and say that no one by that name lives here. If they insist and ask for someone else I say I have a policy of not donating money or listening to business offers from anyone who thinks I'm a male adjunct and not a person in my own right."

"That sounds like something I would say," I objected.

"I know." My sister, in laughing, toyed with the idea of an early death. "I use your exact tone of voice."

"I could do that," I felt very grudging.

"Don't," begged Belinda. "I have a better strategy."

"What is it?" Despite myself, my voice sounded interested. Dammit. I wanted to sulk.

"You have Zoë."

"Yes." Now she was scaring me, "I have Zoë."

"Get her to answer the phone very honestly. Sorry, Mummy isn't married any more and she doesn't want to talk to you if you think she is. But I can sing you my favourite song."

"She'll do it, too!" I had to laugh.

"She'll thoroughly enjoy it."

My mood shattered and shards of laughter fell everywhere. "Belinda, one day I will kill you, you know."

"Judith, one day I will haunt you when you have killed me, you know."

"Did you ring for anything in particular?" I had to ask.

"Mainly to chat, and to see how thing are. You know, double-checking that life is stable again and all that. But partly because I put a box of stuff in the post to you and I wanted you to know that it contains nothing poisonous."

"What is it?"

"Just a few things from recipes of Great-Grandma's," she said airily. "You needed a care package. You were due for a big sulk."

"My waistline doesn't need a care package," was the best witty repartee I could deliver, putting gloom back in my voice.

"Have one piece of each thing and feed the rest to the kids," was her advice.

"Actually, they'll love it," I admitted. There is nothing worse than having two children who adore homemade cakes when your favourite place to cook is the local bakery. How did Belinda become so beautifully domesticated? How did I fail at almost everything I've tried? "Lin, I feel a bubble bath coming on," I said, firmly.

"One of those moods, then — you want to be unjoyous," she said, still annoying. "If I can't cure it then I'll leave you to endure it." Damn her toenails. I couldn't hear it, but I just know she smiled. And I bet it was a charming and supportive smile — damn all her toenails to three hells and back.

We said our farewells and hung up. And all the way through me running a nice hot bath, Zoe doinged the Dr Who theme.

For the record, the Evil Belinda tucked something into that care package. There was a batch of biscuits labelled 'For Judith only'. And each and every biscuit was marbled purple and green. Feminist-coloured cooking. I could live with the manifestation, but that didn't mean I was going to eat the bloody biscuits. I took them to a meeting.

2.

Rhonda needed time with friends, so she went to her weblog.

Phased: "Meme time!

I want all my fanfic friends to tell me five things they have to be happy about. Phased commands it, right royally."

TVwhore: "Meme time!

Am I allowed to stuff it up right royally then?"

Starchild: "Meme time!

Ignore TVwhore. She hit her head when she got out of her bed on the wrong side and she smashed her face into the wall. My five things are chocaolte, chocalte, choacolte, choaclte and chaocalte."

TVwhore: "Meme time!

Ha! Did not. Never got out of bed this morning. Am sharing my bed with my computer and thinking evil right at you. Your keyboard is mine!! Shudder with fear, Starchild.

My five things are autumn leaves, bad grrls, knitting, fan fiction and chocolate. I don't know what Starchild's five things are — can't find any of the words in a dictionary."

MissTRie: "Meme time!

Starchild's things are what you get before you eat chocolate. Once you eat them then the whole world becomes choc and everyone is happy. I know because I saw it in a TV ad."

Phased: "Meme time!

If you saw it in a TV ad it must be true. What are your five things, MissTRie?"

MissTRie: "Meme time!

Five things is an awful lot of happiness. I'm not sure I could stand that much. Nice sunny days: I like nice sunny days. Writing. Smiling at people who just want to hate me. You lot (can't think why, but you lot make me happy — you did know I recently escaped from a lunatic asylum, didn't you?). Can't do five. Run out of ideas. Can I just put chocolate to fill in the gap?"

Phased: "Meme time!

Chocolate fills all gaps. Especially when there is a gap between my waist and my skirt."

3.

Judith was dumping the latest batch of unwanted mail when something caught the corner of her eye. It was some sort of animal and had no right being in her garden. She turned to chase it away, but the phone rang. She swore to check on it later, and forgot.

Later she wrote down: It was a bloody telemarketer. Wanted to know if I supported some charity. I was almost polite, which was very nice, given it is me we are talking about and not some mythically charming person. All the while I was trying to look out my garden to see what that blasted animal was. A small horse? Nonsense. Small horses do not float around private gardens in Newtown. Besides, I'm sure I saw a horn. Small horses do not have horns. Unicorns are fantasies. It was probably Zoë, pretending.

I hung up the phone and thought, 'Dammit'. I was not going to be caught out by anyone's practical jokes. I made my own phone call.

"Hey."

"Hey. What's up?"

"How do you know anything is up?"

"Because, Lin, you always just pick up the phone and say 'Hey' when you feel a bit down. Otherwise you say, 'Hullo, how are things?' Or you pretend to be a market research firm."

"Do not."

"Do."

"Not very often. Well, something's up. It isn't big, but it made me feel touchy."

"What happened?"

"Someone told me today I was a schoolteacher."

"You are, aren't you?" I did a great quizzical when I was Zoë's age — these days it sounds more like querulous. "Unless I have a mystery second sister."

"It's what I do. I teach in a school. It's not what I am. I mean, it's not what they meant when they said I was a teacher."

"It was a man?"

"How did you know?"

"Something in your voice. I still don't understand why you didn't like being called a schoolteacher."

"It was the tone."

Ah, I thought, *she's peeved. Daylight dawns.* It was a fairly murky dawn at this moment, so I prodded. "And?"

"He said he meant I was worthy."

"Worthy." It came out flat, which means at least she couldn't hear me laughing.

"Dull, boring, predictable, dutiful, virtuous."

"Well, you are."

"Careful," Belinda warned, "I'll disown you." I laughed aloud. "I'm going to take up bungee jumping," was Belinda's reply to my laugh.

"Bungee jumping."

"I have a little echo who goes in and out with me. Yes, bungee jumping."

"Why on earth?"

"Isn't that what people do when they cut loose?"

"It has nothing to do with worthiness, you know. And it isn't even very interesting. I would rather be worthy than bungee-jump. I would even rather be a school teacher."

"I love being a teacher."

"You just don't like to be called one."

"Not when it is given to me by my first date in two bloody years."

"You didn't tell me that." I chided. She had a date! And the bloody idiot who had managed to talk my wonderful sister into a date had called her worthy. Stupid twit. "He was obviously wrong for you. He couldn't see your sterling qualities."

"He saw all my sterling qualities," Belinda complained. "That was the problem. He didn't see *me*."

The minute I hung up, the phone rang again. I snapped an almost polite response into the receiver then turned bright red when the voice of my chocolate-provider (aka Rudolph) sounded sexy and bewildered back at me. Not another telemarketer. I found myself apologising and telling him all about telemarketers and Linnie's ways of dealing with them. I concluded by saying, "I'm sorry — I don't deal with them. I lose my temper."

"You lose it with great aplomb," he reassured me. He thought he could cure me of telemarketers, but refused to say how. He also thought he could invite me to dinner. He had backed me into a corner. How could I refuse? I couldn't imagine what he saw in me, but I was prepared to risk a single dinner. It would pay back the gourmet food and then I could wash my hands of him. Besides, he had a come-hither voice.

I didn't know whether to be hugely relieved or totally annoyed when I went downstairs to get a late night coffee and found little post-it notes all over the kitchen. It was a message for me. I do like leaving him irritated patterns of post-it notes to get Nick to do things. It makes my life worthwhile.

It was his best handwriting. Almost readable. Bloody Nick. The note said, "Mum. If you do one more nice thing in the next 24 hours I will run away from home."

I didn't take the notes down and throw them away. I went round every inch of the kitchen and wrote, "Damn your big toenail too, Nick" on each and every one of those notes.

When I came down for breakfast in the morning, Zoë had drawn a picture on each of a big toe with a flower (in pink) bang in the middle of the nail. She looked up from her cornflakes when I was examining one, and asked, "Do you like Nick's damned toenail, Mum?"

That is when I got my coffee, double strength. I also stole one of the notes and put it in my scrapbook.

Later that day I rang Belinda again to distract her. I didn't mention Rudolph, because that would have rubbed salt into her wounds. Instead, I told her that Great-Grandma's papers were mostly to do with some sort of magic. Jewish magic. I asked her if she could find out for me how magic fitted with Judaism. I had a nasty suspicion that it was illegal. Anyway, I needed to know, and Belinda needed a distraction. Maybe magic would be her great creative outlet. Maybe.

Or maybe I had other reasons for making that call. I wanted to know, vaguely, what Judaism said about all that stuff. I also wanted to know if I had genuinely seen that strange thing in the garden. There was no way I was going to ask Belinda directly.

I need to tell you about Belinda's reply. My experiences this last year have been just chockers with life changing phone calls. This one was a beauty. It confirmed things I didn't know needed confirming. I'll stop failing to explain, and just give you the phone call. Don't worry about my timelines. They're erratic right now, but they'll straighten eventually.

"I think I have worked it out for you," Linnie

sounded a little dubious, but spoke with her best I-shall-inform-you-anyway tone.

"Worked what out?" I like showing how dense I can be — it makes a change from achieving the superhuman.

"This magic stuff you're on about. The religious base for it. Where it fits in the world view we're supposed to have."

"Cool. I need to understand. Because right now it makes no sense whatsoever. I can see bits here and bits there, but not the whole thing."

"Bits here and there? You mean here a bit, there a bit, everywhere a bit-bit? Old Great Grandma had a spell, eeyie eeyie oh?" Linnie was far too cheerful for comfort. I ignored what needed ignoring.

"Now I know what it looks like, that tree thing appears everywhere. My favourite bit is on Neon Genesis Evangelion," I said.

"Neon what?"

"You should know that," I said, chidingly. I do love chiding my sister. "You teach teenage boys."

"I teach teenage boys what?" Belinda was frustrated.

"Cartoons. TV stuff. Manga. Anime. Japanese."

"I didn't know you watched these things," Belinda was defensive.

"I don't — but I have a teenage son."

"You're just basking in reflected glory," Belinda was now amused. "Well, so'm I."

"So are you?"

"We had a visiting rabbi in Canberra last weekend and I got to ask questions."

"It wasn't beneath your dignity to ask questions?" I couldn't help teasing. Okay, so I can never help teasing.

"The things you have been talking about get mentioned in the Talmud," Belinda started, in her best instructing voice.

"The Talmud?" Now I wasn't teasing. Talmud was new to me.

"Bother it, Judith, don't you remember anything?"

"I tried to forget everything." Now it was my turn to be defensive. "It's so much easier in my circles to not be Jewish at all, or to be a lapsed Jew." The Left is not always tolerant.

"A lapsed Jew." I should not have told her. She sighed. "The Talmud is what was written down to explain the Torah. You know the Torah." She was getting very sarcastic, and dammit, I couldn't complain. I had earned it, "The five-books-of-Moses Torah? The heart of our religion? That one? Anyway, the Talmud started off as oral law, but it became the collected wisdom of the rabbis. Sort of. We're supposed to study it heaps and question it heaps. I don't know anyone who actually does, though. So what rabbis say about what it says about magic is pretty well what goes. Except that there were later rabbis who also gave advice."

"You mean we have hundreds of years of rabbis telling us how to run our lives. Hundreds of years of bloody men thinking they know everything." This was the best I could do at comeback. I felt small.

"Two thousand years at least," stated Belinda gloomily. "And they still do it. So this isn't the whole picture, it is just what I can make of what I was told."

"Understood," I said. "We don't need the rest of the world picking on us — we manage to confuse ourselves quite well enough." I pulled myself up. I was thinking as a Jew. Hadn't done that in almost forever.

"We do," agreed my sister. "Can I get back to my explanation?"

"Sure." *Anything to avoid my current thoughts. Tell me the moon is made of green cheese, please. Distract me.*

"God controls everything."

"Duh," I replied. It was obvious. I was entitled to be rude.

"Judith, can you behave for two seconds?" *God, she is easy to stir. God-who-controls-everything, she is easy to stir.* "God controls everything, so the closer you're connected to God, the more powerful magic becomes. Apparently you can do the golem thing and other stuff if you're closely connected, or something. I don't get the 'closely connected'. The rabbi said it would take too long to explain." Just when she gets to the magic, she says it would take too long to explain. "But everyone is governed by *mazal*, which is why we say mazal tov. Mazal is the fate of people connected to the world. It's sort of astrology, too — where the planets and constellations and things influence humans."

"Human nature or human destiny?" It was becoming interesting. Sue me.

"I think maybe both," Belinda said cautiously, "But I'm not sure."

"There are twelve mazalot in the heavens," she continued, "which means mazal is feminine, because the 'ot' is a feminine ending, which should make you happy." Why should things being feminine make me happy? Oh, because I am a feminist. Duh. She thinks that I would be happy in a world with no men. A feminist I am; Germaine Greer I never wanted to be. Later on, when someone told me that 'mazal' was masculine after all, it was too late. What a sorrow.

"So the signs of the zodiac are all female and each is a mazal." I was making sense of it. Yes, there are modern miracles. Little ones, but no less miraculous for that. 'Mazal tov' was all about the stars being in alignment.

"Maybe," said Belinda, cautiously. She rethought and said, "Yes, I think so."

"Is there anywhere I can get a written description?" I asked.

Lin's thoughts made me very uncomfortable, but they also made sense of Ada's papers. I had to sort them out. If religious magic lay at the heart of our family secrets, then I would find out more.

"The rabbi said that Maimonides described it."

"Mammon who?" Big Greek name was all I heard. Belinda said it so naturally.

"From Moses to Moses . . . that guy." Oh, she really did think I should know the name. It was still just a big Greek name to me. And she had quoted something that obviously should have been just as familiar.

"Doesn't help."

"One day, I'm going to kill you — you know this," Belinda said, with as little energy as possible.

"I know." I was chirpy.

Belinda hates it when I admit to not knowing things Jewish. Even though a few years ago she only knew a little more than me. I give her a hard time about it. I love admitting I don't know things — I hate the reality of not knowing things.

"Maimonides was this bloke in the Middle Ages— Moses Ben Maimon, or something. Spanish, I think. He was also a doctor. He wrote the Guide to the Perplexed and I think he wrote the thirteen principles of faith. Anyway, he explained things so we could understand."

"And has he been translated?" I was suspicious. Maybe I should have heard of this bloke after all. A Greek Spanish Jewish Middle Aged bloke.

"Yes!" Belinda lost it. "Check him out on the bloody internet! Pretend he's a rotten politician who needs dirt dug on his policies. Go look it up for yourself!"

"Okay, okay, I will." I managed to sound genuine. "Email me his name so I get the spelling right. And I'll look it up. I promise. Now tell me more."

"Maimonides explains all the mazal and stuff, is all. And he doesn't much like astrology. So Great-Grandma probably didn't like him."

"I like her more and more. There are lots of dead guys I hold grudges against, too."

"It would make sense to you." Belinda's tone was tart, then she relented, "Every bit we find about her makes her more real, doesn't it, even with all the wacko things she believed?"

"Yes. Is that all your explanation?" I was more impatient to know more than I wanted to admit.

"Not nearly," Belinda smiled sweetly. I could see that smile in my mind's eye. Damn her little toe. "We now get to the good bits. Magic isn't forbidden in Judaism, not even by Maimonides. It's only certain types of magic or certain ends for magic that are forbidden. Prophecy, for instance, is fine, as long as it's by God's will."

"That goes against everything everyone says — 'Thou shalt not suffer a witch to live' and all that."

"I know," replied my sister. "We're so used to looking at our own world through Christian eyes, you know. Christianity doesn't really understand Judaism."

"I hate it when you're right."

"You live with too much hate, my dear," Lin was quite happy to rub my nose in this little triumph. "Anyway," she continued, "We're not allowed to do magic that worships anything other than God or anything that looks like it worships anything other than God, which is the same reason we separate meat from milk."

"*You* separate meat from milk. I don't keep kosher."

"Nor do I, actually, but it's the principle. Maimonides said it was the memory of a pagan sacrifice, so we don't do it. We don't do it for magic things either."

"So no graven images?"

"I'm not sure. Certainly no worshipping graven images. We still have the zodiac, after all." Belinda sounded thoughtful, "The examples I was given were offering incense to the stars or making images of them. It's not just reading the stars. And there's more."

"More?"

"More," Belinda said firmly. "And this bit is totally crucial. You might even like it."

'Hah' was my only thought. Or was it 'Up Yours'?

"Judaism is ethical," she continued. "We're not allowed to do things that harm intentionally. We do not hurt people."

"Oh," I thought aloud, "that explains why Ada's papers have no aggressive magic."

"Aggressive magic?"

"Stuff that attacks people — don't you know anything?" We smiled at each other from our respective ends of the phone line. We were even.

"The rabbi gave me a bunch of cautions. Important ones."

"Tell!" Because if the magic was Jewish but not aggressive, then what was it?

"We're not supposed to know the future from astrology and stuff because self-fulfilling prophecies and dependency are anti-Jewish."

"How are they anti-Jewish?"

"Judaism is about taking responsibility for our own lives. So if you depend on knowledge you find from predicting the future, it undermines your sense of responsibility . . ."

"Who said this? I mean, who did the rabbi tell you said this?"

"Maimonides again."

"Damn Maimonides: I like looking at my horoscope."

"I bet looking at it is fine; just don't let it take over your decisions for you."

"That doesn't sound quite what the rabbi said."

"It isn't — it's what I say. As long as you don't claim, 'I'm a failure because the Sun-Herald said I would be this week,' you're fine."

"You mean, I can fail at anything I like and as often as I like, as long as I don't blame it on my horoscope."

"Precisely." There was a pause. "Dammit, Judith. Talking yourself into being a failure is just as much not taking responsibility for your life as depending on a horoscope."

"It's not magic related."

"No, but that doesn't make it any less stupid."

"Are you calling me stupid?"

"Yes! And mean!"

I produced another thought, "But if I ask someone for help and don't know how reliable they are or how good they are, and I rely on their advice and don't use my own judgement, then I am —"

"Stupid," was Belinda's conclusion.

"I was going to say, 'Not a good Jew.'"

"I guess that too," ceded Belinda. "That one statement has a lot of annoying consequences."

"You know how I read it?" I offered. I tried to say it without smiling.

"How?"

"Maimonides was feminist." Smug. Smug. Smug. I had not only got even, I had pulled way ahead. Smug prevailed.

Belinda was silent. Yes, I'd succeeded. Internal joy abounded. And more smug.

"He lived hundreds and hundreds of years before feminism was invented." Her tone of voice was everything I could have asked for.

"But feminism is all about taking responsibility for the self."

"Oh." Belinda was thoughtful.

"So you're making me more Jewish and I'm making you more feminist," I was triumphant.

"In your dreams," was Belinda's response.

4.

Tony and Lana had to go to a wedding. Rhonda told Tony over the phone, "Just dump the friends. Don't go. Who needs weddings?"

"I didn't ring you to be told to dump my friends," Tony was grouchy.

He hated weddings, and Rhonda knew he hated weddings and she just couldn't help teasing him. "So you rang to tell me all about it? Two hours before it begins?"

"No, I rang because I'm a man in trouble and only you can save me."

"Let me guess. You forgot to book a babysitter. Again."

"Please, Rhonda," Tony had that edge to his voice. Rhonda thought she'd better be nice. Then she decided that honesty was better, under the circumstances. "I asked Belinda, and she's got some sort of family crisis."

"This is the fifth time this year. Plus I ran those boxes to Sydney for Belinda. I love the kids more than I love anyone, but that's four times you've promised me a few days' notice and not to disarrange my entire life. And now you're asking it again."

"But how much can it possibly upset your day?" Tony was pleading, but using the worst possible words. Rhonda mentally pushed him off a cliff and watched his body drift down to the rocks below. Tony swiftly managed to turn 'bad' into 'worse', "I mean, all you do is sit at a computer and play games."

"So writing articles for journals is games, is it?"

"No," Tony rushed his words out. "Of course I didn't mean that."

"But you assumed it. You also assumed I wasn't doing temp work, and didn't have other plans. You forget to get a babysitter because you think I'm just here, waiting at home."

Tony gave a heavy sigh.

"Is Lana there?"

"Lana's getting dressed. No, here she is."

"Give the phone to her, please. I want to talk about this to an adult." Not nearly cutting enough. But it would have to do. She would babysit. Again. This time, though, she'd make sure Lana knew it was under duress and with no warning. Tony would pay.

"Hi?" Lana's voice was tentative.

"Hi, Lana, it's me."

"Oh, hi," Rhonda could hear the smile in her voice. "What can I do for you?"

"You can kick your husband in the fundament, for a start."

"Oh dear, what's he done?" She wasn't taking it seriously.

"He forgot to book a babysitter and just now rang me to ask me to rearrange my whole day."

"Do you want me to hold him while you strangle him?"

"Something like that. Mostly I just want to know what's happening."

"He's in deep trouble, that's what's happening. I was lining up babysitting last week when he said he'd talked to you."

"Well, he didn't talk to me. I can do it, but it means rearranging."

"Look, I'll find someone else."

"And how much time do you have to find someone else?"

"None. But this is wrong."

"I know and you know, but you're the one who is going to be on the phone to find someone while he moons round and asks where you left his left foot. What can we do?"

Lana laughed. "I will use every evil means at my disposal to make sure that he never does it again."

"But will you? You're sweetness and light compared to me, and he's not listening to me. Why should he listen to you?"

"My poor, innocent friend. Sweetness and light has ways and means. Trust me, he will suffer."

"And from now on I need a week's notice or else I can't do it." Rhonda was adamant. "This isn't the same as meeting you for a coffee somewhere. I need warning."

"And you will get it, my friend. And he will know every inch of what he has done wrong. Every single inch."

There were reasons why the kids didn't come to her. Reasons Tony had obviously forgotten. A few minutes later she was walking around her living area wondering how she was going to get it all kid-proof in a half hour. She couldn't. There was no way. They were too big for her to simply move her oil burner and her glass lantern out of reach. And papers always seemed to get drawn on or scrunched up when the kids were round and their parents thought it was cute. She loved them, but she didn't want her work destroyed.

She rang Lana back. "Lana, I can't have the kids at my place without really mucking up my work schedule. Can I take them on a picnic?"

"Sounds great."

"Picnic and movie and make Tony pay?"

"Sounds fair to me. Do you want us to drop them off at your place still?"

"Yes. I want them to see the work their father doesn't think I am doing."

"Coolies. Be there soon. With every cent Tony has in his wallet. Spend the lot."

Rhonda sat back with a sublime smile. She was going to see her two top people in the world. Tony would be paying for a fine afternoon's fun by being stupid. Occasionally life did appear to have an ounce of fairness.

The impromptu picnic was a hoot. Number Two held Rhonda's hand encouragingly and asked with all the care of a counsellor, "Why are you so sad, Auntie?"

"I'm not sad," protested Rhonda. "At least, I don't think I'm sad."

Number One wanted her to prove it.

"How do you prove you aren't sad?" she asked them, bewildered. "Do I have to give you a goofy grin?"

"No," Number One decreed. "You have to play on the swings and climb the ropes and slide down the slide."

When she'd dutifully done these things, the kids unpacked the picnic Lana had cobbled together and made sure Rhonda only ate things that were good for her. "And no red cordial," instructed Number Two, firmly. "You know it just makes you go all silly."

"But if you get to drink red cordial, then why can't I?"

"Because she's already silly, of course," said Number One.

When it came to the post-picnic and post-movie shopping trip, the roles changed back. Apparently money and driving licenses were unchangeable. Numbers One and Two did, however, get to decide what groceries Rhonda bought. They were an irresistible force and an immovable object when it came to buying Rhonda's groceries. Anything that said

'teriyaki' or 'gourmet' or 'low fat' was firmly put back
on the shelf.

"You need real food," Number One said.

"What's real food?"

"Macaroni cheese," said Number Two. "That's real
food."

5.

BB and Secritmax had spoiled Rhonda's evening online. The two were in the chat room with Kool when
she appeared and they were tediously enthusiastic
about searching for Nostradamus. Kool wasn't tediously enthusiastic. He just saw her new nick and
wanted to talk. Rhonda didn't want to. She wanted to
watch. It was just too much effort to remember what
persona she had invented to go with the brand new
alias, and far too exhausting to actually use that
persona.

Rhonda dumped chat for a while and spent time on
her web journal, blogging all the memes in the known
universe.

First, she discovered that her Hawaiian name was
Lalani Banani. She rather liked it, and was tempted to
use it on the sober and serious Secritmax. Lalani Banani. Rhonda wondered if it really should be 'Lalani
Obsessiva Banani'. Didn't sound as exotic, but it certainly reflected her current self. And it certainly
sounded silly. Rhonda didn't blog it though. It would be
possible to work back from the meme and find clues
about the name.

The next meme she did, however, was worth blogging, for sure: 'What does your sleeping position reveal
about your inner self?'

Rhonda cut and pasted the pretty picture into her
blog and found that she was admitting to the world

how sensitive she was and how shy she was about showing her sensitivity. Private beyond anyone else. Unsure of relationships. Only trusting fully after many reassurances.

Sometimes memes became too close for comfort. But then, right now, comfort was something one found in other people's lives.

Another meme. She needed a final meme to take the bad taste of truth from her mouth. She found one that claimed to spot her hidden talent. "Hee," she typed. "I am apparently a terribly important person. Beware of me. My secret talent is to shake empires and rock boats. Or was that rock boats and shatter empires? The meme questionnaire tells me I am a catalyst to change, but that no one really pays attention to me. I am secretly powerful. So suck up to me bigtime, friends!!"

"Do you believe this stuff?" TVwhore posted, a bit later.

"I wish I did," Rhonda hadn't lied most of the day, so she could make this untruth a doozy. "I blogged those two memes because I liked them. I liked the thought of big and powerful MissTRie, changing the world by fluttering her eyelashes. But if I had believed for even a moment, I would have left the 'Hee' out."

"I wish I had those answers. I did the same memes and got confusion and addled thought. Not the sort of thing one wants to report."

"God, no. We should swap results. Confusion and addled thought sum the real me up nicely."

"I like it. I keep answering 'til I get your answers and then I will paste them as me. 'Twill take lying and foul cheating."

"But the value of the result . . ."

"Exactly."

None of their friends noticed that Rhonda and TVwhore had the same answers. Or if they did, they didn't comment. Memes, Rhonda realised, were just not terribly important in the universal scheme. Maybe she could have got away with telling her friends that her Hawaiian name was Lalani Banani? Then she had a better thought.

Rhonda spent an hour designing and printing. She pasted the exotic result of her labour on the hidden side of the computer tower, where no one could see it. Her computer was now officially called 'Lalani Banani, proud keeper of Rhonda's obsessions.'

I'm like Pharaoh's soldiers, Rhonda proudly joked to herself, *I'm in de-Nile about my own obsessions.*

6.

Judith felt communicative: One of my favourite notes from my box shows just a little of what Ada was like and why she was writing things down. My reading of the papers is that her daughter (my grandmother) had rejected a family tradition. This is the medical graduate from Melbourne University. Mum was just as scientific as her mother. Everything in its slot and everything explained. This is how I was brought up. Very Anglo. We didn't play in rock pools when we were children, we analysed their ecosystems.

Anyway, Great-Grandma wrote one telling note, which showed where she got her knowledge from, and that she really didn't understand it all. The note was a copperplate scribble next to a gigantically long incantation, and that annotation said:

These were what Grandmother used to call magic words. I cannot determine what they mean, but they (and other phrases) appear time after time: Forba Forba braymo azziebua.

Obviously my marvellous ancestress was determined magic would not be lost. This is why the box was kept for so long and never opened. I wonder if they even looked inside the other box? I mean, I wonder if they looked inside either box?

Let me rephrase: I can't think of a single reason why anyone would want to preserve family recipes for cakes and puddings with the same relish and care as they would preserve a secret magic tradition.

Where this thought came from is getting back to where I was up to in my narrative. I do not get confusing on purpose. It was another wonderful gift from the decipherment. This is going back to before Belinda's sage words on Jewish law as related to magical practice.

When I received the scanned centre pages from that scrapbook I worked out that where Great-Grandma wrote, "She said what she said," in a spell, it referred to something on one of those lists.

'What she said' referred back to another set of words, the key words that actuated the spell and made everything work. It was a magic discovery. Thinking about this particular deduction makes me silly and happy and phunny. Even now, retrospectively, it's exciting. She was writing everything down, but not so anyone could understand. Intentional obfuscation.

I sadly suspected the only way of finding out if I were right was by trial and error. For trial and error, one needs trial. But what if something worked? I needed to find an innocuous spell.

This was not the level of magic in the charms that Zoë and I had used to protect the house and ourselves. Those charms were kind of stand-alone — just read what is said and follow the instructions. Like one of Belinda's recipes, in fact. Whether they worked or didn't, they were harmless, so it didn't matter what we did with them.

This was magic that could *do* things. It was testable

in a way that the charms were not. How do you know if the charm worked or if you were going to be safe anyway? So that key to how Great-Grandma was writing her notes was . . . magic. No other word for it.

I thought, *Maybe I should ring my sister. I need an excuse to ring her. She's too much alone.* To think was to do and her phone rang. Okay, my hand pressed the numbers, but I swear it was a telepathy thing.

"Hey, Linnie, I have a rhyme for you."

"What sort of rhyme?" My sister was less than excited. She thought I was teasing, when all I was doing was trying to sort out a bit more of which paper did what. And talk to her. I should have done the talking bit first, perhaps.

I guess I was also trying to avoid talking about the email the Dark Side of the Lin had sent me the day before. It was gruesome. The pictures will go away if they don't get mentioned.

There was one more reason for my racing into the topic without so much as a 'How's your garden growing?' I was still very uncomfortable with the thought of my family the magic-believers. Who wouldn't be? I would rather fight battles that need to be fought, than find that our whole worldview might rest on quicksand. Or that my Great-Grandma was gullible.

She-of-special-awe couldn't be gullible. Ostracised, yes. Unknown, yes. Mysterious, absolutely. But not gullible. I didn't know what my sister knew directly from Mum, but I did know, in my heart of hearts, that Great-Grandma was Larger than Life and had left an imprint generations deep.

"One from Great-Grandma, and it's labelled 'mnemonic'. It sounds Jewish."

"Right now, to you, the whole world sounds Jewish. It's a stage you're going through."

"Am not!"

"Are too. So you thought I could explain it?"

"I thought you might be interested!" She wasn't really out of mean time and into normal time yet. I would just have to live with this.

"So you thought I could explain it?"

I laughed and gave in. "Yes, I hoped you could explain it."

"Give."

"The first line reads: Adam, Seth, Enosh, Kenan, Mahalalel, Jared, Enoch, Methuselah, Lamech, Noah, Shem, Ham, and Japhet. The second line is: Aries, Taurus, Gemini, Cancer, Leo, Virgo, Libra, Scorpio, Sagittarius, Capricorn, and Aquarius, Pisces. The third line says, and forgive me if I mispronounce: Nisan, Iyar, Sivan, Tammuz, Av, Elul, Tishrei, Marheshvan, Kislev, Tevet, Shevat and Adar. The fourth line is: Abraham, Isaac, Jacob. Peace. And the last bit goes: Sally, Rebecca, Judith and Leah. Peace unto Israel. And that is the lot of it."

"Some I can tell you at once — the other bits I'll need to check. I think I know them, but I'm just not certain."

"So tell!"

"There are the star signs."

"I guessed that for myself," said I, impatiently.

"And the Hebrew months."

"Now I feel stupid."

"You're going to feel more stupid. Abraham, Isaac and Jacob are the patriarchs and Sarah, Rebecca, Rachel and Leah are the matriarchs."

"But it has 'Sally' instead of 'Sarah' and 'Judith' instead of 'Rachel.'"

"'Sally' is just a form of 'Sarah', but 'Judith' is curious. You're a matriarch."

I filed that somewhere deep in my brain to be used

against the infants in the far, far future. And then I bugged Belinda further. "What about the first names?"

"I have the nasty suspicion I should know them — let me get a book." It took her about two hours to get that book. "Got it. What were they again — slowly?"

"Adam, Seth, Enosh, Kenan, Mahalalel, Jared, Enoch, Methuselah, Lamech, Noah, Shem, Ham, and Japhet." Do not ask how I pronounced some of these.

"Um. Oh! Sorry. They're the first men, in order." Now we both felt stupid.

"So it's nothing secret or mysterious."

"Just basic Jewish knowledge. The Judith bit puzzles me. But I don't know if that just demonstrates my abysmal ignorance."

"You know more than me."

"Doesn't take much."

"Can I ask another question?" I asked this very cautiously.

"You're terribly polite today." This was said like a puppy worrying at a piece of cloth. She was going to sort it out, even if it meant ripping the cloth to shreds.

"I know." I grinned. "Can lists like that be used in magic?"

"How the hell would I know? Ask someone."

"Good idea." She was joking, but I wasn't. I had my thoughts on understanding some of the more arcane-looking documents from my box of mysteries. Grandma's Little Box of Mysteries — isn't there a musical called that?

"While I think of it, I have a title for my CD." This declaration was out of the blue. Had Belinda taken up fronting a band while I wasn't watching? In an attempt to dispel her high worthiness?

"Why does your CD need a title?" I put on my patient and resigned voice.

She put on her my-sister-is-an-idiot voice. "So that you can identify it when you look for it."

"Why would I want to identify it when I look for it? In fact, why would I want to look for it?"

"Judith," very threatening. I'd better behave, I thought, but I really didn't want to.

"Okay, what's the title?"

"I'm calling it, 'They tried to get us; God rescued us; Let's eat!' — you can see it quoted all over the place when people sum up Jewish festivals." God help me, she was bubbly as she said this. If I were not careful, she would froth at the mouth.

I was amazingly tactful. "Well, the 'let's eat' bit is our family exactly."

"Yes. Sometimes I think if it wasn't for the food we wouldn't get together for Passover even." From bubbly to wistful all in one second. When had the stable sister become moody? And what the hell could I do to get her back on track?

"At least we eat."

"There is that."

"And you do more than eat."

"I'm so good and virtuous I am a danger to humanity."

"Belinda! You sound like me." Sarcastic and dark and . . .

"Well, you're a bad influence. And I'm in a grumpy mood."

"Not because I was rude about your cookbook."

"Not that. You're rude about everything. I stopped taking it seriously when I was about eleven."

"What, then?" I tried unbearably hard to sound supportive and charming and sisterly.

"I don't know. I feel a sort of restlessness inside."

Middle-aged mindspread? Or just the grumps? Whatever, I was going to improve things. By hook or by crook. But it was unlike Belinda not to have ways in hand to improve things herself. "A mystery then?"

"Mysteries sound nice. This is just uncomfortable." And she said that in her own practical tone. Even moody, Belinda was sensible. And down-to-earth. "I'm thinking of going somewhere on holiday," she finished.

"Where?" Plain curiosity at work here. Where does a Belinda go to relieve herself of mood swings?

"I found one of Great-Grandma's old addresses so I was thinking of spending a week or so in Victoria next holidays and seeing where she lived."

"It's only the beginning of term." Advance planning for having fun from the woman who had been shy of a dinner party? Why did it scare the hell out of me?

"Hey, I can dream."

I smiled at that — dreaming was something I approved of. But I would do better. "Can I come?" I was going to sort her out.

"Of course."

"If we do it first week, then Zoë will be at camp. And Nick would adore having the house to himself for a week. He can feed the cat." I was getting her alone. Either to have lots of deep and meaningful discussion or to wring her neck: I could decide later.

"Is he responsible enough?"

"He has amazing depths of humanity. He just grunts and *looks* antisocial."

"Let's do it, then. I'll book one of those budget cabins. We can drive down in one day, and then just spend the week there." Linnie sounded businesslike. My mood improved to match hers.

"Sounds lovely. It's ages since I've had a real holiday."

"I'm paying for the room — since I was going anyway." What did I say? Businesslike.

"Since I have no money, I will accept gratefully."

That was when the trap closed in. Most people think if you are poor you have to be condescended to. Belinda never condescends. She waited for me to invite myself before she said she was paying.

All the same, I found myself wondering what Belinda was unsettled about. Soon we would spend a week together, and I would get to the bottom of everything. Well, maybe not to why I kept running out of carrots. Some things are purely unfathomable.

Naturally, life being what it is, things got more complicated first.

The initial complication was not unexpected. It was Rudolph pretending to be a telemarketer. He offered me the Harbour Bridge for a penny and was very upset to hear that this was not an original offer. He also reminded me that I'd agreed to be taken out to dinner. He was witty and I was witty back, but I grumped to myself when I hung up the phone. My sister wasn't the only person laying traps.

The next phone call was worse. I hauled Great-Grandma's box out of hiding. It was a natural consequence. But gods, I have trouble writing about that phone call.

Why do some people bother to be born, when all they are going to do is spend their lives hurting the hell out of people? Not hurting others is the bare minimum we can expect to do with our lives.

I'm beginning to understand why Belinda joined the Jewish Centre in Canberra. If someone hurts, she has to give support. Our family has never had a tradition of mixing too much with mainstream Judaism, but Belinda's heart takes her that way.

Damnable results, though. For a while she slept on my couch because it made her feel safe. Sometimes it happens still, today. She gets scared, and wants to be out of Canberra.

Every time Belinda comes, Nick cancels his games and gets rid of his friends and stays home, watching TV with her or playing chess or just talking. Lin hates chess. But knowing Nick is there, six feet of pure protectiveness, makes a difference. You can see it when she smiles at him, as he gives her the fifth cup of tea in an hour. I begin to think that Nick inherited a bit of Belinda. That worthiness.

I will get to the point one day; I *will* tell you what happened. My mind is out of order. I'll get some more tea and then I'll talk about that phone call.

"I can't chat," Belinda said. No questions for Zoë or Nick. Just, "I can't chat."

I wanted to chat. I told her so. I wanted to tell her I'd worked out that the papers mostly related to a system of magic. I wanted to gently tease Linnie about it and suggest we play around with it in a purely scientific fashion. I also wanted to mention I was having dinner with Rudolph the next night.

So I started, "I just feel like chatting."

"I can't." So adamant. Her voice was clogged. Not my warm and wonderful older sister at all. "I can't," she said again, in case I didn't believe her. I coaxed and reassured and finally got her to cough up.

"You know the Quiz Night?" she said. "The community thing," she said impatiently. "The fundraiser. Merriment unbounded." Linnie sounded like me. Using happy words to sound bitter and twisted.

"You vaguely said something. I didn't remember it was a quiz night. You were cooking."

"And providing prizes, and helping at the door. The abundant joys of a small community." *Oh dear*, was my thought. She isn't the kind of person who lists all the things she does to help.

"There were about eighty of us," she said. She sounded as if she had climbed glass mountains in iron shoes to get each word out. "About 10 o'clock I was thoroughly sick of it. I'm not competitive and there was too much noise and . . . anyway, I saw smokers coming back in and thought, if they can smoke, then I can go outside for five minutes and breathe the fresh air."

"The icy air," I suggested.

You could hear the shrug in Belinda's voice, "I had a jacket." Another of those bloody pauses. "I went round the back, because I didn't want to run into the smokers. Someone else was there. I didn't know her and she was on the phone. She shushed me and pulled me behind a car."

Grrls' Own Adventure in the Jewish Community Centre Carpark?

"She pointed from behind the car. I saw a group of youths. Eight. There were eight. All rugged up. I couldn't see any faces — all I could work out that they were male. They were making things in a circle."

"One of them turned and threw something. It was a big throw, very high. A strong arc. Red against black. The thing glowed red. It landed on the flat metal section of the roof. It burned away with others that were there already. I just didn't realise that there was a fire on the roof until that thing landed up there. There was a fire on the roof." Her voice faded in remembered shock.

I have never been so silent in my life. I wanted to hear the rest: I didn't want to hear anything at all. I wanted to go straight to my bedroom and hide under the doona and put my hands over my ears and sing la-la-la.

"There was an explosion. They told me later that was when a Molotov cocktail hit a window. The window right next to where the Torah is kept.

"The youths bundled up and left. The woman with me was crying: she kept saying that she'd rung the police three times and they hadn't come. They hadn't come. I went round the front and waited with her. The police took twenty-five minutes to arrive. The fire engine never came at all."

"I never heard about that," I said slowly. I should have known. I should have rung Belinda to see if she was okay. I should have.

"No one did. I don't know why." And Belinda was angry. "Not even the people upstairs were told. They finished the Quiz Night and were ushered out the door and never saw the fire on the roof. The police asked me two questions and took my details in a little notepad. That was it."

"Did they catch anyone?"

"No. I looked the next day, and everything was kind of charred. But the window held. So no one knows except the police and the insurance people."

"That's not such a bad result," I tried to be encouraging.

"Except that it was the fourth bloody incident."

I was shocked.

"And if the police are doing anything they don't tell us and I'm more scared than I have been in years." All her words rushed together as she tried to get them out before the tears took over.

"Come and stay for a bit," I suggested.

"I have school." This was a non-negotiable. Belinda is tediously conscientious about her teaching — she will teach at school until the moment the Angel of Death appears. "I'm booked in to talk to a counsellor after school tomorrow," she said. And that was the best I could get from her.

I thought she would dump the Jewish community thing after the Molotov cocktails. Instead she started to attend large numbers of community functions. The more people condemn Linnie for being Jewish, the more publicly Jewish she will become. I never knew I would have to fear for her life though, because of her religion.

No one ever found those thugs. The incident never made the papers. Belinda, who was a strong and independent woman, was walking scared. Damn all bigots.

Every time I think of it I remember that these youths would have burned my sister alive for being Jewish. Belinda told me later the nice lady wasn't even Jewish, she was a friend of someone who had organised a table — I hope she's okay. Linnie has never said, and I can't ask her.

I have to stop and cry a bit. I'll get back to this later.

7.

Right from the moment she met Lana and Tony at the restaurant, Rhonda knew it would all go wrong. The air hummed. Rhonda felt she would transform into a Cassandra figure during the main course and erupt into unbelieved prognostications of doom and gloom. She made a joke of it with Lana, to relieve her inner tension.

"I feel like an ancient Trojan today," she said.

"Helen of Troy?" Tony looked across in interest. Of course he would assume Helen.

"No, Cassandra."

"Who on earth is Cassandra?"

Rhonda never knew if Lana was genuinely ignorant, or if she put on a show to make Tony feel good. Either way, it was annoying. "The one who told everyone what would happen and no one believed her."

"What do you think will happen?" Tony was acting the tolerant ex-husband. Today she wanted to strangle him with his stupid Pinocchio tie.

"If I told you, then you wouldn't believe me, so I

won't say," Rhonda looked annoying. She could tell because Tony's index finger was tapping on the tablecloth.

"If you could tell, you mean, you wouldn't be Cassandra," Lana's eyes were on Tony's finger, and she was smiling.

"Oh, let's just order."

The whole evening was like that: Tony needling Rhonda, and Lana egging them on. Sometimes being so close to your past wasn't a good thing.

Food helped turn the conversation away from fragile wit to safer topics, but the air still hummed and Rhonda knew that this night was a night of risks. Small risks. Niggling risks. Bitter risks. She just didn't know why, and so she fed the risks into the dinner table chat.

Lana's eyes glowed; there was a part of her that enjoyed being a little bitchy and taking emotional dares. Tony pushed the conversation further because he liked the attention, but each time it slid out of his control his finger went tap, tap-tap.

The dinner went from jumpy to unbearable when the Sleazoid turned up at the restaurant with his wife. Rhonda managed not to vomit while everyone smiled sweetly at each other and drank coffee together.

She excused herself as early as she could without offending Lana. Sometimes life was just too overwhelmingly full of small things that could not be borne.

The next day, Rhonda found herself writing something quite unexpected.

CHAPTER FIVE

1.

"ARE YOU ZOË? I'M HERE TO TAKE YOUR MOTHER TO dinner."

Judith didn't call out to announce that she was sitting on the lounge chair round the corner, trying to develop a bad cold. She kept her gaze fixed on that door, and waited to see how her blue-eyed darling would react to Rudolph.

He looked down at her as if he was looking at anyone else shorter than him. Not a pretty paper doll. Not an adult-in-formation. Judith appreciated this.

Zoë looked him up and down very slowly and carefully. This was unusual. She was normally instantly at home with adults. In the end though, she seemed to approve. "You wanted to sell Mum the Harbour Bridge," she said.

Rudolph took his cue from Zoë and kept everything light. Judith took her cue from Zoë and was cautious but cheeky. The two went to a tiny, bijou restaurant in the middle of nowhere. Everything was green and ferny and comfortable: nothing expensive or intimidating. Judith felt impelled to write about it later.

There was no menu, only a wine list. The owner-chef came out and spent a few minutes asking about us. Then he announced what he would make us. "You are Jewish," he said to me, "no pork."

If it had been anywhere else, I would have instantly demanded blood pudding. But it wasn't. His eye had pierced a soul I wasn't sure I possessed. I meekly said yes to his fish-dish.

Rudolph was not scared into submission. He asked, "Do I look like someone who eats whole cows?" and had his steak changed to a strange confection that should have been in the Art Gallery. If it wasn't for the bed thing I would have demanded a mouthful, since I had never seen anything like it. Despite the lovely creases round his eyes, and the wit, and the disarming smile, I tried to make myself sexually invisible. Except for one-liners.

Just before our second bottle I found him his nickname. The wine was as fizzy and pink as Rudolph. It matched his ever-so-elegant pink shirt. From glass three on, his nose was also ever so elegantly pink. Rudolph the Pink Nosed Date.

I shoved my feminist self into my beaded purse and kindly allowed him to pay the bill. He dropped me home at an oddly sensible hour and I took my inebriation out on Ada's box. I should get inebriated more often, because it helped me work out astrology and Ada.

There are several charts in the box, and a name on them, 'Clare White'. I think Ms White was Great-Grandma's astrologer. Great-Grandma took her astrology seriously. Her comments are written all over each chart.

They are enormously detailed charts. I wished I could read them. I was confused as to why she kept just those two early charts and then there is a gap of years, and why there are only a few anyway. Maybe there were no others. The notes on them are interesting. They hint at story. One of them refers to her foolish sister, who everyone pretended was dead.

She was very angry about her husband in another. She has an arrow pointing to something indecipherable and suggests that, "This might mean change. If it is change for the worse, I shall haunt him forever."

A clue to her? Was she a beaten wife the way I was a beaten de facto? Did he threaten to kill her? I feel sick.

I hope she wasn't. Maybe it shows where I come from, rather than where she was? It had better be that. I use every skill I have to make it distant for me so that I can keep going. But for Great-Grandma? How can I see her objectively? How can I see her at all?

2.

Note from Rhonda: I think that the reason I'm diarising this dream is because it was the most concrete dream I have ever had that summarises my vision-ick-thingie.

The fact that it lingers makes it a dream that has to be written. I feel like a fiction writer who is compelled to tell someone's story, except that the story is mine own. It isn't the same compulsion I normally feel, but it's close.

I experienced the dream as a story about visiting a house. It was only later on that it became apparent that my link with the house was rather special. It was only after I woke up that I realised that my house was my prophetic soul.

Every single person who appeared in my dream was linked to me: the fretted woman who owned it and didn't want us to visit the tower; the young child I explored with; and the guys who wanted to steal all the gold. I am not sure that the miners/thieves were me, unless they were my fear of exposure. The others most certainly were facets of me.

I couldn't hear their voices or faces: I felt them through their personalities. I find it quite extraordinary to have felt people, while my eyes were blind as Justice.

I voyaged in the house. I felt like an early explorer, discovering new inner worlds. Much of the house was Victorian and comfortably homey. Sometimes it transformed into a splendid mansion. I don't remember kitchens or bathrooms. The house was a series of rooms for recreation, not the fundaments of life. There were no bedrooms.

My favourite room was a huge open lounge, where most of the colours (reds and greens and dark browns, late Victorian) were at the edges. It reminded me of my aunt's house. Auntie didn't appear at all, only the echo of her home.

As I try to find words to describe it, details fade.

The dream had clear sequences. The first was me coming to the house to take care of the child. The lady of the house appeared to introduce me to the child and to explain the rules of the house. The child is the one who explained the house itself to me, and showed me the garden from the balcony and helps me explore. The house was there for the child. Because I was with the child, we read books. Big pictures and large print. It was hard work making them out. The child and I both becoming curious about the tower.

The moment I left the child behind and moved along alone into the dream, the woman came back and talked about the tower. She told me that she wished they could access it and could know what was in it. The lady was very unhappy: the house was going to be sold. There was a desperate sorrow around me.

I left the last children's book on a rostrum and also left the lady behind. That is when I went exploring upwards instead of outwards.

Before that, I'd seen so much. I'd recognised the house, too: it was part of my life. It was big, friendly, empty. Tidy. The child and I left stray books in it, but that was all. Empty. Void. Then I was in a room with the child and we were exploring together. I wish I knew why the child came and went so.

From a window, we could see the tower. The tower was nothing like the rest of the house. The rest of the house was pretty normal, all squares and angles and wood and brick. Lots of painted wood. The tower was of spiralling slate and twisted into the air like a unicorn's horn. Very wide at the base, and very complex, as if it had grown and not been built. The ridges in the slate whorled upwards, creating a helix.

The tower had no windows. It was special to the family somehow and looked impenetrable, but unless the treasure in it could be found, the house would be sold. I'd just found a way into that tower when the thieves came.

The thieves were dressed in rustic browns and greens and had mallets and hit the inside of the tower, from one of the upstairs rooms. A part of the tower crumbled, as if an earthquake had shattered the rock into fragments and piles of crumble.

I removed the thieves. There was no violence. I think it was all done in words, but the words have fragmented like the rocks. I know that no one was hurt and that I used my lucid dreaming to remove the thieves, and that is all I know.

I looked at the crumbled rock and realised it was laced with gold, gold in all the colours of the rainbow. It was rainbow gold, not pyrites. My lucid dreamer self then became active. I told the dream that slate and gold didn't mix (the combination distressed me far more than the rainbow hues shimmering through the gold) and so the rock of the tower changed into something more suitable. I was excited, and crumbled the rock a bit more, and made a hole into the tower.

The house was saved because the gold was the treasure. I knew in the dream that there was still a quest to follow. I was to find out what else was in that strange tower. I woke up while I was looking into that dark hole and thinking that the next step was to climb in and explore upwards.

3.

Naturally, *Judith continued*, I rang my sister the next day. I was going to use her investigatorial skills cannily. I was going to be positively salubrious for Lin's mental health.

"Hi."

"Hi, you," Belinda sounded unusually affable. She'd left her teaching voice in the classroom. And she was chatty. She told me that she'd planned to spend Sunday afternoon gardening, but rain was a show-stopper. She'd just made herself afternoon tea, and was curled up comfortably in front of the heater, wondering what she was going to do with the rest of her day. My phone call was perfectly timed. "Ringing for anything in particular?"

"Just to talk."

"Cool. Anything new and exciting at your end?"

My tone of voice had obviously not communicated itself. "In two days?" I need to make it clear that this was not the first call after the bombing. Lin was mostly her normal self.

"Well, I prepared the ground for planting yesterday."

"Why aren't you out there doing the planting today?" I can be polite if I really want to. I just have to work at it.

"It's pouring buckets. I just told you. I'm eating cake."

"You've got a sweeter tooth even than Nick."

"You like chocolate for breakfast."

"So?"

"What aren't you telling me?" Belinda suddenly turned demanding.

The change in her voice was so dramatic, I had to chuckle. "Sprung bad, huh?"

"Yep," replied Belinda, imperturbably. "Can't get away with anything."

"Make a bet," I was suddenly in a better mood. "I couldn't decide what to tell you, honestly."

"About what?"

"The box, of course." Well, I wasn't going to tell her about Rudolph.

Belinda informed me in huge detail why she could not understand why it should be 'the box, of course,' when I had not said a thing about the box for so very long. Which was a great pity, now she thought about it. What had happened to our aim to understand our Great-Grandmother and whatever turned our family into its unhappy, dysfunctional self? Life, Belinda thought, unoriginally, was a mystery. And of all the mysteries that comprised life, my mind was apparently one of the greatest of all. "So what about the box?" Lin finally asked.

"I took a couple of the papers from it to a guy at the Nicholson Museum," I got it out in a rush, before Belinda could plague me with more explanations of all and sundry. Before I could get nervous.

"The Nicholson Museum?"

"Specialises in the ancient world. Based at Sydney University. Took me a while to get an appointment."

"Okay, enlighten me. What has the ancient world got to do with our family? I assume we had ancestors there, but that would've been a long time ago."

"Hah, very hah. Some of the papers had Hebrew, and some had some sort of Egyptian."

"You could have asked someone Jewish to read you the Hebrew."

"Don't know anyone who reads Hebrew," I admitted, totally without regret. "Besides, the Nicholson guy could have been Jewish — I never asked."

"Feminists don't read Hebrew? Sort of like feminists don't have a sense of humour?" Sometimes the smiles in voices should not be so apparent.

"Very funny." Sometimes sisters should be put in a cupboard. A dark cupboard. An airless dark cupboard. A dank and airless dark cupboard, full of half-open disinfectant bottles. "Do you want to hear or not?"

"Okay, I want to hear." I wondered how long before the next fragment of witty repartee.

"I met a guy called Nick."

"Not aged fifteen and your son?" Ah, that long.

"Our age, I think. Brown cow eyes. Big and limpid. And a brown cow brain. Also big and limpid."

"You didn't like him."

"He was okay. He just surprised me."

"I didn't know you could be surprised."

"Belinda, do you know what the bloody paper was?" This was so hard to say. I was going to sound stupid.

"No," Belinda answered, immediately, "Of course not."

"It was a list of spells."

"A what?"

"Like a Book of Shadows," I proffered helpfully. I had talked it over with a Wiccan who was a friend of a friend. In an entirely neutral way, of course. It was bad enough that Dr Cow-Eyes knew. "You know, for witches and warlocks to do their magic with?"

"Books of Shadows aren't Jewish." This was said as if Belinda knew it for a complete and total fact after many years of research.

I ploughed on. "This was in Aramaic and Hebrew. It had other words in, too. Dr Nick wanted to take the original." I could not work out how to say Nick and not confuse things with my son but 'Dr Nick' sounded idiotic. Some days one sounds stupid, regardless.

"What did you do?"

"I nearly snatched it from him and ran out the door."

"A bit extreme," Belinda was worried.

"Well, pretend it was you. That you'd just found out that Ada was a practicing witch. A Jewish witch. That a stranger wanted to take the only copy of what was probably her book of spells. And he wanted to do things to it."

"She might not even have known what it was."

"Hah. There are some strange things in that box," I hinted darkly.

"We need to look properly," Belinda was worried, but also excited. In fact, she was where I'd been shortly after opening that bloody box.

"I've started. Dr Cow Eyes is an okay bloke, so I let him photocopy stuff. He's going to do me a translation. You can come to Sydney one weekend when we have it and he can meet the rest of the box and we can both ask him impossible questions."

"OK."

"Good, because I have homework for you." I loved the thought of giving My-Sister-the-Schoolteacher homework.

"Homework?"

"Why should anyone Jewish be playing silly buggers with magic in the nineteenth century?"

"I can guess," she was making a tentative joke. I think I had put her off-balance. Good. "I can make lots of guesses. I'm a good guesser."

"Can you not guess? Can you find out?" I let a weeny-teeny bit of desperation sneak into my voice.

"I'll see what I can do." She didn't sound so confident.

"Thanks."

"What are sisters for?" Belinda asked, rhetorically.

I ignored the rhetoric, naturally. "To annoy, of course."

Thereafter we reverted. And that is when young Ms Belinda actually remembered to take herself off and ask lots of questions from a rabbi (I bet that was one surprised rabbi) and came back with all that stuff on Jewish magic and ethics and things.

4.

The obvious article for Rhonda to write after the John Law fiasco was the one on its British equivalent. More daft finances. Idiot century, where the future was so much more important than the present and paper was worshipped.

Rhonda sighed. Obviously she was not over the Nostradamus chat room incident. If her damn-fool gift was back then, it was back and there wasn't a bloody thing she could do about it except live with it. And avoid being caught. And write about the South Sea Bubble. Charmingly. Wittingly. Educatively.

The trouble with the South Sea Bubble is that it had too much in common with Tulip mania. Speculation. Frenzy. Greed. And yet she was expected to write an entirely new article.

She'd already done the foolish human beings thing to death with the Mississippi Scheme. Rhonda pondered. While she pondered she wrote a time line to appear in a sidebar and to underpin the piece. Then she looked at the timeline and realised she had her approach: the UK handled its frenzies differently to France.

She was going to use this difference to show how England had a valve for opposition and dissent and France did not. She was going to use the piece to show why the French Revolution did not happen in the United Kingdom. Why the Pompeii of late eighteenth century England was never drowned by Vesuvius, no matter how corrupt and foolish it became. And that was a really good over-the-top metaphor to start the article.

Having sorted out her basic approach, Rhonda moved on to the importance of the bubbles that survived the South Sea fiasco, in creating a state where invention and innovation were more encouraged. She linked the South Sea Bubble to the Industrial Revolution and the rise of British wealth. The evidence was enough to back her claims. Rhonda was very pleased with this. The mood she was in didn't allow her the luxury of proper research, and it looked as if she wouldn't need proper research. Something was well in the world.

"Eighty six bubbles were banned," Rhonda wrote, "in this regulation of venture capital. Eighty six bubbles silenced before they could make a babble and lose people their sanity. My personal favourite is the one for transmuting quicksilver into a fine metal. A bit of alchemy indeed, to render mercury both malleable and non-poisonous."

British regulation didn't stop all bubbles, but British culture held a large element of ridicule. "Laughter," Rhonda wrote, "was a medicine for economic woes."

"Some of the side-effects were medicated against by a satirical chattering class," wrote Rhonda, "But not all. The South Sea was romance personified, and defied ridicule and rationality. Until a few people decided to sell . . ."

She spent the rest of the article talking about the collapse of bubbles and their effect on society and describing the fate of individuals. She couldn't get as taken up with it as with the Mississippi Scheme. Dull and worthy, that was the sum of it. Worthy but dull.

As she re-read the article she thought, *A bit crowded, but it will do.*

Then she realised, with a sinking feeling, that she had triggered one of her episodes. It was close, very close. She could feel it burbling in the vicinity of her stomach. She made dinner in a great hurry. It would be nice to have a full stomach this time round.

This burble turned out to be a revelatory one. On balance, it was more about what had already happened than about the future. She didn't know if she preferred to hate revelation more or prophecy more. Rhonda babbled online about four big venture capital projects. She revealed that they were all of the salted gold mine variety and were doomed to fail and to bring many people down with them.

"They are bubbles," her Nostradamus self wrote, "and they will start bursting when the first auditor turns whistle-blower. The wait will not be long."

Then she threw a punch that surprised even herself. "One of the four 'salted goldmines' is a goldmine in reality. A goldmine with no gold. The tiny African government that bails out this venture by accepting the land in lieu of Western debt has the opportunity to become a happy one, for although there is no gold, there are diamonds. The French government will suggest it take the land back in return for a new loan. Not even I can tell you if the small African country will discover its diamonds before the French obtain the mine."

I handled that one respectably, Rhonda thought and was very proud of herself.

She was about to log into a new chat room and unwind a bit, when a second fit took her.

"March, 2010. Country X will embrace the cause of private ownership enthusiastically. A public communications network will be transformed into a private company. Initially, this will cause no great change, but within twelve months, larger and larger segments of it will be floated on the stock exchange as it lacks the government underpinning for basic functioning, and as shareholders are given 'profits' taken from research and development funds.

"Within fifteen months the country involved will encounter difficulties on several fronts. Firstly, the share prices will initially reflect the standing of the company when it had a solid research and development arm and was an industry leader. There will be a 'bubble' of enthusiasm for the shares that rockets the prices up higher.

"They will spiral upwards, ever upwards, until a government inquiry shows that basic line servicing is a problem, that it takes up to four months for new subscribers to get a basic landline, that some remote regions do not have telecommunications at all, and that the CEO has been given a $6 million bonus payment for establishing this desirable outcome. Share prices will plummet and infect other ex-government institutions on the stock exchange. The big sell off will be given many names, including Grim Tuesday, Sell-Out Tuesday, Tip-Off Tuesday and Toneless Tuesday. Three suicides result.

"Thirty-six companies will fail, simply because of the lack of service from the telephone company and the subsequent unsustainability of their business. Another five hundred and seventy four narrowly escape collapse. Fifty-seven people die when, at the height of the sell-out, the entire system has no telephone service for two days. People relying on telephones to report emergencies are unable to call an ambulance, unable to call a fire engine to put out a fire and unable to call suicide counselling services.

"'We have never felt so alone,' says a national newspaper.

"The Prime Minister informs the nation 'It could have been much worse. We still have our mobile phones.' Thirty percent of mobile phones are inoperative at the time of his pronouncement, as they are linked to the defunct erstwhile national telecommunications service.

"The army will be sent in to re-establish basic telephonic services. Public confidence will continue to plummet.

"Parliament will be recalled urgently and will race through legislation to make all essential services public. Phone and cable lines will now be defined as crucial components of essential services. In the rush they will forget recompense to shareholders, who will lose everything. Two more suicides.

"A subsequent parliamentary review will admit that it was all avoidable and that privatisation of essential services was to blame. By this stage the country will have lost much of its edge and be behind all its neighbours, struggling back into the first world. Then those who have bought the inflated shares and those who have lost family members will sue the government."

5.

Oh! I've caught up with myself, *wrote Judith to her mythical audience*. Now we're back in chronological order, and you don't have to trouble your poor little brain to sort out what happened and when. And if you have a rich big brain it was never any trouble in the first place. And yes, I'm aggravating. I've been told twice today already. My boss wonders why she keeps me on. I tell her I'm a tourist attraction.

I said this to Rudolph when he turned up to buy something. He bought a nice vase, and asked me to dinner again. I told him to come back in a week. He just laughed. I gave him a tatty daisy I stole on the way to work. I told him I'd stolen it from a stranger's garden. He laughed again.

A little later I rang Belinda up with something I'd found out about the box. "I think that list of dates with a name against it and an eye at the top was Great-Grandma's fumigations against the Evil Eye. It was apparently a very Jewish thing to do. But I have no idea how it was done. Pity. I would love to fumigate against the Evil Eye."

"Maybe it would drive the smells out of Nick's room?"

"No, it would take something far more drastic to do that."

"That reminds me," Belinda said, "I've got another quote from GG's scrapbook. You need this one."

"Like hell I do," I said, at my most courteous. Besides, I already had my copy of the bits I wanted.

"There's a little newspaper cutting which has the heading 'How it is Done'. And it says:

"I heard it!" "Who told you?"
"Her friend." "You don't say!"
"'Tis dreadful." "Yes, awful!"

"Don't tell it, I pray!"
"Good gracious?" "Who'd think it?"
"Well, well!" "Dear, dear me!"
"I have my suspicions!"
"And I, too, you see!"
"Lord help us!" "Poor creature!"
"So artful!" "So sly!"
"No beauty!" "Quite thirty!"
"Between you and I!"
"I'm going!" "Do stay, love!"
"I can't!" "I'm forlorn!"
"Farewell, dear!" "Goodbye, sweet!"
"I'm glad she is gone!"

"That's yuck," And it was. Negative in a bunch of ways. Like that misogynist rhyme.

"Either she had a very, very wicked sense of humour, or she was masochistic," was Lin's comment.

"Or it was there to mislead," I retorted.

"I guess we'll never know," was Belinda's wistful reply.

"I guess we can guess," I snarled, and Belinda laughed.

"Would you like a happier quote to cheer you up?"

"Yes, I would," I said. "I want to see Great-Grandma as something other than a mean-spirited person."

"You would rather she was mad, bad and dangerous to know?"

"Absolutely," I said spiritedly, "But not in the way Byron was mad, bad and dangerous to know. George Gordon was a turd."

"If her quotes are anything to go by, then she was a very colourful lady. I like this one," she said, "but I'm not sure it helps any. 'A boy once asked his father who it was that lived next door to him, and when he heard the name, inquired if he was a fool. "No, my little friend, he is not a fool, but a very sensible man; but why did you ask this question?"

"Because," replied the boy, "Mother said the other day that you were next door to a fool, and I wanted to know who lived next door to you.'" Your kids are cooler than this."

"You know what?" was my immediate thought. "That only makes sense if the mother and father are separated and the boy lives with the mother."

"Jokes aren't supposed to make sense," said Belinda. "Besides, you're not supposed to interpret 'next door' literally."

"Oh," said I, feeling next door to a fool myself, "I want one more."

"Why on earth?"

"Just give me one," I said.

"Can a leopard change his spots?" she asked.

"I don't know. I assume a leopard can change his spots with hair dye."

"No, simpler than that. When a leopard is tired of one spot, he can go to another."

I groaned, but was immeasurably cheered. The propensity for bad jokes was inherited. Our strange ancestress would've been able to sit down with Nick and Zoë and joke. Make that Nick and Zoë and Linnie.

Talking about Great-Grandma was Belinda's way of avoiding memories of night fires and my way of avoiding Peter. We were both scared of repeat incidents. It struck me at that point that she would have worn corsets.

"So what?" said Belinda. "All women wore corsets then. And later. Mum wore a corset for ages."

"I hate corsets," I declared.

"You hate lots of things," Lin reminded me.

"True," I reflected. "But I haven't added to my list of hates recently. I've been kind of fixated on bits of government policy I hate and things that annoy me about daily life and . . ."

"Corsets," Lin stuck in, before I could finish.

"I was going to get to that," I said with dignified injury, "I was about to add them to my list of hates so I don't get boring. I would hate to be boring."

"Or worthy," added Belinda.

Aha, an opening. "I don't need to be worthy, you know, you do that for both of us."

"One day I will leave you to your just desserts," Belinda threatened.

"As long as they're chocolate, I'll be happy," I reassured her. "Damn, gotta go. There appears to be a crisis in the kitchen."

"Crisis?"

"Smoke and a scream or two. The usual."

It was, as expected, the usual. Zoë and Nick had dropped something and toast was burning and they were angry at each other. I made them put everything back in order and sent them both to their rooms. Not that sending them to their rooms is a great punishment these days. I looked in on them a few minutes later and Nick was on his computer. Zoë was reading, with the cat curled up on her stomach.

First I did my shopping list for the next day. More carrots. I idly wondered which of my children was eating all the carrots and would turn orange.

Then I went to the living room and spent a charming evening annotating all the minutes of the meetings I had hated attending this last month. This needed doing anyway, and at least, while I was in this mood, the notes would be rude.

A week later all my minutes came of age. June invited me to a meeting in Canberra. She was going to argue with the Attorney General and she wanted me there. My boss was happy enough for me to take a day off.

Rudolph was less happy, as he had planned on taking me to dinner. I offered to steal him something from Parliament House, but he sulked, charmingly. I told him how charming his sulk was.

We left early, but the mail came even earlier. There was a letter from Peter in it. I didn't open that letter. I wrote on it "Return to Sender" and dropped it into a letterbox on the way out of Sydney.

Once it was gone, the day improved. We hit Canberra almost out of time for our meeting. We raced into Parliament House like bats out of hell, and walked into that big office feeling a bit smug. June (as always) had her camera about her neck.

I got to be obstreperous with the Attorney-General. That AG was one of the more tolerable current idiots in Parliament. Sometimes, very, very occasionally, he allowed good things to happen. This is why we went all the way to Canberra: he was prepared to meet with us as long as he didn't have to exert himself. The government was considering legislation that reinforced the rights of men to see their children regardless of the safety of their spouses or ex-spouses and their children.

June led me through the day in a kind of mentoring fashion. Tactically late arrivals and the camera and the sheer presence of June is not who she is. She has a big heart and a frightening capacity for coffee and cigarettes. She personally got me through the worst of my traumas and showed me I could make things better for other people in the same position. I met her in the Nursing Mothers'. Very, very way back then. What a dauntingly old person I become.

That day, I tagged along with her and her little lobbyist card.

It took over a half hour to get our coffee. There wasn't a scrap of a queue: the delay was June. She collared members of our beloved Parliament and loyal-to-death staffers and briefed them. She introduced me to my own Member of Parliament, which was a hoot. He studiously snubbed us (hoping, I think, that June would just fade away) until June cheerfully announced where I lived.

Another guy, the Shadow Minister for Immigration, was very welcoming. He introduced us to a useful person for women's policy and promised June a meeting.

Everything was on first name terms, even the people who gave us the brush-off. Parliament is truly a weird place.

We finally found a little table next to one of those giant windows that gives garden views. The garden was wet and all the smokers were clustered in little alcoves outside. I met my first Federal Minister that day, in a little damp alcove, near that café. I think it was between the second and third cigs that we finally got our meeting. At that point, a staffer from someone's office hailed June.

It turned out there was a very tiny window of opportunity (a few hours) for getting a really nasty new little bit of legislation opposed. A few words from the staffer and June knew what was being referred to, saw its awful implications, and decided to take action. Long distance, I'm very cluey on these things. But I am your ultimate written word person and this happened at machine gun speed.

Another staffer passed with a takeaway coffee clutched in one hand and files perilously slipping from the other. June collared her and asked if the Labor Women's Caucus had started. The staffer with coffee said it was about to begin.

June said we could finish our business elsewhere.

'Elsewhere' was her exact word. I followed her down cold white corridor after cold white corridor after cold white corridor. 'Elsewhere' was in a pale nowhere, but it had giant black armchairs and frozen coffee tables. Every now and again a member of the Labor Women's Caucus walked by. June would call out that person's name and tell them the situation. Eventually the most senior Labor women came out to us from the meeting.

June introduced our little group and we had the nicest conversation. Warm and glowing and supportive. My extra-top-favourite politician sat on a little stone table, while I was ensconced in this huge black armchair with notes all round me. She acted as if she had known us forever. My face was bright red.

Finally the shadow minister for women's issues came and had a chat with us. By this time our papers were away and we stood up to meet her. She was totally charming as she walked us gently to the edge of the public section of Parliament House and waved us out through Security.

We'd saved the day. June told me so, next time I saw her.

I told Belinda about it when June dropped me off and she howled with laughter. Her news was different. A bit strange to hear her all calm and collected, telling me that the gentleman who'd called her worthy had misplaced two weeks'-worth of student corrections. I remembered why I'd encouraged her to take that job in Canberra, years ago. It wasn't just so that Zoë could have her own room.

When I got home, things were happily normal. Nick was out with friends. Zoë was waiting anxiously at the door. There was a rather nice bunch of flowers from Rudolph, which would've made me feel guilty if it had not been completely comprised of daisies, exactly like the daisy I had given him the week before. My floral theft, returned to me fifteen times over, ensconced in very pretty purple paper.

6.

Judith played round with magic that evening. Judith didn't really wonder if magic worked or not. She knew it didn't. Nothing seemed to have happened with the charms or the protection. That scrapbook bewildered her. Judith wanted to make sense of the weirdly misogynistic stuff Belinda had read out. Magic was her solution.

Judith now knew what most of the things in the middle section of that scrapbook were. Reading the lines on hands and on foreheads. Lists of names necessary to basic enchantment. A bestiary of Jewish mythical beasts. They all linked with spells or to other magic methods in the box of notes.

Zoë was beginning to know it a little too, although Judith had warned her not to look at random or shuffle the pages.

Judith was fascinated by Ada. Earlier she had been curious because of the legacy. A forgotten sister. A daughter trained in medicine who never spoke to her mother, but kept her papers and even handed them down the generations. And that divorce. Divorces were not common back then and family tradition said Ada instigated it. Belinda was fascinated by the chauffeur: Judith was fascinated by the divorce.

Now Judith thought of Ada differently. Not in terms of her legacy, but in terms of her shoes. What size were they? What did it feel like to walk in them? A skerrick of sibling rivalry may have prompted Judith to try her own little path in Ada's shoes. To attempt magic.

If a formula said to do such and such or so and so, was it physically possible to do such things? This is what I wanted to know. Because if it wasn't, then I knew she was only interested in it theoretically. If it was, she was maintaining a hidden Jewish women's tradition.

Naturally things weren't so simple. I included Zoë. Bonding. Zoë loves fantasy and magic books. I wanted to know about Great-Grandma. So we did magic together.

Zoë wanted to know about Great-Grandma too. She didn't tell me so. I was too busy being gung-ho about it — all she had to do was say, "yes Mum", in a patient voice. Why do children suddenly turn into preteens when you close your eyes for a moment? "Yes, Mum," in tones ever more resigned and bored. Nick did this too. Teen tones. From, "Oh, Mum, do I have to?" to "Yes, Mum," and bland ignore in the blink of an eye.

We talked about the ethics, not because I thought anything untoward would happen, but because Lin's little spiel of personal responsibility seemed totally perfect for a child Zoë's age. This magic was a very good excuse.

For her first solo effort, Zoë says she chose her bit of magic because it mentioned Hekate and she knew Hekate from TV and books. There was nothing too terribly unethical in what she planned, so I said, "Fine". Mothers say 'Fine' the way kids say 'Yes, Mum'.

Zoë chose something to get her through the next school day. She was being picked on by bigger girls. This was the first I'd heard about it. I was spitting mad about those bullies, but since I'd just lectured Zoë on personal responsibility, I had to give her that spell and time to see what happened.

We had other strategies to deal with those girls once the magic failed.

The Hekate charm was a good one. Unobtrusive. It was against fear. I can see why it would exist in a Jewish magic tradition, what with all that irrational hatred against us over the centuries.

The first step was to have courage. While you were walking bravely forth, you held your thumbs and said, 'I am Hekate'. And if someone came to you and they were doing this, you took hold of your right heel and said a little rhyme to help you overcome them. The right heel bit must look odd, but I didn't say that aloud. I'm the embodiment of cautious restraint.

Zoë wouldn't let me do my magic charm until she'd tested hers. They had been doing scientific method in class. I wasn't to try anything by myself under penalty of something awful. It made me wonder who was the mother and who the child.

After three days of thumb holding and not being bullied, Zoë was radiant. She was a thorough believer in magic. I was a thorough believer in how standing up to bullies is magic. We were both very happy with the results.

Nick was ensconced in his room most of the time and didn't even notice. He was in teenager mode. Except that Lin kept telling me he frequently emailed her. Everyone else thought that she'd recovered from the Molotov cocktail; Nick was there for the long haul. He did this support thing in teenager mode. He spoke in grunts and emerged from his room only to go to school or to scoff his evening meal in silent haste.

Zoë's experiment had worked and it was my turn. I couldn't make up my mind what sort of magic I would try. Zoë and I pored over the English-language material in Great-Grandma's box.

I needed my spell to have a really obvious result. I was to wear a picture and when the good thing happened I was allowed to be happy and had to say 'chaithrai'. I liked the closure on it, and I found I really liked the permission to be happy. Life was wearing me down a bit. I could have wished for Peter to die. But what would that have solved?

Zoë didn't like my spell: she thought I should be happy without permission. She was also not delighted with my wish. I wanted a windfall to give her and Nick good birthday parties this year. She told me bluntly that it wasn't for me at all. Bluntly, loudly and very strongly. Zoë made me do two spells. We did the birthday one first and decided to argue about the other after.

We made the amulet with the requisite picture, and invoked an angel (Great-Grandma's magic has lots of angels invoked, and even God). We said the invocation twice. Then we finished with some very familiar words — they took me back to my childhood. It was a standard thingie, "May he who makest peace in the high places . . ." and so on. Straight from the synagogue service.

This made me feel religious. I only remember where those words come from now — I'm remembering despite myself. Back then, the words felt familiar and friendly, but were also strange phrases written by someone inebriated with the thought of enchantment.

Belinda says that our Jewishness is not the same as most of Jewish Australia's. Which is a whole new reason why Henry and I had a failed marriage.

Henry's parents are Holocaust survivors, and his view of the world is different to mine. Our food is different, our lifestyles are different and the way we bring up children is different. Our politics are the same. Except he's a Party man. Always. Labor Centre-Left, for the record. Bloody factionalism.

I investigated things Jewish once. Years ago, there was a political kerfuffle about Jewish divorce. Being told that it is worse for Catholics doesn't help Jewish women whose husbands won't grant a divorce. Damn, I'm getting angry. Let me go back to the charms.

I know why I'm angry though. This time it's not the problems faced by women whose husbands say 'no' to divorce (I can feel angry on that too — it's a good subject to get angry about). It's because someone called me bossy today. I'm not bossy. I'm just very clear on things.

I am me. I was called Joodles today, too.

I am me, Judith.

Stop being angry, Judith. Go back to magic.

Zoë and I waited a full day for huge amounts of money to fall into my lap as a result of the charm. Nothing happened. Well, Rudolph talked me into a second date. That happened. Rudolph pretended to be a telemarketer selling me "a night on the town with an extraordinarily handsome gentleman."

Zoë and I gave up on the money.

Just after dinner the second day, we sat at the kitchen table and started planning the next charm. The phone rang. Zoë answered it and behaved annoyingly. She said, "Hello," nicely and then, "Yes," a number of times. Then she said, "I think Mummy would like that." Then she hung up. Her face was beaming like a newly burnished sun. There was mischief beneath the smile.

"Well?" I asked. Distrustful, of course. I was betting it had been Rudy. I already wanted to renege on that date.

She grinned at me. "That was the lady from the shop."

My boss had rung? And just told Zoë things? "And?" I did not trust myself to say copious amounts when faced with Zoë looking like she might be sick from a surfeit of joy.

"Say 'Chaithrai' and I will tell you."

"Do I have to be happy as well?" Me at my most sarcastic.

"Yes," affirmed my ever-dotty daughter. "Say 'Chaithrai' and be happy or I won't tell you."

"Chaithrai," I said. I smiled. Sarcastically.

I knew the money existed because of the look on Zoë's face. But for all I knew it was ten cents. In which case she would get five cents for her birthday party and Nick would get the same for his. Even-handedness is very important in high finance.

"Now say the blessing." I had no choice. She'd handed me the right paper instantly from the mass on the table.

Finally Ms Bossy told me, "You won lots of money last Melbourne Cup, and someone forgot to give you the envelope and she just found it when she was cleaning." How could I win money on a sweep and not remember it?

Then it came back to me. Last November a friend's friend was in a crisis and all the refuges were completely chockers (bloody funding cuts) and she stayed at my place and I stayed with her the next day. I missed the Cup function. My boss had collected my contributions on the way there and probably put it all in sweeps.

"How much did I win?"

"It was two hundred and forty-seven dollars. And ten cents." I especially liked the ten cents, under the circumstances. Five for each child. "And it's all for birthdays."

"It is, indeed," I agreed. "Lots of chips and balloons."

"Twisties and jelly babies and chocolate crackles and Snow White cups," was Zoë's view. "Lots."

"All at once," I agreed. If she wanted to make herself sick on her birthday who was I to stop her? Except that the Snow White cups would make *me* sick.

Inside, I was shaken. Magic couldn't work, could it?

Every single one of those damned papers was spread out in front of us. Lurking.

There was a bit of me that wanted it to work so I could get revenge. And be rich. And have all life's wondrous goodness. All the things that you read about in fairy tales. Every single one of them. A genie to do my bidding; a wonderful husband; a fab job; a solid future for my children.

Only a bit of me really trusted itself to dream. Some of me was curious. Most of me was scared stiff. Happiness and Judith are not comfortable sharing a bed. The new me was learning not to hide though, so I didn't make Zoë pack everything up then and there.

We were going to try that next spell. We were. And it would fail. Because magic did not work. It was merely a popular way of escaping sad realities.

A tiny, tiny corner of me wondered what realities Great-Grandma was escaping by writing down spells. Why did she hide the key to the spells in the middle of the scrapbook? I also wondered why so many of the spells were defensive. In our lives there had been Peter (and other Peters for some of my friends) and there were Molotov cocktails. Had Great-Grandma faced violence with magic?

Damn, I was getting totally tangled. And Zoë was sitting there at the table, her face expectant. Waiting for more magic. I couldn't strip that look from her face.

When the day's mail mysteriously appeared in one of the piles I took it in my stride. I wrote 'return to sender' on one of the letters. I did ask her if she would mind running to the corner quickly and posting it immediately. I promised hot chocolate. God knows, I needed hot chocolate.

When she came back we continued with our work. This time we did it methodically. We put away all the papers we didn't understand or that might be danger-ous. Magic was a myth. But children are precious be-ings and you take no risks. None. Not ever. Even if it means running interstate and to another city, you take no risks.

Zoë put every single bloody page that might hurt someone right back in the box. And I sat there drinking hot chocolate and looking like a tailor's dummy, with a fixed smile on my face, hoping Zoë would not notice how hard I was trying to be pleased and happy. And tailor's dummy is not the right simile — because they don't have heads and my head was sporting that fixed grin. Damn all similes to the five hells.

I do not deal well with intangibles. And next time, don't point it out.

Sorry, that last comment was to bloody Belinda, who is visiting this weekend and laughing over my shoulder. I shouldn't have turned the computer on while she was here, but I wanted to get past this sec-tion. So now I have a sister saying that I don't deal well with some tangibles either, namely cooking. I didn't burn the dinner tonight. The stove did.

Belinda and Nick and Zoë have been turning the house upside down. It's more of Great-Grandma's fault. Belinda decided that Ada *might* have played par-lour games. That she *would* have played parlour games. That there was no way she could have *avoided* playing parlour games. So the three of them have been playing bloody parlour games all bloody afternoon.

I came to my computer for refuge and now I want to finish the episode, but they keep telling me that dinner is over and I should play. I don't feel like it. I feel like getting to the end of this bloody narrative. No one told me that baring my soul would be addictive. Or that my family would run gross interference by playing *Hunt the Slipper*.

I'm going to play *Throw the Bloody Slipper* if they're not very, very careful. Good, Zoë read that. She's gone off giggling. Maybe I'll get a little quiet.

Where was I? Oh yes, Zoë and I had the papers in front of us. Zoë picked a paper up and told me what it was or showed it to me (she'd got the hang of Great-Grandma's handwriting, but some of the subject matter was terribly abstruse), and most of it went back into the box.

"Ooh," said Zoë, when she had puzzled out yet another page, "Do this one! I like this one!" She liked it because it began 'Just as you saved Jonah from the whale . . .'

It was to save someone from being forced to convert. It was not a spell I wanted to play with. Lots of people try to convert me, but it's hardly a life or death matter. They're just as much distressed by me being a feminist as me being Jewish.

A moment later, Zoë got excited (again). She found another bloody amulet. I swear she's addicted to amulets. This time, she announced it was a much better one than all the others and that it would give lots and lots and lots of protection. Zoë needs a bigger vocabulary. Thus saith her mother.

I had no objections to the spell. I like making jewellery, and amulets made a difference from the stuff I normally sold at Sunday stalls. This one had a text to be written, which I liked more than the scratched early version. Classier.

Great-Grandma's note said: *Text for placement inside amulet: Great heavenly one who makes the universe move and turn, the God who is Adonai, Lord, ruler of all, ablanalanalba, grant me favour. I shall scribe the name of the great God in this amulet, and it will protect me from every evil creature, I, Eve, daughter of blank.*

Our names would go where 'Eve, daughter of blank'

was. I could do that. And make gorgeous containers. I wrote the correct name for the magical being I was calling upon, but I'm going to respect the beliefs of those more religious than myself, and not tell you what it was. I'm leaving out most of Great-Grandma's angel names, for the same reason. The magic won't work without these names.

I did say it was Secret Jewish Women's Stuff. Wizardly Stuff. No one can do it except myself and Zoë. And maybe Linnie. If she asks nicely. If she continues to keep her Evil Twin away from me.

Zoë then suggested flying through the air. I asked was she prepared to jump from the roof to test it? She said, naturally, "Yes." Damn her pale green scrunchie. I informed her that we were not trying a flying spell, ever. I didn't want to clean up the splatter on the pavement afterwards.

Did Ada-the-indelible ever fly through the air? I had this vision of a Victorian matron holding her skirts tight as they tried to billow when a tail breeze caught her unawares.

Finally we decided on one for gut ache. You say the charm over water and drink the water. It seemed safe enough to me, and my period was due. I would soon have enough aches and pains in that area to sink a battleship. Zoë put the paper aside for when we were ready, and we packed everything up and she went to bed.

7.

Two days later Judith drank her words. Zoe said the charm, her face earnest and her brow wrinkled. If anyone had told Judith she would be unhappy at diminished period pains, she would have laughed in their face. When the drink worked, however, she found herself in tears at the lessening of pain. *It's all in my mind,* she told herself.

She asked Zoë if she thought it was enough proof that the magic worked. Zoë, of course, said yes.

"Hold off on it a bit," her mother advised. "I'm still not sure."

Her daughter — a born horse trader — had Judith create the new protection amulets first. She wanted to wear a new one under her school uniform.

"Why?"

"Because I want to," said her daughter, irrefutably.

Judith understood the imperatives of emotions. This may have been because she herself was still wearing her first amulet.

She made another for Zoë and another for herself. She made one for Rudolph's watch. She could afford to give him a present, she rationalised, since her period saved her from any designs he might have on her person. They were very pretty. The casing for her amulet was purple. Zoë wanted pink. Rudolph got black exquisitely etched with an almost- red nose, and no magic text. Then they both agreed to let well alone until Judith had sorted her mind out.

8.

The next two days were unconscionably long. Rhonda could not bring herself to go online. She had nightmares of being haunted by her own voices echoing around the net. A day or two without chat room and friends won't hurt anyone, she reassured herself, glumly.

"I have friends," she said in firm reminder when the days stretched out, lonely, without online activities. A person passing looked at her comment in stray surprise. But she did have friends. It was worth saying aloud. Two flesh and blood friends, in fact. Their children, heartache and heartlove all in one. And her online buddies. And casual acquaintances.

Rhonda had to remind herself, however, how friendship operated. "Friends don't stand outside the shop window, watching other people living," she told herself, "Friends are proactive. Friends do things together. They talk, they laugh. And no one is going to know I need talking and laughter unless I tell them."

When she'd walked through the front door, Rhonda stopped and juggled her keys in exuberant eureka. She went straight to her computer and switched it on. She then spent the rest of the day and the next day and the day after writing a series of fan fictions. Each of them was a gentle joke. Each of them starred a friend.

Phased was Xena, and Starchild was the unknown Jedi who Yoda turned to for wise advice. Phased could be found running a gift shop in Smallville and Rhonda herself (in even-handed zeal) was on the Battlestar Galactica. The narratives were innocent of sex. All her online friends tended towards femaleness, so really the only option was slash — or changing her friends' genders. Neither appealed.

After she posted her stories, she crumpled. She put a drop of marjoram oil in her burner. It was the wrong day for marjoram, but she didn't care: it would help her revitalise her crumpled self. When the woody scent started seeping into her pores, she went back to the computer and sat back and watched the screen for a bit.

"Sadly boring am I," Rhonda told herself and fell into a wistful screen-mesmerised dream. She wished she could be something, someone . . . different. Not normal. She had tried normal, and failed. In control. That's what she wanted. She wanted to be able to make decisions about her life and to have them happen.

Rhonda wafted towards the television and sat down. Maybe it would ground her. Or maybe there was something on that matched her mood. On top of the TV guide she found a pen and some paper. Of course. She left pen and paper everywhere, why not there?

Instead of checking to see what was on, she let the images and sound flicker in the background. She only looked up when the advertisements blared or when she was looking for a word.

Rhonda wrote another new piece for her fan fiction friends. It had her screaming capitals and pregnant pauses, because if she had left them out then she would have been too identifiable. She was beginning to think she was paranoid about style. Maybe paranoid - full stop. And she yanked herself back into her dream story.

It wasn't fan fiction proper. It didn't feature a hero from her favourite TV and film universes. It didn't steal plots. In a way, it was a Mary Sue. Rhonda was most definitely the heroine and absolutely in wish fulfilment mode.

She set herself as a mad scientist. Brilliant, charming, totally demented. Rhonda cheated and put a precise description of her physical self as that mad scientist. It was the first time she had ever put her eye colour and height in anything for the web. She paused a moment to chew her pen and wonder just how stupid she was being. She changed her eye colour and ploughed on. Dr Bet, she called her character. Dr Bet, Mad Scientist. Who took everyone's secret dreams and made them come true.

She took whole paragraphs from the fiction her friends had written and wrote them back into the story about them. It took her two evenings, and she didn't post it until the third day. It left her very happy. She loved that group.

She was so buoyed up by her love and her writing

that she wanted company. Blogging was no good. Who answered depended on who was online and when, and it was the wrong time of day for anyone to be out there. Well, anyone who counted. There were always people in chat rooms.

She found herself a chat room and snuck in as 'guy'. Stupid nick. She didn't like it and wouldn't use it again.

She talked. She talked more than she had ever talked in a chat room before. It was as if her plug had come unstuck and a stream of babble was exiting her brain through her fingers.

Rhonda didn't know what she was saying. It was a bit like being in prophetic mode, except she wasn't. She was just letting loose a torrent of emotions and foul feelings onto the world. In character. She always used American spelling and carefully remembered to use US syntax and sound a bit Californian from time to time. But apart from that, she didn't care what she said and she didn't notice what she said. Then a comment brought her up short.

"Who are you, really?" someone asked. "And why do you say such stupid things?"

"Who am I?" Rhonda answered. "I am really Pharaoh's foot soldier and I am in de-Nile. It's hard to say clever things from underwater."

She left the computer screen to its own devices while she went to get dinner. Food was a good thing when there were idiots around. Normal food. That's what she needed. Sane and balancing and normal. Instant macaroni cheese. Fifteen minutes later she was back at the screen, fuelled to take on the world.

She took herself and the remnants of her bowl of joy to her favourite chat room: less chance of idiots, she thought. Hopefully she could have a chat with old friends, even if they didn't know who she was. She felt a bit daft and devilish after calling herself Pharaoh's foot soldier, so she logged on as daftdeveil. Kind of Scottish; a tribute to her purported ancestors.

Instantly she encountered a familiar voice. Not one she wanted to hear. Awful timing, too.

"Does M44M ever come here?" asked BB.

"No," said Rhonda, as daftdeveil. She had wondered when BB would meet up with her again in a chat room. She was surprised it had taken this long. Unless it hadn't. Unless he had as many aliases as she did. What a foul thought. "Don't know M44M."

She realised she was in a masochistic mood. She would hang round and ask BB the sort of questions daftdeveil was about to become known for: daft ones.

What a stupid thing to do. Rhonda disconnected before she could get trapped into watching herself being cornered. "I'm going to stay offline all night," she told herself. She had no idea how she was going to manage it.

Lana rang. "Hi." She was bright and cheery. So be it. Bright cheer could be used to its full effect.

"Hi. Are you busy tonight? Can you get a babysitter in a hurry?"

"Why?"

"I'm miserable and depressed and want to do something incredibly stupid."

"That's seriously cool, because Tony needs to be left alone for an evening."

"You're not talking to each other?"

"Let's just say that time apart will not do any harm."

"And so his punishment is babysitting?"

"Got it in one, sister. How about we go clubbing?"

"Because it's incredibly stupid?"

"Because I want to find you a man."

"So that I can argue with him and leave him at home with the kids and go off and have fun with girl-friends."

"That's about it." Lana was insanely merry for someone who was having a marital tiff.

Clubbing might be fun. Dancing and drink and lots of noise had a real appeal. "Let's do it all girlie and proper," Rhonda suggested. "Come over, bring pide and we will do each other's hair and faces before we go."

"Coolies," said Lana. "Be there in an hour."

"See ya." Rhonda felt like a teenager: it was a nice feeling.

———

The hair and the faces and the giggles took her right back to schooldays. How many years since she had done such silliness? Too many.

They decided to catch a cab into the city, because cabs increased the prospect of each of them getting entirely and thoroughly drunk. Lana made sure that Rhonda had enough cash to get home, should they get separated. Rhonda looked at Lana with narrowed eyes and assured her that she had no intention of getting separated.

"I wouldn't know what to do, out alone on the town; I need you with me the whole time. Besides, Tony said to keep an eye on you."

Lana just shoved a fifty-dollar bill in Rhonda's purse, and said, "Humour me. And Tony doesn't know what side is up. He told me he didn't want to pick either of us up at the police station."

The thought of her being picked up by the police for some reason caused Rhonda hysterics. The half bottle of pink champagne she had already consumed might have assisted. "Oh, God," she laughed, almost breathless, "The thought. Would they even arrest me?"

Lana crumbled in laughter too. Even all dressed up, Rhonda looked quiet. Not the sort of person the police take notice of, however drunk. And no matter how giggly and snarky she became, Lana was too nice for mischief.

"Well, we can hope," Lana suggested, "and maybe the policeman will be cute at that. Now get your butt into gear, we're going to paint the town bloody crimson!"

And so they did. A quiet and demure crimson. Not quite red. More like blushing pink, if one were to use Rhonda's cheeks as a guide. Lana flirted with all available specimens of men, then, when they got too interested, gently let it be known that she was married, and threw them Rhonda's way. Rhonda was completely out of her depth.

Eventually, a man thrown in her direction proved familiar. It took her about five minutes to realise where she knew him from, and it took him about the same time to remember who she was. This embarrassed both of them. She had been flirting with her first cousin, Sam.

This was one of those things that were worse to imagine than to experience, Rhonda thought, as she sat across the table from her cousin and tried to delete the background noise. It was so important she hear what he said, even if it wasn't anything important. Ten years was a long time. A very, very long time.

The reason she hadn't recognised him was that he'd changed. He still had that friendly, inquisitive look, but it was subdued by plumpness. His hair had receded considerably, and there was a lot of grey. The chubby cheeks made him look younger than he had last time she saw him, and the grey made him look older. It was the hairline that had thrown her entirely.

She noticed that Sam evaluated her just as carefully as she had evaluated him. Neither of them was very comfortable with this chance meeting. Sam finally said, "I haven't seen you since GAM's funeral."

"No one has seen me since then," and she plunged straight into the truth. "The family cut me off when I went on drugs."

Sam looked a bit surprised that Rhonda was so open about the drugs. She didn't see the use in hiding it, not from him. For sure he knew about them, given the family and its obsession with talking things through until everyone was hurt and bleeding. Besides, she'd been over them for nearly a decade. This was one part of her life she didn't have to hide.

"My husband divorced her too," Lana said. "She was a total mess."

"Except that once I was through it we found we were still friends. You know," and she looked at Lana, "I keep thinking how lucky I was and how nice he is. We weren't at all right married, but we make fantastic friends."

She was being honest too. Tony and Lana had been there for her where no one else had ever been. She loved them more than almost anyone.

"I think it worked out well," Lana said. "I got a great friend along with the man of my dreams."

"Considering the mess I made that year of just about everything, I think it worked out well. Except for the family giving up on me."

"I didn't know about it until years later," Sam defended himself. "I just didn't see you at family gatherings. I guess I thought you were avoiding me." He didn't look her in the face. Rhonda decided to wait a bit before she judged.

"I got so many knockbacks when I went haywire." Rhonda didn't understand why she had to explain; Sam could have asked almost anyone what had happened. "I wasn't going to ring every single family member and be told I was dangerous to be near."

"You? Dangerous?" Lana laughed. "You live in a different world, but you're one of the sweetest and safest people I know."

"Thanks, I think."

"GAM said something about you," Sam said. His face was very inward looking. "I forgot it for years and then it came back to me when Mum wouldn't give me your address because you got the legacy. That legacy upset Mum. She thought it was mine. She thought it very loudly and very often."

"That's Auntie," and Rhonda found it in her to laugh. She also found it in her to be fair. "It maybe should've been yours, too. After all, you were close to GAM, and you helped her an awful lot those last years."

"You lived interstate," Sam defended, but that wasn't it. "I want to tell you what she told me. She made me come round to see her. She said that sometimes someone in the family has particular burdens to bear and sometimes the family was supportive and sometimes it acted nasty. She said she thought she had found a solution in case the family was nasty, but that it wasn't equitable. No one would like it, but it was the best she could do. She said that several times. The best thing she could think of for everyone concerned. She said that no one should bear those burdens without help. She was so earnest and so worried. I can't ever forget that conversation."

"She was referring to the drugs?" asked Lana. Openness sometimes went too far: Rhonda wished Lana had not said that.

"No, this was before then. I mean, I never knew about the drugs, so it must have been before then. It was just after you got married." He looked at Rhonda. A mean little bit inside Rhonda was glad Lana had got a tiny comeuppance for having mentioned drugs as if they were the only thing in Rhonda's life. Six months out of three and a half decades? She was more than that. "It didn't make any sense to me because I'd just been to your wedding. You had your husband and your scholarship and you were happier than you'd been in years. GAM didn't make sense."

"Have you noticed how amazingly cool we are at discussing topics that are fearfully sensitive?" Rhonda asked.

"Do you mind?" asked Sam.

"Sorry," said Lana, at the same time.

"No, no." She waved her arms in the air to fend off blame. "I don't mind at all." And she didn't. She really didn't. "I was just impressed. And I'm not sure what GAM was talking about."

"So we're not talking about everything then," and Sam looked across astutely. "I'm the family history person, remember? I know about our Jewish great-grandmother who was dumped by her family. I also know there is something from that side that we never talk about. And I saw GAM looking at you. It was a funny look. Almost pitying. Once she said to your mother that you were not really able to handle it without help. Auntie said that she would always be there for you. GAM didn't say a word. I could see she didn't believe Auntie would. I kept thinking how glad I was that I had Mummy and you had Auntie, because Mummy was always there for everyone."

There was a silence in the small circle. The clash of the music in the background expanded the halt in time.

"Mummy wasn't, though, not for you," Rhonda was surprised to hear Sam admit it. It was quite true, but she never thought she would hear it said. Sam was a very decent guy. "She was there for everyone else, but never for you. I feel so bad about it."

Sam's confession took an ache from Rhonda's soul and blew it away with its honesty. It was Sam's mother who'd led the hate crusade. Sam was right, though. In most other respects, she was lovely. Just not to Rhonda.

Rhonda focussed on her own painful history. "I wish I'd had that close relationship with GAM." She tried to steer this dangerous conversation back to slightly safer waters. Guilt-fests were not good things to share. And Sam was entitled to love his mother. "I always thought she avoided me."

"I think she did. I think that whatever she saw, she was running from it just as much as the rest of the family. And that the legacy was given out of unadulterated guilt."

"It should have been yours," Rhonda said.

"I used to think so," Sam admitted. "But I still have the family."

There was an empty silence. Sam was the one who broke it. "Can we swap phone numbers? I don't want the burden you have. Anything that scares the older generation that much is something I want away from my children. But maybe we could phone from time to time and I could keep you in touch?"

"I would like that," said Rhonda. "I would really, really like that."

Sam excused himself once the ritual number swapping was complete. He was leaving for home first thing the next morning — this had been a quick work visit.

Rhonda felt bereft. It was easier to pretend there was no such thing as family, than to find and lose it in such a rapid space of time. At least she would know a bit more about what she was missing. Still, she felt lonely. A big cocktail appeared magically at her left elbow.

Lana smiled. "You look as if you need it," she said.

"Now you know about my family," Rhonda replied. "More than you ever wanted to know."

"Well, I've been plaguing you for long enough.

Sounds like a good family to be shut of. Even GAM (whoever GAM is) sounds a bit batty. If they have cut you off forever because of something so stupid as a few months of being an idiot, you're missing nothing."

"Thanks," and Rhonda gave a feeble smile.

Another thing struck her. Lana'd missed half the conversation. She had also missed that Tony had not sought a divorce because of the drugs, but because of the secret the drugs hid. Rhonda treasured Lana's innocence and she treasured Lana's friendship, even as she felt callous about making her family out to be monsters. Fear makes monsters of everyone, after all.

Then Rhonda changed her mind. She sipped her drink and felt her anger build inside. The older generation knew about her curse. And they had stood by and let her think she was mad, or possessed. With just a little support, she might have been able to find a way through it. She might still have a husband, a career, and a family. Everything, instead of nothing. That moment of happiness she had experienced in her twenties, but for a lifetime.

No. She didn't have nothing. She had two best friends who knew her worst and still included her in their lives. She had two honorary children. And she had an entirely geekish side to her character that had evolved from the loneliness.

"Who on earth was GAM, anyway?" Lana interrupted her thoughts, "GAM isn't a name, it's a trademark."

Rhonda felt a wave of nostalgia hit and she explained GAM. "Great Aunt Mabel with a gammy knee. We all called her Auntie Mabel until her knee started playing up, then somehow the whole family started calling her GAM. The family likes acronyms. Until I got the legacy I thought she hated me. Now I think maybe she hated me and felt guilty."

"I wish more people would give me guilt money," Lana replied. "You can buy the next round and we'll drink a toast to gammy knees."

"I've never drunk a toast to gammy knees before," Rhonda admitted.

"Well, it's overdue. Go, get the drinks."

At the bar, Rhonda found herself standing next to the last person in the world she wanted to see. Mr Ick. How on earth did he manage to be so bloody ubiquitous? She was mellow and simply avoided eye contact. He wouldn't notice her. Tonight was her night.

Tonight wasn't quite her night. He said warmly, "Rhonda, what's a nice girl like you doing in a place like this?"

"That line," Rhonda replied tautly, "was old even when you were young."

She saw his hand moving for a part of her he had no rights over. Rhonda took one step back and was out of reach. She paid for her drinks and made a strategic exit. It was indeed her night. She was on a roll. She giggled as she sat down and she also announced, "Everything's going my way. We should go play the pokies!"

So they did. Rhonda won $35 and they both resolved it would be spent on drinks.

"Luck is to be enjoyed," Lana said. "No use saving it for a rainy day."

"Besides, we aren't nearly drunk enough," Rhonda said.

"True," and the two contemplated their glasses for a moment.

"Do you know," added Rhonda, "that I won a very symbolic amount of money just now?"

"Symbolic how?"

"I turn thirty-five soon and I won thirty-five dollars. And does it prove that I am drunk, for me to feel pleased as punch about it?"

"No," Lana dismissed. "You always say things like that."

"Oh." Rhonda felt deflated. "But I don't always know I am saying things like that."

"Not important." Lana had a question in her eyes. "When exactly do you turn thirty-five?"

"Let me count. Oh!" Rhonda was definitely drunk, whatever Lana said, because she couldn't stop herself. "In thirty-five days. That's so cool."

"That's so wacko. Everything is thirty-five tonight."

"Yep. Happy silly coincidences. Love 'em."

"What are you going to do for your birthday?"

"Not one damn thing." Rhonda was cheerful about it. Nothing could dent her on this night of nights. "I'm growing old gracelessly. I hate organising things."

"Well, if you're sure," Lana said, and asked her if she had killed any pot plants recently. Rhonda had a sad record with pot-plants and Lana loved twitting her about it.

Tony rang her the next day. He started off with the usual acerbic comments about girls and nights on the town and how relieved he had been that the police hadn't been involved.

Rhonda replied, "You're just upset you weren't with us."

"Next time I will be," Tony said. "Next month we are going to do something for your birthday. I know you don't want to, so you just keep any protests to yourself. I don't want to hear them. If you don't dress up we'll take you out naked. So get some glad rags together, and trust us."

He expected her to have something ready for a celebration? Rhonda rang Lana on her mobile and said, "If Tony is serious about doing something then I'll need clothes."

"Didn't he tell you?"

"Tell me what?"

"That half the plan was to make you buy something pretty."

"He did not."

"We're going to have fun — you need to find a wow-dress."

Rhonda found this heartening. "I will," she said, "I'll find the wowest dress I've ever owned. If you get one too, we can blind Tony with our splendour."

"With our wowness. We will blind Tony with our wowness."

Rhonda had to laugh. And then she had to plan a shopping trip.

Rhonda decided she wanted a girlie frock, with bangles and big earrings. The trouble was that whenever she walked into a shop, the girl helping wanted to steer her to something more suited to an older woman. "Something with a bit of drape," one lass suggested.

"I wanted to do the cleavage thing," was Rhonda's reply. The look she was given suggested that cleavage was not allowable after one's twenties.

After such looks from three different shops, Rhonda felt aged and woeful. She rang Lana and explained the problem. Lana brought the kids and they descended on the most likely of the shops that Rhonda tried earlier. Lana played the card they had nicknamed 'the noxious infants'.

"Ben and Val," she said, loudly enough for the shop-girl to hear. "We need to make Auntie Rhonda look sexy for her birthday. What clothes should she get?"

Ben wanted Rhonda to wear a cowboy hat, and Val said, "She has to look like my Barbie." The shopgirl took one glance at the kids and left them. Kids were very good at keeping shop-help at bay.

The ritual trying on of dresses included some very honest comments from her two favourite almost-relatives. Rhonda would always treasure Ben's "That's yuck" when she found the low-cut dress she had been yearning after. She bought it. Ben held her hand on the way back to the car, despite her bad taste.

CHAPTER SIX

1.

I'M BACK AND I'M ALSO TOTALLY LOST. I NEED TO WORK
out where I was up to in my astounding narrative. It's
Zoë's fault. I caught her on the phone to her father,
singing him a silly. It took me right back to when I
caught her singing the silly to Rudolph (he of the pink
nose). Zoë had made up her mind.

Rudolph hasn't met Nick yet. Nick will hate him on
sight. I can't possibly have a boyfriend who my son
hates.

Anyhow, while Zoë and I were magicking away, Belinda did a bit of work to find GG. I know I'm usually
scathing about Lin's recipe project, but this time it produced the goods. It really did. We found out something
about being Jewish in Australia prior to the 1940s.
Something that shocked our socks off. Horrifying in a
quiet, householdly way.

Lin has also, in her ineffable way, divined how it
happened. My loving sister informed me that everyone
Jewish became a tad more European and sophisticated
when bunches of Holocaust survivors arrived. Other
things changed too, she said. She said this in one of

those enthusiastically educational phone calls she loves giving me from time to time.

It makes sense. We're Anglo and have an Anglo culture. No bagels, no gefilte fish, no lokshen kugel. I discovered all these foods when I moved to Sydney. We would have honey cake for Jewish New Year, and we would eat chops and three vegies every night for dinner. We still do. Nick likes his chops and vegies. Zoë prefers Neapolitan ice cream.

Plain food for plain people, Mum used to say. I stick to what Mum taught me. It's very hard to muck up cooking good plain food. When I burn things, it means I've tried to make food like other families eat. Not grilled bloody sausages.

I'm having trouble saying it. One thing we know for certain about Great-Grandma is the extent of her Jewishness. In fact, Great-Grandma's oldest sister had been dumped by the family for marrying out. Miriam renamed herself Mary, forgot she was Jewish, and we all forgot she existed. Linnie found a family tree online that told us about her and about her daughters, Mabel and Clara and Betsy, but hasn't chased the next generations yet. This wasn't the shock.

Let me list you some of the recipes in Belinda's collection. That's the easiest way to lead into the problem. This is tougher than the magic stuff or the lost relatives.

2.
"Baa! Baa! My turn!" posted Rhonda. "This isn't a meme I've snurched. It is my very own invented by yours truly. I want to know your five best words. Everything is in fives this year. My five best words are: snurch, historiography, cleavage, maturity, addiction."

TVwhore "Consider me tagged: love, writing, internet, secrets, stories."

Starchild "And me! chocolate, TV, knitting, friends, sleep."

Phased "Children, women, chocolate . . . that's all."

3.

Here's how it starts: Pancakes, French pancakes, brandy butter, Tea cake, Fig jam, condensed milk tart, Royal icing, Almond icing, Chocolate icing, Chocolate soufflé, Dundee cake, fruit punch, mushroom soup, Chocolate sauce, Devilled almonds, sponge sandwich, Welsh Rarebit, apple crumble, apple snow, cheese straws, Macaroni cheese, scones, sausage and apple casserole, sponges, egg au gratin, lots of sauce recipes, a ton of ice cream recipes and biscuit recipes and other sweet stuff (I am bored with typing names of recipes so let me put in a pause for dramatic effect), and . . . Christmas pudding.

Yes, that was it. Jewish Christmas pudding. Belinda said that the Anglo-Jewish community might have had Christmas dinner as a social event way back then. Belinda is a bloody know-it-all. Belinda informed me that it didn't make us less Jewish. How can that be? Christmas bloody pudding is as un-Jewish as un-Jewish comes!

I went for a long walk in Newtown to cogitate the contradictions of being Anglo-Australian and Jewish. Christmas pudding and magic. I found myself in that nice old churchyard.

I'm obsessed with being surrounded by gravestones when I need to think. I know that little cemetery better than almost anyone. None of the people in it can be related to me in any way, shape, or form, because it is a Christian place in Sydney, and my family is Melbourne

Jewish. That little graveyard was the safest place on earth for tough thoughts.

Until then.

I now had Christian relatives: Miriam/Mary's descendants. Then I found myself wondering how Christmas puds had become Jewish and then suddenly lost their Jewishness again. Belinda said this latter was survivor guilt. She said this with huge cheer. We would never have known there was a family Christmas tradition if GG had not noted those recipes.

I wove my way around the graves and found myself wondering what other aspects of our heritage had been lost. I was suddenly looking forward to that trip with Belinda in a few weeks and finding out more about GG's environment.

Maybe Zoë and Nick and I would make the pudding and cake and the brandy sauce. I found myself chuckling. Maybe we would do it next week. I would let Nick and Zoë decide. Nick had obviously big things on his mind, and this would help remind him that he is crucial to our lives.

I wondered what those big things were that were on his mind. I mean, I wondered where he was up to and if everything was okay. I knew *what* they were. *What* they were was scaring me silly.

I arrived home rather pleased with myself. Not inordinately pleased, just rather pleased. Nuances are important. Especially when I had another dinner date.

Within five minutes of arriving home I wanted to return to the graveyard and scream my head off. If a grave is a fine and private place, then a graveyard is brilliantly fine and amazingly private and therefore a good place for screaming.

Nick'd written to his father. He showed me the envelope.

In theory, if you bring a child up properly they're

equipped to handle all sorts of impossible situations. In practice, the proof is in the pudding. And we could make Great-Grandma's pudding tomorrow night. Another kind of pudding entirely, but one that also needed proving.

I couldn't scream. What I had to say was, "You're doing the right thing, Nick. I completely understand." And I had to say it with true honesty and fine rapport. And then I had to dress up fine, ready to go out.

Sometimes, being a mother stinks.

That weekend, he was flying down (at Peter's expense) and meeting his father and his stepmother and all his little half brothers and sisters. It was his right. I gave him Dad's phone number in case. I always keep Dad's phone number on hand, in case.

Nick put together a photo album and some clothes. If he took presents, he didn't tell me.

I went with him to the airport (still crying inside) and saw him and his little bag off in safety. He had his school uniform with him so he could go back to school from the airplane. I didn't want to wait until Monday night. I didn't fuss, though. Or cry. I was trying to make it easy for Nick. It was very hard to be civilised, putting him on that plane.

I guess I had this big fear that he would not come back, that he would adore his father and decide to stay with him. It was perfectly possible. It was his right. Would his father play the all-round good guy, the way he used to do? Was he still violent, and was he still such a damned hypocrite about that violence?

I started missing my son the moment the plane lifted off.

I had to make an urgent phone call. My whole year was just a series of phone calls. I wished I could rip the thing out of the wall. I wished I could turn the outside world off.

I didn't waste time on politeness. I wasn't rude, but I went straight to the point. The date had to be cancelled; Nick was in Melbourne and it was too late to get someone to mind Zoë. I was not even going to try — Zoë needed her mother.

Rudolph didn't reschedule. If I'd thwarted any deep-laid plans, he didn't indicate. I was always off-balance with this man, and I never understood how he did it. This time he said, "I'll be over in an hour with dinner," and hung up.

I was expecting something movie star. It was in character, after all; bringing one of everything on a menu so that we could each find something we liked. Instead, he carried a picnic hamper and a rug and Scrabble. We sat on the rug in the lounge room and played Scrabble. Zoë made a solid pretence at enjoyment, and so did I.

When it was bedtime for Zoë, Rudolph left. He let me know his intentions. He walked out the door with a "This time next week," and a very lingering kiss.

Zoë was a misery all weekend. No matter what we did, she moped. I suggested we try the Queen Victoria Building. The look on her face suggested grave robbing.

"Nick doesn't come all the time anymore," was my feeble response.

"If we don't ask him, we can't go," she informed me, haughtily.

"It's just a fun morning," I said, "Not a religious ritual."

"Nick isn't here," she repeated, "We can't go." Ms Broken Record. Who nevertheless needed cheering up.

Dammit. We watched stupid TV and played idiot cards. We caught trains to Bondi. We were not happy bunnies.

I found out more about our poor lemon tree that weekend. I've left it out of the story until now because I'd rather that the whole series of events that concerns it didn't exist. Another excitement I could have done without that finally reached a stage where I couldn't hide it. I suppose it meant I didn't have much energy to get worked up about Ballarat. Or worry about Rudolph's intentions.

My mind tangles the events of the tree. It didn't happen chronologically for me, because Zoë kept things to herself. That's another reason I didn't mention it earlier. That Saturday afternoon the dam burst. She stopped looking like a wet weekend, but she couldn't stop talking because she was still so damned unhappy.

You remember I said we had noises in our bathroom? I never did get in the plumber. Those noises stopped all of their own. That's what I thought. Zoë said differently.

She said there had been a strange whoosh from the bathroom when she finished the protection spell. The branches of the lemon tree had rustled and then the birds stopped singing. And that she hadn't told me straightway because I'm easily frightened and would stop making lemon tree jokes. She didn't say it as directly as that. In fact, the whole tale was rather tangled and roundabout.

So there were noises in the bathroom. And there was a whoosh when my daughter put the protective spell around the house. And the whoosh went to the lemon tree. Then Zoë discovered that the tree was giving out gold coins. Zoë and her friends saw someone making off with their swag, but didn't find any coins themselves. They weren't quite sure what to do, so they kept quiet.

I'm still sorry I didn't believe her that afternoon. In my defence, she was terribly giggly. Zoë kept saying, "It went whoosh, Mum, from the bathroom. Whooosh!" The crucial bit happened when I came back late Saturday night, not having listened to my daughter.

I'd decided that a drink with June would help my miseries. My daughter had announced that if Nick could see his father then she was big enough to baby-sit herself. I maintained a tiddle of personal responsibility. Two drinks. That was all I had. Two bloody drinks.

I came home via the back door because June had walked me in that direction. I could see someone in the laneway, so I trod warily. I need not have.

A man was cursing that tree with fine colourful language. It had given him bad coins, he said. It had got him into trouble with the police. It had deceived him. He was not going to give it presents any more. He was, in fact, going to church the very next day, and when he was cleaned of his idol worship, he was going to sort that tree out.

It was only a few minutes before he left, going the opposite way down the lane to me. I crept through the gate, eyeing off the tree and staying as far from it as the gate allowed.

My initial thought was how drink can addle the mind. It wasn't until I had talked to Zoë again (who needed warning about the stranger and not to use the back door for a bit) that we both realised there might be more to it. Whooshing and bathrooms and trees and gold coins all finally entered the same sentence in an intelligible fashion, sans giggle.

The next morning Zoë and I investigated. At the base of the tree, thrown in over the fence, were all sorts of small things. A pack of cards. A few coins. Three candles. That sort of stuff.

Tree bloody worship. In my backyard.

"Magic," breathed Zoë.

"Idiocy," I breathed back. We collected the presents and donated them to charity.

Zoë and I looked up every reference book we could lay our hands on. We wanted to find out precisely what the hell it was that had departed our bathroom in disarray and taken up residence in our lemon tree. And if cutting my once-adorable tree down would assist matters.

If this stuff had come on a different weekend, I guess it would have contained its own terrors. Men cursing by night. Idol worship in Aussie backyards. But that weekend had a special worry and the lemon tree was a distraction.

Nick came back early. Sunday night early. By train. He caught the day train (with his own money) and returned late Sunday night. Zoë and I picked him up at Central Station. He was glowering until he saw us, and then a giant relieved smile descended.

He wanted to talk to me, he said. I gathered that he didn't want Zoë to know what had transpired. I was relieved about that too. I was not relieved about the miasma of gloom.

Before Zoë went upstairs and to bed, she gave Nick the longest hardest hug. It brightened the air. I had no idea what he or Peter had done that made Nick come back so soon, but to come back to his sister was obviously a plus.

I'm still not focussed. I keep seeing his face as he got off that train. My mind's eye needs training in how to forget. Nick does not race into things and does not race out of them. He had obviously planned this time with his father carefully: something had gone wrong.

What I got, straight up, was an apology. He was sorry he hadn't asked my opinion. I apologised back, which cracked a little smile. I was quite honest: I said I knew things were difficult and I'd been trying to give him space. I knew how scared I was of Peter, I said, and didn't want that fear to get in his way.

Nick looked me straight in the face then, and said, "Would it help to know I don't think he does those things to his wife?"

Yes it would, and yes it did, and yes I said so instantly. Nick smiled properly then. But he was still not ready to speak. "Do you want a cuppa?" I asked. He nodded.

I got the teapot out. Mostly these days we use teabags, but there are times when we need emotional sustenance, and that is when I get out the old family teapot and make proper tea. Nick's eyes lightened when I brought out the big pot. He reached up high into the cupboard and pulled down our special chocolate biscuits, which are also for times of succour.

I put the pot in front of him, and the cups too. I said, "You get to pour. You've earned it." I never let anyone else pour from that teapot; I always tell them it's mine as boss and they had to earn the privilege. What I wanted, desperately, was to give him my support and to create a silence big enough so that Nick would fill it.

Nick poured the tea slowly and deliberately. He did everything properly, just the way my mother taught me, from slowly rotating the teapot to settle the leaves, to putting the milk in the cups first, to filling the cups just the right amount. And yes, the tea was perfect.

I nodded at Nick once I had sipped mine. He gave me a little smile back.

It's a strange thing to realise, but him making the tea from that teapot, in just that manner, well, that was the moment when he was fully adult.

Nick let snippets drop on the table, like crumbs. He hadn't realised he looked like his father, he told me, earnestly. Where his size came from. He looked more like his father than his half-brothers and sisters did. There were five of them. They were nice enough, he shrugged, but Zoë was more fun.

"I'll have to go back," he said, "but I might ring Grandpa and stay with him. I don't want to stay there again."

"You spoke to Dad?" I asked. I had never heard him say 'Grandpa' before. It had always been 'Your father'.

"I rang him on Saturday night. I stayed with him and he drove me to the train in the morning. He helped me a lot."

I was very pleased to hear that.

"He's wrong though," and suddenly Nick was very fierce.

"Who's wrong?" The fierceness confused me.

"Grandpa. He doesn't *know* you," Nick continued. "I had to tell him all about what you do and how you help other people. He thinks that the shop is all of you — and it never has been. I had to tell him how you always ask Auntie Lin about him. Every time you ask you look as if you really want to hear. Every time. I even told him about your secret photo album."

"You're not supposed to know about that album," I grumbled. It held photos from my childhood; Belinda had copied them, since I'd left with so very little. She had managed to move out of home with more dignity and a lot more luggage.

Nick had some solace. "Grandpa said your album needed some more things. He doesn't know what you have, but he'll post copies of things as he makes them. He's not sure about speaking to you, but he's going to send you some of your old stuff too. Next week."

My face was perfectly straight, but my eyes were

suddenly swimming. I could almost thank Peter for that stupid note. Almost. There was someone I could definitely thank though.

"Thank you, Nick. This is very special." My voice was soft.

"You owe me big-time, huh?" and he smiled as he looked across at me.

"I owe you very big time."

"Can I see all the photos then, when they come, even the ones of you with zits?"

I laughed and he laughed and I said he could see the photos. There was a pleasant silence.

"I'm not sure I like Dad," Nick ventured tentatively. "I'm sorry."

"You know," I was thinking aloud, "I'm not sure you have to like your parents. It is better if you *can* like them, but not all parents are likeable."

"I liked some things about him," ventured Nick, also thinking aloud.

"What did you like?"

"I liked his big laugh, and how he's really passionate about cricket. I like the work he does, and I like his new wife. She's a bit like you, you know." His voice sounded surprised.

"She's a feminist?" I wasn't just surprised. I was astonished.

"No. Things run smoothly round her. He gets really angry if they don't, and he blames her when someone else mucks up." God, but this brought back memories. I put my teacup on the table carefully, for safety, my fingers curled round its warmth. "One of my half-sisters dropped a glass on the floor and he got mad at his wife. You would just have stopped and cleaned it up; he got mad. You know," and this bit was hard coming out, "I can see how he could have been violent. His temper is like a flash — it goes off so very quickly."

"Hair-trigger," I agreed.

"That's exactly it." Those were the words he had been after. I felt almost useful. As a parent, I was feeling very fallible. As a woman, I felt very frail.

It took another chocolate biscuit before Nick was ready to go on.

"He said he bashed you, you know," he finally volunteered. "I had to leave. We were getting angry with each other, and I didn't want to stay there. I needed to come home."

"Can you tell me what happened, or would you rather not?" I asked.

"I want to tell you," he sounded very positive. I do like this son of mine. "He said he bashed you, but that you'd deserved it. He couldn't understand that he did something wrong. When I told him how scared you were, he said you were wrong, that he had never done anything to hurt you. But he admitted he bashed you. He talked about the thing with the knife and the threats. He just didn't see *anything*." That last 'anything' came out in a big gush.

"Damn," was my answer. "That makes it so tough for you."

"What about you?" he asked.

"As long as Peter doesn't plan on ever seeing me again, I'm fine." I was intentionally cheerful. I had a lot of stuff to sort out inside myself before I was fine and it might take all my life, but I was a great deal finer than I'd been even a month before. My main worry is you — how you deal with it. I've thought and thought and thought about it."

"And?" Nick looked hopeful. I gave him the hard truth.

"There's no instant answer. You're the only one who can sort out your relationship with your father. Just don't become like him in the violence aspect and whatever you do will get my hundred per cent support. Take your time and think things through. Come to me if I can help. If you want professional help, I'll find the money for it."

"You're being the dream mother, aren't you?" he said wryly.

"Damn your big toe," was my reply. "You weren't supposed to see through the self-sacrificing perfection act."

Just because I had decided that the world was going to be a clear and nice and peaceful place for a bit and let us get on with sorting out the problems thrown out by recent happenings, didn't mean that the world had decided that it was going to listen to me and let us get on with sorting out the problems thrown out by recent happenings. In fact, the world and time were both against us.

Rudolph decided I needed to go out with him. Rudolph was forever deciding this and never actually asked me whether I wanted to date. This is why he got away with it, of course. He also got away with other things.

I wasn't wrong about the next date with Red-Nose being bed. He is a patient and subtle man, but it was going to happen. We went to another bijou restaurant then somehow ended up at his place for coffee. I felt very wicked, slinking home at four.

My work the next day was all shattered and in pieces. So was a glass figurine I dropped. There was something about Rudolph, even if I was fighting it every inch of the way.

June thought I had time to spare and decided I needed to read Anne Rice writing about witches. It was all women's stuff, she said. "Those trinkets you make," were her exact words. Not the magic. June didn't know about the magic. In fact, almost no one knew about the magic, though I suspect Dr Cow-Eyes might have had some thoughts. He was translating a third document for us with great gusto. Nick said he just liked coming over to dinner.

It wasn't the marvellous cooking; he was much happier munching on the results of one of Lin's care packages than eating grill and vegetables. His eyes lingered on every paper, as if it could grant him immense treasure.

4.

Rhonda rubbed her hands. Time to write another of the Mackay articles.

This was the good bit of her week, before the aftereffects of the excursion into history. It was like a drinking binge — great merriment followed by even greater regret. For the next few hours she could rejoice in the fascination of magnetisers. Not that she could remember anything about magnetisers. It was too long since her initial perusal of Mackay. And for some reason her brain had not stored information on magnetisers the way it had on tulips and Mississippi gold and British bubbles. Time to haul out the yellow book and reread a chapter.

Mysterious magnetisers mean massive merriment. Rhonda smiled at her alliteration and she cuddled up in the big chair and read.

Her first line of thought was that this would be an easy piece to write. Magnetism, Mackay implied, was a form of faith healing. What he was really implying was that only the weak and credulous fell for such things. Rhonda decided to position the article to explain how the ancient worldview changed and gradually metamorphosed into the modern one. Magnetism was perfect. It was at that precise juncture where all things were possible.

Rhonda really loved this thought: that humans moved from having the Earth as the centre of the universe and obeying God's will, to humans as a small component in an impossibly huge cosmos, but that those tiny new humans demanded the power to control the universe. It was a good idea for the article, too. Rhonda made notes.

She bit the pen hard, as she realised the personal consequences of the change in worldview. While they lived in a universe surrounded and encased by God, there was an acceptable explanation for people like her. The voice of God. Or the voice of the Devil. Either way, a clear place.

There was no room in a man-controlled universe for mystic visionaries.

She wasn't heading to a good place with this train of thought, so she stopped biting her pen. Instead she took up some clean paper and wrote a rather cool sidebar quoting Mackay on Paracelsus and talking about secret societies. Rosicrucians and their ilk were always joy to the pop history public.

Rhonda typed up her sidebar and the very first section of her article and took a break. The longer before she finished the whole thing, the better. Happiness maintained. Sort of maintained. Her merriment had a manic edge.

It was two more hours before she could bring herself to look at that article again. The moment she did, the rumbling began. Damn that gift of hers. It poisoned everything.

Rhonda didn't write any more that evening. She sat in front of TV and let herself feel drab. If she wasn't going to enjoy her history, then she was not going to be forced to write it. Deadlines be damned. Inner prophets be even more damned.

The next morning she thought she had a safety rope. Her rope was that strange transition from ancient to modern medicine. She wanted to rewrite the whole article and make it about pre-modern medicine. It would fit the subject. It would also have been dead boring, because she could feel her mind slipping into 'I am a pedantic historian'. Inner excitement didn't always translate to the outside world. It was still a rope, though: it had changed her focus and filled Rhonda with a vast current of energy.

Mackay used that magnetising thing as an excuse to tell stories about a few major personalities. Unlike the other topics, though, this one rested upon a really drastically changing worldview over too great a span of time. In fact, the whole thing was rather a nonsense. Mesmer and magnetism. Two subjects a hundred years apart, with just the word 'magnet' in common? There was no guarantee of them being linked. And Mackay gave no proof. Just fascinating tales and scathing criticism.

Mackay had even fudged the principles behind magnetism by spending an awful lot of time showing how Mesmer made his money even while he was being examined and how the examination proved he was a fraud. That didn't prove anything about the earlier period. Nothing.

Rhonda suspected that Mackay was doing his best not to ask questions about his own worldview that he didn't want to see answered. Magnetism could be a fad. Or it could be deeper.

Anything not just a fad, in Rhonda's book, needed a more contextual treatment. She was skating on thin ice with the history of science and even the history of the philosophy of science. They weren't her areas. And even more besides, the deeper she went into research, the deeper her revelations from that rumbling within.

Not a good idea. All she could do was write something that raised queries in the minds of readers. So that's what she did.

"I am an evil child," she informed herself, "And will no doubt come to a bad end. Hang on. I already did the bad end. No wonder I'm happy. This is the afterlife."

And she was able to finish editing the article in peace. Just when she was about to send it out, the phone rang.

"Hi, it's Sam."

"Hi, Sam," and she had a nice chat with her cousin about life, the universe and everything.

Well, maybe not about everything. First they chatted about Sam's genealogical work. He had entered their grandmother and her two sisters into a database and found some cousins.

"One of them's in Canberra," he said. "I'll get you details sometime."

"Thanks," said Rhonda, with a polite pretence of enthusiasm.

The rest of the conversation concerned Sam's children. He seemed determined, as did half the world, to include her on the joys of child-rearing by discussing it at horrendous length. Rhonda felt this was unfair, as it wasn't by choice she didn't have children. It was a safe topic though, and she knew all the right questions, so she wheeled them out and half-listened to his answers. Boy, boy, girl. Grades, hobbies, after school activities, school camp, plans for holidays. The only time she actually paid any attention was when Sam admitted that his daughter was staying home instead of going on school camp.

"She has a few problems with some kids at school," he said, "But that will pass. She says it isn't anything important; she just doesn't want to be with them twenty-four hours a day."

Rhonda could relate to that. Imagine having no place to escape to if things went wrong inside. Damn. Speak of the Devil and he shows his horns.

"I need to send my article," Rhonda lied. "Before cut-off. Sorry. I wish I didn't have a deadline."

And the conversation was safely over. Barely in time. Her rumblings had become grumblings, and she needed to empty her mind into her computer immediately. And if she emptied her mind to Sam, she would lose the only relative in the world who would talk to her. She dashed for the computer and vomited her poison.

Poison was the right word, she thought later, as she read it back. This particular night in Revelation Town was about medicine. Instinct had taken her to an unusual venue to publish it, as well. She had gone to a medical blog and posted anonymously. She wondered if she should stay online a bit longer and see if anyone answered her comments. Or if madness lay in that direction. Or if she was already mad and should therefore give up and just get coffee.

Coffee was the answer, Rhonda thought, as she pondered on how her subconscious could possibly have known that three big US medical establishments had faked test results. That those three were linked, and also linked to a major drug manufacturer. She hadn't even heard of the names she had keyed in, so maybe the whole lot was a fraud.

Rhonda sipped her coffee and pondered some more. She liked pondering, because the process rhymed with Rhonda. Rhonda in ponder. And she was in a strange mood.

When she realised the cause of the strange mood, she was not delighted with the universe. It appeared that posting to a blog was not the same as posting to a chat room. God and the seven heavens only knew why, because she certainly didn't. Rhonda found herself drawn to the web and into chat rooms, and typing the whole damn prophecy again. Word for word. She knew it was word for word because she checked it before she wasted time typing it out yet again for her record.

"The trouble with using chat rooms," she tried to tell her unruly innards, "is that I need new aliases. It's really much more sensible to be 'anonymous' on a blog. And I can just copy and paste from a blog; I don't have to rekey all those words." But her innards didn't listen.

Rhonda spent the rest of the evening inventing new aliases. If she could only remember, she could use one-off names just for prophecy, but, well, the mood didn't allow for niceties like thought. It was more likely that she would post as someone she had already been and be caught in the act, if she didn't plan.

Rhonda contemplated doing something to rail against the unfairness of life. It was like her late teen rebellion: when the family didn't notice, the whole thing became an exercise in nothingness. She had to do things that felt good and made her life less of a cesspool, not plague herself by rebelling against . . . who?

Rhonda was all written out. It had been a long day for writing. Her history article and then one of her episodes and also a new fan fiction. What an extraordinary set of objects to share a day. What an extraordinary set of objects to share a computer.

She posted her latest fiction in a different group to usual. Of her close friends, only Starchild was an habituée of the Harry Potter fan fiction message board. TVwhore and Phased had sworn foul revenge on all things Harry Potter a long time ago.

The JK Rowling fan group was the only other one

she posted to as MissTRie. Because she could and because it gave her a sense of daring to say she could. She wrote in her blog, "I have just sent a new story to the Harry Potter message board place. Come and look! Yes, even you, TVwhore. You can expand your repertoire of reasons to hate Harry. I will make it easy and give you a direct link — you don't have to look at the rest of the board."

All in all, Rhonda thought later, this had not been one of her most genius of fictions. Her close friends liked it. Almost everyone else in the fan fiction group was unimpressed.

They started off by saying, "Yeah, well, each to his own, I guess," and, "Not my thing." A few days later the gloves came off.

"Snark," Rhonda announced, viciously punching the clothes she was washing by hand. She sprayed sudsy water all over herself, but it felt so cathartic she punched the clothes again. She had temperament to get out of her system and the only way she could think of was by wringing and twisting and vigorously getting rid of tough stains One velvet dress would never be the same, but at this moment she just did not care. "I have been forced from the group because of snark."

At least she still had TVwhore and Starchild and Phased. It was TVwhore and Starchild who had conspired to set up a little group of the four of them. The day the snark had hit its worst, there they were, inviting her to join an exclusive group.

"Since we are exclusive," Phased had said.

"Very, very exclusive," TVwhore had added, "We thpeak with lithpth and only drink from the betht china."

Rhonda still had to sort her temper out and kill her velvet dress, but at least she was not alone. There was chat and there was cat, she decided. Chat was what she did with her friends. Cat was what the snarky set did. She was well rid of them.

When someone on her history board asked if anyone in Regency England read Voltaire, Rhonda stepped in with an answer. She felt the need to assert herself.

Someone new said, "Yes, but do you have any qualifications? Or did you pick up your history by reading Georgette Heyer? I am sick of everyone here speaking up about things they have found on Wikipedia."

"Thanks for the vote of confidence in my opinions," typed Rhonda, wishing sarcasm and fury would rip down the line and cause bile to rise up in the critic's throat. "I did not look it up on Wikipedia, though I do enjoy Georgette Heyer almost as much as I enjoy Walpole. And I do have that undergraduate degree you seem to want so desperately. I also have, however, an MA and a doctorate in the subject. I understand if you want to do your own research and don't like my suggestions, but I am rather tired of people disparaging my qualifications."

To her surprise, she received an abashed apology. "I am so used to people spouting off about things they don't know that I didn't even think to check if you were right. I did check, because I value my pass degree in history. I know what I am talking about." *Bloody cheek*, thought Rhonda.

Dr Jane Smith had lots of ideas about what she wanted to do to the poster, but she had lost her rights to the Harry Potter group and she decided to remain silent. Silence proved to be a remarkably good strategy. The poster was flamed. Rhonda was not the only one who thought that 'I value my pass degree' was a bit up themself. One poster called himself 'Bertie Wooster'.

"You have a pass degree in history," he said. "That's wonderful. I wish I had a pass degree in history. I left school when I was fifteen and I learned the history I know from reading and thinking. You do need to know, since you're a newcomer, that Dr Smith has been here for three years and has always been spot-on. She has never waved her qualifications in our face. She has answered questions and asked them and been rather nice even when we're stupid. You didn't need to know she had a doctorate: all you needed to know was that she is a good egg and always generous with her time. You should not have tried to make her look bad or made her justify herself. You don't deserve the help of a professional historian."

"Yes, you moron," the next poster said, "She's a professional historian, and you are a professional idiot. If you don't know how to be polite, then go somewhere else. I read Jane's articles and am a fan. So shut the hell up or get the hell out."

"Thank you, everyone," Rhonda wrote, her brain whirling round the idea of her having a fan, a real live fan, someone who read things she wrote and enjoyed them. "I do appreciate being appreciated and I especially appreciate all your support. Can we get back to talking history?"

She felt good, though. And she took that good feeling to bed, hoping it would carry over obligingly to the next day.

5.

Judith was ensconced in the lounge chair, reading Anne Rice. She was trying to convince herself she was enjoying it.

The phone constantly interrupted her reading. Rudolph, for instance, had cautiously arranged another date. Judith was curious about the caution: why should it matter so much to him? He was a man of many women, after all. He couldn't see a female without falling into flirtation.

Belinda rang, and Judith was happy to be distracted. She was a very professional Belinda. "I'm just ringing to tell you not to worry."

"Worry? I never worry," she joked.

"Good, because it's all okay."

"What's all okay?" Judith had sudden fears of Peter making visits to Canberra to plague Linnie.

"About the latest attack."

Judith's whole body went on pause. "Latest attack," she said slowly.

"Another thing lobbed at the Community Centre. There were about nine children playing in there at the time, so I assumed it would make the news. But no one was hurt, and I was only there for the early part of it."

"The early part of it?"

"When we saw youths in the distance digging something into a sandpit. So you see, I'm fine and everyone I know is fine and there is nothing to worry about."

"Why don't these things make the news?" Judith asked, since Belinda had cut off all other avenues of concern.

"It didn't?" Belinda sounded curious. "I was certain the fact that kids were in danger would have made it newsworthy. But Jewish things aren't news. I suppose I should have broken it to you more tactfully." Belinda was unrepentant. She was also very calm.

"How are you?" Judith asked. Judith didn't trust that calm.

"I'm okay, I suppose," was Belinda's answer. A bit slower than her earlier cool explanations; she was genuinely thinking it through. "I'm scared and not sleeping. I'm going for more counselling."

"And that's okay? Can't you unaffiliate and become less Jewish again and be safe?"

"A lot of people are doing that," she said, again thoughtfully. "But I'm finding I can't."

"Don't let terror win." Judith laughed weakly.

"Well, you do the same thing."

"Now I do," Judith had to agree. "But at first I ran like hell. I believe you fight, but not when you're going to be hurt. I believe very strongly in not being hurt. That was a hint."

"And you think that, because I'm now at risk, I should also run."

"That's the sum of it."

"No." Very simple answer. But said with force. That was when Judith realised how very angry Lin was. Belinda's inner self was spitting fire. If any attackers came within her reach, it would not be the Dark Side that mauled them, it would be the Demon Aspect of the Dark Side. "I hate what's happening, but running isn't going to change it." She paused. "I know what it is," and her voice took on a small wonderment. "I have my share of your social conscience. I do *not* believe people should hurt, and I want to be there for other Jews."

"And risk yourself." Judith was not happy.

"If the rest of Australia gave a damn about what was happening, then there would be a hell of a lot less risk."

"I wonder why it wasn't in the press?" Judith tried to change the subject.

"I know." Lin was bitter. "I asked one of your journo friends. I forgot that. I should've know it wouldn't be in the news."

"You rang a friend of mine?"

"No," she explained, carefully, as if Judith were a slow student. "When you were up here last year, remember the dinner party?"

"These incidents were happening as long ago as that?"

"These incidents have been happening for two years

now. Before that it was just graffiti and grave desecration and that sort of thing."

"Just that sort of thing." Bitter Judith. She heard her bitterness and admired it for a microsecond.

"Compared with now, it was 'just'."

"I guess so. What did my friend say?"

"That if something happened to Jews it was not news unless the Jews did the doing — that is why Israel is always portrayed as an aggressor, and Jewish victims there are numbers, not people. Anti-Semitism here isn't reported unless someone dies." Belinda was bitter.

Judith couldn't blame her. "I need to think about this," was what Judith said, finally. "But I'm glad you're not hurt. Really, really glad."

6.

It was her birthday. Rhonda could feel it even in bed, her eyes not awake.

She had the feeling of a special day that she had carried from her childhood. Birthday cake, and friends and presents and various relatives jumping on her bed to sing, "Happy birthday to you, you live in a zoo." She kept her eyes closed. That was her duty as birthday girl.

Then she woke up fully and her mind dutifully ticked the 'None of the above' category. She got out of bed and refused to shower and dress. Instead she made herself the biggest pot of coffee she could, singing herself the unbirthday song she had composed when she was twenty-two. Turning thirty-five was going to be the same as every other birthday since she turned sixteen, a bloody awful day to live through.

She remembered she was going out that evening. It didn't cheer her up entirely, because there was a part of her that had wanted her mother to come into the bedroom in the morning and say, "There's a strange parcel on the kitchen table. I wonder who it could be for?" Or maybe her father to look at the mail and say, "Who is this person who has so many letters?"

The family had made a special deal of birthdays. Her parents and grandparents had always posted cards to the children, so that listening for the postie's whistle was a treat.

"You're too old," they had said when she turned thirteen. The others weren't too old when they turned thirteen, just her. But the others were simpler beings.

When she had complained, her mother had taken her aside and said, "You need to be adult about this, dear. Treating you as a child is not going to help. Your father and I had a long talk about it." But she had been given no adult recognition, just the deprivation of treats. And oh, she was still bitter about it, this birthday of hers.

Rhonda couldn't stop her feet walking to the mailbox. Every year she did this. Every year she hoped that the cards would start arriving. That her family would remember her and take up where they had left off. Today she hadn't even put shoes on, so enthusiastic were her feet about getting to that letterbox.

When she got there, she couldn't open it. The postman had been. Something was poking a sliver of envelope out the edge. It was probably a bill. Rhonda drew a deep, deep breath and pulled back the lid to the letterbox. Inside was a square-ish envelope. A card. Maybe it was a card. It had to be a card. It couldn't be a card. She stood there looking down at it, tears rolling down her cheeks, hot and wet and happy. Gingerly, carefully she lifted it out. Gingerly, carefully, she opened it. It was from Sam.

"Happy birthday, cousin. May you grow older gracefully."

Rhonda sat down next to the letterbox, not caring

who saw or what she looked like. Not caring about the nightgown or the bare feet. Not caring that the letterbox lid was as open as the front door. She held that precious card in her right hand and wiped tears away with her left. This was her best birthday ever.

She gave the card pride of place on the mantelpiece. She brought all her dress-up clothes for the evening into the lounge room so she could look round at the card whenever she needed reassurance. Every time she looked, she absolutely had to go over and hold it and read the words again.

Tony and Lana were early to pick her up. Rhonda was mostly ready, including having donned her much-revealing dress, but she had not put on any makeup or sorted out a handbag. She hadn't even worked out what makeup she should wear.

"My mind hasn't been where it should be all day," Rhonda explained, as she ushered them in. Out of the corner of her eye she caught a glimpse of cardboard and gave her happy-smile.

Tony took one look at her fluster and said, "Mind if I watch the cricket?"

"Be my guest," said Rhonda. He switched on the TV and switched off his brain.

Lana asked, "D'you want me to do your makeup?"

"Please," said Rhonda. "You do a much better job, and I am all a-flurry. I don't know how to makeup for this dress, or which perfume to wear. And I can't help thinking this dress is not a good idea."

"I like that dress," called out Tony, from the safety of the lounge.

"You shut up," Lana said. "She's my friend, not your wife. You gave up ogling rights years ago."

"I can ogle."

"If you ogle," suggested Rhonda, "Lana and I might

have to do something drastic. Something with cold water, perhaps."

"The dress is fine," Tony said, and subsided back into cricket.

Lana was very efficient with the makeup, and Rhonda soon felt as if she were wearing a party mask. She was emerging from being birthday girl into a more normal state of nervousness. A night on the town.

Dinner was fine. Somehow Tony had rustled up some friends she hadn't seen in almost-forever. She was touched when a birthday cake appeared, made by Belinda, and even a few presents. She put her new bead necklace around her neck immediately. Lana explained that the kids had bought it from their pocket money.

Thirty-five was not an impossible place to be, after all.

After dinner the friends went home, and Tony and Lana and Rhonda did the threatened clubbing.

"I really don't want to," Rhonda had said.

"Nonsense," replied Lana. "We don't want you growing old before your time."

"Besides," Tony got in, "I need more time to admire that dress. I'm out of practise at leering." His reward for this comment was a light slap by his wife, and then they shared a kiss.

Every moment of happiness was balanced by a thread of 'I wish', Rhonda thought, as she watched them cuddle. The necklace from her two favourite children was a reminder that she could have had children and should have had children, and the cuddling reminded her of her great aloneness in everyday life. But she had the children as her honorary niece and nephew, and she had Tony and Lana as friends. Bitter sweet, but more sweet than bitter. And she had that card. She was not without family. That thought gave her dignity, even as she held a bizarrely coloured cocktail in her right hand.

Her almost-unalloyed joy was impregnated with impurities just two hours later. The impurities could be summed up in two words: 'Mr' and 'Ick'.

He spotted them once they were past dancing and had settled down at the Holy Grail. Rhonda couldn't say "Buzz off, it's my birthday." She couldn't say anything, in fact, because of Tony. Tony liked to control things. He liked his women to be sweet and well-behaved. Rhonda had valued what Tony gave her so very highly that she had tried intensely to be his dream wife. Subsumed her personality to match what he wanted. And there were some legacies of her sacrifice.

Even though the marriage had failed, she was still in his protective orbit. Normally, this was a wonderful thing. This evening, though, Lana was the designated driver. Tony was all set to drink. A lot.

Rhonda sighed. Having Tony scare off Mr Ick would have been perfect under normal circumstances. Just not when he was drunk. Never when he was drunk. When he was drunk, Tony had to be kept jovial. She remembered one time when he had beaten the living daylights out of someone who had tried to feel her up while they were at a bar. It wasn't that she would've minded if Mr Ick had the living daylights beaten out of him. She just didn't want to see Tony in court.

God, this was what thirty-five was, remembering incidents that had happened when you were someone's first wife, and basing your current actions on those incidents.

As Mr Ick slid in to sit beside her, she felt self-conscious. Every inch of her felt exposed. She slid away from him. Her next half hour was spent repositioning herself, getting rid of his hand from her lap, and smiling almost desperately. She felt trapped.

The trouble with clubbing in a group is that there's only one car. The trouble with clubbing in a group is that, unless you plan in advance, there are no easy ways out. She could taxi home, but that would mean finding the others and announcing, "I'm going." She knew what Lana would reply to that, and it made her cringe inside. She had to pretend to be sociable, to make sure Lana couldn't say, "Just try for a change, Rhonda — you weren't born reclusive."

She had a few minutes' respite when her nemesis went to get drinks, but at the end of it she had to accept a random drink and smile in thanks. It was very hard to smile. It was very hard altogether. Rhonda sat on a too-small chair, crowded by Mr Ick and his attitudes. She nursed the bright blue beverage he had given her for as long as she could without so much as sipping it. Her eyes flitted around possible exits.

Another group of people moved over in their direction, obviously intending to join them and make a mob. Rhonda started in on her drink. Maybe the alcohol would give her fortitude.

7.

I was in a meeting to help refugee women. These women had suffered enough to be forced into becoming refugees and now they were being dumped into bloody containment by the Federal Government. And yes, I am a bleeding leftie. Sue me.

Over coffee I mentioned what had happened in Canberra. To my horror, a woman who I have trusted and admired for almost forever said, "It's their own fault."

"What have those children done to deserve having fireworks shot at them?"

She had the grace to say, "Not the children." But then she said things that were almost worse. "It's the whole Jewish problem. If it were not for Jews, Palestinians would be safe. Jews deserve to be scared."

I was determined not to get into an argument over Israel. We were talking about Australians in Canberra, not something over the other side of the planet. I said so, forcefully.

And was told that I had been brainwashed.

I didn't stay for the second half of the meeting. Instead, I wrote an angry email and copied it to all my women's email lists. I never do things like that. Never. But I was very angry.

Several women attacked me. I was told by some that by supporting Judaism in any form I was supporting patriarchy. I was told that my sister was lying and that the Jewish community was only in danger of dying of greed and too much money. I was told a lot of other things that were pure bigotry. 'Zionist Conspiracy' appeared.

On the mail lists where I was supported (at least to the point of my differences of opinion being accepted as legitimate and me not being called a liar for recounting my sister's personal experiences), on those mail lists I stayed. On the others, I am no longer.

I had to choose between being Jewish and being a feminist. I do not see that there was any choice to be made. I should be both. I am both.

It wasn't the whole women's movement that was at fault. Most of the women were, as they always are, wonderful. Supportive and thoughtful. I got a flood of private emails expressing horror at what happened. This matched the bitterness of the flood of public emails condemning me and Israel and hating all things

Jewish. The bigots won the public battle and I had to console myself with, "At least I have private support."

This was why Belinda still attended Jewish things. We were reclaiming Ada as a kind of hobby, but this bigotry attacked part of ourselves too. We had done no one any wrong by being Jewish. Our social consciousness came from our bloody Jewish upbringing, in fact. Our family are upstanding solid and civilised human beings. Good people. The sort you should be happy to invite to dinner.

I was not going to give up being Jewish. I would rather dump the bigots from my life than forget my upbringing.

I am a Jewish feminist. And if some of the far left hates me for it, then some of the far left is bigoted and stupid and needs to stop navel-gazing and look at the real world. I am a feminist Jew. I'm proud of it.

The effects of me ardently declaring myself as belonging to two unloved minorities might include nasty rebound for my children. I didn't want to tell the kids. Nick had enough to bear, Zoë more than enough. But the children who were targeted in Canberra were even younger, Belinda had told me. The oldest was nine.

I told them I'd lost my temper. They'd deserved a view on it before I wrote that email. I was too angry and had done it instantly.

And Zoë, my own sweet Zoë, said, "I already told everyone at school I'm Jewish. There are three other Jewish kids in my class and I want to learn how to make honey cake. Becca brings some in every year and she makes it all by herself."

"We *talk* about making it every year." I'm good at feeble justification.

"But you've never taught me and I want to make it. And dip it in chocolate."

202

We were getting off track if the conversation was turning to chocolate.

I explained anti-Semitism to Zoë and she wasn't worried. I said that maybe I wasn't explaining properly. She said that she'd talked to Auntie Linnie about it last year, because she had heard things. And they had a class on racism last year too, she hadn't told me because she thought it might worry me. Zoë said all this with a slightly superior manner. As if she had doubts about my intelligence. And my capacity to make honey cake. Bloody smug. Like her aunt.

Nick was amused I'd lost my temper and emailed everyone about being Jewish. Nick was not quite as condescending as Zoë. Not quite. He was in supportive mode. And he wanted to read all the emails.

I had nightmares that night. The twitchy sort where you move from one frightful scenario to the other. Sometimes I was saying magic spells and caging bigots and putting them in a museum where people could look at them and say, "An extinct species." Sometimes I was putting Peter into a little glass box and hiding him in the wardrobe. Every now and then a flaming ball would land at my feet and I would jump on it and jump on it and jump on it to put it out. It would not be extinguished, it kept burning there and my feet were going black. And all I could do was jump and jump. All the time I was jumping I was saying to Zoë, "Don't grow up, it isn't safe."

I woke up feeling bruised. I didn't want to go to work. I wanted to turn round and sleep without any dreams. Neither was possible. Work demanded I be there, and more sleep would have meant more nightmares.

The thing that bothered me most was how angry I was. I wanted to scream obscenities at the world. I wanted to get Great-Grandma's spells and use them.

But I couldn't. I had to be true to who I was first, and hurting other people was not a part of that. This is when I fully understood what Lin had been saying: Judaism was ethical; you did not hurt others.

I grabbed the curse papers though, and took them to work to look at during my lunchbreak. It was bothering me that they were in the box. If I couldn't bring myself to curse people who were hurting us, then why did Great-Grandma have them at all?

It was a quiet morning in the shop and I was left to take care of things by myself. This gave me the time I needed to look and to think. What my looking and thinking showed me was that Great-Grandma had left every single one of the curses incomplete.

Why did she have them in the box then? Did she need to know they existed?

I needed that consolation. I copied out a couple of phrases that I could mutter if I felt like cursing someone. These phrases would not damage the tip of a cat's tail. Or even damn someone's toe. They were still reassuring.

It irked me that we could protect, but not attack. What Belinda was going through, with the violence, was what Jews have gone through since forever. The longest hatred and all that. Yet this Jewish magic exists. Imagine, a weapon that was never taken out of storage, even during the Holocaust. Those with the knowledge could use aggressive magic or remain Jewish. What an awful choice.

I needed action. There were those right-wing newsletters that mysteriously appeared in my letterbox. Feminist got junk mail from the far right. It's one of the predictable aspects of everyday life. Normally I'd just throw it out. I found a phone number on one of them. "Hi," I said to a voice at the other end, "I'm sorry to trouble you, but think there's something wrong with your address list. I keep getting your newsletter and I haven't subscribed."

"I'm so sorry," the woman at the other end said. "Someone must have been over-enthusiastic. It does happen. Are you sure you are not a member?"

"I am not."

"Would you like to join? I can give you a special rate."

I was the soul of tact. She'd left me no openings for righteous anger. "I'm sorry, but my life is quite full right now. Teenage children and the rest of it."

"I quite understand. I'll make sure that you are off our list. Keep us in mind though."

"Oh, I will," I said.

Nice anti-Semites. Neo-Nazis are human beings. Dammit, why couldn't the lady at the other end of the phone have been a bitch? The biggest drawback of putting the phone down was that I still needed to explode.

Since exploding over the phone had been such a dismal failure, I decided to explode on paper. I wrote several letters that night. Rudolph looked over my shoulder and made caustic comments, since I was supposed to be having yet another elegant dinner with him. His hand rested lightly on my neck the whole time. Between us, we wrote to every far-left newspaper and organisation I could think of. I was not expecting any answers.

I think the only things that kept me from breaking down that evening were Rudolph's comments and his hand caressing my neck. Now I'm gung-ho and engines on fast forward. Mixed metaphors, but lots of energy. Then I was operating on angry adrenalin. I was facing the fact that racial hatred happens in Australia. And that it happened to me. And that people who accepted it were complicit. Bloody hypocrites.

All week I was askew. Tuesday I actually panicked. I was a half hour late back from work. I forgot Zoë's dance class. I flurried into the house, trying to think of how many things I would have to do in the next few minutes. The big killer was that we had missed the train. This meant a taxi and $45 from the emergency funds. Damn it to all hell.

The phone rang. I nearly damned the phone to all hell as well. It was Rudolph, wanting to know if he could come round for coffee. I told him it was Zoë's dance night and we were about to order a taxi because we'd missed the train. I sounded as if I didn't control the universe. He sounded sympathetic. Damn him. Sympathy took two minutes and I didn't have two minutes. I stared at the phone in loathing.

He said to wait ten minutes before calling that cab. I waited and lo, there was Rudolph at the door with car keys jangling temptingly.

While Zoë and her class were being good students, he murmured rude things about everyone except Zoë in my ear. This calmed me right down. It was nice to know that there was someone in the world who was bitchier than me.

He drove us back afterwards, and demanded coffee. I offered him dinner as well, if he could deal with my cooking. He was so pleased he became all wry smile. And this is how he finally met Nick.

Nick liked him, which dashed all my hopes of losing Rudy in the wash. They developed an instant camaraderie, in fact, outdoing each other in pretend condescension about my cooking skills and about women in general. Zoë and I said rude things about them, until we all gave up and played board games.

I feel very strongly that I have earned a life free from fear next time round.

I have had a lot of comings of age. I turned eighteen

with a nice big party. I turned twenty-one with a quieter party — the terrors of life had begun to hurt and placating Peter was important. When I was twenty-five, I turned feminist. I was in Sydney and was attending university as a mature age student, with Nick by my side in his stroller at every single lecture. Now I'm in my forties, and I have come of age Jewishly.

I am Judith, therefore I fight. And argue. And explain at great length. And have a special corner ready for Lin when she gets too scared because of the bloody Molotov cocktails. I am Judith. I'm magic in all sorts of important ways.

CHAPTER SEVEN

1.

SHARP LIGHT AND A HEADACHE WOKE RHONDA. SHE didn't want to move. If she didn't move then the headache would stay outside her body. If she didn't move then everything awful would cease to exist.

The feel of the sheets against her naked body and the warmth of the bed helped lull her into believing the headache would go away entirely if she just slept a little more. Alas, her stomach wouldn't allow it.

She bolted for the bathroom and spent the next little while leaning over the toilet, emptying the contents of her gut. Eventually she flushed the toilet then moved her very bare self to the basin, washing her face and bending over it, face down, hoping the nausea would pass.

All she could see was white and chrome. White basin, chrome plug hole, white wall, chrome taps. Every molecule of white and chrome hurt her eyes.

A hand gently stroked down the length of her backbone, over and over. Warm. Friendly. Calming. Rhonda let herself be soothed by it until a voice asked, "Are you okay?"

"No, I'm not okay," she snapped.

This was the moment she realised that the warmth of the bed had been a shared warmth. But who had she shared a bed with? Tony? Who else would be that familiar with her? God, what would Lana say? Rhonda wanted to hate herself, but it was too hard. Everything was difficult. The voice sounded unfamiliar, but her brain was mush. She wasn't thinking at all straight.

Please, God, let it not be Tony — not with Lana and the children. She would pretend it wasn't Tony. Better it was a stranger. She would deduce whose voice it was when she could think a bit more clearly. No, she wouldn't. She would find out now, before not knowing became a bogeyman.

She tried to sneak a look over her shoulder, but the movement set off the vomiting again. The hand gentled her and soothed her body and the two of them stood by the sink for a long while, Rhonda feeling about as sick as she could. The man had moved in close and his warmth became her warmth as his hand helped stabilised the turmoil of her stomach.

A big being who radiated heat and was patient and very quiet, that was all Rhonda knew and all her brain could handle as she stared at white and chrome, white and chrome and wondered how her night on the town had faded and become such a strange pale place.

As the nausea subsided Rhonda had to face a new truth. That body next to her was far too big to be Tony's. She was naked in front of a complete stranger. A complete stranger with whom she had obviously been to bed. And she didn't remember a thing.

"I need a shower," she said. "I'm not dealing with this at all well."

"Go for it," the man said. She still couldn't focus on his face or body or anything with more colour than the bathroom plughole. She didn't want to know. She just wanted the whole situation to go away.

Rhonda stood in the shower recess, unable to move. The pressures and pains were combatting each other and she was caught in the crossfire. Eventually her body calmed. She had her shower and struggled into leggings and tee-shirt and wobbled as far as the kitchen.

"Food?" suggested the stranger, who was now wearing clothes. Nothing else was really making any sense. She felt as if she was in a bad crime novel.

"All I can cope with is coffee."

She tried to make a pot for the two of them, but her hands were clumsy and disconnected. She found herself mopping up dry ground coffee with a sink cloth, and leaned over it into the floor, wondering how this was happening.

"Allow me," the voice said, and she was gently moved aside. She gave up all pretence of competence and sat at the kitchen table, dizzy and disconnected. It didn't matter how hard she tried to exclude the man in her kitchen from her existence, she couldn't help noticing him. How could anyone not notice him? He was a big man and had a big presence.

He also had a big accent. American or Canadian. One of those neutral ones that could go anywhere. No regional distinction. Like an actor's accent. Universal US.

She found herself wondering how she could be concerned about regional distinction in accents when she was so damned sick. And when she had lost her memory. When she had obviously lost a whole evening of her ever-so-important life. Sarcasm. She noted her own sarcasm. She could manage sarcasm. Then the sarcasm and the memory of it slipped away as she started processing where things had gone wrong.

Rhonda focussed. It was difficult to cast her mind back. A lot of connections seemed missing. Not missing. As if they had not existed. It was a peculiar feeling. The last thing she remembered was being handed a fancy drink by the Sleazoid and sipping it cautiously. She remembered feeling trapped.

"I can't," Rhonda said.

"Excuse me?"

"I can't remember anything. My mind is all white and blanked out."

"What do you remember doing before it all blanks?" his voice was warm and gentle. She found his acceptance of the strangeness of everything reassuring.

"Drinking."

"What sort of drink?"

"It was blue," Rhonda offered, "I don't know anything about it. Someone bought it for me."

"Blue," and his voice was thoughtful.

"I want to know what happened," Rhonda said. "I can't remember. And it hurts. I'm dizzy and I have a headache and I've lost a part of my life."

"I can help with the headache," suggested the stranger, and rustled round in his pocket until he produced a couple of pain relievers.

"Thank you," said Rhonda. "I was in bed with you, wasn't I? I wasn't imagining it."

"You weren't imagining it," he echoed.

"Did we have sex?"

"Yes," and his voice sounded amused.

Rhonda found she could not look up at him. She had had a one-night stand. She was so embarrassed. So incredibly embarrassed. "Would it be terribly stupid to ask if it was safe sex?"

"It would be very sensible to ask, and yes, it was."

"Why can't I remember?" wailed Rhonda. "Tell me something about what happened, anything."

"I remember you had hiccups," the stranger said, helpfully. "In fact, I used them as an excuse to extract you from the people you were with and to get you home."

Rhonda looked up and made a suspicious face. The stranger looked back, gaze innocent. His eyes were big and brown, and his face was comfortable and lived-in. If it wasn't for his huge presence, you might miss him in a crowd. Then she looked at those brown eyes again and thought, *Only if he were wearing sunglasses.*

She wished she had sunglasses right now. The room was too bright.

Rhonda wondered how she could be looking at him when the world was not being as settled as it should be. She was moving through it, her only connections with it were through her symptoms. She sighed. Then she focussed on what he had said.

"Hiccups is not what I was expecting to hear," she said. "In fact, hiccups are an exceptionally mundane way of getting someone into bed. There must be more. Lots more. And you're going to tell me, I hope."

"I'm not sure I want to tell you the rest."

"It was that bad?"

"It was all good. It was all very good, in fact. It's wrong that it's gone."

"It seems sick from this end of it. I don't even know your name. I might have known your whole life history and now I don't even know your name."

A silence. The man looked unhappy. She'd shocked him. Rhonda thought, *Men.*

Rhonda gathered that he was handling the memory loss thing capably, until it included his name. He was not used to being forgotten. She could understand that; he was a memorable man. How *could* she have forgotten a night with him?

"You know, you can take that as a hint."

"I'm Dave," he said, "You're entirely right: I told you my whole life history last night." Rhonda felt relieved that he seemed to regret her not remembering that more than the sex; that life history had been part of the 'very good'. "You were so relaxed and easy to talk to."

"I'm not a relaxed person," Rhonda said, as dismissively as she knew how. "I'm not a people person. I was bloody drugged."

Dave reached to put his arm round her then, encountering her glare, thought better. "I didn't drug you," he defended.

"No," and she softened a little. "I bet I know who did. And I bet he was mightily mad that you ran away with me."

"It was the hiccups," Dave said. "If you are referring to the fat guy. He didn't know how to handle them. He moved to the other side of the table and fumed at you."

"I wish I could prove it," Rhonda said. "He's been totally ick as long as I have known him."

"Why did you go to a club with him?" Dave asked.

"Do I look that stupid?"

"Should I answer that?" and Dave looked her straight in the eyes.

Rhonda found a tiny smile lift the corner of one mouth. She felt a little lurch somewhere in her gut and damned herself for finding this stranger so attractive. She should have kicked him out the door the moment she realised he was not Tony. Instead she was holding polite converse over coffee. She turned the conversation back to Mr Sleazoid.

"He's my case manager when I get temp work. I wouldn't go out with him in a pink fit. He just turns up places."

"He's stalking you?" There was more than casual interest in the way Dave leaned forward.

"Not that I can prove. It isn't every day. He's just a sleaze."

"If he did use rohypnol on you then he must have been prepared."

"Or he does it to other women as well. Totally yuck." And then the term caught up with her. "Rohypnol?"

"Flunitrazepam. Date rape drug."

"Oh. Is that what melted my brain? Even more total yuck. But how did you know what it was?"

"That's why I asked about the blue drink," Dave explained.

"And why do you know so much about it?"

"I know all sorts of strange medical information; it's my work."

"Work does bizarre things to people's minds," Rhonda sighed. "I need to write fifteen hundred more words by the time offices open in the US. And my mind is mush. Total and complete mush."

"Give it time. Take it easy."

Rhonda looked up at her companion miserably. "I still feel sick," she said. "I'm a stranger in my own body."

"I'll take you to the police station when you feel a bit better and you can lay charges."

"No," said Rhonda, adamantly. "I already told you that it would be hard to prove."

"I bet we can prove it, between us," Dave's lips went thin and stubborn.

"You know," admitted Rhonda, "I suspect we could. Maybe. But I still don't want to."

"Why?" This was not curiosity, it was frustration.

Rhonda realised that she ought to be thinking this way too. It was suddenly important to reach past the muddle that was her mind and find out why she didn't want to pursue the matter.

"I need to think this through," she explained, since

Dave was obviously about to start arguing with her. "And I'm slow and sick. There's something important that my brain can't quite get at. There's a reason I don't want to get the police involved but I can't *think* of it. Do you know how *annoying* that is?"

"Take your time," and Dave's whole face softened again. "D'you mind if I make more coffee?"

"Make as much as you like. Have breakfast as well. Or lunch. Or even dinner," Rhonda tried to gesture to the kitchen generously, but her coordination was all fouled and all she did was upset her coffee cup.

"Leave it," Dave said. Rhonda just nodded. "Why don't you go have a nap?" Dave suggested. "I'll be here when you wake up."

"Don't you have work?"

"I want to finish this conversation. You're really mad at this guy and you have the best reason in the world to sort him out, but you don't want to take him to the police. I need to know why."

That was fair enough. Rhonda could understand the pursuit of understanding, just as she could understand that her body needed sleep.

"Help yourself to whatever," she said, amazed at the level of trust she was putting in a total stranger. "Just not the silver."

He laughed. As she drifted back to the bedroom she was thinking about Dave and not about pursuit of criminals. There was something about him. Not only those big brown eyes and those amazingly long lashes and the way his face reflected his inner judgements. The fact that she could focus on him through the haze that had replaced her brain.

What had happened last night? She would have sworn on the Bible that she would never ever find herself in bed with a total stranger. Never. Rhonda knew she was not a trusting person. She had reason not to trust. Too much reason. How had 'never' turned into this big man?

It was like turning lead into gold; it ought to be impossible. But Dave wasn't impossible. Dave was for real. She gave it all up as a bad joke and slept.

When she woke up her brain was much clearer. She knew what she had to say to Dave. If he was still there. And if her silverware was also still there. That was a joke she shouldn't have made.

She needed a shower. As the realisation of the drug sunk in, so did the need to play Lady Macbeth and clean herself over and over and over.

Before Rhonda even entered the kitchen, she knew Dave was standing by the stove. It was the scent of food that did it. Spice scents mingled with rice and vegetables and just a hint of chicken.

She saw his back first. He was very big, hiding the stove and half the kitchen behind his broad shoulders. He turned round and his eyes flicked over her. It was mostly an 'is she well yet?' flick, but there was a little bit of something else below the concern for her well-being. Rhonda found herself going pink.

"I hope you're recovered enough to eat?"

"I'm feeling fine," Rhonda said. "Totally embarrassed, but well."

"Good," and he turned back to the stove.

"Dave," Rhonda said this hesitantly. Maybe she had the name wrong. She was suddenly not sure of anything.

"Yes?" and he turned round instantly.

"I said I would tell you why I don't want to prosecute. Why I don't even want to chase the mongrel."

"Yes?" and his eyes became gimlets.

"I need to explain why."

"You don't have to," he said. "I was out of line. I've been reminding myself that I took advantage of you."

"You didn't know I'd been drugged. *I* didn't know I had been drugged. Let's leave it at that."

"For the moment, anyhow."

Rhonda began to wonder if Dave ever left anything alone for long. He was one of those blokes who just had to have answers. Just her luck. Well, she could give him some answers. He was certainly owed them.

"I don't really want to tell your back all my deepest thoughts," she commented. "It might be a very intelligent back, but it's hard to talk to."

Dave had a glorious laugh. Big and comforting. "Give me a moment, then."

In a few minutes he came to the table, two cups in his hands. "Coffee?"

"Thanks," and she was grateful for it. The warm cup and the hot drink helped soothe several aches. She let her thoughts settle and her emotions find their still centre.

"I was trying to find a way of explaining it," Rhonda said. "Why I reacted so strongly. It's not that I don't want him to stop being a prick. It's not that I don't hate what's happened. I do. But bringing him to court will hurt me more than it will punish him."

"You're saying that justice for him is not redress for you."

"In a way it would be. I have a bit of a messy past though. That would come out. And I hate being seen. I hate public notice more than almost anything."

"Yet you have a writing deadline," Dave noted.

"I use a pseudonym for my writing," Rhonda explained. She felt a bit pleased with herself. She was telling the entire truth, and yet hiding everything.

"Really private, then."

"Really, really private."

"Okay. I think I get it." He understood. Rhonda

looked up from her cup in surprise. She caught his eye and they smiled at each other.

"You need protection though." Rhonda felt she had walked from a clear path onto quicksand. "Not by the police," Dave obviously read her look correctly. "From this guy."

"Protection?"

"You're stuck with me, honey."

"I don't know you!"

"We know each other Biblically," and his smile took on a tint of wicked.

"You know me Biblically. I didn't know you till this morning."

"I know," and his face showed his amusement. Wry amusement. Dave had the most expressive face she had seen in anyone. "I fell in love with you at first sight and you forgot me the first instant you could."

"Fell in love?" Rhonda was totally out of her depth.

"Bear with me, honey. I'm not going to move in. I just want to keep an eye on you for a bit."

"Then stop bloody pressuring me."

"Why?" He was very calm, but not quite in control. "It worked last night."

"So you say." Rhonda let her irritation make her tone tart. "I can't recall, if you will remember."

Dave reached over the table and picked up her wrist. He kissed her hand. "Give me time," he said. "And let me play knight errant."

"I don't understand this," Rhonda stated. Dave kept hold of her wrist. He looked at her, and kept on looking until Rhonda gave in. "God," she said, "You're better at pressuring people than anyone I've ever met." He smiled.

"I don't believe in love at first sight," she warned. "And it scares me to let a stranger in my life. I'm just about the most private of private people."

"But?"

"Oh, you could hear the 'but'?" She was at her most sarcastic. Dave still smiled. "The fact that I didn't snatch back my hand the moment you grabbed it," and she looked accusingly at her recalcitrant appendage, "suggests that maybe something in me says it's worth giving things a go." Dave's smile grew.

"You can be my knight errant if it will make you bloody happy. But I want to start this dating thing all over. You remember having slept with me. All I remember is having woken up in bed with a stranger."

His smile dimmed. "That's fair," he said.

"Damn right it's fair. I hope I haven't burned your dinner."

Dave raced for the stove. "And anyway, I understand articles," he explained. "I'm a journalist." Rhonda regretted giving him that second chance. Journalists were not something she needed in her life. Him being a journalist explained a lot: his inquisitiveness, his accent, his knowledge. "I'm in Canberra on an extended assignment."

Rhonda shrugged off implications. She had to take chances sometimes, and she would rather take a chance on him than on anyone else she had met in years.

"Just don't tell me about life at Parliament House," was her safe reply. "Ever since we got this government I haven't wanted to notice the Hill. Unless you count sliding down the grass on top of it. Except the security guards are strict about stopping that. Abuse of public property. Disrespectful. No, there are no redeeming features of that Parliament anymore."

"There are some beautiful gardens," he prompted. "I can show you some. I know all the private places."

"Maybe," Rhonda answered. "We'll see."

He fed her and washed the dishes then went home so that she could get her article in.

2.

I'm magic at opening boxes. I know this because Zoë
tells me so. She could not believe the way I just ripped
on into them. Layers of paper and packing just thrown
out onto the floor until they were so deep we were
wading.

Those boxes were from Dad.

Zoë kept me company when I opened them. In fact,
she was of major assistance for the initial unpacking.
Nick just hung around in the background. Zoë loved it.
She hadn't realised I had a childhood, nor that the
childhood had included a tutu just like hers.

She brought hers out and she measured them very
carefully and showed me every single difference. The
shade was particularly different. Mine was a yellowed
pink, because it had sat in a Melbourne cupboard for a
million years. She stuck her face right into it and then
complained that it smelled funny.

The frills were in a box with a whole lot of other
dress-up clothes. I used to love wearing Indian skirts
and very Bohemian cotton prints. Peasant blouses.
They all smelled funny — way too long in storage.

Zoë put each and every piece of clothing on and
twirled round to show me them properly. Twice the
skirts of my late teens fell from her, because these
skirts were far too big. Twice she fell in a happily
laughing heap.

Nick was totally startled by the thought of his frilly
pink feminist mother. He hung around for ages,
watching us closely and making occasional snide comments, but he never came through that doorway. Girl
cooties.

Ten boxes of stuff. My whole childhood and
teenagerhood. Belinda used to call it 'teen-angerhood',
because so many of our friends were angry back then. I

wasn't one of them. I was happy being me. And hanging around Peter.

Linnie would say I'm imagining the past the way I want it to be. But me, I looked at my pink tutu and thought, "This is not the dance costume of an angry child."

Peter and I moved out together the moment I turned eighteen. I hadn't taken much with me. Peter never liked my clutter. And when I left Peter, a suitcase and a box tied with string was all I had.

Dad had not thrown a thing out. All my first eighteen years was in those boxes.

There were four batches of books. I hefted them to near the emptiest bookshelf. Zoë took several for reading immediately. I read science fiction when I was in my teens. Girls from science families do that. Nick had never read Doc Smith, and I had the whole Skylark series. And Cordwainer Smith. And Sylvia Engdahl. I forget what else he took, but there was a big hole in the collection before he left for work.

My diaries were there. Not with the other books, thank goodness. Imagine if Nick had got to them! I'd kept a diary from when I was twelve until when I moved out of home. I called my first diary Kitty, in honour of Ann Frank. 'Dear Kitty,' I read on page one of the very first one I was ever given, then closed it in a hurry. I shut my eyes and just felt the musty warmth of the cover.

I was at home in Melbourne, with a mother and a father and a big sister I argued with all the time. I was in high school (just) and was average height and a bit tubby. I hated the fat. I wanted blue eyes, not brown. I wanted long, long black hair. Black with a fine red-brown sheen. Curly, bohemian hair. I didn't know what I wanted to do when I grew up; I had my first diary and it was my new secret self.

That was the first of many diaries. I found every single one of those diaries in those boxes. All wrapped in tissue paper. I gave the tissue paper to Zoë and I hid the diaries in the drawer next to my bed.

In two boxes was my collection of records and tapes. Dad had packed my life the way it was when I left home. Frozen in time.

Lin's first record player all of her own had been a little blue portable one. I wondered if she still had it? And, if she did, if I could borrow it and listen to the Bee Gees and to Sherbet again?

I grinned as Zoë held up an old pair of jeans and made rude noises. She made rude noises on principle, I told her, because those outfits were back in. "Oh, Mum," she said.

In those boxes were some strange things. A little phial of my old violet scent: I used to love that smell. Now it's sickly and too sweet and too floral. Zoë snaffled the phial.

Schoolbooks and letters from friends. All the ornaments and jewellery I had been given when I turned eighteen. A string of pearls. An opal pendant. Three vases.

Lots of things. Every single one with memories attached. Our little house would be strained to store all this past. And yet . . . and yet it was so lovely to have it.

After dinner Zoë went to bed and Nick came home. We decided to find homes for everything, somehow. We did this put-away at once, because next week was Ballarat and I did not want things left around. It was a late night because Nick and I kept stopping to look at things while we were finding homes for them. In the end though, we found places for everything, except one box of unbelievably miscellaneous possessions. Nick got into the roof and hid it there. He pretended to be lost while he was up there, and then he started making ghost noises.

I got to do my mother-scream, "Nick, you bloody well get down here this instant," into a black hole.

3.

It was a strange couple of weeks.

Nick had his father and was not happy about it. I had my childhood and proof my father had not forgotten me, and was happy about it. Zoë and Nick were teaching me how to be Jewish. And Belinda was having nightmares about burning buildings. My dreams were part nightmare and part Rudolph.

It didn't seem right somehow that Belinda and I were to go away and leave everything. It was Ada's time.

Maybe Lin could talk Dad into coming and having a picnic with us. Melbourne is only a couple of hours from Ballarat, after all. We used to go there as kids. Sovereign Hill and the diorama and all the grue of the goldfields. More memories.

I rang Belinda the next day and asked her if she could thank Dad and say how wonderful it was to get all those things. And to suggest the picnic.

She said she would try. In the meantime she had collated some of GG's jokes — lifted from that scrapbook — and was sending them to me by email.

I printed the jokes off for Zoë and Nick. They read them out over dinner, cracking up with laughter. They both got their sense of humour either from their respective fathers or from their equally idiot aunt. Certainly not from me. These are jokes that are not worth even a demure giggle, in my humble opinion.

The reason why a drunken man staggers is because he is dizzy-pated.

Why is the figure nine like a peacock? It is nothing without its tail.

Why is the Prince of Wales, musing on the Queen's government, like a rainbow? It is the son's reflection on a quiet reign.

Why is a cigar-loving man like a tallow candle? He will smoke when he goes out.

How many dog days are there in the year? 365. Every dog has his day.

What is that which every one can divide and no one can see where it is divided? Water.

What is that which divides by uniting, and unites by dividing? Shears.

If you should meet a melancholy pig, what animal's name might properly be applied to him? Pork, you pine (porcupine).

My boss had a small surprise for me, three days before our holiday. She admitted while we were re-stocking shelves that Rudolph was an ex.

And the next thing I knew Zoë had the sniffles. I rang Belinda, and she said she would go on ahead and meet me in Ballarat. Just before she left, she emailed me a curious question.

"I don't think this is something to take with us," she said in her email, "For one thing, it's too depressing. I have all sorts of other things arranged for our holiday (just you wait). If I leave it till we get back, though, I'll forget, so here it is, for your delectation. Just a sample of a theme that I found running through the scrapbook and on a few recipe papers. Some of the mottoes were scribbled below the recipes. They made me wonder. We can talk later. See you down south when Zoë realises she wants camp and de-sniffles."

He that has lost his conscience has nothing left that is worth keeping.

A bachelor is a man who has neglected his opportunity of making some poor woman miserable.

It is suggested that one reason why so many marriages turn out unhappy is because the bridegroom is never the "best man" at the wedding.

The clergy in a certain town, as the custom is, having published the banns of matrimony between two persons, was followed by the clerk's reading the hymn beginning with these words — "mistaken souls, who dream of heaven."

The mass of mankind is uncommonly slow
To acknowledge the fact it behoves them to know
Or to learn that a woman is not like a mouse
Needing nothing but cheese and the walls of a house.

Don't be in too great a hurry, girls, to fall in love with the young men. It often happens that your hearts are no sooner theirs than theirs are no longer yours.

It costs a great deal more to be miserable than to be happy.

"Your inconstant temper would make me miserable."

Never witness tears from a wife with apathy or difference. Words, looks, actions — all may be artificial; but a tear is unequivocal; it comes directly from the heart, and speaks at once the language of truth, nature, and sincerity.

Well, that was her email. For me, it was patently clear that if Great-Grandma had not actually suffered abuse from her husband, she certainly did not like him overmuch. I wondered what the grounds for her divorce had been? And what her parents thought about it?

Lin would find out. Because for me, it was the stuff of nightmares.

Zoë didn't have the sniffles. She had the heebie-jeebies. Those school bullies were also going camping, and she didn't want to be near them. I rang Belinda and suggested that Zoë come with me to Ballarat, and Lin wondered if Zoë would not enjoy visiting her father more. I asked what sort of ex-wife I was, to dump Zoë without warning. I hardly saw Henry these days. Belinda, being such a sane and rational person, asked me which Zoë would like.

I asked my daughter. Zoë simply picked up the phone and rang Henry and asked him if she could stay for a week. He wanted to speak to me, and I explained the situation a bit further.

Of course he would take her. She could follow him round and help him at work. Everyone was happy. I was happy in a discomfited fashion, but I was happy. Poor Nick has a toad of a father, but Zoë has a nice dad and I still regretted things not having worked.

He could only take her the day after next. To fill the extra day, we went to the Queen Victoria Building. I was feeling mellow, so didn't choose the mean crown. Then we walked all the way to Circular Quay and bought milkshakes. Eventually we bussed back home and Zoë helped me pack.

While we were packing, Nick stalked round the house in a proprietorial fashion.

Zoë insisted I put lots of extra things into my cases for Belinda. Even Nick had some things for Belinda — a bunch of recipe books he had picked up at a trash and treasure and three pot plants. Carrying those pot plants on the train was not my idea of the start to a dream holiday.

4.

"I need a meme," Rhonda typed in her blog. "Can you hear the plaintive lilt?"

"Go to one of those quiz sites and do a quiz," said TVwhore. "Can you hear the sultry snap at your silliness?"

"How about an old meme?" Phased asked. "How about we all tell a fear we've faced. I can start. My fear was that people with more education than me would look down on me. I went back to university and got an education."

"That's good," said Rhonda. "That's really good. Something to be proud of. Mine is newer. I got given a date rape drug on my last birthday and woke up in bed with a stranger." And as she typed Rhonda found out something very important, "I didn't know I was angry at myself. I thought I was angry at the person who gave me the drug. But I was angry at me."

"I lost a lot of friends through being honest," Starchild said. "I did the right thing, too."

"I told my parents my big secret last year," said TVwhore. "Does that count?"

"Of course it counts," said Rhonda. "It counts bigtime. It doesn't even matter how they took it, because you having told them is the hard bit."

"Why is it the hard bit?"

"Because, TVwhore, what they say or do is up to them. You can't be your parents. Can't live their lives. Can't stop them from being stupid or from being wise. I never got to tell my big secrets to my parents. We don't even have each other's phone numbers anymore. It was their fault. They couldn't deal with me. And they were idiots for not even trying. Does that make sense?"

"Something like that happened to me," said Phased. "It makes sense."

"God, yes," said TVwhore. "Me too. My father doesn't talk to me. My mother sends me messages, secretly, as if it's some sort of wrong thing she is doing. You're entirely right, MissTRie. I told them and I can live with myself. Maybe one day you will be able to do the same with your family."

"Maybe one day. My next big thing to sort out, heh?"

Phased admitted, "I like that."

"It's good, heh?" from Starchild.

"I meant it selfishly. I like that MissTRie has things to sort out still. If you aren't sorting things out, I'm not sure that you're living. And we're all haunted, in a way."

"I know what you're saying," Rhonda found tears dribbling over everything as she typed, "None of us is alone."

"Oh! I like that," said Starchild. "None of us is alone."

"Being alone is the worst thing in the whole universe," said TVwhore.

"Thank God for friendship, then," said Starchild.

"I hear you, sistah," said Phased.

And Rhonda worried about humanity. From the outside, everyone except her looked fine. Normal lives. Happiness. Scratch the surface and everyone she knew had hurts. Fractured humans, flawed humans: just like her.

5.

Rhonda saw Dave a lot before their first date. He would ring up and drop round for a chat. He'd arrange to meet her for coffee and a bite to eat. His excuse was that he was keeping an eye on her. He didn't mention love again. He didn't repeat the wrist holding.

She hadn't met anyone like him before. She told him that, and he answered, "Well, you're not going to meet anyone like me again. I'm an original."

After two weeks of gentleness and support, Rhonda found she almost wanted to go out on a date. She wanted everything and she wanted nothing. It was like standing on the edge of a precipice and wondering if she would fly or fall. In the end, the only thing Rhonda could do was jump off that cliff.

"Dave," Rhonda said.

"Hey, Rhonda."

"I do know my name."

"I'm always glad to hear that."

"I'm being courageous today." There was a silence on the far end of the phone. "Don't you want to know how I'm being courageous?"

"You know I do." His voice was almost a whisper.

"If you're interested, I thought we might go see a movie."

"Are you saying what I think you are saying?"

Rhonda thought that she was jumping off a cliff, but now it seemed that it was Dave in mid-air. "Dave, you can use the 'd'-word — I won't faint."

"Is this a date?"

"If you want it to be, yes. But just a movie."

"Drinks after?" His voice was as hopeful as Number One's. He was as serious as on the first day she met him. This was a good sign. If it was such a good sign, why was she so scared?

"OK, drinks as well."

"What time?"

The only way of dealing with fear was with sarcasm. "You can't work out a time yourself?"

Dave laughed his big laugh and the tension was broken. "I'll pick you up at eight, then. And Rhonda?"

"Yes?"

"You're a doll. Thank you."

When she'd hung up, Rhonda just stood there, looking at the telephone. She was a doll. And she was scared.

She'd seen Dave every day this last two weeks. It shouldn't be different tonight. But it was. It was a date. A first date. Rhonda suddenly let out a huge whoop. Then she quietly went to her wardrobe and spent two hours trying to work out what she could wear.

When Dave came to pick her up, he had the biggest bunch of flowers Rhonda had ever seen.

"Thank you," Rhonda said. Hiding behind the roses

she felt suddenly courageous. "Dave, can I ask a daft question?"

"Sure, shoot."

"Are you as nervous as me?"

"I feel as if I'm fifteen. Is that how you feel?"

"Something like. And I keep telling myself that it's irrational and I'm still fluttery as a whatever."

"As a whatever," Dave smiled. "I like that. Go put your flowers in water and then let's go argue about what we want to see."

And they did. They took out their nerves in exhaustive analysis of the various offerings.

A few minutes into the film Dave's hand carefully took Rhonda's and he didn't let go until they both stood up after the credits. As Rhonda sat in the dark, her hand happily held, she wondered at Dave's contradictions. A man who could sleep with a stranger, then be scared of a date two weeks later.

It was when he brought her home later that night that the penny dropped. He didn't ask. He went into the kitchen and made coffee. He already knew her better than Tony ever would. And he knew that her asking him for a date was a signal. Rhonda wasn't sure what she was signalling. Not yet. All she knew was that he was a very good person to sit over coffee with, late at night.

6.

Rhonda pretended she wasn't herself. She pretended she was a person who was all fine with the world, who could stand up for her rights and who had nothing to lose. She walked into the temp office, her courage afire. She didn't wait to be directed to an office or a noticeboard. There was only one place she was going, and she was going there now. Nothing would stand in her way. Nothing.

She caught the Sleazoid gossiping with another staff member.

"Sorry, mate," the skinny man said, "I didn't realise you had a client appointment."

"I didn't realise I had a client appointment either," and he stood up to his full height, crossed his arms over his big chest, and stared Rhonda down. Just thinking of Dave cut Mr Ick to size. Rhonda smiled up at him, with all the sweetness of her soul.

"I've told a journalist what happened that night," she said, her smile never faltering. "He has written an article." She was lying, but she betted that Dave would follow through if necessary. "If anything else happens to me, anything at all, including you leering down the front of my dress, or if I hear of anything else happening to any other woman who uses this office, then trust me, he's going to get his article out. You want a future, you clean up your act."

Rhonda was amazingly impressed with her courage.

Shortly afterwards, a knock at her front door startled Rhonda into several typos. Something inside her announced that it must be Dave at the door, and that he must be bearing dinner. There was no logic in the assumption, just a little incline of her heart towards the door. She followed that inclination and there was Dave.

"I hope you eat Chinese takeout," he said.

"I eat anything I don't have to cook," Rhonda replied, "Well, anything cooked. I don't, for instance, eat raw liver or the hearts of unborn children."

"You don't know how relieved I am to hear that," and he put his bags on the floor and scooped her into a warm embrace. "Are you tempted to skip dinner?" he asked, hopefully.

"Tempted, yes, but very hungry." Also not quite

ready to have sex. Rhonda wondered what it had been like that first time, with this man. Knowing she could never retrieve that memory made her very shy.

"You win," Dave laughed and opened his packages while Rhonda found eating implements.

"Chopsticks?" she asked.

"Spoons," Dave said firmly.

"Funny, I had you down as someone fond of authenticity."

"Honey, I am. But not with hot and sour soup."

They got down to eating as if neither of them had seen food before. After the meal, Rhonda collected the plastic, catching faint whiffs of spices and oil and chicken as she filled a rubbish bag. Dave stood up to help her, but then his phone rang.

"Damn," he said, "Do you mind if I get it?"

"Go ahead. I'll just finish cleaning."

Dave went outside to take the call and was gone a long while. When he came back, he looked five years older. Rhonda didn't want to ask what was wrong. Her mouth dried and her throat clogged when she tried. She gave him a hug.

He looked down at her in surprise. "He's dead," Dave said. "He was killed by snipers in Iraq."

"Come sit down," said Rhonda, and she led him by the hand to the couch and held him, cradled and safe. They sat like that for over an hour and finally Rhonda realised she wasn't doing much good. She brought out her port and two glasses and filled them. Dave looked up when she gave him one of the glasses, but there was no light in his eyes. It wasn't until he had finished the third glass that he started to talk.

His best friend was dead. They'd been to university together and started on the same paper, six lifetimes ago. Robert had become a bit of an expert in transition governments and so he had been sent to Iraq. And he was dead.

Rhonda wanted to find something she could say. There was nothing. This was something she would not lie about: she would not give false wishes about resting in peace, or being in the hands of some deity. Her lies didn't extend to hypocrisy or false hope. She couldn't even distract him with something witty. All Rhonda could do was get Dave drunk. And so she did.

Dave didn't say any more about his friend, but eventually, he talked. He told Rhonda about the most inconsequential things: a ball game he wished he could have got to, the weather in his home town at this time of year and how he kept forgetting to pack his socks when he had to go somewhere in a hurry. Once he had let all this flow out in a gentle stream, his mind started waking up.

Dave awake was Dave asking questions. He reminded Rhonda of a little boy asking 'Why?' all the time. Except he asked what and who and how. Questions for Dave were like online aliases for Rhonda.

After three-quarters of a bottle of port he was only slightly drunk. He must have the hardest head in all Christendom. Rhonda was envious until she snuggled in closely and nearly fainted from his rich breath.

In his mood of faint sobriety his questions were probably not as focussed as usual, and she was not his usual victim. They were definitely questions needing answers however, and Rhonda wondered what sort of project he was working on that could require such common-as-mud knowledge.

He wanted to know about fan fiction. He started by telling her that he knew about it, but didn't know about the sort of person who read it or wrote it. He didn't even know what to look up to find it. He had tried 'fan fiction' but it gave too many results. He didn't know enough, he mourned.

"I need to find out about you lot," he said.

"Us lot?"

"People from Canberra. Why would someone so close to the snowfields go online and write illegal fiction?"

"You're a confusing man," Rhonda said. "Why the snowfields?"

"I missed winter here," Dave mourned. "Skiing."

"Thredbo isn't Aspen, you know."

"I know. It's still snow. And I got a day off and got there just after it had all bloody finished."

"I don't know snow," Rhonda admitted.

"Bloody Aussies."

"We are, aren't we?" and she smiled.

"If you don't know snow, you know fan fiction." Dave was persistent. Like a little terrier. An oversized little terrier.

"Why should I know fan fiction?"

"I dunno. Journalist's instinct?"

"Huh. I don't think it's illegal, though. As long as you don't make money from it."

"I thought it was stealing intellectual property."

"You would know about that. All I know is that lots of people do it and they seem to get by."

"That doesn't make it legal."

"So check with a lawyer. How am I supposed to know if it's legal?"

"I don't want to check with a lawyer. I don't care if it's legal. I want to know who writes it."

"I guess a whole range of people."

"What sort . . .?" and Dave's next question was interrupted by the phone.

Lana or Tony. Had to be Lana or Tony. Especially at this hour. Rhonda sent up a quick prayer, thanking

God for ex-husbands, extricated herself from Dave, and answered the phone.

"If that's your ex-husband," Dave growled, "tell him I hate his guts."

"Who on earth is that?" asked Lana at the other end. "And why does he hate Tony?"

"He's drunk, ignore him. You met him at my birthday party, I think. Big American called Dave?"

"Well, that certainly explains a lot."

"I'm not going to tell you any details, you know," Rhonda said tartly.

"But you're seeing him?"

"Yes."

"What's he got against Tony?"

"God knows. He's drunk."

"You have a drunk boyfriend."

"I have a drunk American boyfriend," and Rhonda looked over at Dave to make sure he was listening. He raised a brow to show how much he cared. "Wait a second," and Rhonda covered the phone. "Dave, go make yourself some coffee."

"Don't you have any more port?"

"I doubt it. Whatever there is, is in the wine cabinet. I would rather you made yourself some coffee."

Dave helped himself to an old bottle of Cointreau, and Rhonda chatted to Lana while watching him systematically work his way through it. It was a real floor-show, because his open face reflected every moment of intent to render blotto. Eventually, he was going to keel over and collapse, Rhonda thought, and wanted to get off the phone and force him to drink coffee, but Lana was chatty and there was a kind of morbid fascination in watching Dave. Especially as he obviously hated Cointreau and his faced curled up whenever he downed some.

As she put down the phone, she wished he would

talk. Not that she was any good at hearing true confessions, but she rather thought he needed to make some. He hadn't even told her his friend's name.

The Cointreau was a worry. The more she thought about it, the more it worried her.

Rhonda eyed Dave up and down and asked him, "Are you trying to kill yourself?"

"Can't forget."

"Alcohol doesn't help you forget. It just hazes things so they're tolerable. If they're not tolerable you'd better get some sleep."

"Can't be alone. Hurts."

"You don't have to," she sounded as practical as she could. Like a nurse. And, like a nurse, she helped him walk to the bedroom. She put him to bed like a child, and held his hand until he was fast asleep. His helplessness made her ache, and she sat next to him most of the night, watching.

When Dave had finally left the next day, Rhonda had a fit of conniptions about the state of her house. This was entirely irrational. But if one has conniptions, one must do something about them. Not that her home was bad by her standards. It was just that there was so much paper lying about. She'd done all those drafts and redrafts and printouts and checks and just left them strewn around. Artistic. Bohemian. Rhonda sighed. Excuses just didn't cut it when other people walked into the place and saw the pigsty she lived in.

When Dave was there her perspective on life changed. It was when he was suddenly absent that she noticed mess.

She stacked her papers high, into a toppling tower. She plunked the tower by her big armchair, made herself a giant cup of tea, turned on the TV, and methodically sorted. Some went straight into the recycling box, some went into a pile for filing, and some she looked at in bewilderment, wondering how a letter from her MP inviting her to a consultation, or a gas bill, or an offer of a free personality test could have mingled so promiscuously with her history articles.

When she had taken the second batch of papers out to the recycling bin and dumped them with a resounding thud, she felt as if things were happening. Tables were almost visible and the floor showed dusty spots that had not seen sunshine in weeks. Rhonda sang along with the week's top hits and mellowed.

The next paper shattered her peace. It was handwritten. And dated. She had written it the day after the date rape drug. The day after. When her memory was full and functioning. She didn't remember writing it. What was worse, the Rhonda who wrote it knew that the Rhonda who read it would not remember writing it. It scared her.

Remember through this page. When your mind will not allow the ideas to appear. Use the writing to jolt yourself into awareness where awareness is needed.

Sometimes the dreams grow within me. And they grow and grow and grow. I knew it when I took drugs in my twenties. I knew it when I could not lose myself in my history and knew it even more when my history warped inside me and became a part of the problem.

I tried to escape it. But now I cannot. What is within blossoms again.

I have tried to talk with myself through dreams, but my self will not listen. My self is scared. I am not afraid. Accept the gift or find death.

Rhonda stared at her words. She looked at the paper until the telephone rang and then she put the paper away, delicately and with care, until she could bring herself to understand what it said.

It was Dave on the phone. He had tickets to the ballet and wanted her to come.

"I don't see you as the ballet type," Rhonda teased. He must have the head of an ox and a stomach of steel, to have got through the previous day with no hangover. Suddenly she was not worried about the Cointreau.

"I'm not," he admitted. "But I kinda suspected you were. And I owe you for last night."

"I am," Rhonda said, "But I keep thinking you have ulterior motives."

"Honey, you keep thinking I have ulterior motives because my motives are ulterior. Just accept it and we'll be fine."

"If I come to the ballet with you, you'll be frustrated," Rhonda warned. "I have a phone call to make at 11 p.m."

"US?" he asked.

"How perceptive of you," Rhonda smiled at the other end of the phone.

"A man?"

"God no, I eschew men."

"Uh-huh."

"Well, except you. And you don't allow me to eschew you."

"Damn right, I don't. I'll have you home in time for your call."

She realised when she put down the phone that she had accepted his pursuit of her. She should have known that when she asked him on a date, but she was slow.

The biggest problem was that she was keeping her secrets from him. The second was that she was having trouble admitting to him that she was a geek. She had lied about the phone call. Half-lied, Rhonda told herself. Only a half-lie, which for her was almost a truth. It was a phone call to the US. Surely there was an element of call in an online chat with Phased?

Dave didn't know that Rhonda did geek things. Whenever he was round she pretended she was playing computer solitaire. There was a kind of euphony about a woman alone playing solitaire, Rhonda thought.

The next night she went home with Dave. She told herself that it was purely because she wanted the sex. "Sex is a fine recreation," she informed herself, carefully. And besides, a steady boyfriend gave her protection against Mr Lewd and Awful. And besides, Dave needed her.

CHAPTER EIGHT

1.

WHEN JUDITH HEARD A LIST OF WHAT SHE HAD DONE SHE
wondered when her sister slept. Maybe she hadn't.

Belinda had bought passes for all the biggest attrac-
tions. She had also obtained the keys to Great-Grandma's childhood home. Apparently the house was on
sale. Judith blinked in astonishment.

There were maps and leaflets as well, but that was
to be expected, argued Judith with herself, *You cannot
criticise a born organiser for organising. Just for doing things
like paying big sums of money and sneaking off and getting
keys to houses.*

There was also the genealogical research.

2.

"GG never divorced!" were her first words to me.

"What?" was my intelligent reply.

"I'm serious," she said, "GG did not divorce. She
went with her parents to Melbourne in 1900 and her
husband stayed behind."

"You could at least say, 'Hello, Judith, my dear and wonderful sister,'" I grumbled.

"Hello, Judith, my dear and wonderful sister," she dutifully echoed, and then raced back into, "She must've separated. And her parents must've supported her."

"That's bad news."

"Why?"

"Because she and her parents moving to Melbourne sounds awfully like me moving to Sydney."

"You mean,"—and you could hear Belinda's excitement turn to dismay; I felt like a pig—"that her husband was terrible."

"I'm prone to think that."

"I wonder if court records show anything."

"Write a letter when we get back." was my suggestion. "I don't want to think about it now."

"I can understand this," she said slowly. "But we need to know."

"We need to know," I echoed, "But you get to find out."

We spent the rest of our trip carefully not talking about why the family took their only child and moved to Melbourne in 1900, with young baby and without new husband. How the scrapbook had an undertow of misery. Could magic be an escape from memory?

We did more in Ballarat than have a conversation about Great-Grandma. But because of that conversation and my late arrival, and because of Belinda having got us into family right from the start, day one in Ballarat was not spent eyeing off black swans warily or hunting for gold on Sovereign Hill. It was spent exploring a very empty house. Belinda says it was built around 1865, so it must have been. Since she thinks she knows everything. And she checked with the estate agent, and our family were the first owners and lived there until 1900.

I wish I were money-minded. I would have bought that house as it stood vacant. I could have sold my Sydney home and moved myself and the kids. I justified to myself that it would not have been fair on the kids, but a little bit of me was thinking of Rudolph.

Let me tell you about this family home I drooled over. This was the home the family had moved to when they had made their money by supplying the goldfields with the stuff of everyday life. It was tapestry brick. I admired the patterns the brick made when my sister pointed them out. I also wondered if Ada had known what tapestry brick was.

I guess we're talking about a heritage building. I guess this makes my family a heritage family. What a heritage, though: strange beings in lemon trees, possible domestic violence, and being Jewish. Always a burden, that being Jewish.

I digress.

There's a big two-storied veranda at the front, and it's framed by some lovely white iron lace. I covet that iron lace. Much nicer iron lace than ours.

There's a big front door in the middle of the veranda. Very presentational, stained glass and all. A bit daunting. If my family had not had serious money way back then, they made a good pretence of it.

To the right as you enter is a huge lounge room. The ceilings are amazing. Victoriana to die for. Decorated to a dream. I bet the rooms were all reds and browns originally, but in this big empty house everything was painted white. So I don't know the original ceiling colour, except that the white created a space Zoë would want to dance in. Lin and I did some steps in that big room, just for Zoë. We decided we would send her a postcard the next day, telling her we had danced in her honour in the ancient family lounge room. She would call us silly, and give her little happy smile.

The lounge room had a big arch leading to the dining room. Belinda said that the arch was not the original link between the rooms. I dreamed giant double doors, then I imagined an ordinary doorway, just in case one of them worked to present me the original mental image. Psychic understanding of homes, this is called. Or maybe just me imagining things. Psychic misunderstanding of homes.

Other things had been tampered with. The original kitchen would have been a lean-to. At some stage the lean-to had been transformed into a real kitchen, at the back of the dining room. Belinda had done some chatting with the estate agent. The estate agent suggested it was probably around the same time as the bathrooms were made internal. So the whole back of the house had changed since 1900. Better kitchen, better plumbing.

The laundry was still out back. Like my place, except for me it's the bathroom/laundry that's out back. You went out from what looks like a family room, but which Belinda said was probably the quarters of the poor maid who would have lived in.

Above the stairs was all bedrooms. Four of them in their expansive entirety. And a big bathroom, obviously recent.

Imagine Zoë and Nick and me with a big room each rather than piddly little ones. Imagine a room for the computers instead of them jammed into corners where everyone always trips over cords. Imagine nice old fireplaces with wooden mantles. Imagine enough power points. Power points may be taking imagination a bit far.

Great-Grandma was a favoured child. She grew up as the only daughter in a family wealthy enough to own this home. From that to being deserted by her daughter and dying alone. Money isn't everything.

There was an inscription in the cemetery (we visited there next), which made me wonder if some others of the Jewish community practised magic. It said: GUARD US FROM EVIL — FROM FEAR — FROM ILLNESS. It was on the grave of someone who had died in her twenties. Great-Grandma has those same words down in her magic notes, as a part of a charm. I found myself thinking about secret women's traditions again.

I wanted to worship at the Eureka Memorial, for the record. I wanted to sing, "Remember the flag and the stars that she bears, the white stars of the Cross of the South," and relive in my mind the rebellion of the goldminers against the government. Instead, my domineering sister dragged me to the Jewish section and we spent a very wet ten minutes looking for graves. I found my inscription then, and quickly scribbled the words down while Lin was not watching.

To my surprise Lin found the graves we were looking for. I'm not surprised she found them; I'm surprised they were there at all. Ada's grandparents. Our great-great-great-grandparents. Dead.

"Judith," she said seriously, as we looked at them. "Do you remember Rhonda, who delivered those boxes?"

"She's buried here?" I asked.

"Her ancestors are. Right in front of us. I need to find a way of telling her that we're cousins."

Our ancestors had respectably long lives. Born in England, died in Ballarat. Given nice big white marble weights to hold them down. With flowers on. Well, one of them had a nice wreath of flowers around the edge. I got Belinda to take a picture, just for the decoration.

She thought I was being sympathetically ancestral. Hah. I was being frilly pink.

She was not happy when I wanted to go get flowers for the grave. In fact, she turned bloody decorous. Poor etiquette, it seems. Far be it from me to insult the dead with sad lack of etiquette. I whispered a "Hi, from us" to my ancestors instead, and we moved on to the next family, who bore the name Hamburger and whose tombstones were made by MacDonald and Son. I said "Hi"to them too. I'm not ancestral, I'm just talkative.

Linnie coped by taking photos. I did a bemoaning or a bewailing or a beweeping pose in front of each and every tomb. We went and got coffee to sober me up. She got coffee. I got a big old-fashioned pot of tea.

Bloody Belinda was up at an unholy hour the next day. Lin was quite sympathetic to share a room with when she was nine. These days — hah!

She tapped on my shoulder to wake me up and I looked up at her. She looked blonde and slim and fit and annoying. So annoying, in fact that I blinked one eye slowly at her (the other was being inscrutable and refusing to work) and I turned right over and tried to go back to sleep. She woke me again to get me to jog with her. I pulled my pillow over my head.

She laughed at me under my pillow. She also lifted the corner of my hiding place and asked what she could bring me for breakfast.

Holiday was turning into holiday camp.

"Something unhealthy."

Too soon she returned bearing a huge coffee and two chocolate covered doughnuts. All for me. My healthy sister had an apple-bran muffin and a mineral water. Now you know why she's a natural blonde. Bleached of all nutritional interest.

"By the way," she said, offhandedly, just as an aside,

when I was almost awake, "I forgot something yesterday."

"Another Hamburger buried by Macdonalds?" I asked.

"Much more exciting." She sounded arch. I swear she sounded arch. Lin rummaged through her folder. Finally she hauled out a computer printout. Never leave them on their own, that's what I say.

"I ordered proper prints," she explained, and she handed me the black and white page. "It's the Ballarat Bicycle Club in the late nineteenth century," she said, equally helpfully.

"And this is supposed to delight my eyes and rejoice my soul?" I asked.

"Look to the right," I was instructed by my sister-the-infernally-wholesome. There is a special place in hell reserved for eaters of apple-bran muffins.

"There's a penny-farthing," I noted, with acute insight.

"Behind the penny-farthing. Sitting on something."

"There is a Woman in White. Very Wilkie Collins."

"Thank you for your literary insight." Goodie, my attitude was beginning to annoy her. Between that and the second chocolate doughnut my day was looking up. Sisters bring happiness, everyone says so. I verbally admired the layered white dress and the way the black belt reflected the black band round the white hat.

Belinda had been building up to a Pronouncement. Serves her right for going jogging. Unholy activity. Mind you, if I was right about her Pronouncement, it was an amazing piece of detective work. Zoë might have to create something, I thought. Zoë is the official maker-of-nice-things-for-Auntie-when-Mummy-is-impossible.

"It's Great-Grandma," she finally said.

We really do look like Ada. She's there in Belinda's

eyes and my jawline. I'm assuming this is a good thing. I have her figure. So even without those boxes and stuff, Great-Grandma left us all sorts of goodies. Yum. I always wanted rounded shoulders and a big bottom. Dream of my childhood.

"I guessed. It is a brilliant piece of deductive research, but you went jogging and I hadn't finished giving you a hard time." Then I wondered, "How old was she?"

"Young single, I think."

"So young Ada was a daring cyclist."

"It appears so," smiled Lin, "And I bet she would've jogged if she had been born a hundred years later."

"Huh, she would've been a feminist."

"She would've done both," my sister said, very firmly. "And when you get dressed we can go look at plants."

"Not tourist spots and black swans?"

"Not today. We're going to explore all the nurseries for things for my garden."

"Why?" I was genuinely bewildered.

"Because I've spent two days getting keys and pictures and things and I am GG'd out. I do not want to pan for gold. I need vegetation."

"You *are* vegetation." I went to have a nice hot shower.

Belinda's local nurseries were miles and miles away. And miles and miles. And lots more miles. Nice views. Obscure roads. I gave directions. This means we were never lost, although we often took the scenic route. Sometimes the very scenic route.

And all this travel and not getting lost and swearing at maps was for what purpose? Belinda bought lavender. She enthused about a dog that greeted us at the bloody lavender farm, and about box hedges made of lavender. Worth every bit of effort I don't bloody well think. Lavender. One pink, one purple, and one with funny leaves. Lavender.

At the end of the day our motel room was chockers with potted plants. Smelly ones. "In your next life you will be a salad herb," I informed my insane sibling, "And I will eat you with sliced tomato and a touch of balsamic vinegar."

The next day we pretended to be tourists. We were walking along the main drag and Belinda stopped. "Look at the streetscape," she said. A moment ago she had been laughing at Athena on the roof of the Mechanics Institute. All I could see was a broad street with lots of floral thingies and green strips and statues and other historical garbage. I said so. I used those very words, in fact.

"No," Lin breathed, "You're not seeing it properly. Take your eyes up and back."

I saw it. Everything was different. Even the sky changed. You could see the old city underlying the new — generous and wealthy and welcoming. Expansive and expensive. Extraordinary.

3.

The weeks Rhonda had been away from chat rooms faded the instant she logged in. Maybe chat rooms were eternal, or existed in a special kind of present, or had their own time continuum. It felt comfortable, as if no personal history had elapsed and the outside world wasn't quite real.

She didn't like the current inhabitants of the room. They were full of stupid innuendos and trying to work out gender and sexual preferences so they could play sex games. Rhonda got out. She could not abide virtual pornography.

The next chat room looked promising at first. There

were five people, and they were talking current affairs. She made sarcastic remarks from the right wing persona she was developing to go with this nickname.

Soon the subject turned to revelation and prophecy. It seemed that people came into chat rooms these days just so that they could announce, "I was in a room with that new Nostradamus person."

"How to ruin a chat," Rhonda typed.

Despite Rhonda's scorn, the discussion turned to identifying the new Nostradamus. Everyone started to describe their theories and techniques. It appeared that some were developing it into an art.

"If you're going to talk this garbage, I'm out of here."

Rhonda suited action to words when one of the self-described hunters used her comment as a reason to start questioning her about what she knew. "Because you know something," Nostrahunter said. "It's obvious."

"The only thing that is obvious is how boring this topic is. I'm going. Good morning all."

Rhonda was entirely annoyed. Not only was a perfectly good chat session entirely spoiled, but open season had been declared on her secret self. They were a bunch of bastards for wanting to deprive her of her privacy. The only good thing was that Nostrahunter and his mates thought that she was a he and in the US.

The first thing she did was work hard to make her cover more secure. Rhonda decided to change her TV diet for a time so that her writing would not have even the hint of a British or Australian twang.

Hopefully it will help, she thought. Nothing else was doing much good, not even a bottle of white wine. Not even a date with Dave. Thank goodness there had been no repetition of his late night visit. She was impressed he trusted her, and worried she might not be able to handle what she needed to do for self-protection if he were round. This split consciousness was a distraction.

Research, thought Rhonda. Research is the way to deal with all the trials and traumas and tribulations of this world. If she could establish some patterns for who was following her then she could avoid them. Rhonda started her research with four search engines and groups of words from all her known utterings. She cross-tabulated stacks of information. She worked through a list of fifty search terms to hunt for hunters, and cross-tabulated them, too. When she had done this, she revived several of her old aliases and asked around. It was dangerous in its own way, this hunting, because it exposed her.

Rhonda rang Dave two days into her investigation and pleaded illness. She had to sort herself out. "Selfish bitch. That's all I am," she told herself as she dialled.

"You don't sound well," he said.

The emotional drain on her was too intense. "I have a massive headache," she admitted, truthfully. "Maybe I'm coming down with flu." Flu was a good excuse. Lassitude, too, invaded every joint and every bone as the hunt for her pursuers grew and took shape.

After a week and a half, Dave asked if she had been to the doctor.

"No," Rhonda admitted. "I just need rest."

"I'm coming round," he said.

"Mr Knight Errant?" she asked, feebly funny.

"No, Mr Bloody Worried."

Dave came in and instantly loomed. Had he always been this big or was her guilty conscience magnifying him?

"You need more exercise," he pronounced, holding her chin lightly and scrutinising her intently.

"I hurt," Rhonda said, with as much dignity as she could muster. "And you're treating me like a child."

"You're not taking care of yourself," Dave said.

"It's a worry, then?" Rhonda allowed herself a smile.

"Yes."

"I get like this from time to time, you know," Rhonda said. "I bet it's entirely gone within a week."

"Last time you had it, you saw the doctor?" Dave asked.

"Yes," and this was the truth. "If I'm not better within the week, I promise to get it checked."

Dave looked concerned still, but caved in. He treated her like fine bone china the whole evening, however.

"I always thought it would be nice to be treated like a fragile female," Rhonda said wistfully, when they were settled down watching TV.

"You don't like it?"

"No, I don't."

"Get well, then," and Dave sounded fierce.

"How can I not get well, when you tell me to like that?"

Dave laughed. He visited her every day, and the enforced time off the computer made Rhonda's headaches abate.

It was hard, though, not knowing when he was going to drop in. She had to whisk her research away at the merest hint of noise near the front door. Every time a car pulled in she would jump in startlement. The sooner she finished her little investigation the better.

It took her three weeks. By the end of the three weeks, however, the results were quite clear. At first there had been a host of people chatting about her. They all thought she was male and American. Eventually most of the chattering had dropped, and the subject just came up from time to time as a curiosity. Serious pursuit had begun.

Someone had been documenting her before she had

begun documenting them and she had met at least one of them, personally, in a chat room. BB and several of his mates had combed the Net very carefully: the tables documenting their questions showed a system at work.

As far as she could read it, there had been three groups. Either that or the patterns made three overlapping systems by chance. Rhonda sighed. She would rather the latter, but the former was more likely. The three groups had been forced out of action by the buzz, it seemed. This wasn't the first time the world at large had been interested in what she had to say in her more insane moods, but this time it had spread. Saved her from inquiring fools, too, so she couldn't fault it.

At first the buzz had been pretty sporadic, and then it started to feed on itself, as good gossip does. Once blogs started recording what was happening in chat rooms and millions of people became curious, it spread almost everywhere. Even to the newspapers.

"If I read newspapers," Rhonda reflected bitterly, "I would have known all this earlier. I hate it. I'm not the New Nostradamus, no matter what the Washington Post declares. I'm not even the new Rhonda. I'm old and embittered," and she continued to check her findings on herself, pleased with her anger.

A little after the furore reached its peak, most of the searchers dropped out. She assumed they'd given up. The advantage of a free press. Everyone gets bored if you leave them to make a fuss. Just like children.

And now there was just one person or organisation systematically hunting her. Just one persistent busybody. There were other mentions of her in various places, but when she crunched them it looked as if they were random. With one pursuer, life was simple.

Lies were simple, too. She could stick to her old strategies, tried and true. A US accent online for chatting. Male identities for chat rooms.

She could retain MissTRie and her friends because there was no link between them and her lone pursuer. If there was, it was TVwhore and she was just too clever and Rhonda might as well give up now.

Despite the pursuit, she was free. And she could remain so. She wondered if she should ritually burn her notes. Instead, Rhonda celebrated by ringing Dave to say, "No headache tonight."

He responded with an invitation to dinner and a sleepover.

"Like kids," Rhonda giggled. As she heard herself, she despaired. What adult woman giggled? What was Dave doing to her?

"Hardly," the man himself answered. "If you bring Daffy Duck PJs then I might have to rip them off you."

"Sorry, no Daffy Ducks."

"Pity," Dave said, sadly.

Between the evening and the present were several hours. In contemplating this, Rhonda realised that she needed to unwind the coil from inside her. If she didn't, it might unleash itself in temper or mood. Giggles were one thing, temperament was quite another.

Rhonda made herself some coffee and went online. She posted a message to her three closest e-friends, telling them they could find her in a particular chat room. She kept it open while she surfed, and just checked from time to time. It was unlikely they would turn up. Time zones and work and private lives were all killers.

Rhonda was lucky though. Not only did two of her friends appear, but while she was waiting for them she had an idea. Even if one of them was her lone pursuer (and even if it was the terrifyingly perceptive TVwhore, which it couldn't be, given that TVwhore knew her name and hadn't done anything with that knowledge), distraction was perfectly possible.

4.

Rudolph demanded that I make up for lost time. I suggested a movie. He suggested a weekend of wild sex. We compromised with a movie and a night together. Something for everyone. I'm not saying if we had wild sex, just in case Zoë reads this.

Then I rang Linnie. More of that porno spam came (as it always does) and I suddenly realised that it used abbreviations. And that quite a bit of the stuff in Great-Grandma's material was a completely different set of abbreviations. And that there was a cure for abbreviations, even though one has not yet been found for porno spam. I'm not entirely sure Belinda appreciated the phone call.

"Hi," I said. "I need you to go through Great-Grandma's recipes and tell me what the bloody culinary abbreviations mean."

"You can cook," she chided.

"Hah," I said.

"For you I will do this great thing."

I got my abbreviations and light was shone in some dark places. The most obscure abbreviation of all turned out to mean 'repeat this two more times'. More of Ada's magic was revealed.

Now I have to give you the first note I wrote for Great-Grandma's box. The one that led eventually to this all-purpose narrative.

———

I've been wicked and must atone. If I were Catholic I would confess.

Peter rang. I said I did not want to speak to him, but would get Nick. He said he wanted to speak to me, not Nick. I couldn't. I dropped the phone.

I retrieved it and I hung up. He rang back. I walked away. The phone rang out.

I went to Great-Grandma's box. Something inside me was prepared for that moment when I hung up the phone and my mind went that awful blank.

I made cakes of bran and shaved sandalwood and that ghastly vinegar. I wrote Peter's name on each cake in my neatest handwriting. I looked up at the light as I hid them away and I said, "Hekate, take the sleep from Peter."

Now he will have insomnia and it's my fault. Those resolutions to take responsibility for my own life fled the minute Peter rang that second time.

I needed a spell for strength. I held both my thumbs and said a kind of nonsense thing to Fnoube and Abrasax about giving me strength. I said it seven times. I should have done that before I gave Peter insomnia. The repetition calmed me down.

My first love sounded just the way he had just before I escaped the house, carrying Nick. He always sounded as if he were in the right.

There were recipes for exorcism in Great-Grandma's box, but I left those alone. I had not even known Judaism had exorcism until I saw that formula. I made amulets. I convinced myself it was just to make a change in my offerings for the next craft stall. I could dress Zoë up in scarves and things and make her look as mysterious as a bubbly, cute, eleven-year-old blonde can look.

This is how I moved from being a shop girl to someone with a car. It's because I was scared. I did quite a few amulets for pregnant women and for protection against violence.

I told Rudolph I was in a frenzy of exotic jewellery making, and if he wanted to see me he would just have to put up with it. He laughed, of course. He also brought coffee and chocolate and ran an entertaining monologue when I became too quiet. Twice he cooked us all dinner. I wanted to damn his left heel when I found out he cooked to perfection. Rudolph is gourmet through and through.

I made Rudolph another amulet and told him it was for his love life. He laughed at me. I didn't tell him any of this was magic.

5.

"I have a friend who logs chats," TVwhore said, out of the blue. Rhonda stored this away for later worry.

"So what did I miss?" asked Phased.

"I was just saying that I am busier than you. I am a busy, busy, busy bee."

"Doing what?"

"You are such a curious little Phased," TVwhore mocked. "Don't you know MissTRie never answers questions like that."

"Tis true. I don't. I am a very perfect MissTRie indeed. My secret self is my very own."

"You're in a strange mood today," said Phased.

"I am, aren't I? Sorry," but Rhonda was unrepentant. What was there to repent? Especially since she was here with great plans and plots and they were unpacking themselves quite nicely. Silliness was a great shield.

"Well, don't be," Rhonda could have sworn that Phased's typing communicated crossness. Impossible. Typing was soulless, Rhonda had frequently betted her hidden side on that fact.

"I have a secret self, too, you know," said Starchild, the great peacemaker. "I really like my secret self."

"Tell!" TVwhore said.

"Yes, tell," said Phased.

"It's my iceberg," Starchild typed, the words loading on the screen phrase by phrase. "You already know the tip of it."

Three friends lined three question marks vertically:

"?"

"?"

"?"

"My knitting," Starchild explained. "I have a knitting business. I make fireman booties and funky baby teddy bears."

"You dress babies."

"I dress babies *beautifully*."

Rhonda laughed aloud and found herself translating that laugh into print, "LOL, Starchild. I love it."

"Except I'm not selling anything to you three."

"Why not?" from TVwhore.

"Because that's why I was keeping it secret. There's one corner of my life where I don't have to be continually meeting targets or checking colours and sizes."

"And if we want funky booties?" Rhonda found herself with a sudden yearning for tiny, tiny clothes.

"Then I'll refer you to a friend."

"I have a secret life, too," this was from Phased.

"Tell!" said TVwhore.

"I can't," Phased confessed. "Well, I can tell a bit. But it's hard."

"Why is it hard?"

"I'm sorting out a Past. My ex was . . . interesting. "

"In what way, interesting?" asked TVwhore.

"In a way we shouldn't be asking about," Rhonda typed, as repressively as she knew how. "Some secrets are secrets because they preserve sanity."

"Okay, I get the hint." TVwhore seemed unrepentant at having pushed Phased. "If ever you want to talk, sweetie, we're here." There was an extended silence.

"Drabbit," Rhonda said, "You really want my great secret."

"Of course we do," said TVwhore.

"Yep, indeed," said Starchild. Phased was silent.

"I play lawn bowls," Rhonda said. Her first decent lie of the day.

"That's IT?"

"Hey, lawn bowls are uncool. It took me great courage to admit I'm a closet player. Until then I was like Pharaoh."

"?" said Starchild.

"Huh?" said Phased. TVwhore was silent.

"In de-Nile."

"LOL," said Phased.

"My secret life is sexier," TVwhore finally said. "Makes lawn bowls look so wimpy."

"I'm biting my thumb at you, TVwhore," Rhonda typed.

"Hope it tastes nice," TVwhore said, and logged off.

"Damn, she's a tease," said Starchild.

"She'll tell us," said Phased. "I bet it is something to do with MissTRie."

"Why me?"

"She talks more to you than to the rest of us."

"She does," Rhonda admitted, "But that doesn't mean I'm linked to her secret life."

"You guys," said Starchild, "I have to go. Looking forward to your next stories!"

TVwhore posted a locked message in her blog. Rhonda had the really nasty suspicion that it was only visible to her.

"Have you worked out my secret life yet?" TVwhore said. "It should include you. You're important to me."

Rhonda suspected she was supposed to be reassured. She wasn't. She didn't respond. In fact, she hoped that if she ignored it long enough any growing problem with TVwhore would just fade into the woodwork.

6.

Rhonda was due a respite from life, the universe and everything. Especially everything. She was determined to force life, the universe and everything to give her one. Especially everything.

She wanted play money, and she needed to write without the looming fear of her talent manifesting. And she didn't want to go into the job agency. Rhonda wrote an article that was different to any she had written before. It was going to be her triumph over entropy.

The article had hardly any history. It took the heat off her innards. No roiling stomach. "Every good Rhonda deserves fruit," she said, and rewarded her virtue with a tart apple.

She walked with a lift to her step and showed off her literary skills to her boyfriend. Even the word 'boyfriend' added lift to her step. Her life was on the mend.

Rhonda was rather proud of the article. It was a bit literary. She wasn't sure she had ever managed literary before. It included a lie, just as every other article she had written recently. Her lies were little and meaningless, but she liked them. For no good reason, she liked them. Or maybe for a very good reason.

The lie in this article was that she still travelled. She admitted this to Dave, "I'm like the lady who wrote 'Hans Brinker and the Silver Skates.' I've created a pretence of travel." Dave said it was interesting but he doubted it would find a market.

"Bet you?" Rhonda asked.

"Sure," he laughed, and they recorded their bets on a

blank piece of paper stolen from the printer. "I'm certain the printer won't object," Dave joked.

Despite the fact that the article was pretentious and based on a lie, she sold it almost immediately. Rhonda was surprised at herself. Without even thinking twice about important things she needed, Rhonda spent the money on a new game for her computer. Dave's lost bet had helped buy a better quality game, so she magnanimously allowed him to play it with her.

One night when they were crowded close at the keyboard Rhonda's scores took a nose dive. "Goddam it," she said, and tried to redeem the situation.

Dave commented, "I didn't know you lived in the US of A."

"I thought it would scream out at you, given how many Americanisms creep into my speech. I did my doctorate in Syracuse, New York."

"No," he said, "It didn't even whisper to me until just now."

"'Goddam it' isn't really American," she defended herself.

"It wasn't the words, honey, it was the accent."

"It's your fault. You're infectious. Until you came along my US accent was dead as the dinosaurs."

More than his accent was infectious. Rhonda never thought she would find herself sharing her computer. She finally admitted to herself, clearly and without doubt, that she was in love.

"A forever love," she told herself, giving the emotion a romantic spin. She was exaggerating it, and knew it. He was the man of her affections, not the man of her dreams. "I wish I knew why these things happen. What a stupid thing to do with my life so precarious, to fall in love." She was smiling however. She smiled a lot, whenever she thought of Dave or saw his eyelashes cast his eyes into shadow or heard his voice on the phone.

Just his presence was enough. His big, comforting presence.

The next day, Rhonda absentmindedly tidied the paper recording the bet onto her 'All finished — need to dispose of thoughtfully' pile. As she placed it there, she noticed there was writing on the back.

She turned the paper over. It was her handwriting again. The date was today's and the time was one a.m.

7.

Belinda finally came through with information about the sefirot and the tree of life diagram. They make sense of Ada's note that complained they were nothing to do with magic and just another way of understanding the universe (both masculine and feminine). Great-Grandma was practical rather than mystical. Anyway, Belinda's email said that sefirot named aspects of God. Ada refers to I Chronicles 29: Binah is understanding, Chesed is mercy, Chochmah is wisdom, Gevurah is strength, Hod is majesty, Keter is the crown, Malkut is sovereignty, Netzach is victory, Tiferet is glory, Yesod is foundation. If I type it enough, maybe it'll stick. No wonder Ada wrote notes.

There's so much non-Jewish magic around that I'm trying to sort out what's genuinely from my tradition and what isn't. GG has a list called Nephilim (sounds Greek to me, but then everything sounds Greek to me) where there are beings with strange names. She explains what they can be called for. Azazel was the one I called for my jewellery work. She notes that he is bound head and foot in the dark and may not come. She also casts doubt on his existence. Which to me suggests he would not come if you called. Even though I called him.

I thought that was funny, but Zoë is looking over

my shoulder and said, "Mummy," in the exact tone of voice that suggests I was being stupid. When she's older and less cute I might be rude when she uses that particular tone of voice on me. And yes, Zoë, that was a warning. I'm not sure what I'm warning you about, but I'm definitely warning you. Now shh, I'm writing brilliant prose.

I was going to list them all, but I've changed my mind. There was a second list that included more familiar names. Raphael was linked with men, for instance. These names are not important in some ways, because the magic recipes suggest they're substitutes for the names of God. Lesser substitutes. If you call on them in their own right — not as substitutes — then you're worshipping them. Which is, of course, un-Jewish.

Anyway, the really fun bit of this long note in Ada's box was what came after these lists. She says what I just said, that the names of angels are mostly a perfectly good substitute for the name of God, not as powerful, but less theologically worrying. She also says, and this time I will give her own words:

How you make certain that knowledge is not abuse: a good education in ethics is an improvement on seeking great power. So does one have a responsibility to pass down knowledge to children? Not always. One must give the following generations the core, however, otherwise all is in danger of being lost. Without ethics, what cautions do you give to ensure your daughters use their knowledge wisely? Scientific training is not the answer. Women with big hair are just as troublesome as men with beards, when they confine their thinking to science.

I bet she wrote that note in anger. My daughter, the doctor who won't listen.

Great-Grandma wrote things down with explanations and I'm systematising it. Everyone in our family analyses: myself, Belinda, and Ada. No wonder the family moved into science.

Anyway, back to demons. They're much more ambivalent than Christian demons. The thing that seems to make them demons is not how good or bad they are. It's because they do not work for God. If you call on them you are worshipping false gods. Simple. Nothing to it.

Some are quite nasty — there are *sheydim* who are violent, *mazikim* who destroy things, and *ruachim* who are spirits. Some of them are good for fortune telling and sometimes a *ruach* talks directly to you and teaches you deep secrets of the universe. That's all I know. I don't know what sort lives in lemon trees and bathrooms.

Great-Grandma didn't leave names. She wasn't encouraging her descendants to worship false gods, I expect. She might not have appreciated those neighbours who gave idiot gifts to my nice tree.

Which brings me back to the history of the lemon tree.

8.

There was a knock on the door. Isn't that a nice opening sentence for a story? It was early evening and we'd just got in. There actually *was* a knock on the door.

Zoë was pretending to do her homework — you could see her feet tapping out a dance rhythm under her desk, if you looked from the right angle.

Nick wasn't visible. He wouldn't appear until I yelled out 'dinner' at the foot of the stairs. I could probably call out from the kitchen with the same effect, but I like going to the stairs and screaming at him.

The tap was so quiet I didn't hear it. Zoë was

opening the door before I noticed anything. Standing quietly at the front door were two kids, a couple of years younger than Zoë. I know they were unknown because, instead of talking to them, Zoë looked them up and down and called, "Mummy!"

I said, "Yes, dear," from right behind her.

They were nice children. They wanted me to have something they had been given by someone hiding in our tree. I took a look at the coins. This was not small change from Belinda's overseas trips. They looked like solid gold. And they were no currency I had ever seen.

"I'm sorry," I said, and handed the coins back. "These aren't ours. Whoever was in the tree was playing some kind of joke on you."

"What do we do with them?" asked the taller girl.

"Ask your parents to take them to the police for you, perhaps," I suggested.

"They're from your tree," the shorter child said. "They're yours."

"What did the man in the tree say when he gave them to you?"

"He told us where to find them and said there would be lots more if we prayed to him and gave him presents."

"That's a stupid thing to say," Zoë said, voice full of scorn.

"I know," said the girl patiently. This was one well-brought-up girl. "But he left the coins next to the foot-path so we thought we should bring them to you."

"That was very thoughtful of you," I said. "Why don't you come in and Zoë will find you biscuits and cordial and we can ring your parents and talk about what to do."

The kids told me their names and address and I used the phone book intelligently. Their mother came over within short order, and Zoë entertained the visitors in the kitchen while the mother and I discussed the coins over coffee in the lounge room. I told her how impressed I was with her children, but said that the coins were not ours.

"I suggest you take them to the police. If they get claimed as lost property then the real owner gets them back. If no one claims them then your children should keep them," was my learned opinion.

"You're sure they're not yours?" The lady was anxious. If it had been Zoë and Nick who had done the finding I would have been anxious in exactly the same way.

"Absolutely." What I wasn't sure about was that man in the lemon tree. However, I couldn't share the truth with a stranger. I had a thought. "We've been finding all sorts of things left at the foot of our tree for a little while now — we just leave them a bit then give them to charity when it gets too cluttered. The kids and I will keep an eye out at this end, but it sounds to me that this is not just an idiot playing practical jokes. You might want to warn your children to stay clear of the tree, and let the police know."

"I find the whole thing worrying," said the nice lady.

"So do I. I'm going to find out who is using our tree and what on earth they mean by it, and I am determined to stop them." She looked reassured.

"In the meantime, take those coins and leave them with the police," I insisted. "That way we're all in the clear if some idiot is doing something illegal."

She did what she promised and I did what I promised. The police didn't take it seriously. They thought the whole thing was a prank. In fact, they thought it was Nick.

Our family never found anything at the base of the tree. No coins; no gifts; it did not talk to us. This fitted with it being whatever thing had fled from our bathroom.

This mess had one really bad consequence. Like the police, one of our neighbours decided that the whole thing was a really stupid practical joke by Nick. Nick is not into really stupid practical jokes. So he was deeply offended and, naturally, went into sulks. The police came to warn him off his tricks. He went to school, he went to work, and the rest of the time he spent in his room being miserable.

I had to take action. I was not going to tell the whole world we had a demon-infested lemon tree. I checked all the instructions we had on making demon bowls and it fell short of what we actually needed. But I felt that a demon bowl might still be what we had to do. So I sought expert advice.

I yelled for Zoë. She was getting very good at magic. I waved the paper at her and said it had a mention of a devil and maybe it was related to our lovely lemon tree.

"It's not a lovely lemon tree," she snorted.

"It was until it took on its own personality," I said.

"Sure, Mum," she replied, sounding dangerously teenagerish. She read the paper aloud, just in case I had missed anything. I presume that is why it was read aloud. She could not have assumed I was that stupid. She read:

Sneeze on a Monday you sneeze for danger;
Sneeze on a Tuesday you kiss a stranger;
Sneeze on a Wednesday you sneeze for a letter;
Sneeze on a Thursday for something better;
Sneeze on a Friday you sneeze to your sorrow;
Sneeze on a Saturday your sweetheart tomorrow;
Sneeze on a Sunday your safety seek,
The devil will chase you the whole of the week (unless you trap that devil in a bowl).

"We used to say the sneezing rhyme when we were

kids," I explained in my most motherly tone. If she could be supercilious, I could be condescending. In fact, condescending was rather fun. "It's the little bit after that interests me."

"Great-Grandma says we trap devils in bowls," she thought aloud. "And Auntie has that bowl."

"That is what I was thinking. I checked on the Net and it looks like there's an exhibition of demon bowls in the US." I refrained from saying how old the demon bowls were — they were neither nineteenth century nor English. But they did look like Great-Grandma's. "We need to find how to catch it in a bowl. Then I can make lemon marmalade."

"And I can make pancakes with sugar and lemon."

"And we can all live happy ever after."

"I will look through the box tomorrow," Zoë promised. "And I'll write down every time it mentions demons and devils."

"You will do your homework first," I instructed firmly.

I have to admit, Zoë worked hard at collecting information. She did indeed write down every single mention of devils and demons from Ada's papers. She used highlighters to show where they all fitted together. She even went on the Internet and checked in an encyclopaedia.

Alas, we were missing something crucial. Four days of hard work and we were back where we started, with a strange creature in the lemon tree and no way of getting rid of it. I did something I'd been longing to do ever since the thing started tempting the masses into worship, and I went to the backyard and swore at it.

The lemon tree laughed at me. Deep and resonant laughter. Like the rumble that had previously haunted our bloody pipe system. It's very humiliating to be laughed at by a lemon tree.

It also threw slices of lemon at me. Elegant slices. I damned its toes and ears and eyes. Then I found myself wondering if it had ears and eyes and toes.

I refused to be treated in such a cavalier fashion by a bloody tree. They were my lemons, and it was my corner of the garden, and I wanted it all back. I did not have the courage to cut the tree down. I went back to GG's papers with the intent of reading them laterally.

What I found was curious. I didn't know whether it would help. The papers had a spell for learning seventy languages. All the languages of the world, it claimed. I looked up the seventy language bit in my rather odd reference book collection.

Solomon spoke seventy languages. They were not the languages of people. They were the languages of wildlife. All the people (men, which made me grumpy — the kids got macaroni-cheese for two nights running, so grumpy was I — and yes, I made them eat all their salad, and no, there was no dessert) who learned the seventy languages were given warnings about impending doom and could thereby avoid it. One rabbi learned of a demon in a tree. Just like ours.

Zoë and I decided we would spend the weekend learning seventy languages. I do love saying it like that. I'm not even capable of learning one language, and here I was trusting in a spell to teach me seventy. If we were going to live surreal, we might as well think surreal, I said to my daughter. My daughter paid no attention to me.

This spell worked beautifully. I do hate it when spells work. I would rather that my ancestress were deluded and half mad.

I don't know how we understand birds and animals and insects — it's not like they use speech or even think rationally. But if we talk about something, there are certain thoughts that come to us, or phrases, and we know they are from birds or rabbits or whatever. It took another week of talking and thinking and asking before we put together what the currawong thought with what the pigeons thought with what all sorts of other stray creatures thought and got some sort of answer. And it was just as confusing as it sounds.

It made Rudolph a little jumpy, because I kept reacting to comments from under the floorboards. He started watching me as if I were someone new in his life. He even started sending chocolates again. I didn't have time for that. I didn't want to make time for that. I ate the chocolates and paid no attention to the rest.

Nick didn't notice a thing.

I was right with my initial thought: demons, it appeared, get trapped in demon bowls. Like the one Belinda had of Great-Grandma's. The exhibition on the world wide web on demon bowls said something about them coming in pairs with eggshells, so we put that to the various wildlife and received the oddest strayest thoughts.

I wish it were possible to turn the skill on and off. I know exactly where the termites are headed. I am safe from attacks by killer magpies. But they never shut up! Perpetual babble, in every crevice of the damn house! Bloody Zoë says we can't use pesticide on creatures we understand. I nearly used it on her when she said that. Being nice should not include termites and silverfish.

Ada and her daughter must have seen the world differently. Ada listened to beetles and her daughter listened to stethoscopes. I have a scene in my mind where Great-Grandma tells her daughter about something important, and the daughter asked sarcastically, "And just how did you find that out? From the pigeons?" and Great-Grandma answered, "From your daughter's pet rabbit."

I told Zoë my little scenario, and she worried about

Belinda not knowing the seventy languages. I got the world's most distressed phone call from Linnie the next night. Belinda had followed a set of instructions Zoë had emailed her, saying, "It's for school." That weekend Zoë and I and Great-Grandma's box went to Canberra.

Linnie says it's great. As a teacher, it gives her eyes in the back of her head. My suspicion is that she suspends disbelief for short times only. For her there is no perpetual wall of talk.

Linnie took Zoë out to buy clay, while I wrote out instructions. Belinda insisted on those instructions, because she complained that Zoë and I babbled. Babbled! All we were doing was copying the bowl. I was offended. I used my angriest handwriting:

1. Take clay
2. Mould 1/3 of clay to shape one bowl.
3. Mould 1/3 of clay to shape second bowl.
4. Copy writing from ancestral bowls onto new bowls.
5. While bowls dry, stuff rest of clay down Linnie's throat.
6. Write notes for Linnie on the importance of clay as a source of roughage in a healthy diet.

We only got as far as item four on my list. I was bribed with chocolate truffles to forgo the rest. Later I found that the truffles had been my own, stolen by Zoë from my secret hoard.

When we arrived home, we put our eggs in the bowl as bait (eggs are to demons as chocolate truffles are to Judiths) and said the incantation. The whole tree quaked and shivered. Zoë and I quaked and shivered along with it. We held our ground and our bowls and we said the spell again. The second time there was a whoosh into Zoë's bowl. I clapped my bowl quickly over it.

It was trapped. We sealed the bowls with pitch in classic tradition. Stinky stuff, pitch. It'd already killed Zoë's tee-shirt. We used Zoë's defunct top to wrap the bowls containing the irritating creature and we buried them very deep.

It's done. No one gets strange coins from our lemon tree or offers it sacrifices. I've not been pelted with lemon slices for so long I am almost over the experience. I have to say though, that if you want bumper crops, you cannot do better than bury an unhappy demon in a set of bowls at its base, nicely entombed in a tarry pink tee-shirt.

9.

Close one door and another opens. Or rather, choose your path with care. My message to my poor innocent self.

And another message to my self, that you/I may choose consciously: remember Auntie Jane. We use the name to share history with the world — do not forget her.

After that think on the family tree.

Rhonda threw the paper to the floor as if it were a serpent. She couldn't remember writing or thinking any of the substance of the note. Its existence gave Rhonda the creeps. She hated, hated, hated the thought that her mind could do things without her. Drugs had been bad enough.

And why Auntie Jane? She could find out about her aunt, even if the rest remained a bit of a mystery.

Rhonda resolved to ask Sam about Auntie Jane next time he rang. Then she realised. The family tree. That was what was tugging at her memory. It was her mother's family. GAM's family.

CHAPTER NINE

1.

"No CAN DO."

"I'm sorry?" Considering the question, Rhonda was perplexed.

"Do you want me to spell it out?" The Sleazoid looked across his desk, with a pretence of boredom. "There are no jobs that fit your skill sets."

"None at all? Are you absolutely certain?" Rhonda didn't believe what she was hearing. She wasn't sure that she could do anything about it either. The agency had made it very clear that case managers were gods. She knew it was supposed to be an affirmative action agency, she reflected, but the longer she knew it the more closely this place resembled a cesspool. "Not even for data entry?"

"Not a thing," and he smiled and leant across the desk confidentially. "And I'll tell you what. There won't be anything for two months. Maybe three. It depends. And after that, it also depends."

"Thank you for all your efforts." Rhonda tried to sound sarcastic, but ended up just sounding small. She had to get out before she did something she would regret, like tip that carafe of water over his head.

She found the nearest café. Coffee was the source of all good, and her brain really needed that good.

Rhonda was not going to bring Dave in. Her bluff had been called. Damn Mr Ick.

After the coffee she was still short of money. More coffee wasn't going to secure her a job. Nor peace of mind. She had the choice between surviving without the extra work — which was possible, but made life with Dave a little awkward — or doing something drastic. She thought of not paying her ticket at the movies or her share of dinners, and her mouth went tight. Her pride was at stake.

Rhonda girded her loins with that pride and went back to the temp agency. She asked the receptionist if it was possible to see someone more senior than Mr Ick. The receptionist gave her a pitying look. Rhonda ignored the look. Rhonda ignored everything except the pale green corridor to the senior manager's office. She knocked. Her knuckles sounded faint on the glass.

"Come in," a male voice said. Behind the desk was another Mr Ick. Oily and well fed. Satisfied with life. Looking her up and down as if she were a prime cut of meat.

Rhonda sat down and explained that she thought that there was a personality clash between her and her case manager and that it was minimising her chances of work, which was reducing potential agency income. She liked that last bit.

Her brave declaration was answered by a shark's smile.

"I was told you might come and see me," the manager said. "It's against our policy to change case managers for trivial matters. You'll have to sort out any problems you might have directly." In other words, buzz off, girlie, you are his.

She went to get another coffee, to think more about her options. Most particularly, any options she could drum up which would avoid her walking through that door. To help her think, she used a pen and paper, and her diary.

The ideal approach, Rhonda realised with a heaviness, did not include any other temp agency. This was no big city.

Her pen bit into the paper as she contemplated. She found herself drawing columns. What expenses did she have coming up? How much of her expenditure was used on a social life with Dave?

A half-hour later she had rows and figures in her little notebook. If it weren't for GAM, work would have been essential and Rhonda would have had no choices. But the numbers worked out. Barely. She might have to swallow her pride with Dave in terms of who paid the entertainment bills, but she could balance that by cooking. They could have lots of home-cooked meals. Very romantic.

That was how she'd do it. Polish her candlesticks and give him a romantic dinner and get them both out of the going-out-to-dine habit.

The big issue was Dave's birthday. His present was the only item on her list of expenses that was starred as essential, but didn't fall within the GAM-based budget. Rhonda drank the dregs of her coffee, rolling some chance-found grounds over her tongue as a thinking aide. Her tongue didn't enjoy the grittiness and she said to it, "Tough, tongue." Then she smiled a satisfied smile. There was a happy solution, even to this. She swallowed the grounds.

Rhonda didn't have to buy him a silver-plated whiskey bottle. She didn't have to — when she thought about it — buy him a thing. She would make him something. It was not second best, but a much better idea all round. Dave's reading glasses would have an embroidered case.

The only loose end was Sleazoid. Rhonda wanted to sort him out. Truly she did. She should've taken the date rape thing to the police as Dave had wanted. She really should have. Except all the Sleazoid had done was feed her the drug in a drink, and even that was not provable. Dave had been optimistic and she had been scared. Now she was pessimistic.

Rhonda drew little daggers dripping blood next to each and every line in her table. She nearly drew another picture, with the daggers dotted nicely over different parts of the Sleazoid's body.

She went home still cursing, and started to embroider the curses into her embroidery pattern. Very Gothic. Very angry.

Rhonda looked back at her handiwork two days later and pondered on it. Something was missing. It was too much grey and black. Gothic, yes, but boringly so. Rhonda used her silks and a needle to paint a little red rose in one corner. It was a declaration to herself as much as to Dave.

Somehow, the cursing and the anger had transmuted into something softer while she had been working on his gift. In the transmutation she had made an astonishing discovery. Dave was the bedrock of her world.

He took her past the Sleazoid's latest without even batting his long eyelashes. Most of this was because some article he was chasing up was going astray, and so when he came round he was quite happy to snuggle in front of TV with home-made dinner.

Rhonda worried about this with a part of her brain, but when she quizzed him he just said that he needed to come up with a new approach to a problem. And in trying not to let Rhonda worry about his concerns, he never focussed on hers. Which was unlike him, but his quiet support on the home front was quite sufficient to her needs.

Dave's birthday dinner was perfectly elegant. Everything was white and silver. Rhonda explained that that the colour scheme was in memory of their first meeting.

"I don't recall the club being those colours," he said, puzzled.

"I meant the bathroom." Rhonda was pleased at the way she said this, all dry amusement.

Dave laughed and laughed. Then he held her tight, and said, "God, I'm glad I found you."

"I always wanted to ask," said Rhonda, from the safety of his arms, "if you really fell in love with me at first sight."

"Not quite." Dave's breath warmed her ear. "It took a full five minutes."

"Then you're quite mad," Rhonda declared, and kissed him. "And the birthday present I made you is perfect."

"You made me a present?"

"Don't sound so astonished."

"Honey, no one has made me a present since I was ten."

"Don't sound so hopeful, either. I took artistic liberties."

"Gimme!"

"After dinner," said Rhonda primly, and skipped away from him to serve up. He followed her into the kitchen and wrapped his arms around her. "Out," she said, "You're in my way. I'm spoiling you tonight."

"I am spoiling for another type of spoiling," Dave hinted.

"Maybe later," Rhonda said, as sternly as she could. "Go sit down now so I can serve."

He went. He sat. He conversed nicely. The whole evening, however, she was the centre of his attention. It felt warm and comforting. More warm, Rhonda realised around dessert, than comforting.

After dinner she gave him his present.

"You made this," he marvelled.

"It would have been a bit prettier except it turned to Goth and it stayed Goth."

"I like it like this," Dave admitted. "I would never carry anything pretty. Is there a reason for the flower? It kind of draws the eye."

"Don't you know the language of flowers? Red roses mean passionate love," Rhonda mocked.

As she said those words she felt a rumbling inside, but suppressed it. Not even a subterranean roar could worry her that night. She was far more interested in the large gentleman who was suddenly looking at her with very specific intent.

2.

The next episode in our roller coaster year was more enjoyable. Not for me. God forbid I should ever be allowed to enjoy life. My boss had started to drop dark hints about Rudolph, which had turned me wary of him again. I was still returning mail to Peter unopened and looking very carefully at phone numbers before picking the phone up.

Anyway, one day the phone rang. It was not Peter.

Dr Cow Eyes was ringing to tell us he had a job interview in Canberra and had to cancel dinner. That dinner had its own importance, because he was nearing the end of the translations. Soon all the strange papers in Hebrew and Aramaic would be equally strange pa-

pers in English. We were lucky that he had a low
boredom threshold, or was a bit lonely, or whatever it
was that had got him interested when I went in to
see him.

I decided to push our luck. I reminded him that I
had a sister in Canberra. I pointed out that she was single, heterosexual and a natural blonde. He laughed at
me. I asked if he would invite her to dinner anyway.

"Will she tell me lurid stories about your childhood?" he asked.

"Sure to," I said despondently.

"Then consider it done. What's her phone number?"

I know things went swimmingly because Belinda
refused to talk about it at first. Dr Cow Eyes didn't talk
about Belinda either, when he came to dinner the next
week. I was hoping this was also a good sign. It might
have been that they hated each other's guts, but I had
my doubts. My doubts were based on a phone call from
my sister a few days after Dr Nick dined with us.

She had a night out with other teachers and they all
got very drunk. I need to get her drunk a few more
times and find out how much of poetic obscurity was
her being drunk and how much was me leading her on.
A scientific experiment.

She started the conversation with a very fairytale, "I
found the perfect man, oh sister mine. Taurean, meek
and mild."

"Does he have long lean thighs, as Grandma would
have wanted?" I was guilty of encouraging her. And
that Taurean meek and mild thing was almost word for
word what Grandma had said when we were children,
about the perfect man.

"Yes, all the things that a gentle man is supposed to
have."

"And this time are you going to listen to your heart
or your family stereotypes?"

"I don't know yet."

"Does he have long lean toes, too?"

"I don't know yet."

"When you find out, tell me."

"No way. If I see him naked, I'm not giving a report to my sister."

"You know, a swimming trip would reveal his toes just as effectively as getting into bed with him."

"You're denying me all my fun in life!" This was not going to give me where he lived. "Just because you met him first doesn't mean you get to know everything about him. He thinks you're a laugh a minute, by the way. He suggests we go to Sydney regularly for the performances in Newtown."

It was Dr Nick.

3.

I have no idea why I feel it essential to tell you all about the magic Zoë and I did. It can't be because I feel guilty whenever I do any magic. Because I don't. Well, yes, I do. God, I'm confused today. I poured boiling water on my toast this morning.

I could take a break from typing and clear my brain that way, or I could tell you more about Great-Grandma's box. The cause of all evil. I was never confused about things before that box came along. And I'm a chronic liar, yes, I am.

Tonight I'm on my own. I never let myself get on my own. Bloody awful thought. On my own is when I think that it's Peter at the door. I'll just find something from that box and get myself carried away by ancestral strangeness. Safer. Much safer. I don't want to talk about what happened next with Rudolph.

My boss happened next. She gave up on dark hints and told me straight out. Rudolph was not reliable. Or rather, he had reliably slept with half my friends. She said he said he liked feminists because of the challenge.

Now, some of this matched the Rudolph I had seen, and some of it didn't. The trouble is I was in no state to sort things out. I didn't want to face him on it. I didn't even want to think about it. I wished my boss hadn't told me. I wished Rudolph had never walked into that shop and decided to chat me up. Damn his winning smile.

And so much for dispelling a bad day by talking spells. All I've done is make myself worse.

I'm going to steal whatever fiction my kids have left lying around, make some hot chocolate, and read. That won't help at all, will it? I need to do something useful. Make my spot in the world secure. I have no submissions or anything on the boil. Damn. Damn. Damn.

I'm going back to Ada. That other Ada, the non-magic variety. I'm going to write down all we know about her. We know she went riding on bikes, and that she was separated but not divorced. We know her family disowned her sister, who turned Christian (and was possibly a bit strange). We think she hated her husband, and that she was such a mistress of misleading that we aren't sure if half the things she said were true. We know she loved her single child, and sacrificed her to the Gods of Modern Science. We know her solitary child hated her. We know I have her figure (damn her roly-poly shoulders).

And we don't know much more. In every kid's book with magic there's a way of calling up the dead and asking them questions. Why doesn't that Great Spell allow me to call up Great-Grandma, ask her questions, then damn her toes for not writing things down properly in the first place?

Why did she leave us that box at all?

While I'm distracting myself with magic and its various linked ideas (like Zoë's obsession with using spells), I shall redeem my promise to talk about the Jewish zodiac. All that mazal.

Ada deplored living in the southern hemisphere. There's a note on the back of one of her astrological readings saying that, and at great length. Lots of lovely round phrases and immense sentences. Also some gloriously long words. The southern skies were a source of distress. None of the lore her mother taught her applied. She couldn't just replace Sirius and the constellations. I wonder why she couldn't ask someone to teach her?

What's strange is that somehow, over the years, the family has managed to apply the northern sky knowledge to the southern skies. We have an inordinate number of family sayings about the moon in Scorpio or thunder from Gemini. I checked it out, and our attributions bear no resemblance to real astrology, so it's another thing that our family does differently.

Anyway, this made me think that the reason we have so few charts may be that they were done for her, and in England.

The mazal thing Belinda explained ages ago, but I still get tangled on the philosophy side of magic. Because it comes up over and over again in Great-Grandma's papers, and because it now underpins my life one way or another, I thought I should explain that our zodiac (our family one) isn't quite the same as the modern zodiac. Besides, I feel amazingly guilty that I put hints of spells in here without actually giving anyone enough material or do any magic. So a bit of nice throwaway knowledge might assuage my guilt. Then again it might not.

Bad memories and even badder children. Both of them are in their rooms sulking. And no, it is nothing I did wrong and it is very much something they did wrong. Together they wrought great mischief. They flooded the bathroom and then nearly burned down the kitchen. I still feel guilty. So here is the Zodiac. As described by MTGG.

There's a ram or sheep, which must be Aries, and a bull for Taurus. Gemini is Siamese twins, and cancer is not a crab at all, but a feminist. Actually, she is a queen on a throne and wears purple shoes, and any enthroned woman wearing purple is a feminist in my book. So Cancer is now the official sign of Jewish feminists — I say so.

Libra is a man holding scales, Sagittarius is an archer (human), Capricorn is a goat, Aquarius is someone androgynous getting water from a well, Leo is a lion and Pisces is a fish. And that's it for my series of detours into theoretical magic.

4.

Witchcraft was worrying Rhonda. She didn't want to write about it. But she was committed to an article.

The trouble was that she had given a blanket 'yes' to the series based on Mackay's book. When she'd said she would do it, she was given a list of topics to cover in the introductory articles and then told to do the rest in any order she wanted. Her eye had focussed on the cool subjects and the safe subjects. Her eye had entirely skipped over the heading 'The Witch Mania'. What a clever eye I had, Rhonda informed herself ungently.

She made up for her discomfort with sarcasm about ancestral witches. Ancestral demons. Ancestral anything she could name that fitted in with the witch craze. She had still a niggling feeling that she would have been burned as a witch if she had been in another place and another time.

Rhonda had revelled in studying the witch craze as

an undergraduate; that was the lunatic element in this whole equation. That was the year she'd decided to face the inner demon. For a full six months she had thought, 'I can defeat this thing by understanding it'.

Part of the problem was that the university subject had been named to get students. Witches had hardly come into focus that whole semester. Nor had witchcraft. Not a single magical potion or mystical formula in sight. Nor any thoughts on the culture and thoughts of the women in question. They were reified. Women made into objects.

Instead of looking at the women who were being accused of witchcraft, the class had scrutinised how society acted towards people they thought were witches. And she'd already known what society thought of people like her. So all she learned that semester was that there was a long history of people acting the same way people always acted. Stupidly and cruelly. And that the moment one was accused, one stopped being a real person.

The story of her adulthood: look it in the face, fail; drug it into oblivion, fail; flee it, fail; hide her face from the world. And retain humanity. Never let the world decide who she was. Remain Rhonda.

And now she had to look at witches again. Must write an article about witches.

Rhonda didn't. She went to a movie instead. She stole the money from her grocery budget, because she really, really needed that movie. A magic-free movie, with no superheroes and no extraordinary powers. It was, in fact, a very bad movie. It fitted her mood divinely. She employed her sarcasm tearing it to pieces online.

The movie and the verbal massacre of its many failings calmed Rhonda down enough so that she could open Mackay the next evening and see what he had to say about witch mania. She had a bottle of whiskey and a glass ready in case she couldn't stomach it.

Before she could read even a word, Dave rang. Rhonda joyously used him as an excuse for more postponement. "Hi!" Rhonda let her voice demonstrate her joy.

"Have I saved you from yourself?' Dave asked.

"No, you saved me from worrying about work. I have a bottle of whiskey at hand should I need saving from myself."

There was a silence.

"I rang last night and you didn't answer."

"I didn't answer because I was out. I had the screaming meemies and the conniptions and a pink fit all at once, and so I took myself to the movies."

"Alone?'

"Of course alone. Dave, what's wrong?"

"I could've gone with you."

"I didn't want company, not even yours. I just needed to be stupid."

"Well, I think it was stupid, very stupid. And now you're working with a bottle of whiskey. I think that's damn stupid."

"Dave, is there something wrong?" The line crackled but Dave was silent. "Dave?"

"You're self-destructive sometimes, you know that? And you hide things from everyone. I don't know even a tenth of you."

Rhonda didn't know if she should laugh or cry or scream. "I haven't changed. I'm the same person as a week ago and a month ago." Dave was a gaping hole on the end of the phone and Rhonda kept talking to fill the void. "I do things by myself a lot," she explained, as if she had been caught shoplifting. "It isn't a big deal. I've been single for a long time. And anyway, no one owns me. Not Tony, not Lana, not the kids, not my friends, not you."

He didn't say a word.

"Can you come over here?" Rhonda could hear the desperation in her voice. "We need to talk."

"I dunno," said Dave. "I just don't know. Give me a few days."

Rhonda had no idea what to make of any of it. She didn't know if Dave's work was getting him down, or if he'd been told to leave the country, or if he'd suddenly seen what a true loser she'd always been.

Sometimes, there was no escape in lies. Sometimes, there was no bearing the truth. She looked at the whiskey on her desk and was tempted, very tempted. She looked at the computer and wanted none of it. In the end, she went to bed with a vampire novel. It was the sane solution.

CHAPTER TEN

1.

I'M NOT THE ONLY ONE WHO FOUND MAGIC STRANGELY
addictive.

You remember our lemon tree? You remember that
there were two nice children? And that there was one
man who was not so nice and yelled at the tree for
giving him coins he could not sell?

One day, not long after the demon was safely
buried, Nick found the man lopping branches off our
tree with a pruning implement. All the while he was
swearing at it for mistreating him. Nick shooed him
away. Gods, I was glad it wasn't Zoë who came home
by the back lane that day!

We called the police and said he was a loony and we
were scared of him. We showed the branches in the
laneway and the devastation done to the tree. Not that
it didn't need pruning, mind you, but not really at that
moment and certainly not in that lopsided and vicious
way. The police promised to keep an eye out. Day after
day, more of the overhang onto the laneway was cut
off. Soon the tree had a vertical line up its side. The police didn't seem to be able to do anything.

None of us saw the man after Nick sent him packing. That was something. But our tree was gradually being demolished, and every few days we had to clear up the new debris and moan the diminution of its glorious self. Rudolph was good about helping us clear up, and I tried to forget what the boss had said about him. I tried incredibly hard. I watched his beautiful smile and smiled back and made bad jokes, and every joke was hard labour.

I may not be a gardener, but I've loved that lemon tree since we moved in. It smells so fresh and gives such fabulous fruit. In season, you can see its sunshine from the other end of the lane: it's how I know I am home and safe.

What we needed was a warning system. What we wanted was something that would wreak havoc and let loose the dogs of safety. Damn, Shakespeare didn't quite write it like that.

I had a secret consultation with my clever younger child. She reminded me that we understood the languages of the birds and the bees. Damn those birds and bees, they are ubiquitous. I looked at her suspiciously and asked if I had talked to her about those things. Zoë said to me, "Don't be stupid, Mum. Those sorts of talks went out with the dark ages." And yes, I was quoting.

Not that I wanted desperately to give her a talk on sexual awareness and stuff. Trying to talk with Nick about it a few years ago had been tough enough. But being called stupid was not harmonious. Besides, I was simply asking an important question as it occurred to me.

I asked her if she couldn't leave off being a teenager for a bit longer, and if she was going to call me stupid, to do so safely behind my back where I couldn't hear. Because she was grounded that weekend. She smiled a little smile. I need a new punishment for her, one that has the desired effect. One that has any effect at all would be nice.

Anyway, she was right about the birds and the bees. I told her to listen for changes in their song; she wanted me to be more specific. I said, "Whatever," in my most articulate manner and moved on to the most important aspects.

When the man was in sight, she could ring the police. And she was not to stay outdoors to watch him heave into sight for the opportunity to ring the police. Nor was she to peep out from the windows and be seen. Zoë was to run into the house and pretend no one was home.

She got that.

2.

Rhonda checked her email and found that there was a comment on a blog post. It was from TVwhore. Rhonda was too emotionally fatigued to let it worry her.

TVwhore "Hi, you — if you can come online I'll meet you in this chat room."

TVwhore was obviously just going to hang online until Rhonda turned up to chat. Rhonda felt obligated to check out what TVwhore wanted. Not merely a strange thing to do, but a very odd way of doing it.

In her abstraction she nearly logged herself in as 'Rhonda', but she caught herself, and replaced it with MissTRie. Her hands knew she didn't want to be in a chat room; she had other things to think about. Her brain knew that if a friend needed her then a friend needed her. And there, in the chat room, was TVwhore, waiting patiently. She ignored her disquiet.

"Hi there. Hope I haven't kept you waiting."

"It's fine. I had lots to keep me occupied. Caught up on my reading."

"You didn't say what you wanted to see me about. Is anything wrong?"

"You're a sweetie. Thank you for being concerned. Nothing's wrong. I just needed to chat."

"Okay then."

There was a long pause. Rhonda racked her brains for safe subjects. "What've you been up to?" she asked.

"Oh, this and that." TVwhore claimed nothing was wrong and yet was having trouble talking.

It was all too much. First Dave and now TVwhore. Although at least TVwhore wanted to spend time with her, she wished Dave could be persuaded into the same thing. Rhonda sighed.

Time for a diversion. What was the absolutely safest subject she could think of? "What's the weather like?"

"I live in England. What do you think the weather is like?"

"Hot and humid. You have tropical plants creeping down your chimney pot."

"Why do I have tropical plants creeping down my chimney pot?"

"Global warming, of course."

"Thank you, MissTRie."

"For a bad joke?"

"No, for coming here."

"So nothing is actually wrong? You just need company."

"Yes."

"I can deal with that. How about we do something really stupid?"

"How stupid?"

"Did you ever play 'I spy' when you were a kid?"

TVwhore let a smile-icon sneak onto the screen. "Of course."

"Then how about we play it right now?"

Three smile icons lined up in a row. Rhonda breathed a sigh of relief. Whatever the problem had been, she had averted it. "I like it. I'll start. I spy with my little eye . . ."

3.

Being constantly aware of who was walking through the gate was tiring. It didn't matter who it was, I jumped as if it were that piece of walking slime. The first couple of times it was Nick, and then it was one of Zoë's friends, and Rudolph kept appearing as well. Rudy's appearing was beginning to distress me as much as the weirdo's: I just couldn't shake those comments about him. Every disarming wrinkle about his eyes, every smart comment, every winning way was especially designed to make me hurt.

It took us a little while to sort out what the creatures of the fields were saying. I don't know how Belinda handles it, but the way I handle it is confusedly. If you ask me for a race tip, I will tell you that the sun is going to shine nicely for a little.

When he ran out of sections of tree that he could reach from the lane, Mr Weirdo came into the yard. Bit by bit, he was hacking things down and pulling out plants. A little at a time. He never stayed long enough for the police to catch him.

I was not impressed. But I was scared. As his depredations took him closer and closer to the back door, I got more and more scared. Once he came right to the back door and upturned pot plants then threw the empty pots at the wire screen. The police just missed him that time. We were out of the house by the front door, just in case.

The next time he came to the front door. He didn't

actually do anything. He looked at the door. A neighbour told us this. He examined the door carefully, looking at the hinges and everything. Standing a little behind him was another man. Unkempt and in tatters.

This was the last straw for Nick. Nick knocked on every door and told each of our neighbours about him and asked them to ring the police if they should see him. The lady out the back of our place, who could see every bit of the ruin that was once our yard, said he was a disgusting excuse for a human being, and promised to do her best.

We told Dr Nick, because he had remarked on the gradual degradation of the yard. He was stupid and told Belinda. Damn Ol' Cow Eyes. Damn all his toenails and all his toes and damn even the joints of his toes. May they all suffer acute rheumatoid arthritis for fifteen minutes and thirty seconds a day every day for three years.

Which reminds me. Be proud of me. Be very proud.

Throughout all those attacks on my poor innocent backyard, I had all the preparations for a curse against the nasty guy who was doing it all, and I kept them in my big handbag, ready to wield. There was lead, and lead, and lead. I could have written a curse on a gemstone or paper, but the strongest curses are written on lead and thrown in a grave. I was in my favourite cemetery, sitting on a gravestone and longing for peace. And I did not do it. This is my source of pride.

I was so good: it was killing me to be so virtuous. Just with a little unwonted lead weighting down my handbag. And a piece of stray metal, to scratch the lead with. I have now officially buried the recipes for cursing where Zoë cannot find them easily. Just in case you're reading this, Zoë, don't even think about it. No cursing. Cursing is not something a nice and well-brought-up young lady does.

Belinda worried. It was inevitable. I said encouraging things. What else could I do?

After he had killed all our pot plants and thrown the pots at the back door, and thoroughly investigated our front door, the stranger left us alone. I was walking wounded, and glad of the reprieve. I even ceased caring about Zoë's pet geranium, which had to be repotted. I just left the Rudolph problem floating, and let him come when he liked and do what he liked.

Zoë wasn't walking wounded. Zoë was as mad as I have ever seen her. She investigated Great-Grandma's papers and online and said she would tell me if her work came to anything. I had to extract a promise from her not to do a thing with magic without my permission. She promised.

We all knew the police phone number by heart. And there was peace. And soul-emptiness.

You would not believe what happened next. I got another letter in the mail. When Zoë opened her letter, very excitedly, there was a letter to me tucked inside it. It was to me from Peter. Peter, my beloved. Hah!

There was no reason for him to write. He had access to Nick. He had a lovely, organising wife, who dealt better with his tantrums than I ever did. Unless she was divorcing him, in which case all I could say was good on her. And if he wanted me as a character reference he was a . . . Damn. I was about to be very crude.

Using Zoë was low. She had such a look of disappointment on her face when she found that the only thing in the envelope was something for me.

I got my friends to write another letter for me. My friends, on all their lovely letterhead, said that I did not want to see him or talk to him directly and that any business left over from however many years ago could go through them. Any further direct contact would be regarded as harassment, and follow-up action would ensue. Or words to that effect. I don't know the words, in fact. I couldn't bring myself to even look at the letter.

Next thing I knew, the bloody idiot rang Nick. I was in the kitchen and Nick was watching TV. I have no idea what Peter said, but I heard every word Nick said.

"'How can she be serious?'" I heard Nick echo back into the phone. "Are you a total moron? Why should she ever talk to you again? Why should she even want to listen to you say anything? Do you know what you did to her? Do you know what she does? She works in a bloody gift shop: you're the one with the big house and the nice car." Nick didn't let Peter get a word in edgewise. He ranted on about how wonderful I was, and how Peter had done nothing except make me scared and how he could leave us the hell alone. I was so sad for Nick.

My son said, "If all you want is to see me, I can visit Melbourne once a year. But that's it. If you try to ring Mum or write to her, I will never speak to you again. Every time you try she shakes for days. She doesn't deserve what you did to her."

He listened a while and then, "That's a fair compromise. I can do that. But it's all off if you try to talk to Mum. All of it." And he hung up the phone.

I expected him to go up to his room after that, or to sit down and watch TV. It was big stuff he'd been handling. Instead he came into the kitchen and just stood there, looking at me. I looked back at him for a moment. Then I held out my arms and gave him the warmest and longest hug I could.

"Your tears are ruining my outfit," he said, after a bit. We cracked up with laughter. God, that was a moment.

Nick had one more thing to say. "He was trying to tell you he's sorry. He asked if I could tell you for him."

That started the tears again, and this time Nick opened *his* arms.

"I'm so lucky I have you," I said. "You're fabulously wonderful."

"You shouldn't say things like that," he reproved. "I might believe them."

4.

The next day (don't you love all these 'the next days' — last year was more than a bit like living in a soap opera) the phone rang again. It wasn't Peter. Thank God.

It was Dr Cow Eyes. I know I should stop calling him that, but honestly, his eyes are so big and liquid and pleading, they just turn me into a giggling teen every time. Not the drooling sort, the cynical sort. Because such eyes usually have no brain behind them. I can't take him seriously. Fortunately, he can't take me seriously either.

Anyway, he was ringing to say he had accepted that Canberra job and to let me know he would be dining with my sister from time to time.

"And why did you tell me this?"

"So you wouldn't be shocked when you found out any other way," he grinned. I swear he grinned. "I live in awe of your temper."

"I have no temper," I defended myself bravely. "I'm as mild as a gentle kitten."

"I won't argue with you," he said, meanly.

"Can I help with anything?" I decided to be nice, since he'd done all those translations and since he was obviously besotted with my sister.

"It's all under control," he said, then put in one of those loathsome pauses some guys add to a conversation when you just know they are going to say something they think is funny. "And Belinda is cooking dinner for me my first night, so I should eat well."

"Are you implying anything about my cooking?" I asked indignantly.

"No. Why would I do that?" Damn his pinkie. I finally find a man for Belinda and he thinks my cooking is a laughing matter.

"I'm very pleased you like my cooking," I said with dignity, "Because I plan to visit my sister heaps and take over her kitchen."

Silence. Well, that would change as he knew us better. I should take advantage while it lasted. I decided not to. As Peter's apology was sinking in, I was beginning to feel almost mellow.

It was only when the phone was back in its cradle and I was staring at it contemplatively that I realised that Ol' Brown Eyes had just announced he had serious intentions towards Belinda.

Did this mean I was going to be the Newtown floorshow to both of them for the rest of our natural lives? Or in my case, my decidedly unnatural one? Who knew? All I knew was that if he called me the Newtown bloody Floorshow to my face, he would suffer, direly.

This phone call brought me to a resolution about my own love life. I couldn't take any more. Life in general was too rich and varied, and needed simplifying. Urgently. I rang Rudolph with the intent of breaking off our relationship. I used the 'just friends' line. He laughed.

"I'm serious," I said.

"So am I," said he. That was the end of the conversation.

He came round the next day, pretending to be visiting Nick. Nick, unfortunately, fell for it. They had a grand old time, while I stood in the kitchen and glowered.

5.

Way back (lo, those many moons ago) when the wacko had investigated our front door with intent, he wasn't alone. He walked round the house from other angles for a bit after that. He did nothing — he just walked. And a bit behind him every single time was a bare-headed man who looked poor and tattered and fragile. If you smiled at him, you would see a mouth that once had lots of teeth. That sort of poor. Well, we hadn't seen his teeth, but we assumed that they fitted his general air of trampness and destitution.

The wacko and the tramp never actually talked to one another. Nick watched them closely and noted that it looked as if the loony did not even know the other man was there.

Zoë announced to me that this was a case for super-Zoë. She said she remembered reading in one of GAM's papers about a poor man, dishevelled and in tatters, and she had looked up dishevelled in the dictionary.

"Find me that paper," I said.

It was that list of angels and other amazingly odd beings and what they did. The one I refused to explain at great length. He was one we could have done without ever seeing. The Angel of Death.

First we rang the police again and let them know the guy was turning his attention to the house itself. As ever, they promised to keep an eye out. The minute the phone was on the hook again, Zoë and I sat down with that whole bloody box and worked through it. There was nothing useful. I sent Zoë to bed and had a fit of the conniptions, quietly and obsessively, in the kitchen.

About a half hour into my conniptions, when I was reduced to my grade three swear words, I saw the corner of a nightie showing at the edge of the door.

"Zoë," I said, threateningly and motherly, "what are you doing out of bed?"

"I was reading, Mummy," and the nightie emerged into the kitchen with her in it, "And there was something useful."

"Go get your slippers," I sighed. If we were in this state because of the Angel of Death, then at least she should not get a cold.

"Mummy, you have to read this," and she waved a blue book in my face.

"I'll read it while you get your slippers," I said. "And your pink dressing gown," I called up after her. We were going to get through this episode without sniffles, even if we lost life and limb.

The Angel of Death meant death, Zoë's book said. There was a solution, however. I mean, there was a story that contained a solution. If you could see him, then he could also be persuaded you were not for killing.

I digested what we were supposed to do and decided that it was feasible. Scary, but feasible. I got Zoë to get Nick. That took longer than her getting her slippers, because he was settled in front of the computer. It needs strong measures to prise him lose when he is in front of that machine. I promised hot chocolate.

When the chocolate was in everyone's fists, I started in on the serious stuff. "Nick, Zoë's done some research on the guy standing behind our loony." Zoë was on edge — she patently did not want me to give away our magic secrets. "I have a strategy for dealing with him."

"And the wacko?"

"I have no idea how to deal with *him*," I said, reluctantly. "Apart from cursing his pinkies to stop him throwing things." Nick laughed, but Zoë looked worried.

"The next time you see the tramp-guy, invite him in. Be very, very polite. Give him food and drink."

"We should be very, very, very polite," piped up Zoë.

"Just as polite as we know how," I said grimly. "If I'm the one who sees him, I promise I won't swear."

"My God," said Nick, teen cool betrayed by a chocolate moustache, "It must be serious".

"I'll pretend I didn't hear that," was my stern reply. "We're going to be so nice and so generous and so welcoming to the tramp-guy that he refuses to help the other guy."

"And now, Zoë," she looked at me expectantly, "bed."

Her face drooped, but she went, hot chocolate in hand.

6.

Damn life, Rhonda thought bitterly. Things just happened all at once. Witches and arguments and friends with undefined issues and being chased by people she didn't know. At least it was a different sort of chasing to the usual, she reflected. Then she remembered where she had hidden the whiskey that night she'd been avoiding getting drunk.

Rhonda got well and truly sloshed and redeemed her entire wasted day.

The next day she rang Dave.

"Dave," she said, "Would it make you happy to know I have a perfectly awful hangover?"

"Why didn't you ring me and we could have shared the hangover?" he asked.

"On the principle that a shared hangover is half as bad?"

"Exactly. And the process of causing the hangover is far more than double the fun."

"Well, I wasn't sure you were speaking to me."

"I was mad as hell with you: that's not the same as not speaking."

"It is with my family. They're mad as hell with me and haven't spoken to me for years. It took me all my courage to pick up the phone and ring you."

"Hung over *and* an emotional wreck."

"I am," admitted Rhonda. "I rang to say I was sorry."

"Are you?"

"I don't know. I'm miserable and missing you and altogether a mess, so I must be sorry, mustn't I?"

"Your logic is appalling."

"Everything is appalling."

"How about I come over and bring my patent hang-over cure? When you're less miserable you can apologise properly."

"Okay," said Rhonda, in her littlest voice.

"And in the meantime I want you to drink about a pint of orange juice. You do have orange juice? And you know what a pint is?"

"Yes."

"Then drink it all. And take some pain meds."

"And I won't be hung over," said Rhonda, following the thought to its conclusion. "So your patent hangover medicine won't be any good."

"See you in about an hour."

He was true to his word. Exact and to the minute, he came, bearing sushi.

"Hi," and Rhonda gave a watery smile as she opened the door more widely to allow him and his trays entrance.

"How are you?"

"Weak at the knees."

"That's how I like my women," Dave said, and came in. He handed the stacked trays of sushi to Rhonda and went to the stove.

"Sushi is your hangover cure? There's an awful lot of it."

"Sake is my hangover cure. The sushi is so that we don't have to do it all again tomorrow."

"Oh." Rhonda put everything on the side table then sat herself in the armchair. She felt her eyes go blank.

"My God, you're a mess," Dave observed, coming over and looking down at her. Rhonda was sure that he was hiding amusement.

"I did everything you said," Rhonda defended herself. "And you're not supposed to tell me that I am a mess, you are supposed to tell me how beautiful my eyes are."

"No deal. Your eyes are bloodshot. What've you been doing?"

"I drank the best part of a bottle of whiskey."

"Why?"

"Because I remembered where I'd hidden it."

"Okay." Dave drawled the word, slowly, and looked at her measuringly. He knelt so he could see her face better, "I'll bite. Why did you remember where you had hidden it?"

"Because I couldn't work out what was going on the other night with the two of us, and I didn't want to get drunk so I hid it. Then I found it because I can't work out what a friend is doing. I don't like not understanding things."

Dave laughed. Dave always laughed. "Are we friends again?' he asked.

"I guess," Rhonda shrugged. "I can't sort you out, either."

"So you're going to drink more whiskey?"

"Run out. No more whiskey," and Rhonda felt the sadness well up inside her. "And she wanted to meet me online for no good reason. I just don't get her. She's following me round online and acting needy and I don't understand it."

"Maybe she likes you," Dave was amused still, but gentle.

"Sure she likes me. We're friends."

"God, you're naïve."

"You keep *saying* that," and Rhonda's voice rose in a whine. Sometimes she just hated herself. "You never *explain* anything."

"Oh, honey," said Dave, and picked her up out of the armchair, carried her to the couch and just held her.

"Have we made up, then?" she asked, after a long, long time, "And what happened to the sake?"

"I can heat it when we're ready. I just think you need to sit quietly for a little."

"You're right. Why are you always right?"

"Because I'm omniscient."

After another quiet bit, Rhonda asked Dave what he meant by her friend.

Dave asked Rhonda a surprising question. "Is this friend a lesbian?"

"Why?" Rhonda couldn't see Dave's logic. "Surely you aren't a bigot."

"No," he said. "I was just wondering if she wasn't interested in you."

"You're in love with me, so you think the whole world is also?"

Dave laughed, but denied Rhonda's logic. "She's stalking you. Gently."

"Oh." Rhonda felt stupid. "I never thought about it that way. I just thought she was needy."

"Needy, yes."

"Oh. "What do I do about it?"

"You aren't secretly in love with her?"

"How can I be secretly in love with her when I'm secretly in love with you?"

Dave gave her a perfectly fatuous grin. Rhonda found herself gazing at him and lost time and the conversation. "Dammit, Rhonda, this isn't a solution."

"Smiling is a solution for a lot of things."

Dave didn't laugh. "Maybe I should post an 'I own Rhonda' notice."

"Own me? Didn't we have this conversation before? And didn't it go somewhere really dreadful when we had it?"

"We did and it did," now Dave was sober and unhappy. He looked away.

"I know," she said, and Dave looked down at her, hopeful as a puppy dog. "Let's wait until the right occasion happens. I chat with my friends on the blog all the time. Something will come up."

"On the blog? This whole thing is happening online? Do you mind if I read it?"

Damn, thought Rhonda. So much for hiding nerdishness. Might as well be hung for a sheep as a lamb. Besides, maybe this was the cause of that dreadful phone call. Maybe all he needed to see was her geek side.

"Of course not. How will you help me find the perfect moment if you don't read it?" Rhonda noticed how serious Dave was still looking. "What's wrong?"

"I didn't realise how damn jealous I was, that's all."

"So keep an eye on TVwhore. Because, honestly, you have nothing to be jealous about. Even if she's interested in me, which is unlikely. I'm a one-guy woman. Seriously."

7.

Since she was going out that evening, Rhonda had to finish her witch article in a hurry. It was more of a challenge than the others, on all fronts. The subject matter would just about kill her emotionally, and she had to allow for a break on the inner self front between writing and evening. The subject matter was also very dense: Mackay had a hundred pages on it.

Rhonda chewed her lip and pondered. There was no time for sorting out deep problems and no time at all for discursions. She had to do the whole thing sharply and sweetly.

Rhonda made several up-front decisions. She noted them for the editor and said that she could write articles on those facets of the subject later, if the editor so desired, but that a topic so popular couldn't be too academic, and she feared that she would become mired in technicalities if she went down these routes. It was an excuse, and she knew it. But without the excuse, the article would never be finished. The subjects she listed as problematic were Mackay's notion of spirits and otherworld as contrasted with those in effect at the time, and the relationship of prophecy with the Church.

What Rhonda ended up writing was very straightforward. She described the use of techniques for identifying and punishing heretics and how they developed into techniques for identifying and punishing witches. She talked briefly about the traits used to identify witches and how those traits developed, but she refused to glamorise.

She also refused to get caught up in how many innocents were killed. Nor was she going down the path of discussing the lives of Mother Shipton and other prophet types. She wormed out of talking about both Joan and Mother Shipton by commenting that these people on the borders of society, and yet whom society follows with a morbid fascination, are often tangled with the larger problems that gave rise to persecution of witches.

Rhonda read it back and cut her sentences down to

size then gave a little nod. It would pass. Even though it boiled down to an excuse for not writing about the topic properly, it would pass. *Excuses and excuses and more excuses still*, she thought, *are the only things I am bringing to this article.* And she was finished. She rested her forehead on her hands and wept.

Rhonda wept because of the descriptions of her that were spreading through the internet: people wanted a prophet so they described what they thought a prophet would be like. They had nothing to do with what she was like. And she could never be what people wanted her to be, either. Rhonda could only be herself. And her self was no defence against the modern equivalent of a Matthew Hopkins, Witchfinder General.

Eventually she emerged from her self-pity. She looked at the time and made a resolve. "You're going to perform now or not at all," she told her gift.

Rhonda went onto the computer, logged into a chat room at random, and began typing. If it wasn't her inner prophet talking, then it was her imagination. She couldn't care less which. She was going to type garbage until the inner damn fool let loose. And then she was going to type more garbage except that it would be visionary garbage. And she was going to be over the whole thing soon enough so she could have a shower and put makeup on and wear her prettiest dress and have an entirely delightful dinner party.

And she was never, ever, ever going to actually read Mackay's hundred pages about witches.

"Type," she told her fingers. "Quickly, damn you — I have more important things to do with my life. Starting as soon as I get offline. So get a move on." Rhonda smiled.

Her gift got a move on.

When Rhonda returned to normal awareness and read back what her fingers had recorded, she was horrified. She worked furiously to make her permanent record, but she wished that this particular emergence from the pit had stayed repressed.

Rhonda's misbegotten gift had uncovered a cabal. A small group of influential people whose power crossed borders. She named every single person involved and every single organisation they had infiltrated and gave places and dates and even times of meetings. She listed where the secret minutes were kept by the one member of the cabal who was recording proceedings. Rhonda even pointed out that the other members of the cabal didn't know about the recording and that the government agents who had stumbled onto them had been bribed into submission. All of this was within Rhonda's capacity to deal.

What she was having trouble with was the fact that this secret group was achieving results by hurting people. It was creating a new witch craze, though it gave another name to what it was doing. "Creating a better society," they proclaimed. "Destroying fear."

Rhonda revealed scapegoat after scapegoat: students, scholars, government employees. All of them were in jail as part of the wider plan. And there her muse had stopped. She knew that innocents were in jail and who had put them there, but she had no idea why these people were stirring up hatred. It was all against one ethnic group. And it was three countries. Maybe she could work it out.

Rhonda pulled back. "Don't get involved," she scolded herself. "Bad enough to have a gift that runs your soul without letting it run your bloody life." Rhonda was disturbed, though. She was even more disturbed when she realised that the person chasing her was probably in the chat room watching the words flow. It was all too much.

Rhonda logged off very quickly, saved her text, then

went offline. She resolved to spend the rest of the week as far from the computer as she could get. Then the phone rang.

"Hello?"

"Is that Jane Smith?"

"Yes, it is," Rhonda thought back to who she had given her number to along with the Jane Smith pen-name. It had to be someone she had written something for. An editor.

"I'm sorry to ring you, but I just wanted to know when you were likely to be finished with the next Mackay article. We're having to bring our deadlines forward this month."

She couldn't go back on the computer and finish re-vising it now. She just couldn't. Rhonda fell back on her tried and true way out of everything: she lied. "There's more research with this than the others. The earliest I can get it to you is Monday."

Monday, it appeared, would suffice. On Monday she duly dared the computer and revised the article and emailed it.

When she went to check the news feed she had so carefully set up in her moment of confidence, she wished she hadn't. She was famous. She even had a new nickname. The New Nostradamus was old hat, the international press announced, Revelator was changing the world.

Rhonda decided she might as well be killed for a sheep as a lamb and took the time to check the news stories out. To her surprise they dated to within two hours of her original revelation in the chat room. Damn. She'd been right about that chat room presence. Maybe the pursuer would be run over by a car. She could only hope.

It was time for a new tactic, she decided, since the running and hiding were not solving much. Mind you,

she would still run and hide. But she would use her
brain, as well. Rhonda asked around in chat rooms to
see if anyone knew anything about the news frenzy.
She found out that there was a site where a paper had
generously published its core data.

On the website, she found the exact words of many
of her oracular statements, going back two years. Along
with the texts her inner rumblings had produced, the
paper had kindly provided linguistic analysis to prove
that the same person was responsible for all the out-
bursts. They had traced how each statement had been
proven to be true and accurate and what ructions each
one had caused.

It was especially foul because Rhonda had been so
very certain that she was unrecordable in chat rooms.
She had keyed thousands of words manually under that
assumption. She checked her records against the report. She found that there were even records from
rooms where she'd been the only person present. How
was this possible?

Rhonda ran some words through a search engine
and found out more about chat rooms than anyone
needed to know, ever. Along the way she found out
about chat logs. Someone had logged hundreds of
rooms for tens of thousands of hours, and checked for
her prophecies.

There was money and knowledge behind this investigation. She'd known that already, but there was a
harshness to the knowledge now. She wasn't just being
chased with those vast resources, she was being
recorded. Rhonda was scared.

At the keyboard her fingertips felt cool and slippery.
They slid over the keys and transformed her words
into a travesty. It felt as if the slick plastic was jolting
waves of fear from those delicate fingertips right
through her hand. The shudder trembled through her

bent fingers and through her wrists and her arms and into her shoulders. She carried the burden of it on her back, every minute of every day.

Not even the most soothing bath of lavender and rose could gentle her nervousness. Rhonda had structured her whole life around those fingertips touching that keyboard. Whether she went online for work or for pleasure, she couldn't escape.

After two days the taste of fear left a slight acid in the back of her mouth, and the scent of it dwindled even the smell of fresh-brewed coffee to a lingering memory.

Rhonda tried to run from it in chat rooms. She went from one to another, reading desultorily random conversations about sex and about the opposite sex, about the state of the Red Sox. Eventually her fingers took her with them back to the chat room she used to visit as M44M.

BB was in that chat room. Rhonda looked at his two initials lined up with other visitors on the side of the screen and wondered if she should leave. He was obviously an agent for the newspaper that was hunting her. And he could be Dave. It wasn't terribly likely, but it was possible. Even 'possible' was too close. Rhonda knew why this hunt had given her such a tangible fear. It could be Dave. That could be his special project in Canberra.

Die in a ditch, girl. Give up. Jump over a cliff. If Dave goes, there's nothing left. Life is dust. Then she thought, *I have to know. I have to know if Dave is BB. I can't continue like this.*

BB was his obvious self. He wasn't doing his 'I can see through lies' stunt, he was asking, "What do you really know about the people in chats with you?"

Rhonda started inventing and posting histories for every nick BB presented, and soon the others in the room were joining her. She kept an eye on everything BB said. He couldn't be relied upon to be honest, but he might just give himself away.

And he did. Scattered inside his questions about known Netizens were assumptions about time and weather. It was daylight where he was.

Rhonda suspected he was chatting from work, even though he claimed to be lazing about the house, because he talked about coffee and getting the day started. Several times he went quiet, and came back saying, "Sorry, on the phone." And when he left, two hours after Rhonda came in, he left with a joyous, "Oh, cake! Must be a birthday." Not very bright was BB. Also in entirely the wrong timezone. Unless it was Dave practising dissimulation. She stayed online in case BB came back.

An hour later, there he was, in the chat room, bright and vapid as ever. And there was a ring on her mobile phone.

"Honey, are you asleep?"

"If I said yes, would you believe me?'

"Can I come round?"

"Why?"

"You have a suspicious mind."

"You know I do."

"I've spent the whole damn night web searching for pictures and stories and obituaries and . . ."

"Ssh," said Rhonda. "You're in a bad way. I'll see you when you get here."

"Thanks, hon."

Rhonda didn't think that this was an act, but, just to be safe, she watched BB make a fool of himself in the chat room until Dave let himself in the front door. She gave her boyfriend a hug, and asked, "What can I do?"

"Nothing," he said, sheepishly. "I just don't want to be alone."

"How about you choose a movie while I make coffee."

"Sounds good."

While the coffee was busy making noises and hiding her actions, Rhonda sneaked into the computer room and logged off. BB was still babbling away, right up to the moment the connection terminated.

The next day she made a plan. It was a very tired plan, because Dave had stayed watching movies the whole night. When she had sent him home to get ready for work, he had looked less as if the earth was about to swallow him. His eyes were tired and forlorn, but that would pass. At least he was facing things now.

And Rhonda wished her mind would not go in circles when she was tired. She'd formulated an important plan over breakfast. All she had to do was recall it. Or sleep. Maybe she could sleep then see if it recalled itself?

She remembered! Rhonda found some paper and a pen and wrote herself a little note. "Jane Smith = me." It was the perfect hiding place. She would only go online as Jane Smith except when she prophesied.

Her persona as independent historian was very dense and detailed. It was a part of herself rather than a pure invention, but used a richer vocabulary and was full of ideas and opinions. Her language use was different as Jane Smith. Very different. And her best bet at safety (since she couldn't stop the garbage that spewed out in prophecy and revelation) was in that language difference. Rhonda found herself almost purring in satisfaction as she went to sleep the day away.

She was cat-content when she woke up in the middle of the afternoon. She stretched tall and wide and felt the ripple of her bedclothes over her skin. Life was good.

8.

Only Zoë and I were home when the Angel of Death came to our back door. He looked disconsolate. I invited him in. He said nothing, but he seemed surprised.

Zoë did her sweetness and light thing. She wears her bravery with a flourish of guilelessness. She even got her ballet dress out and demonstrated her favourite dance, as if his life had not been worth living until he had seen her twirl pinkly. She showed him her box of secrets. It was stones she had picked up and shells and dead leaves, plus a Barbie doll outfit (goodness knows why since she doesn't actually have a Barbie). While I fed him, she took him every bloody thing from her box and told him all about it. She charmed his socks off, I do believe, because he was smiling fondly at her.

I acted as a backdrop to my beaming daughter.

It's just as well Zoë didn't understand how important all this was, because I was so petrified throughout the whole thing that I nearly threw up three times. I fed him cake and chocolate biscuits from our special tin and I made him nice coffee. I was a gracious hostess. Pale green, but otherwise perfect.

After about twenty minutes of being treated royally, our angel excused himself nicely. He thanked us for our hospitality. He smiled, showing us perfect set of teeth and two very sharp eyes. Then he left by the front door.

Zoë was watching him and she told me, "He's gone to the back again."

She was puzzled. So was I. He waited at the door, looking towards the back gate. Zoë and I watched from behind the curtain in my bedroom. She hid her eyes, but insisted I whisper every single thing that happened as it happened, in case she missed something. We made the mistake of blinking — and the Angel was gone. We still waited.

Next, the madman arrived. "He's coming up to the gate," I whispered to Zoë. "This is strange: he's carrying something. Lots of somethings."

"What are they?" She was curious and excited and, yes, just a little scared.

"I can't tell. But whatever he is doing looks serious. Damn. Zoë, get my mobile!"

She raced downstairs and was back in a twinkle. The police number was by now on autodial. They advised we stay in the house and that they would be there as quickly as they could. Zoë listened to my end of the conversation, her eyes wide. At the end of it she whisked downstairs.

"Zoë! Where are you going?"

"To check the doors," she said. All the downstairs doors and windows were locked and bolted, she said, when she came back up. I felt a little safer, and wondered if this was all.

The man had obviously dropped his various somethings at the gate whilst trying to get in, and was laboriously picking them up when we went back to the window.

The Angel of Death was there. I hadn't seen him return, but as the guy moved in through the gate, there he was. Bedraggled, unkempt, and surprisingly authoritative. The madman stopped and talked with him for a little. Then he tried to force his way past the Angel, just barging on through, his arms full of possessions. Then came the weird bit.

The Angel simply held his hand out flat, in front of the other guy's face and the guy stopped there, totally unmoving. For about five minutes. It was uncanny.

Zoë and I stared at the silent tableau.

Finally, the police came. They couldn't see the Angel of Death, but they could see the stuff the man had in his arms. They talked with him — vehemently. Two of them hauled him and his possessions off to the police station, the third walked right through the Angel of Death and knocked on our door. The Angel looked up, winked at Zoë, and gently faded.

I raced downstairs and opened the back door. The policeman said all was well, and that the man and his explosives would be taken care of. I was restrained and all I said was 'Dammit.' My inner turmoil had to be repressed because of the children. But I said "Dammit" for there had been a reason for the Angel of Death appearing. I thanked God, and Zoë and her imagination and sweetness and bravery.

Then I thought how cool it was to have given afternoon tea to the Angel of Death.

CHAPTER ELEVEN

1.

THERE ARE SOME WEEKENDS THAT ARE REALLY NOT VERY nice. We had a spate of ghastly-hot weather, and everyone was talking water restrictions. Belinda rang me because there were bushfires on the outskirts of Sydney. Nothing near me. Never near me. I live far too inner-city for that. But she rang me to check that things were okay.

I guess it was all that stuff that's been happening around her; she wasn't her usual calm and managing self. And she always worries about me when she gets disorganised. This has been happening since I was five. She would get nightmares about things that went wrong with me, although back then it was jumping off her bit of the double bunk and being bitten by dogs.

The double bunk thing was a genuine concern, because I used to put my dressing gown on backwards like a cloak and shout Superman-sayings as I leapt from on high. This is why I was so adamant Zoë should not try the flying spell. Landing from on high hurt.

I reassured her by cursing her roundly. If I'd been

polite, she would have turned from a worrier into a panic merchant. Belinda laughed at me, and she said she'd ring back on Saturday afternoon when she was less jumpy, and we could have a real chat. She had an early morning wedding to attend, so she'd call after that.

It did sound good, so I sat by the phone all afternoon. I suppose all the stress got to me. I sat by the phone because I wanted to talk. I didn't ring because there was something quavery in me.

I was in a slightly vague, hazy mood. In a drift. Alone. Zoë was out with her father, and Nick had tagged along. It was nice to just sit and wait to chat with my sister. But the phone didn't ring.

When it reached early evening I started to get worried. Belinda always rings when she says she will. Boring but reliable, that's my sister. Unreliable is Evil Twin. I waited a couple of hours longer. Then I rang her. The phone rang and rang and rang and no one answered. I tried ringing her mobile.

Yes! She was there. A worry I had not quite verbalised lifted its weight from my shoulders. "Have you seen the news?" was the first thing she asked me.

"No," I said.

"Watch the news, and ring me back at Nick's," she commanded. She has never, ever, ever used that tone of voice to me. 'And ring me back at Nick's'? I almost jumped out of my chair to turn on the TV.

I didn't have to wait. It was the top story. It was the only story. Flames had engulfed Canberra. The city was swept by bushfires. The news showed walls of flame thirty metres high and balls of wildfire.

Damn. Damn. Damn.

I'd spoken to her. She was alive. But the sheets of flame on the news wallpapered my mind when I telephoned her back. Bushfire is something we take for granted in Australia: it will happen. But not like this. Not tornadoes of fire exploding our homes.

2.

Dave was being inquisitive. She told him so. "You're a sticky beak, you know."

"Tell me something I don't know," he said.

"See," Rhonda answered, "You're even inquisitive in admitting you're inquisitive."

"Yeah, sure. But I still want to know about the research side of you."

"Why?"

"If I have to call you doctor, I want to know why."

"You don't care about calling me doctor. You don't want to know anything in particular," Rhonda said, "You have this deep drive. You have to know everything. Preferably yesterday. And my bloody thesis is so far in my past that yesterday is too recent."

"Your bloody thesis? It was about violence then?"

"You never give up?"

"I'm a reporter, honey, I'm trained in tendentiousness."

"You're a stubborn bastard, you know. You don't really want to know about my bloody thesis. You just want to fill in gaps about my life."

"I want both," Dave admitted.

"Why?" Rhonda asked, "Apart from the needing to know everything yesterday bit." His answer was crucially important to his future with her.

Dave slowed down and thought a bit. "I guess," he said, with pauses that seldom entered his shotgun speech, "I guess I hadn't really thought about why. I just need to know. But . . . there's a reason."

Rhonda looked at the distress on his face and felt a little guilty. "Can you talk about it?"

"I just never thought about why before, is all."

"I didn't mean to upset you," and Rhonda rubbed her head against his shoulder in reassurance.

"I don't think I'm upset," Dave admitted, "Just thoughtful. Give me a minute and I'll have an answer."

"That sounds more like me than like you."

"It does." And then there was silence.

"God, I'm an idiot," Dave said, after the silence.

"Yes?" Rhonda tried to make her query not sound as if she was agreeing. She often thought men had idiot patches, though, so there was some agreement in there.

"It's the way we met," Dave said.

"You want to know about my bloody thesis because I was stupid enough to take a blue drink from someone I mistrust."

"Yes, I mean no. I mean, dammit, Rhonda, don't derail me."

"What then?"

"I don't fall in love at first sight. I don't do what I did to get you into bed that first night. I don't do things like that."

"You were drugged too?"

Dave looked down, not entirely comfortably. "You Aussies will joke about anything."

"I'm really glad I can joke about this thing, anyhow," said Rhonda.

"You're there now. Making jokes."

"Yes, I am." Another short quiet moment. Then, "Oh!" said Rhonda.

"What?"

"I think I understand. You want to know everything about me because you can't understand how all this has happened. I'm not your type."

"You've turned my whole world round," admitted Dave.

"Good," said Rhonda. "Because my world is all

shook up too. Think for a bit. If you really want to know about the thesis I'll tell you, but it's really not germane to understanding me. I'm not going to tell you unless you care about knowing it for its own sake."

"You're irrational," Dave objected.

"I am, and my irrational self wants to make a chocolate cake. If I make it will you eat it?"

"Do we have cream?" Dave asked.

"Yes."

"Then I'll whip the cream up with a bit of your port."

"Um. I think we finished the port. I might be able to find sweet sherry though." And the conversation was finished until two days later.

Rhonda found herself impelled to ask, "You sure you want to know about my thesis? Have you thought about it yet?"

"Your bloody thesis?" Dave smiled. "Shoot."

Rhonda smiled back. Trust him to pick up the fact that she never said 'my thesis'. It was always 'my bloody thesis'. Trust him. She was caught in his eyes and lost coherent thought. She said the first thing that came into her mind, just to get some words out and prove she wasn't an imbecile.

"It's all about history," Rhonda started, then stopped to think. Mental blanks were not useful for describing things.

Dave snuck in with, "What a surprise," so she hit him lightly with the back of her hand.

"Behave," Rhonda instructed.

"Give me three reasons why," and Dave gave her that look and she melted all over again.

"Do you want to hear about my thesis?"

"Dammit, you know I do."

"I could've sworn your mind was on something quite different just now."

"Later," he promised. "Now tell me about this thesis of yours."

Rhonda poked out her tongue. It seemed like the right thing to do. "It's all about how people imagine the past," Rhonda was on a better path now. It was hard to describe something she had lived with for so long then pushed so very far out of her life. "I called it 'Imagining History', but it was partly an edition of a piece of historiography by Walpole and partly an analysis of the text. Does that make sense? Do you know who Walpole was?"

"Sure does. Sure do," Dave was looking very big and comfortable and Rhonda had a sudden desire to just cuddle up. She had this urge far too often. She had never felt this secure with Tony. It was quite extraordinary.

She suddenly realised how much of her life had been spent running. With Dave she had a place where she was no longer fleeing. It was an odd thought.

"Tell me more," her rock of strength encouraged.

"Truly?"

"I need to know reasons and meanings and detail, and all you've given me is the heading."

Rhonda gave him a lunatic grin and proceeded to share something very private with him. "Headings are good. I just find it hard to explain the rest because no one really wants to know. They want pretty-pretty."

"Rhonda," Dave growled warningly. She began all over again, falling into almost-jargon in her attempt to explain.

"My basic idea was that our forms of scholarly expression simplify how we imagine history. That they are cultural artefacts and as such change how we see the past." She was going to stop there, but Dave was leaning forward and focussed. He was definitely interested. None of this had been an act. She kept explaining.

It was slow, sharing her deepest self, but it felt so good, so very good to have someone who listened and who cared about her words, her ideas. This wasn't fan fiction, or popular history. This was her inner self. Rhonda pure. It was soul-stuff.

"There are lots of reasons for this simplification." Her voice picked up a bit. Of all the voices she had, this one was the most rusty. "Part of this is necessary as a communications tool and for teaching. Part of it is because Walpole was consumed by a desire to make a coherent argument and state a case. There is something else that needs to be added to the mix, though. There is something else in his work and in most historical work, things that aren't covered by the driving argument and scholarly analysis. History is not that simple. How we analyse history is not how we actually see the past or describe it."

She realised that she was almost quoting from an early draft of her thesis. Those words had lain inside her, dormant all those years, waiting for someone to say, "I want to hear them." And they were not digestible. They were better read on the page than heard. Yet here Dave was, head slightly forward, mouth slightly open, absorbing it. Making her life mean something.

"I love these concepts." Rhonda explained why this was important. It became crucial to answer the question in Dave's eyes, "To me it was a realisation that literature, as a cultural artefact, embodies lots of lovely complexities and that simplicity and elegance can ignore the reality of the cultural content being presented."

"I need to think about that," Dave said, slowly.

"I can say it really simply," Rhonda suggested.

"You're an evil woman. I dare you to say it in less than fifteen words."

"I don't do dares," said Rhonda primly, her mind ticking over.

"I'll buy you dinner."

"You were going to buy me dinner anyway."

"Just do it," he growled.

Rhonda gave a dramatic sigh and paused to collect her thoughts. "The world of people's cultural consciousness isn't tidy, or logical. It's like chaos theory. There — fourteen words."

"I'll buy that. People are messy."

"We are," said Rhonda, her gaze encompassing the papers that had somehow grown back since her big declutter. "And because we're messy we imagine history is messy. But we like to pretend it isn't and to make nice clear patterns when we describe how people write it."

"Did your thesis ever get to the whys and wherefores?"

"Pretty much. We use writing history differently to the way we use it. There is a gap between the theory and the reality. We're not really deciphering the past when we write history, we're using the past as a means of imagining present history, of placing ourselves in time. Does that make sense? It's a way of pretending the world is orderly, even when it isn't."

"I like that," Dave said.

"You do?" Rhonda's eyes sparkled. "And here I was imagining I had wasted all those years of study."

"Seriously?"

"Well, I wasted the years after I did it, so it seemed logical to assume I wasted those years as well."

"You were just trying to make it tidy in your mind.

GILLIAN POLACK

You need to know an important truth — people are messy. Don't laugh, I can prove it."

"I thought I just explained it."

"Ah, but I can prove it."

"How?'

"Come over here."

3.

I rang Nick-in-Canberra. He insisted on talking to me before I could speak to my sister. I wanted to damn all his toes to nine hells, but if he was taking care of her I had to be polite.

"She's safe," he said. I knew she was safe physically — I wanted to know everything else. So much everything else.

"And her house was standing last time we saw," he continued, as if it was nothing too serious. Very nonchalant voice, damn him. Calm as two toads. "But fire reached her garden and she had to evacuate. We won't know anything until at least tomorrow. So be careful." His voice was full of dire warnings. I almost loved him for that voice.

When I got Lin on the phone I had absolutely no idea what to say. So I let her do the talking. She needed to talk.

It had been a foul day. Grit everywhere. The sky was cream. A very dirty cream. The winds were dry. Everything was frightfully hot and uncomfortable. Everyone at the wedding stayed in the church as much as possible and they were grateful it was early in the morning. It had been a strange decision to have a wedding so early, and then a barbecue reception at dusk, but it was a good decision.

The minute Lin got home from the church, she changed into loose, cool clothes and went into the gar-

322

den. The sky was a bit darker from all the grit. She hadn't worried, Lin told me, because there had been grit in the winds for a few weeks, from the fires in the Snowies.

"Nothing to worry about," she said. "I was more scared about the heat and my plants. It was going to be a scorcher. Damn. I didn't mean to say scorcher. I did not." My heart reached out. I kept listening.

It hurt like hell not to be there, holding her hand and feeding her cups of tea. I've never heard Belinda talk so much. It was like an outpouring from her soul, as if she would forget what happened if she did not explain it. So I listened.

As I listened I kept thinking about all the things she should have done and could have done. Of the radio, and the television. Of birds and bees. Of how easy it is to think about reacting to an emergency and how hard it is when the crisis actually hits.

"I came inside for an early lunch, then went out again. While I was inside, I got a phone call saying the reception was postponed — some of the country people couldn't get through because of closed roads. I just thought that now I wouldn't have to change."

Somewhere at the back of my mind I kept hearing Linnie's phone ringing. I was annoyed that the phone could ring and ring without proving her house had survived.

"It was darker. I mean the sky was darker. It was dull orange. I hated it. I kept looking up and thinking I'd never seen the sky that colour in my life. Just after lunch it changed to a Darkover red. The clouds were so thick that you couldn't see the sun. But they weren't rain clouds. It was hot and dry and so very full of bluster. Things were flying everywhere through the air. I kept thinking how alien the world felt.

"It was hot. Super-hot. I went outside to bring the

smaller pot plants in. And to keep everything else wet and watered. I was so worried about my garden, I forgot to turn the radio on. I didn't know that the red was the fire reflecting off the sky, and that the whole of the mountain behind me was on fire. I didn't know. I was so worried about my garden. It lost all the moisture I gave it within minutes.

"And then the world was dark and I thought that something serious must be wrong.

"I went inside and filled water bottles and my bath and my sinks and hunted out my emergency kit. Then I went back to the garden. After a bit the blackness passed and I could see again. I started using the hose, despite the water restrictions. Everything was so hurt by the heat — it needed real water.

"As the sky paled again, I could see that more and more of my plants were in trouble. And then the sky was cream — the same shade it had been all morning. I went indoors for a tea break and discovered that the electricity had gone. It was too late to turn on the TV and find out what was happening. No power.

"I didn't know what to do. I thought the worst must be past because it was daylight again outside. I tried to ring you, but I had no phone. The news says that the whole network just melted. I didn't think of my mobile.

"All this was before five o'clock," she said with wonder and grief. "It was awful. I went back outside. Everything looked hurt and hot and blown.

"And the air. It was dark and choking and full of flying embers. For ages I stood outside with a wet tea towel over my mouth and nose and attacked spot fires in my garden. I had to wet that tea towel every few minutes.

"And the wind. It came from so many different directions. Sometimes it spiralled and sometimes it swept. All the ashes and embers it carried swirled around in patterns. I've never seen the wind before."

"Nick came round late in the afternoon. He found me in the backyard. He did the ember spotting and made me go inside and pack my valuables. We filled both our cars. He scolded me, you know, for watching the garden and not listening to the radio." She laughed, but it was not a happy laugh. "Apparently we were on evacuation alert.

"We wet everything as much as we could and my Nick checked my gutters and filled them with water. He climbed all over the roof and cleared things. I closed everything and moved flammable things away from the house. Then he made me leave. I came to his place."

"And here you are," I said, gently.

"And here I am. And do you know what the worst thing is, Joodles?" Her voice hurt. "I don't know if I have a house left. I won't know until tomorrow at the earliest. I don't know. I don't know about me. I don't know about my friends."

"Your house is fine," I told her. "Zoë and I put protective magic on it, you know."

I was only half-joking. Belinda thought I was completely joking and gave me a watery chuckle. She was not amused, but she was so distressed that she was prepared to pretend to be. "Protective magic, sure. Around all my rare plants, I bet."

"Sorry, Linnie, we were just doing the house. It was in case Peter came."

This triggered tears. I so wished I could be there and give her the biggest, biggest hug. She just needed quiet comforting at that moment.

The moment passed and we talked again, this time about other things. My children and sport. What we were all eating for dinner. Nothingnesses. Serious conversation was taboo. Linnie had to get through till the next day to find out if she still had a home.

She still had her recipe collection, she reassured me, somewhere in one of the cars. She'd saved that. And Great-Grandma's box and that coffee table book. I would have saved my computer hard drive and my photos. The first things she saved were recipes. I guess she knew I would help with the photos.

Damn those fires.

Sorry, I need time out.

————

I'm back. This is hellishly difficult to write. The closest I've ever been to bushfires is about two hundred metres, and that was on a windless day. The air smelled like a bonfire, with eucalyptus thrown in. Pleasant smell. This was nothing like that. Forty-plus degree heat. Roaring winds. And the air so black that it's darkest night in the middle of the day.

And Linnie was living through it. And there was nothing I could do. Not a bloody thing. If there was just one day in the last twelve months that could be got rid of, it would be that day.

Great-Grandma had no charms against bushfires. I know this because when Zoë and Nick came home, Nick went to his room to keep an eye on things via the web and shout us updates, and Zoë and I went right through the box, looking.

We found out that there were warning signs for events as bad as this, and that we had missed them. Zoë held out a paper which mentioned a halo round the moon and Jupiter, and asked if that was like the thing she had pointed out on Wednesday. With a sinking feeling I said, "Yes, it was" — because yes, it was. Our capital city was burning and no one knew how many had died.

If we'd known more we could have taken more care. But could we have predicted exactly what would happen? I doubt it. And could we have done anything to help Lin? This was the totally crucial question. What could we do now and what could we have done before?

We could conjure spirits, we worked out. There was a nice formula that included a laurel leaf. Zoë found a formula that called on the angel or being or whatever responsible for the sun. Very Donne-ish — the sun was everywhere and therefore knew everything. Busy old fool, unruly sun, why doest thou thus? Sneaking everywhere and seeing everything.

Alas, it was night in Canberra.

We talked about it for ages. Whether we could ask a magical being for information. And we decided against it in the end. Because we knew Lin was safe. We really didn't want to know the rest.

4.

"Sam, hi!" Rhonda had been thinking about family a lot recently. Her cousin ringing was a definite plus. She wasn't ready yet to think of Belinda as a cousin or to admit Belinda's sister into her life at all, but she missed Sam.

"Hi. How're things, cousin? You're clear of the fire."

"Things are good, I think. The fire is the other end of town. Though our brand-new cousin has taken refuge with her boyfriend, I think. And you?"

"Very well," Sam laughed. "I solved my job problems and my wife and children remembered my birthday. What more could you ask?"

"What more indeed?" Rhonda said, wondering when she last had a birthday remembered by anyone.

Except her thirty-fifth. Her thirty-fifth birthday was in a category of its own.

Thinking back to it reminded her that she had a question to ask. She had put it off now for two months, not wanting to dredge up the family issues, but she really had to sort it in her mind. "Sam, can I ask you a difficult family question?"

"If you must." Sam put on a long-suffering voice, to show her he was untroubled by the request. Rhonda had to laugh.

"There are two things that have been haunting me for years, and no one I could ask."

"Serious, huh?"

"I don't know. I'm probably inventing some sort of wild imagining."

"I see it every day," Sam said. "Our family is mostly pretty normal though, so I would guess whatever it is might be in your imagination. No wild incest or unsaid adoptions or anything."

"Nice to hear," Rhonda said, "But that wasn't the sort of thing I was thinking."

"Oh?"

"Two things," and Rhonda struggled for words. "Firstly, I thought GAM and Grandma had a kid brother, but can't remember anything about him. I keep wondering if I'm inventing relatives."

"Oh," said Sam. "That sort of thing."

There was a silence.

"I was imagining it," Rhonda said.

"No," said Sam, the family history expert. "But it's not easy to talk about. He committed suicide when he was twenty-three. When I did the family tree, that's all I could find out and we weren't allowed to ask any questions. Every person I asked gave exactly the same answer. They even used the same words. I wish I knew more."

"You did the family tree? That explains Belinda's phone call." Rhonda wasn't surprised. Sam had always been the one to chat to the older members of the family, and to find out who did what and when. They had joked about it as early teens, when Rhonda had decided she had to be an historian.

"On the non-GAM side, we're particularly good on mad Irish ancestry."

"I couldn't imagine any Irish ancestors being less than mad, somehow. We're a crazy mixed-up family."

"That we are." And there was a silence as they both contemplated the sadness of their genetic heritage.

"Oh!" Rhonda remembered. "I was wondering what happened to Auntie Jane." That was the other question. Important. So important she had not even been able to articulate it to herself without blanking out. Her self to her self. She remembered Auntie Jane and the truth of Auntie's brown gaze.

Auntie Jane had always known what everyone had done, and had looked her in the eye many times and said, "Now I think you need to put that toy back," or "Don't be greedy," or, just once, "If you're interested in reading Shakespeare, have my copy."

Rhonda had taken a copy of Hamlet from the second shelf in the living room and read it a bit and put it back. No one had been in the room at the time. The lust for Shakespeare had been inside her mind, and Auntie Jane had somehow seen it. Rhonda still had that Hamlet.

That volume of Shakespeare was, in some ways, the only proof she had of Auntie Jane's existence. Like her missing great-uncle, Auntie Jane had faded. Once Rhonda had turned eleven it was as if she had never existed. Except that Rhonda had a volume of Shakespeare next to her Nancy Drew.

It was clear that Auntie Jane had a version of Rhonda's own gift. Clear now anyway, with the glorious purity of hindsight.

"I'd forgotten Auntie Jane," Sam admitted. "I think we all try to forget her. Even more than our missing great-uncle, in some ways. I can wonder about him because I don't have a name. I try not to wonder about Auntie Jane."

"But why?" asked Rhonda. "What is it with our family, forgetting and disowning every second member and then proudly declaiming normality?"

"I don't really understand why. Auntie Jane was never disowned."

"Then what happened to her?" Rhonda felt frustration rise in her throat, warm and acrid.

"Our parents all went to visit her regularly. Mum still does. We weren't ever allowed to go with them, not even when we had kids of our own. I went to see her once, by myself, two years ago, because I felt so bad about it. I can't go again. I just can't."

And finally Rhonda understood why Sam had taken her phone number, but would never visit. She was his Jane. He had a responsibility to keep in touch. "You don't have to ring me just because our parents visited Auntie Jane," she said, her voice as soft as her meaning was harsh.

"I never meant it that way," protested Sam. "I don't ring you out of duty. You're one of my favourite cousins. You always have been. Even when I lost touch with you, I thought fond thoughts, you know."

"But?" prompted Rhonda.

"But there's always a chance, that what went wrong with Jane could go wrong with you. And I don't think I could bear to see it."

"What exactly happened to Auntie Jane? All I remember is her looking me in the eye and scaring me silly with the things she said. Is she even still alive?"

"Oh yes," Sam said, voice sombre. "She's still alive."

"Well, you didn't say. Where is she?" pursued Rhonda.

"In a lunatic asylum."

"What?" Rhonda's whole body went still as her soul went into shock. "She wasn't mad. I am totally certain she wasn't mad. She didn't act mad . . . she was different. I'm certain-sure she was just different . . ."

"I saw her two years ago. She was sitting in an armchair. Just sitting. She didn't say a word for a long while. When I asked her why she didn't talk to me, she said, 'Words cause hurt.' The nurse was surprised that she'd said anything. The nurse said she was almost catatonic most of the time, but the doctor said it wasn't that at all. When I asked what it was, he shrugged and said that she was just silent. No one knows what's wrong. Nothing helps."

"I'm so sorry," Rhonda said, "I didn't know. She wasn't like that when I knew her."

"Not your fault, "said Sam. "She was always strange. You have to remember some of the things she said. Like when she scolded Dad for a car accident two days before the car accident happened. Remember that? And when she knew we put that mouse in my brother's shoe. She'd just come in from the garden, so there was no way she could have seen us. You used to call it 'Auntie's sense'. Maybe you don't remember it as freaky?"

"I don't remember it as freaky," Rhonda admitted. "To me it was just Auntie. It wasn't enough to get her confined, though, surely, no matter how upset your father was?"

"Not what you saw. She started to go stranger and stranger around the same time as you did drugs. Everyone decided that you were going to go where Jane went, and that's why they disowned you. Mum said that the family couldn't face that tragedy again. Better not to see you than to see you become Auntie Jane."

"It wasn't the drugs at all, then?" Rhonda asked.

"Not for most of the family. They were the excuse we gave each other."

"So they left me behind because our great-uncle had committed suicide and Auntie Jane was quite, quite mad."

"Yes."

"Thank you," said Rhonda.

"What is there to bloody thank me for?" Sam exploded at the other end of the line. "I'm as guilty as the rest of them. Especially since I saw you, and you're not mad at all. My teenage daughter is crazier than you."

"Teenagers are crazier than almost anyone," Rhonda pointed out. "I'm different, though. It's quite obvious that I'm different. And knowing why makes it easier to sort out how to deal with my difference."

"You always were the most sensible one of the lot of us," Sam said.

"Maybe that is why I'm sane?"

"Sane, but different," Sam was obviously thinking about it.

"Can you live with that?" Rhonda asked.

"Yes," said Sam, "I think I can. Over the phone, at least."

"Over the phone is a huge advance on my last few years." Rhonda couldn't help sounding acerbic. "It's been lonely."

"I bet."

"Sam? Can I ask you one more question?"

"Sure," said Sam.

"If I go crazy, will you let me know, somehow? No matter how difficult it is to say. Please?"

"Why?" asked Sam.

"I don't think it's craziness," explained Rhonda, "I

think it's just not dealing with that difference I have. If I'm not dealing with it, then I want to know. I need someone who will be honest with me. And there's no one here who can tell me." Since she wasn't going to confide in Dave. What a tiny world she had built for herself. Suddenly its intimacy seemed terrifying. People were important.

"Sensible bloody Rhonda," Sam said, a faint smile in his voice.

"Absolutely," but sensible Rhonda couldn't mask her fear.

"I'll tell you," he promised. After a quiet pause, he added, "It scares the hell out of me, though."

"That I could end up in a lunatic asylum?"

"No," and the rest of the sentence was a long time emerging, "that the family condemned Auntie Jane to a lunatic asylum. Maybe she could've been helped."

"I don't think our family is good at support," Rhonda admitted. And neither of them referred to the missing uncle. Neither of them wanted to pursue the idea that there were even worse paths open to Rhonda and her 'difference' than the one forced on Auntie Jane. Loneliness was better than death. Even insanity was better than death.

5.

TVwhore was in a strange mood. She was posting teasers on every thread of Rhonda's blog. "I have a secret," TVwhore said. "My emotions boil inside me."

If it wasn't for the 'emotions boil inside me', Rhonda would have done a disappearing act. She decided to wait and see. TVwhore hadn't taken advantage of her knowledge of who Rhonda really was, after all. She hadn't even sent a letter. And Rhonda felt a curiosity burning inside her to know TVwhore's secret. And, to be honest, she didn't quite believe what Dave had said, that TVwhore might be interested in Rhonda. And so Rhonda's mind was trapped between realities and she didn't run.

To every post she replied, "Tell me?"

Then she signed out and left TVwhore to take her next step. Rhonda wondered particularly what the emotional stuff was. Love, she hoped. Then she wondered who TVwhore was in love with. Love was a good place to be. Less paranoid, less fretful, less insecure. Just as long as it wasn't love with her. She was spoken for.

Dave was in a mind-reading mood, because just as she thought 'less insecure' he came in and kissed her on the head. "Coffee?" he asked.

"Always," Rhonda answered. "Don't bring it in here, though. I'm just finishing up."

"Will you be long?" Dave obviously remembered what had happened the last time she had said 'just finishing up'.

"I'm finishing with this group then I just have one more I want to check on before I go offline."

"Take your time, I brought work with me."

"Don't trust me to give you 100% attention, then?"

"Nup," he said cheerfully, and settled down on the couch. Life with Dave was easier now he knew she was Rhonda the Geek.

Her final task was to check up on the history board. Rhonda wanted the coffee first, but when she settled down for an evening with Dave she did not want work to raise its head. This was how she had kept her secret self so very carefully secret, despite the relationship. It was effective and happy, both.

She settled down to read what her history colleagues had written and was soon immersed in a sequence of bickering about literature. She forgot Dave was in the room and started commenting to herself about various posts.

"Wrong Walpole," she said once, then, "Wrong century entirely, you stupid idjit. How can you even think Charles Dickens? Good lord, some people are morons."

She was drawn into the argument about reading and modern interpretations and finally let loose with, "It's in my book. It's all in my bloody book, goddamit. I'm not going to post excerpts. They can drown in their own bile. I have to explain though, dammit. Let's see . . ." and she started typing.

Eventually Rhonda heaved a big sigh and logged off. "Finished," she said to herself, quietly but firmly. She shut down her computer and then turned to find Dave watching her thoughtfully.

"You're writing a book?" he asked.

"You're eavesdropping," Rhonda accused.

"Hard not to eavesdrop," he pointed out.

"True," and Rhonda smiled.

"I still want to know about the book."

"You always want to know about everything. I need coffee first." Dave pointed to the table where a steaming cup was waiting. "How did you know?" she asked.

"When you said 'Finished', I pressed 'Start' on the coffeemaker."

"You're evil, you know."

"I know. Now tell me about your book."

"My book is about how literary works bring the past to life," Rhonda explained, sounding happier than she felt. For too long she had been hoarding this project, as her guy rope to her academic self. "It's very slow going because it has to fit round everything else."

"Pity," Dave said. "Can you tell me a bit more?"

"I guess." Rhonda didn't want to get into an explanation. Explanations could trigger strange things and she wanted to keep him very clear of that oddness. "I can give you my outline? I'll just go print it out." And Rhonda made her escape before he could object.

"SHADOWS OF THE PAST," said her printout, boldly.

From there on it was all notes and unfinished ideas. Dave read out the bits that appealed particularly. "This book is about shadows. The shadow of the past on our past. The shadow of history in our history. It traces how the shade of an earlier past left its mark on the eighteenth century and looks at the shapes of the stories that people told each other about their own history."

"And that is all you know and all you need to know," said Rhonda as she took back her meagre pages.

"Dammit, Rhonda, there must be more than this."

"Dammit, Dave, there are one hundred and twenty eight pages of pure research, uncontaminated by a single node of thought. And you're not seeing it. You have the outline and some of my introductory thoughts, and that's more than anyone else has ever got to examine."

"Aren't you going to publish it?"

"One day. Maybe," said Rhonda. "But this isn't like one of those articles. It has to be perfect."

All she got for that was a darkling glare.

————

Writing was in Rhonda's ether. It surrounded her and infused her with the need to create. This time, she felt compelled to try something entirely new.

MissTRie: "I've written the intro to a children's story. Who's game to write the next bit?"

Starchild "Me! Me! I want in!!"

MissTRie "I'll post it then."

MissTRie: "Once upon a time there was a child. This child was special. He thought he was normal. He thought he was average. Every child thinks he is normal and average unless his parents tell him he is special. His parents did not tell him that he was special, so he made mud pies perfectly happily."

Starchild: "What he didn't know was that his parents were magic. Yes! Their special magic was light. If they didn't control themselves, then everything they touched glowed in the dark. Look at them carefully and you will see that their fingernails have a soft glow. Glow in the dark nails. This is how a stranger could tell they were magic. They were careful to wear knitted gloves so that strangers couldn't see their fingernails. The boy's mother was very good at knitting gloves."

CHAPTER TWELVE

1.

IT WAS A BLOODY TELEMARKETER. NICK SAYS I SHOULD BE polite about telemarketers forever more. And to them. He says they earned it because of what I put that young man through on the phone that Sunday.

"Do you know I'm waiting on a phone call from my sister? And that she's in Canberra and only just escaped the bloody bushfires? What the hell is it you want me to buy?" That was the polite bit. If that young man retires from telemarketing with compensable injuries, it will probably be my fault.

Belinda's suburb was lucky. Only a few houses destroyed. Her friend in Duffy, the one who was going to be our safe house if things got hairy with Peter — she lost everything. Everything.

Linnie's place was a mess. All her curtains and soft furnishings were damaged by water or smoke. Enthusiastic fire fighters had turned pot plants over and trampled them into the carpet. But all that was small beer. Liveable with. Three of her friends lost everything and one of them was uninsured.

The second thing Lin did when she got home was to

see what she could spare for those friends. I brought some odds and sods to Canberra too, when I came to help her clean up. In the end we put everything in the major collection area, to go to whoever needed it when they needed it. But that was the second thing Lin did.

The first thing she did was walk around her garden. Gone. Lost. It was a miracle the house made it. Linnie lives her garden. It is her soul, the way politics are mine. And now she would have to start again.

Lin kept saying things like, "Compared to what other people are going through, it's nothing at all. Compared to what you have been through it's nothing."

I wanted her to pick up and move elsewhere.

Nick and she were adamant. She was staying. The fire threat was not over, so she had a radio with her, and an emergency kit, and her mobile phone. She and Nick were prepared to flee to each other's places at a moment's notice. Canberra must have been a hell of a city to live that fortnight.

Eventually the fire threat faded. Belinda made the mistake of saying she was going to spend a weekend cleaning things and getting her home de-ashed. I volunteered all our services. My Nick volunteered to get rid of the ashes from the letterbox. Poor Lin had to explain that the letterbox was not ashed: it was cindered.

I rang that lavender farm I had hated visiting in the spring and explained about Linnie's garden and asked about that fancy decoration she had so admired. I was confusing, it seems, for they sent me to my local nursery and faxed the nursery instructions directly.

And my darlings travelled. Nick and Rudolph shared the back seat with all sorts of plant clippings from our rather trashed yard. Rudolph had invited himself. Nick had to make sure that the lavender didn't crash over and mess up my borrowed car. I didn't mind if they crashed over and mussed up Rudy's pristine elegance.

The men also kept an eye on Belinda's surprise new letterbox. Nick-the-younger chose it. This is how he got the back seat, because Zoë took one look at it and refused to go near. It was lurid. It still is.

I had to shut my eyes as I drove into Belinda's driveway. Honestly. I shut them. I nearly hit things, but I couldn't bear to look.

I have to stop crying. I will write more soon.

2.

Dave read the two paragraphs from the online story and wanted to play. "It sounds like fun," he said, and his voice was wistful.

"I didn't know you had a silly side," Rhonda commented.

"There's a lot you don't know about me," he answered, and gave her a meaningful stare.

"Uh-huh," said Rhonda. "Like that that look of yours that gets so overused? I know that about you."

"Rhonda, let me play."

"Okay, but they don't know about you, so expect some surprise."

"I can use your nickname?"

"No," Rhonda felt very firm about this. "You play as yourself or not at all."

"I can't use a nick?"

"You can, just not mine."

"Okay," he agreed meekly. Rhonda was suspicious. He sat at the computer and registered. He typed enthusiastically but slowly, frowning and revising and changing his mind over and over. Rhonda couldn't see what he was typing, but it was certainly taking forever.

Eventually he said, "Ready. Now where do I put it?"

"You can't," said Rhonda. "I've friends-locked my account. Hang on a tick and I'll add you to my friends' list."

"You mean I'm your friend," and he gave her a goofy smile.

"No, I mean that you're an idiot, and idiots need looking after, so I will let you in where I can keep an eye on you."

Dave didn't laugh and Rhonda wondered why. When she asked for his user name to add to her friends' list she discovered exactly why. He had registered as Misstriesman.

"You got the capitalisation all wrong," was all she said.

"You did say I needed looking after."

"You do. Anyhow, now you can post stuff to my blog."

Light casts darkness into disrepair. The boy's parents were crusaders, seeking the foulest and deepest places on earth and bringing light to them. They were relentless in their hunt and relentless in their illumination of the midnight places.

Misstriesman: Light blinds. The boy's parents were blinded by their own light and they could not see that their son needed them.

"Hello, misstriesman," posted Phased. "I have no idea what comes next, but I'm being polite today so I thought I would greet you. It's the first time I've been polite in five days. Tell us all MissTRie's secrets."

"If he does that, I will have to scare him. He's a tiny thing, easily terrified, my boyfiend."

Dave raised his eyebrow at Rhonda after reading this. "Boyfiend?" he asked.

"Oh, damn," Rhonda said. "Let me go back and correct it. It's just a typo."

"Leave it."

"So you're not going to cause me trouble with my friends?"

"Are you kidding?" and he bent over the keyboard and slowly typed.

"How can a journalist be so slow?" she asked him.

He tilted his head round and gave her a very wicked grin. "It's not how fast I am," he said. "It's the end result."

Rhonda read. "Of all the things MissTRie said, the only one you should trust is the boyfiend. I am not human. Beware!"

Phased answered. "You're almost as mad as the rest of us — you'll do. Nice to have been online at the same time as you two. I'm the first one to meet the boyfiend!"

"We'll have to come back from time to time and see what the others have to say for themselves," Rhonda said.

"I guess so. God, I could kill for a cup of coffee."

"Do you know," Rhonda went to put on the kettle, "that between us we keep the world coffee industry very healthy."

"It's a hard job, but someone's gotta do it," and Dave moved up and wrapped his arms around her. Rhonda snuggled close to him, happy.

The next day was less secure. Rhonda was in a chat room with a bunch of people she didn't know. And one of them was asking difficult questions.

They were not the usual difficult questions. This questioner was like a vulture, circling closer and closer and closer over the dead. It was her old chat room, though, and Rhonda was stubborn.

"I won't be driven out," she told herself. "I'm anonymous. Mr Vulture can't get me."

The sudden rush of loneliness kept her silently avoiding anything but the merest pretence of an answer to questions, while the pursuer found out more and more and more about three of her previous personas. Three. Everyone in the chatroom remembered bits and pieces about them: M44M from Ohio, Trud who loved computer games, Dame who dropped French words into sentences from time to time. Memories of them sprouted from the woodwork.

Rhonda had an urge to get offline and ring Dave on his mobile. Except that he was working. She sighed and typed another question mark. She wondered what she should do about this person. The fact that he had brought together three of her nicknames was worrying. There wasn't much she could do, however. Except log off.

She logged out of the chat room and wrote a bleak little continuation of the Child of Light tale.

MissTRie: There in the dark, he learned that light was loneliness. Year after year he relearned it, until one day he ran away from home. The boy found a job in a morgue, and there, in the peace of the night, he found that death could be companionable. He found that blackness was friendlier than the bright glare of neglect. The boy discovered what he wanted to do with his life. He wanted the world to be dark; he wanted the light to go out.

3.

Rudolph faded into a man of all work. He stopped making caustic comments, and spent the weekend doing solid cleaning. Every moment he was nice twisted the knife.

Nick was gruesome. He and Cow Eyes Nick went on a special driving tour together with camera and documented stuff. I overheard him telling Zoë with great relish about a burned old ironing board standing on the nature strip near a church. He told her how the pews of the church were warped with the flames and the glass had all blown out and that the roof had caved in, but that the plastic children's playground was fine. Linnie had been in that church for the wedding.

He talked about how sad the kangaroos looked on the highway, starving and with nowhere to go. No water. No shade. Nothing but charred earth.

I stopped him right there. "You give your sister nightmares, Nicholas, and I will give you nightmares."

"Yes, Mum," he said, and saved his photo collection for his friends at school.

Belinda put all our little pots of cuttings in a safe place. She said she needed time, and that maybe some of her other plants would grow back. I looked at the desolation that was once one of the most gracious gardens imaginable, and said, "Yes, of course they will," dutifully.

She laughed herself into hysterics over the lavender. She never thanked me; her exact words were, "Only you, Judith, only you." Nick reassured me on the way home that he thought those words were good. But he was snickering himself silly. Family.

Anyway, that was the start of 2003. Totally uneventful.

Damn those bushfires.

4.

Dr Nick moved in with Belinda the minute we stopped taking up all the spare room. We were just told it as a fait accompli. "She needs a keeper," was his comment to Zoë and Nick and me. "And I want to save on rent."

"Mum needs a keeper too," Zoë said.

Both Nicks just laughed and said I was a lost cause. I will get even.

All the way home Nick muttered dire things about

Dr Nick moving in with his aunt. Rudolph slept. Then it finally dawned on me that I had wanted a man for my sister, and someone who thought I was hugely entertaining would not stop her visiting us. I said this to the kids, and they said, "Oh, Mum!" So that was all right.

We hit the outskirts of Sydney and started planning for school the next week. Which means, yes, you guessed it, we spent an hour arguing. Zoë and Nick and I spent an hour arguing. Rudolph was awake, but being self-effacing. It scared me.

Rudolph turned up one evening soon after the bushfires. Zoë suddenly didn't like him anymore, so she faded from view instantly. I went up the street, solitary, for milk. I left Mr Look-How-Charming-I-Am with Nick. I nearly bought the out-of-date milk, but that would have been petty, so added some chocolate for sensible Zoë and even more sensible Judith to my purchases, to console us for him turning up to console me.

I found Rudolph lounge-lizarding away when I got home, talking about war games with his mouth and watching me walk through the door so he could send quite other messages to me with the rest of his body. This was a new tactic. He had given up on self-effacement.

Nick didn't look happy. The three of us had singularly uncomfortable cups of tea. Whenever Rudolph tried to insinuate himself into a late night, Nick would send him an ugly glare. Rudolph left with grace, as ever, and just the least hint of delicate self-deprecation.

It took a lot of prodding to find out what had happened.

Apparently the conversation had only turned to war games when I opened the front door. That evening, in the post-fire comfort zone, Rudolph finally started telling Nick what he truly felt for me. How he admired certain body parts, but that it was a shame about my legs. Nick told me that much. He didn't confide in me just how graphic Rudolph had been, but I can guess. Rudolph has, after all, whispered in my shell-pink ear once or twice.

My suspicion is that Nick was not quite ready to discover that his mother had private parts and that they were functional. I have the strong suspicion that Rudolph told Nick what the private parts of women are for. And that Nick objected. Mothers, after all, are not like other humans.

Nick's prudishness is the single biggest piece of evidence that there is a God and that she is looking out for me and mine.

I think I should stop this writing here and get myself a cuppa. I find myself also somewhat prurient, even though they were my private parts under discussion.

For me, once the kids were back at school and Rudolph had no excuse to appear every other day I suffered a kind of reaction. I got headaches and nerve pain and the miseries. Nothing terribly grand. Nothing worth complaining about. I went to work looking strained and I came home looking drained. The kids didn't realise anything was wrong.

Two weeks of feeling as if my nerves were shattering was quite enough, though. Pain relievers did not help, and going to the doctor would have alerted the kids. Besides, I would probably have been given some sort of happy pill. And happy pills go so against my basic personality I refuse to take them.

So what else was left? Magic. I made myself an amulet. And rubbed myself with olive oil that had the same spell said over it as the one in the amulet. I looked a bit like a Christmas tree, with my three amulets hanging. Or an ageing hippy. I smelled like an Italian noodle factory. It did help the nerve pain though. And my life could continue in its inexorable way.

Maybe we were due for something good. Maybe the next crisis that would happen would be a killer. I was basically at the stage where I couldn't give a damn. I not only looked like an ageing hippy, I decided to act like one and just live from moment to moment for a bit. No fires. No angel of death. No anything.

5.

"Zoë!" I called, when I heard her walking in the front door, "Could you please ring your aunt? She wants to talk."

"She liked my present?" Zoë looked innocently enthusiastic. As if she had never, ever sent a parcel. Mail order magic to her aunt, to help the ruined garden. Without her mother's permission.

"She liked your gift, and has buried them, but I'm not very happy. When you've rung her and thanked her nicely, you will come here and talk to me. This is non-negotiable."

Zoë sighed. This was not one of the cute sighs she used to give, but a whole new variety. At this rate her twelfth birthday party was going to be spent eating twisties and chocolate crackles and drinking coke from Princess cups in her room, alone.

At least Rudolph wouldn't be turning up for that twelfth birthday party.

Anyway, Zoë made that phone call and sounded happy and chirpy and totally delightful all the way through it. She always sounds that with Lin though. Their chirps just bounce off each other. Two sunny little tweety birds.

Then I made tea. I remembered back to the phone call with Lin, ages ago, when she told me all about the ethics of being Jewish and practising magic. It's just as well I have a good memory for phone calls. I didn't trust myself to steer us both through this morass.

"Zoë, you know magic can be really dangerous, don't you?" Start with the sledgehammer, Judith.

"It can hurt people." Clever child.

"Yes," but not clever enough. I put years of suffering into that 'yes'. "But it can be bad for you as well as for the people you hurt. It's not as simple as you taking a paper from the box and doing spells whenever you feel like it."

"So you're mad at me."

"And you're amazingly clever and perceptive." No, I did not sound sarcastic when I said that. I am the least sarcastic person you will ever meet in your whole born existence.

"You're going to listen to me very, very carefully, Zoë. I want to know you understand it before you try any more spells."

"But I can still do spells with you?" She sounded hopeful.

"Maybe," I said. "That depends on you under-standing me."

She nodded and we started the explanation. It was long and involved. Tortuous, in fact. I belaboured points until Zoë could repeat them back from three different directions.

"Maimonides was a great Jewish sage who told us how we should use magic safely and so it would not hurt people. He says that it's better not to practise magic if you're not sure. If you can do something without magic, it's better to do without it. And there are some types of magic we don't do at all."

She knows that she should never hurt people with magic. I said, "Great," and forbore to tell her about my attack on Peter's capacity to sleep at night. That's the trouble with explaining things to children, every single lapse in your life shines back in your face in full technicolour.

I explained to her about not doing magic that includes worship of any God but the Jewish God. I said this didn't mean that we criticised other people's worship. It was just that we could only do what we believed in, and we were Jewish. I asked her if she had any knowledge of Judaism apart from what I had taught her.

She said, indignantly, "Of course not!"

"Then we need to work on that before you can do magic by yourself."

"Oh," she said intelligently, sounding just like her mother.

"Besides," I said, "If we're going to be attacked for being Jewish we might as well know more about it."

"Does that mean you'll be studying with me?"

She sounded so bloody hopeful I had no choice but to say, gloomily, "Yes, it does."

And we talked about graven images. And we talked about names of God. Zoë promised she would not do any of the Names of God spells.

The enormous thing I shoved down her throat was the enormous thing Linnie had shoved down mine. Ethics. Doing good to other people. Thinking about consequences of actions. I used the demon as a case in point; he did badly by us even when he was giving gifts to other people in the hopes that they would worship him. Or that we would worship him. Or whatever.

"I liked the sliced lemons, though," she said wistfully. "And the Angel of Death winked at me."

"But if we had not been super-nice to him, he would have let that man kill us with the explosives. You only see the Angel of Death when you're probably going to die, you know."

"Yes, Mum, I told *you*, remember?" She gave me a pointed look.

I sighed. I got her to explain back the ethics. Then I moved onto prophecies and things. And personal responsibility. And taking charge of one's own actions. Heavy stuff.

I knew she would sneak other spells out of the box. That's Zoë. Just like I knew she would do it all on her own. I didn't know whether to be grateful or worried that she's such a solitary child. I made her promise to ask permission.

"What about the things I already did?" She sounded anxious. Good.

"Can you promise me you did absolutely nothing that would hurt anyone?"

She nodded vigorously.

"Then this time I'll forgive it. But you have now promised to check with me first, is that clear?" It was clear. We were clear. Life was a little less terrifying.

As an aside, all this little sequence happened without Nick. He'd done some fast talking at school and told them about his work experience offer and had been given a week in Canberra. During the day he worked in Shaz's office and at night he came home to Lin and Lin's Nick. His spare time, so my sister told me, was mostly spent getting rid of fire debris. A very laudable week, all told. Very educational.

6.

I think the whole world was sick of secrets that week. Well, except maybe Nick.

June rang me the next week wanting me to come over and give solace. Those were her words. Give solace. Her past had caught up with her and she needed uncritical comfort. She turned to me? What the hell was the world coming to? The original Ms Razor Edge as comfort?

When I got to her place I saw white swastikas daubed all over the red brick. I thought of June's age; I thought of her background: I felt sick to my stomach. It took an act of will to walk past the swastikas and ring her doorbell. It took an even greater act of will not to react to the small, frail woman she had suddenly become.

That was an evening of real secrets. June was a Holocaust survivor. I had not known that. I knew her only as a champion of those in need.

She told me about it over tea. She insisted on making me tea. Dammit. At first, when she was new in Australia, she had hidden that she was Jewish. Being Jewish meant dying; it meant torture; it meant not having permission to belong to the human race.

Eventually she let people know more about her background. Not the whole story. Never the whole story. She wanted to be Jewish, she said. She knew many others who denied everything, because they were scared. June said she had decided that life was too short for that. She had kept up a pretence of being Australian Jewish, part of the natural left wing that her generation belonged to in Oz. She intentionally lost her accent and, to all intents and purposes, her past. Most people assumed she was local and had always been local.

June told me now that she had been in Theresienstadt. The Glamour Concentration Camp. Where children sang charmingly in operas the day before they were murdered. But someone from either the neo-Nazi far right or the anti-Israel far left had discovered her. They'd daubed swastikas all over the front of her house. I was the one who had written that angry email. I was proud to be Jewish. That's what she said. I wasn't sure I was even proud to be human when I saw what had been done to my friend.

I was honoured. I felt guilty as hell. I hadn't suffered what she had suffered. I hadn't survived what she had survived. When she was a little less crumpled and torn, I told her to watch TV. She said, "Yes, Judith."

June is not a "Yes, Judith" person. Dammit.

While she was watching TV, I raided her laundry. With buckets and every skerrick of bleach in the house, and big thick rubber gloves, and a face mask, and, when necessary, a scraper and a knife, I got rid of all those swastikas. It was past midnight before I was finished, but when June woke up in the morning she would not be faced with the symbol of those who had murdered her parents and her sisters and her brother and had come close to murdering her.

In the middle of the clean-up, a boy came along with a paintbrush to do more of his nasty work. I yelled, "Boo!" at him, and asked him if he killed his own grandmother for fun.

He ran.

Maybe that was not wise or nice. But I'd been cleaning walls for over two hours. I smelled foul and felt fouler. All I cared about was that June, who'd escaped Europe with no childhood, should be allowed a dignified old age.

The next day Zoë and I came and visited. Zoë distracted her and I did a protection of the house. Then I distracted her and Zoë did a protection of the garden. Zoë pretended to be playing. Both of us agreed that this was an ethical use of magic. And that what that foul kid had done the day before was an unethical use of whitewash.

———

Dave appeared again on Friday, looking smaller than usual.

"Can I take you out tomorrow?" he asked.

"Only if you tell me what's wrong now," Rhonda said.

"You're a cruel woman," Dave said.

"You come in here looking about four foot tall, and I get worried. When I get worried I ask stupid questions. I told you I have no people skills."

Dave smiled and some of his presence came back. "I'm just not getting anywhere with my story," he confessed. "I pulled all kinds of strings to get the funding and it's going ratshit."

Rhonda considered, "Can I do anything?"

"Let me see you behind candles in a good restaurant and I will know that coming to Australia was worth every dime."

"Okay," Rhonda said. "I can do that. I will even dress up pretty."

The next night found Rhonda dressed up to the nines in a very formal restaurant. No candles, but enough mood lighting to put diners to sleep. Dave looked more himself, but still, somehow, smaller than he ought to be.

She resolved to get to the bottom of it. She also resolved she would pretend she had normal social skills. In order to achieve all this, she had to avoid asking all the questions she wanted and needed to ask. Finally, over dessert, she admitted that she had a burning question.

"What went wrong?" Dave asked for her.

"Something like that. I've never seen you less than charismatic, and right now you look . . ."

"I guess I just don't like myself as much as I did," he said slowly.

"But why?" asked Rhonda.

"I lied." Dave didn't look at all happy about admitting this. Rhonda wasn't sure she wanted to hear. But she was the one who started this. And now he had started, the look on his face suggested he wouldn't be content until he told her.

"You're still you," she said consolingly. "Tell me and we can pretend the lie never happened. Or something."

"Give me a little," he asked. "I'm getting there."

And she gave him until they were both back at her place before she asked, "What did you lie about, anyhow?"

"My work."

Rhonda was confused. "You're not a journo?"

"Oh, I'm a journalist all right. I'm just not based at Parliament House."

Rhonda patted the couch to indicate he should sit next to her. He walked around the room restlessly, as he confessed. "I do government stories, but that is my way of keeping a bit of an income stream and developing contacts. I have a big project. Whiz-banger."

"It's giving you giant problems, by the look of it," Rhonda observed.

He whirled around. "Why did you say that?" His eyes bore into hers.

"Because your feet stopped standing still the moment you started thinking about the thing," Rhonda commented.

"Oh," and Dave went off the boil. This man could handle a date rape drug and just could not deal with his own perceived failure.

"I don't even know what the whiz-banger is," Rhonda pointed out.

"Oh, right."

"Come here." Rhonda stopped hinting. He sat down, and she put her arm around him, and said, "Now, tell me."

"It's big. Very big," Dave said. "I'm after someone. I've been after him for years, but I thought he was in the States. Then something he said made me think he had come Down Under."

"An American?"

"Almost certainly. He's very well-known, but no one knows his real name."

"Sort of like the Scarlet Pimpernel?"

Dave laughed. "He doesn't free aristos; he uncovers drug deals and tells the future."

Rhonda did her best to appear relaxed. "You mean the New Nostradamus guy?"

"Sure do. And I thought I had him this week. I thought I had him."

The clever pursuer in the chat room earlier in the week had been Dave. Her boyfriend was still not himself, which was something she was truly thankful for. He was entirely focussed on his near-miss.

"Last year," he said, "when the Nostradamus guy blew open the lid on US and Aussie relations, that's when I realised he might be Down Under. He knew his stuff. I've never seen anyone who knows so much. I started tracking him from what he knew, but that just led to dead ends. Recently I tracked him on where he appears and this week, God, I was so sure I had him. And then he disappeared on me. Damn well disappeared. Like snow in summer."

Rhonda found she rather liked snow in summer.

Dave being her pursuer was just about the worse news imaginable. No, it wasn't. The worse news imaginable would be life without Dave. God, what if she had to choose? Why the hell had she fallen in love? Why, if she had to fall in love, did it have to be with someone who could ruin her life?

CHAPTER THIRTEEN

1.

ONE EVENING, COMING HOME FROM JUNE'S, I LOOKED UP at the sky. Mum taught me this. I saw a halo around the moon, and Scorpio was within it. And I could not for the life of me remember what that meant.

I was expecting, after all the talking I had done at my daughter, after the number of times I had been through that box and trawled the internet for information, that I would know things. No way. I had to trawl through the bloody box yet again to find out. Even things I knew I'd seen before.

It took me far too long. I found the bestiary scan that Lin had done me from Great-Grandma's notebook. I realised I had imagined I had seen a unicorn (the kosher variety) in my garden. Sometimes I am so slow it takes me months to put together pieces. Even at my most gullible I couldn't imagine a unicorn descending into suburban Sydney, so I decided that it was a figment of my imagination, brought on by too much magic. My brain, in other words, was addled.

That important issue being settled, I finally worked out that a halo round the moon with Scorpio inside meant a high ranking marriage and it meant traffic jams. Fine, we would all leave a bit earlier for work and school the next day. Bloody traffic jams.

The week after was not a great deal better. Some things ought to be predictable though. I mean, when Dad sent Lin all of Great-Grandma's stuff and then me all of my stuff, didn't I take the hint that he might be clearing a bit of house space?

Not only did I not take the hint, I was flabbergasted to open the mail that Tuesday and find an invitation for me to attend his wedding. On cream paper with gold lettering, and cupids. There were cupids. Bloody cupids.

Nick and Zoë got separate invitations. That was his fiancée, I bet. Getting in good with the old family. Or maybe finding out that the only way she was going to meet us was to get us invited to the bloody wedding.

And where had we been when he got engaged?

A wedding. In Melbourne. At Easter. No, that is not sarcasm. It is me imitating a stunned mullet. I rang Belinda up that evening and asked her what the hell he was doing.

"I don't know what Dad is thinking," she confessed.

"But you knew he was engaged?"

"No," she admitted, obviously reluctantly. Her lack of knowledge preserved her life for one more day.

"I'm not mad Dad is remarrying," I said

"You're not?" and yes, she was laughing. Bloody Belinda. And Bloody Ol' Cow Eyes. Bad influence on her. She never used to laugh at me this openly.

"No," I said. Still firm. Totally calm. In control. "I'm mad because I have not met my stepmother-to-be." I let this seep in. "Have you met her?"

"Yes," she admitted. "There was a lunch thing when I had the high-school reunion weekend."

"And you didn't tell me?"

"I was so busy avoiding talking about you-know-who that I completely forgot."

"You were so busy trying not to talk about you-know-who that you completely avoided talking about you-know-what?" I asked

She sighed. "You know, Judy, if you'd just rung Dad once in the last few years, he would've made sure you met her."

"You know this for a fact?" I sneered. I didn't know you genuinely could sneer in saying something, I thought it was just something you read about in bad novels. It was a good sneer, though I say it myself.

"What?" she asked.

"What do you mean, 'What?'" I answered, in all innocence.

"What is it you're plaguing me about? Why are you really upset?"

"I'm really upset that Dad could give bloody Peter my address and not think to tell me he was giving me a bloody new mother. That's what I'm really upset about."

"Damn," Belinda said. "I am so sorry, Judes."

"I'm supposed to be happy with him and pleased for his future?"

"You could still be happy for him," she suggested, more patiently, "but I can understand why you didn't ring him."

"You can't understand the years of not ringing though, can you?"

"No," came the answer, finally, "I can't."

"Dammit, Linnie, why not?"

"Because you and Dad had such a special relationship."

One more secret I hadn't told anyone. And unless I told Lin, she would never understand. "Linnie, I need to ring you back."

She just said, "If you don't ring me, I'll ring you. Tonight. We have to finish this conversation."

Maybe it was nothing much. Maybe I'd magnified everything in my mind. Maybe I was the guilty party all along. We tell ourselves these things, you know, even when we know lots of other women who have told themselves these things. Domestic violence tears families to pieces.

I had a long cup of tea. I made sure the kids were out of the way. I left it very, very late. But I did ring my sister back. "Hi, you," I said, a bit watery.

"Hi, are you okay now?" The voice of sisterly concern.

"I will be. Look, there's something. This was just between Dad and me and I didn't want to let it get between Dad and you, so I never told you. It was a joke he made. And I said I would never speak to him unless he apologised. And he never has."

"What sort of joke was it?" Linnie was wary.

"Remember I used to go and stay overnight with Mum and Dad, when things started to get hairy?"

"Yes," and her voice was measured, holding back her views.

"And then I stopped doing it and came to you. And then we decided this was not good enough and we both moved."

"Well, having Peter knock on my door in the wee hours carrying a knife was not my idea of happy families," she commented.

"And I refused to bring Dad into it, and Mum was totally a mess about who to support?"

"Yes." She was sounding worried. "I never understood why you kept Dad out."

"Because of the joke," I said, patiently.

"I guessed that," and she sounded nearly as teary as me, "Just what was this joke?"

"I was reading in the kitchen and Dad came in and wanted a cup of tea. He asked if he had to beat me up to get it."

"Oh God."

"That wasn't the first joke."

"Oh God."

"Sorry, Linnie, I didn't want you to know. But I can't ring Dad. I can't."

"Dad will apologise," was all my sister said. Her voice was tough and determined.

I put my sister through hell.

———

I slept that night. I was surprised. No nightmares. I hadn't realised how much that one small secret had poisoned my life. As I told Nick, we're supposed to love our parents, but sometimes we can't find it in ourselves to like them.

I made another discovery that night. I'd forgiven Dad years ago, provisionally. But I had to hear that apology.

The next few days I obliterated myself in work more than somewhat. I also did something rather drastic. I rang up Rudolph and arranged to meet him for coffee.

I didn't know what to think about him. Even today, I have no idea. He hadn't acted as if I was a trophy. Sleeping together was only a part of what Rudolph and I had. A small part.

I might've been another trophy, or I might've been a good friend he happened to sleep with. My men are never any good at declaring love, so, who knows, he might even love me. All I knew was, it was too much.

The coffee was to simplify matters.

I told him we were no longer an item. I was even a

bit apologetic about it and gave the excuse that we just didn't suit. Which was a sort of half lie. I had no idea whether we suited or not, because I'd been fighting against the relationship from the beginning. I didn't tell him about what the Boss had said because I didn't want to hear his answer.

He was silent. Terribly silent. I wondered if I'd done the right thing. Maybe the Boss was wrong? But she'd dated him. And the first time we met he was buying presents for multiple lady friends. Multiple — not just one. No, I'd done the right thing. Even if I didn't like this silence.

"Judith," he finally said, "This is not the end of us."

"I'm sorry?"

"Girlfriends don't dump me," he warned. "I dump them." Of all the things he could have said, this was probably the most annoying.

"So break with tradition," I snapped back.

"But we're very good in bed together."

"Are you trying to sound like the guy from Bridget Jones, or would you rather I remembered you as a human being?"

He laughed. The man laughed. "I'll give you six months," he said. "Then I'll be back." He put money for the coffee on the table and walked out. Men don't walk out on me: I walk out on them.

I was furious. I kept thinking that he was a sleaze and a slime ball and that the six months was his ego being massaged. He knew though that I wouldn't be certain. Damn him.

The next day, my sister rang. I hate telephones. "Hi," she said, intelligently. She's such a bright spark, my sister. She even says 'hi' with great wit. "It seems ages since we talked."

"It *is* ages," I pointed out. "At least three days. You're still alive, I hope."

"I'm still alive. Things are coming back to order, in their own sweet time. We're all agonising over the past few weeks."

"And?" I prompted, because she seemed to be leading to something.

"I've finally reached the stage where I'm sick of agonising, and sick of being supportive. All I can do with my garden is take care of everything, and then see what comes back to life in autumn."

"There's a chance of that?"

"Not much," she admitted with surprising sangfroid. Which meant she was killing herself inside and there was not a thing I could do about it. I couldn't even damn her plants because they'd already burned in hell. "We have water restrictions back and all the danger is past. All I can do is wait and see."

"Well, you can camp outside and watch for signs of green," I suggested doubtfully.

"Judith." Oh, damn, I went too far, I thought. Her tone was somewhat recriminatory. "Nick wanted a good one-liner from you."

"Your Nick wants a one-liner from me, does he?" I said, savagely. I'm not an amusement park. Not when I'm trying to be supportive and gentle and all things sweetness and light. "You know what he can do with his one-liners?" And yes, my voice was sweet and gentle. "He can take them and . . ."

My threat was interrupted by a male laugh. Until that moment I hadn't realised that both of them were on the line. Dr Cow Eyes had not said a thing. That must be what she'd rung me to tell me. A second phone outlet. Such a charming way of informing me, too. You know, Dr Nick is a shockingly bad influence on my sister. I'm positive her halo's slipping and her level of worthiness has fallen two notches.

What else could I do? I offered to tell Linnie's Nick

where to go and how to get there unless he hung up so I could talk to my sister. I promised him it would take a lot longer than one line.

He laughed again, and said, "It's always a pleasure to talk to you, Judy," and hung up. Bloody cheek.

"I rang about Ada," Belinda said.

"I would never have guessed," said I, still thrown by their practical joke. It put paid to me telling her about Rudolph. "I gather you got an extra outlet put in for the phone."

"Two, in fact," she admitted. "It makes it easier, and they had to fix a bunch of things anyway."

"More damage than it looked?"

"Yes, and no," Linnie replied, thoughtfully. "But we decided to improve things anyway."

"Can I ask difficult questions about Ol' Cow Eyes?" I wondered aloud.

"If you do, you won't get any answers," was the cheerful response.

"What can I ask you about?"

"I've sorted out a whole bunch of things about Great-Grandma," Lin said. "Remember I sent out all sorts of queries ages and ages ago? Well, we have the best answers we are likely to get."

"And so we know a lot more?"

"Not so much, I'm afraid," Belinda admitted.

"Tell me!"

"I have a birth certificate for Grandma," she said. "She was born on 6 May, 1899. Late in 1900, the whole family packed up and left Ballarat and moved to St Kilda. I have several papers showing the family business was sold, and the house, and then they took out membership at the Charnwood Grove Synagogue. A nice lady from the Jewish Museum in Melbourne wrote me a note about Anglo-Jewry at that time and said the family would have been very English in attitude."

"Norah of Billabong, except Jewish?" I suggested.

"Sounds about right," my sister admitted. "Except they would've gone to synagogue more regularly than we do."

"Not hard," I commented.

She laughed, and said, "They dressed up to the nines and went to show off and gossip, the nice lady said. It makes sense that Ada was a socialite type rather than a praying type, doesn't it?"

"You're right," and I was thoughtful, "it does. And for them to all have left Ballarat like that suggests a troubled marriage."

"Definitely no divorce though," Lin commented. "I checked it from every angle."

"Maybe they couldn't get one, so took Ada and the baby to safety," I suggested, "Or is that just my bias?"

"I think you're right," admitted Lin, "But we won't ever be able to prove it."

"And that's everything?"

"Not quite. Grandma graduated in medicine from Melbourne University in 1923, and it seems that's when she stopped speaking to Great-Grandma."

"So she waited to have all her fees paid and graduate and then dumped her mother?"

"Worse. Great-Grandma paid for her to start up practice as well."

"I don't remember Grandma as being that vindictive," was my only comment.

"Nor do I. But I can think of one thing that would have done it."

"What?" I was genuinely puzzled.

"The magic."

"But denying your mother because she is superstitious is not likely, surely? Oh," and light dawned, "I'm being stupid. I bet Great-Grandma proved that magic worked."

"That's my theory," agreed Lin.

"Was she living on her parent's money, Ada, I mean? Because what about the family story about a chauffeur and everyone being jealous?"

"She had a business," said Lin. "She went to Europe from time to time to source supplies."

"Which is where she got her stars done and why they're northern hemisphere." Finally, things began to make sense.

"Yes," agreed Lin. "And she used to show off by being driven to family events by her chauffeur. I asked a cousin; she did that right to her death."

"Very in everyone's face," I commented.

"That's our Ada," smiled Lin. "I don't know anyone in the family who might have inherited that. You, for instance, are such a shy and wilting lily."

"Oh, go jump off a cliff with a rock tied round your waist."

"You know, we could spend our whole life looking for more," commented my sister.

"I'm happy where I am now, but you can keep looking. After all, you have Mr Researcher for a boyfriend."

"Dr Researcher, if you please," she said, with dignity.

When I had hung up I caught a glimpse of Zoë through the doorway. "Hey," I called out, "I just had an idea." She peered round the doorframe inquiringly. "We have to celebrate," I said. "Get Great-Grandma's box."

"What are we celebrating?" asked my daughter, as she huffed the box onto a chair a few minutes later.

"Auntie Linnie just found out a bit more about Great-Grandma. I'll tell you it all when Nick comes home, but I thought you and I should have a little private celebration."

"Because we're mother and daughter?" she asked.

"No, because it ought to be a magic one, for Great-Grandma."

"Oh," she said, "and Nick doesn't know about the magic. Can't he be an honorary woman?"

"I'll think about that," I promised. "Would you rather put the celebration off till I have thought?"

"Can we have a little celebration now and then a big one if you decide Nick can be an honorary woman?"

"So what's our little celebration going to be?"

"I want glitter," pronounced my daughter. "I want to know why we are celebrating, though. Just a little bit of why."

"Persistent, aren't you?" I grinned. "Well, the things that Auntie Linnie found out are all about our family. Our family has this lovely secret."

She nodded. "The magic."

"More than that," I said. "It's a whole different way of looking at the world. We have a very special family."

"Family secrets," another grave nod.

"Not so much secrets," I replied, to my own surprise. "Just a family way of doing things."

"Like the way we peel oranges."

"Exactly." A bright spark, my little one.

"Does that mean that the way we peel oranges is magic?" Well, maybe not quite as bright a spark as I thought.

"No," I sighed, "it's not. Everything we are helps us be the sort of people who can do magic, but not everything we do is magic. Peeling oranges using a fork is just a thing we do."

"Does that mean our family is really, really, really strange?"

"No stranger than most, Zoë," I tried to explain, "Other families have their secrets."

"Ours are better," she said, with an air of superiority. I think she got it then, because she turned to the box.

Glitter. She wanted glitter. I was puzzled as to how

we could achieve it. I watched in fascination as she methodically hauled out certain pages and wrote down instructions. She was already adept at working out how Great-Grandma had broken spells into different sections to make them unworkable, and at moulding them together to get them to operate.

When she'd written it out laboriously, I had made and finished a cup of tea. It was very relaxing, just sitting there and watching her work away, a slight frown on her face and many words crossed out.

"We're going to summon a spirit who will make the glitter," she finally said.

"What sort of spirit?" I reached for the papers and checked everything carefully.

Finally we did the invocation. Sparkles of light and colour descended from the ceiling for long enough for Zoë to dance in them, and for me to reach out my arms in wonder and let the luminescence flicker over me. We never saw the spirit who did this, but we thanked it politely. More sparkles were our reward. Someone liked being thanked.

Zoë was all radiant beams when she went to bed. She hugged me to pieces and had a gentleness inside her I hadn't seen in a long while.

_____

Dad finally apologised. It came very late in the piece, but it was no token apology. He rang me, about a week after I had told Belinda. He said that Lin had been on the phone every night, explaining and explaining. Finally, he said, he got off his rear end and started to listen.

He asked if he could come up sometime before the wedding and bring Jan to meet us. I said, sure. I could have the couch and they could have my room, I calculated. It would be tough, but worth it.

Jan rang a day later and introduced herself. She said we needed to talk. Her voice was very soft and gentle. Worryingly soft and gentle. One of those sweet voices that blinded you to what the owner was saying. I got the feeling she was a woman used to having her own way.

They were coming, she said, because she really wanted to meet me. But they were staying in a hotel. She hoped I wouldn't be offended, but she wanted a bit of space between me and Dad. She'd noticed that we had problems — what a remarkably perceptive lady. Sorry, sarcasm just dripped onto the keyboard when I wasn't watching.

This was a relief, in an odd way. Not to have Dad sleeping under my roof when I had not spoken to him since longer than forever. For Zoë to meet her grandfather in a neutral place — all of this was good. Zoë had not met him before, you see. Not ever. Damn, but it was difficult.

Fifteen years is a long time. He'd grown old. He moved more cautiously and his voice lacked the resonance I remembered. His face wasn't wrinkled and it was crowned with a casque of white. Pure silver. Daunting. Until I saw him, all white and dignified at my front door, I didn't realise that he'd been middle-aged when everything had happened.

Jan was not with him, that first visit. The kids had absented themselves. If being ordered to, "Go do the grocery shopping and take your bloody time over it," can be called absenting yourself.

I invited him in. I was stiff as plasterboard, and my mind was about as deep as plasterboard too. I brought him into the kitchen and made some tea. I had trouble talking, and so did he. This was not the child-parent relationship I remembered.

When we had drunk our tea in silence, I asked if he would like to see the house. He said he would love to, and so we did the grand tour. Upstairs and downstairs and in my lady's chamber.

"You own this outright?" he asked, "Where did you get the money from?"

"Grandad's inheritance," I said. "Linnie and I combined the money."

"What did you do then?" He was seriously interested. I found it strange that he hadn't asked Linnie. But maybe he had and was trying to break the silence. Or maybe he just wanted to hear it from me.

"I got a job in a gift shop. I still have it. And when I was a bit more settled, I did an Arts degree at Sydney University."

"And found someone to mind Nick?"

"Gods, no," I laughed. "There was no money for that sort of thing. I did a big emotional blackmail stunt and brought Nick to class with me. Nick learned Arts by osmosis."

"I'm glad you got your degree," he commented. "I always thought you would be in law or something."

"Well, I'm in a gift shop," I said, with a certain amount of rabid glee.

"Even after the degree?" Well, he could've helped if he had wanted to. No one had prevented him.

"Dad, you have to understand," and all my soul went into trying to make him understand, "where I was, no one should ever be. I use all the lessons from university, and from what I went through, to lobby and work on policy and agitate to make things better. It was not a wasted degree, and I do not have a wasted life."

"But can't you use the degree and get a decent job?" Dad was genuinely bewildered. I think he'd just expected me to pick up where I had left off when I moved out of home.

"It wasn't possible then, and now I'm doing other things." I was a bit dismissive, I felt, and tried to explain. "Look, Dad, I get to go to Parliament House and talk to ministers." Not often, but he didn't need to know that. "I have a friend who is a senator." That much was entirely true. "I talk to people and influence things in a way that would never happen if I was in a regular career."

"And the kids?" Dad asked, a bit hesitantly.

"Both committed feminists," I said cheerfully. "Nick understands so very much."

"He shouldn't have to understand these things." Dad was stiffness personified.

"*No one* should have to understand these things. Nevertheless, we grow from them where we can, and hide the things we can't face."

"Like me. You hid me."

"No, Dad, you hid yourself."

"I was always there if you wanted to talk," he said.

"When did you ever believe what Peter was doing to me? When did you sufficiently respect how deeply I was hurting not to joke about it?"

Silence. A very long silence.

"I'm not sure I know what you went through even now," Dad said very slowly. "But I didn't mean to hurt you. I was trying to make light of it."

"And Peter is your drinking buddy."

"Was my drinking buddy. I thought it was important not to judge a man by just one of his actions."

"Even if one of his actions was to take a knife to your youngest child?"

Another silence.

"Joodles, I am so sorry," he whispered. "It was impossible to believe."

"I dealt with it my way," I said, "I got away. With Linnie's help. And I've missed you."

More bloody silence.

"But," and I was resolved this would be said, "I'm sorry, Dad, I love you and it hurts not to have spent these last years near you, but I can't have you back in my life. Not close. There's too much between us."

"Can't we work on it?" He sounded so hopeful, damn him.

"No," I said very slowly, "I can't see it. Some things are too deep."

More silence. It was killing me.

"But I'll meet Jan and you can meet Zoë, and Nick and Zoë can spend holidays with you if you all want. We'll all come to the wedding."

"Thank you," said Dad, and wisely didn't press things. I wished I could have given him more, but what I said was true. Sometimes, love is not enough. Even forgiveness is not enough.

Zoë was very hesitant when she got back in from shopping. She and her grandfather skirted around each other.

Nick was fine. Whatever had happened with Peter in Melbourne had given the two a rapport. Even if I couldn't talk to Dad, it was wonderful to have a son who could.

Jan turned out to be delightful. A bit like Mum, and a bit very unlike. If she's really as warm and generous as she looks, then Dad will be as placid as a cat in front of a fire.

She and I have friends in common. No one was happy but us two after we discovered this. Jan and I took up the kitchen table and just sat there and swapped stories of people we knew, and gossiped and talked politics and bewailed the state of the country and gave each other phone numbers and email addresses of people who absolutely needed to be contacted.

This stuck Nick and Zoë with having to entertain Dad, and they all soon left us and went to the lounge room. I have no idea how they did. I had a whale of a time with Jan.

Except when she admitted that they'd invited Peter to the wedding. Invitations had gone out before Jan had heard the whole story. She told me she had raked Dad over the rocks, and nearly refused to marry him at all. He wouldn't take back Peter's invitation; the compromise position was that Peter would be put at the furthest table from us, and that both of them would make sure they saw us before the wedding.

Dad was supposed to have told me all that, it appeared. I could see from the look in Jan's eyes that he was going to get it. Jan loved him dearly — it was strong and clear — but she took no nonsense. I thought we might get on.

I pushed the whole Peter issue to the back of my mind. I was in an untenable position. I couldn't deny my kids Dad's wedding, and I couldn't let them go alone.

That was Saturday. Sunday was better. We all went to the city and walked around. We went to Circular Quay and the Opera House and the Botanic Gardens instead of visiting the clocks. Very nice. Very safe.

Which is where we left it. We were going to their wedding and, as I said to Nick, we were going to enjoy ourselves even if it killed us.

What's very, very funny is that Dad was marrying out. Jan isn't Jewish. And it had never come up as a concern or a worry or a problem. It wasn't relevant.

For the record, Ol' Cow Eyes is Jewish; Lin was being a good little girl and earning lots of accolades from her dead relatives. Well, she would have if they had known. And if she had got married. So Dad married out and Belinda is not married, but is with someone Jewish. Life is just like that sometimes.

2.

"There was no happiness. There was no joy. When the Child woke up and became adult, he realised that gloom was with him forever. He killed his parents. He killed himself. There was peace."

CHAPTER FOURTEEN

1.

EASTER CAME VERY QUICKLY. THE NICEST PART ABOUT
preparations was Zoë. She was very excited about getting a dress for the wedding. We broke into our emergency money to get her the flowered creation she'd set
her heart on and to get Nick a decent suit. We got out
of a sulk by convincing each other that it would be
useful for job interviews.

Now, once we'd dipped into our emergency funds
there was nothing left for me. And this is where you
start thinking sympathetically about Judith-the-poor-
mother who puts her children first then comes to her
father's wedding dressed like a dowd. Alas, I am not
that. I refuse to be. Wonderful, yes. Self-sacrificing to
the point of idiocy, no.

Since the swastikas, June and I have had coffee together once a week. When I told her about the Cin-
derella problem, she introduced me to the boxes in her
spare room. There were some gorgeous fabrics just
higgledy-piggledy in those boxes. My mouth watered at
the thought of wearing that sixties mauve and cream
fabric, in a mini-skirt.

My dress cost the price of the pattern, of the trim-
mings, of thread, and of the amulet I made for June as a
thank-you. It was a mini-skirt, though not so mini as to
make Nick disown me. My legs looked almost as good
as Belinda's. I needed Rudolph to inspect.

June and I were both happy. She had an amulet, and
insisted on ordering more, to be done for money, because she could then do what she wanted with the
amulets without compunction. And I had a dress to die
for. Even Zoë was awed by my dress. Nick looked me
up and down and said I was okay, but I noticed his eyes
avoided my legs.

Belinda talked me into a few days in Melbourne.
She argued that both Nicks were with us and that it
was a chance to revisit scenes of our childhood.

I was very hesitant. She was right, though; it
was time to face fears. Some people reclaim the
night, all I wanted was to look over the gate at my
old primary school and tell the kids, "Look where I
went to school." Frankly, if you had told me, two
years ago, I would even be able to go to Melbourne, I would've laughed in your face. I was
terrified.

The wedding came first. We hit Melbourne and Dad
got married the next morning.

Dr Nick was very smug. Not only was Belinda
looking tall and blonde and leggy and lovely, but he'd
arranged a house-swap for the week with some university friends. I don't know how his friends felt about
swapping a Melbourne home with a green and verdant
outdoors for a Canberra cottage with a cindered
garden.

I have to admit, financially, it was not good. Three
return fares to Canberra are a hell of a lot better than
three return fares to Melbourne, after all. We are not
poor-poor — I mean, we lack for nothing essential. But

we're not good on luxuries and hotels and plane fares and meals out are most certainly luxuries.

We didn't even get as far as Canberra, in the end. Nick-my-son discovered discount rail tickets a couple of weeks before the wedding. He bought us return rail to Yass and Lin and Nick picked us up there. One worry less in my ocean of frets; I could afford this week in Melbourne.

2.

Rhonda read the latest addition to the Child of Light series and sighed. She didn't need this. She rang Dave. He logged on at once and laughed.

"What's so funny?"

"Honey, I don't think she's happy with me."

"Well, I'm not happy with her. She killed everyone!"

"I told you TVwhore was interested in you."

"I don't care. She didn't have to kill everyone. Do you know what I am going to do?"

"What are you going to do?"

"Sulk, that's what." And she did. It was bad enough knowing there was going to be big trouble one day with Dave, without there being small trouble with TVwhore right now. She re-read the Child of Light stories. They hadn't lasted long, but she was attached to them.

Rhonda finished reading them in about three minutes. There truly was not much to them. It was not the world's greatest tragedy that TVwhore had engineered an early demise. Except that Rhonda wanted to sulk. She printed off all three pages of the epic saga and sat down in front of the television, to luxuriate.

When she put the last page on the coffee table, she felt pensive. She thought, maybe, she'd not quite reached that dead end. She thought, perhaps, she could do more than just hope that Dave didn't realise who she was. She thought, perhaps, she had a brilliant idea. Rhonda smiled.

What she'd noticed in the Child of Light tales was that her other writing styles were quite different in tone to her prophecies and revelations. She suspected she could lay a really awesome red herring. All she had to do was print out something old before she met Dave for pasta the next day. Simplicity itself.

"Hey, you," called Rhonda across the street.

"Are you trying to pick me up?" asked Dave, as he stood up to give her a hug.

"You're too big. I brought you something."

"A Rolex?"

"More obscure."

"I don't feel obscure today. I can't guess."

"I need lunch. I'll tell you as soon as we've ordered."

When pasta was promised by a young lady who looked as if she should still be in school, Rhonda passed over a folder. "Shh," she said. "It's top secret. A leak from obscure and nefarious places."

"Huh," said Dave. "What is it really?"

"You said you were interested in my writing. I found a piece when I was doing something else, so I printed it for you."

"Cool. Seriously cool."

"Read it later though," she instructed. "I want to have lunch with you, not with my bloody article."

"It must be secret, if you call it 'bloody'."

"Absolutely." And Rhonda smiled a self-satisfied smile. This one was so very far removed from her oracular voice that it belonged in a different universe. It was also incredibly pretentious. She couldn't wait to see Dave's reaction.

3.

Dave took the screed away and read it. He didn't want to comment as extensively as usual at first. In fact, he didn't want to comment at all. His defence was that it was dense.

"Like your brain," Rhonda said, exasperated.

"Perhaps," Dave admitted cheerfully, "Or perhaps I want to understand it."

He took his time. It was three days before he said anything, and even then what he said was ambiguous. Whatever happened, the piece had served its purpose and derailed him. He wouldn't think she was the Hidden Nostradamus. He might think she was an idiot, but she could wear that. He might even think she was pretentious, and she could wear that one, too. She could wear almost anything, except Dave discovering her secrets and leaving her. Rhonda let her thoughts drift and fell into a half-sleep.

"You know, honey." Dave was lounging on the couch with Rhonda sheltered inside his arms. She knew she was trapped, but it was comfortable. "I've been thinking about that last piece of yours."

"Uh-huh."

He gave her an exasperated kiss. "You can say something more than uh-huh."

"Okay. Something more than uh-huh. Happy?"

"Ecstatically."

"Okay," Rhonda said. "I'll behave. Look, I'm listening."

He gave his beautiful laugh and she smiled up at him. "I was just trying to tell you that I like your voice in that last piece. Very pleasant."

"My voice? You mean, my writing voice? Cool."

"No, not your writing voice." She could hear the

struggle in his voice as he tried to puzzle it out. "Your everyday voice. One of the many?"

Rhonda tried not to go still. He would spot that she was scared. "What do you mean, many voices?"

"One of my great delights in you," he said solemnly, "is that I never know which voice you are going to talk to me in, or write in. You joked about it the other day, but it's for real. Sometimes you're just a cheeky child, and sometimes you have almost-American phrasing. Sometimes you are a silly female, and sometimes the wisest and most educated human being I have ever met."

"I thought you meant I was like Joan of Arc."

Dave made a very rude comment about certain things that Joan of Arc had never got around to doing. Rhonda turned bright red. Dave followed up his words. The conversation was finished.

4.

The next day, Dave threw an annoying thought in Rhonda's direction. It was a passing comment, nothing more, from his end. "That Revelator guy ought to be put into a comic," he said. "Superhero"

"Can't see it."

"Secret identity, changes the world. No thanks from anyone."

"Um," said Rhonda, "I like your clever use of complex syntax."

"I bet he wears a fancy costume," Dave continued.

"Privately? Keeps it hidden where no one can see?"

"Okay, I give up. You're really not interested."

"Sorry." Rhonda tried to sound sincere, and failed.

The minute Dave left, she did a methodical fade from most of her on-line homes, both new and old. The place she faded the most from was her fan fiction site. She couldn't decide about her MissTRie identity, because Dave knew it and he was certainly capable of spotting any denials about it from her end. Everything else, though, had to go. She took all her prophecies and revelations and most of her fan fiction and saved it to disk. She hid the disk where it would never see light of day. Then she cleaned her hard drive. Lots and lots of files gone, forever.

She had to get rid of as much of her writing as she could. *They can crunch numbers to prove writing style. What a stupid hobby fan fiction is for someone like me. But then, I'm terminally stupid. Every single one of my voices has known that for a very long time.*

It was not only fear of discovery that prompted her big deletions: it was fear of losing Dave. This was disconcerting. Tony had accused her, time after time, of possessing a vast capacity for selfishness and secrecy. He had said she was incapable of walking even one step for someone else. She rather thought Tony was right. But if he was right, then what was she doing switching her life around so that she could keep Dave in it?

5.

The last leg of the journey to Melbourne didn't take forever for the kids. Nick pointed out things he knew or guessed to Zoë. Both Nicks pointed out things to Zoë. Linnie tried to keep things boppy and happy.

I fell into a sludge. It was all so familiar and so many years past. And things had changed so very much. Built up, got older. There were strange roads doing this, that and the other, and making all sorts of new traffic jams.

We found the house. It was a three bedroom house and there were five of us. I looked at the three bedrooms and lost any capacity to cope. I didn't know if Lin's Nick was actually sleeping with her or wanted to be seen sleeping with her. Three bedrooms, and one double bed. Perfectly normal. So why couldn't I suggest any way that people could sort things out? I was sludge.

Belinda watched my face and got the Nicks to bring the bags in. I like carrying my own bags, but wasn't in the right mood to protest even that. Not good. I could say 'not good' to myself and still not get myself out of the sludge.

She told her Nick to put both their bags in the double bedroom, mine in one single and Zoë's in the other. "And you get the couch," she told my Nick, as if she was bestowing an honour.

He did the ritual, "Why do I get the couch?" grumble.

Lin was mean enough to say, "Because otherwise we won't be able to get you up in the morning."

I'm glad she took care of things. I don't know where I was that night, but it was not a good place.

6.

"Never think of Tony," Rhonda said, savagely. "Because if I think of Tony, he will ring and tell me something stupid."

This time had been particularly nasty. Tony had been drunk. Alcohol was always responsible for the worst decisions Tony made. He had walked out on her when drunk, though his decision not to come back had been made while sober. And tonight he had rung while drunk. He was a volcano of fury. Her new man drank more, but he was a pleasant drunk.

"What have you done to the kids?" he asked.

She didn't know, and said so. He kept asking, over and over, "What have you done? Where are they?"

Finally Rhonda hung up the phone. She screamed. She was so scared and so worried. The kids were not supposed to be with her, not this late at night. Not ever. If she babysat at night, it was at their place. Never hers. And she hadn't been asked to babysit. And she had no idea what had happened. All she knew, really (after taking a deep breath and telling herself to slow down), was what Tony had said.

She rang Lana.

"Hello?" and there was clinking and chatting in the background.

"Hi, Lana, it's me. Tony just rang."

"Is something wrong?"

"I think so. He kept asking me where the kids are."

"Aren't you at my place?"

"Is there a reason I should be?"

"Tony said he would ring you and ask if you could babysit. He had a work dinner and I'm at a preview of an art exhibition."

"Lana, he never asked me. The first I heard about it was when he rang just now. He's very drunk. And very angry at me. And he wants to know where the kids are."

"Oh God. I'll ring you right back."

While Rhonda was waiting for Lana to ring on the landline she used her mobile to call Dave.

Dave said, "I'll be right there."

"Don't you have a dinner?"

"I'll be right there," Dave repeated, and hung up. And he was. Rhonda let him in the door just as her phone rang.

She raced to it, and left Dave to his own devices. He ambled in and watched as she picked up the phone. "Hello?" Rhonda said, her voice echoing sharply in the mouthpiece.

"It's me," and Lana sounded terribly, terribly tired. "I don't know what to do."

"Tell me what happened."

"Tony forgot to call you. And he forgot that he forgot. He's crying in a heap. I've never seen such a useless pile of shit in my life. He left the kids alone and he told them that Auntie Rhonda would be there soon. And then he went to his dinner and got stinking drunk. And then he came home and the kids weren't there."

"And so he rang me."

"And so he rang you," Lana sounded defeated.

"Have you rung the police?"

"I can't. I just can't," and Lana burst into tears.

"Go get a glass of water. Drink it slowly, then come back and we will talk it through. Don't hang up."

"Okay," and there was a silence at the end of the phone.

Rhonda turned to Dave and told him what had happened. Dave was silent. "I can't help thinking," Rhonda was surprised at how tentative she sounded, "that Ben and Val were told that I was coming round. And that they've walked from their place to here three times."

"God, I hope it's something as simple as that."

"I need to be here when Lana gets back, but if I show you the route, could you drive and see?"

"Would it have taken them this long?"

"I have no bloody idea. But if they're there we have to find them."

Dave nodded. Within three minutes he was out of the door. In the background, she could hear Lana and Tony arguing. *Thank God*, Rhonda thought, *for Dave*.

Eventually Lana came back to the phone. "I'm sorry," and she started weeping again.

"Lana, Dave has gone to see if the kids started walking here. Have you checked the house, or did you rely on Tony?"

"Tony."

"So go and check the house. Every corner, every nook and cranny. They could have locked themselves in your office and gone to sleep for all we know. Or they could be in the garden. Check everywhere. Ring me back when you have."

Rhonda was not happy at waiting, but she had no choice. She sat down with a pen and paper and tried to list other places the children might have gone, or friends who might have rung up and found they were home alone and come to take care of them. She drew a blank. Lana might have better luck, but not until she had calmed down.

What a mess. What a bloody, bloody mess. Rhonda put her hands in her arms and shuddered. A gentle hand touched the back of her neck. Rhonda jumped.

"Sorry, sugar, it's just me."

"Any luck?" Rhonda turned round and looked up. Dave looked very formidable.

"I found two children, but the boy said they don't know me and won't tell me their names."

"Okay," and Rhonda stood up. "Where are they?"

"I'll take you." He drove her to the little park where she and the kids had their picnics. A boy was sitting on the bench, with a smaller child curled up beside him, asleep.

"Number One?"

"Auntie!"

"Auntie?" Val's voice was sleepy.

"Why didn't you come?" Ben's voice was reproachful.

"Because I didn't know you needed me." She came to the bench and sat down next to Ben. Val wriggled over him and onto her lap. The three sat very close.

"Who is he?" Val whispered.

"He's my boyfriend, he came to find you."

"I didn't tell him our names," Ben whispered.

Dave sat down on the other side of them. "You did the right thing," he said, "You didn't know who I was. I could have been an evil stranger."

"Except you're not." Ben's voice was sounding bigger.

"I'm not. But you did the right thing."

"You didn't do the right thing in coming to find me. You could have tried ringing me," Rhonda scolded.

"Val was making phone calls for her stupid TV show when he told her not to, and Daddy told us he'd made it so the phone would kill us."

Damn Tony. And damn Tony again. Rhonda took a deep breath. Life was just full of occasions for taking deep breaths. "So you came to find me," Rhonda said, as conversationally as she could manage.

"Except Val got tired, so we stopped to rest."

"Do you want us to take you home?"

"Did Daddy drink tonight?"

"Maybe," Rhonda was not going to say what she thought of Tony. These were his children.

"Can we go back to your home? Please? I want to sleep on your couch."

Damn Tony. Damn Tony. Damn Tony. When had his drinking gone so far? What the hell was he thinking?

"Okay," said Rhonda, "But I'm going to ring your Mum and if she wants you to go home, you're going."

"Yes, Auntie."

Dave picked Val up and carried her to the car. Ben held Rhonda's hand as if he had found his forever-refuge. As soon as they were safely seat-belted in the back for the car, Rhonda rang Lana.

"The kids are safe. Dave found them," she said, without preamble. "They've asked if they can sleepover."

"I'll be right there," said Lana and hung up.

"How about I make some hot chocolate when we get to your place, while you talk to your friend," Dave suggested.

"Do you two want hot chocolate?" Rhonda flung the words to the back seat.

"Do we get a chocolate biscuit?" Val's voice sounded as if she knew she was trying to push her luck. The kids would be back to normal in no time.

"Maybe," Rhonda said.

In the end they had two biscuits each and stayed the night. So did Dave. The look on his face when Ben careened onto him first thing in the morning, announcing, "Number One is storming the fortress," and Val bounced up after him declaring, "Me too, me too. Number two too," was almost as funny as the look on the children's face when they realised that it was not Rhonda they had woken.

"This isn't a fortress," Dave growled, "it's an ogre's den." Val squealed and there was mayhem. By the time Lana came to pick her errant offspring up, they were ready to go home. Rhonda didn't ask if Tony regretted any of his actions. She was still too busy damning him. None of this showed on her face as she hugged the kids goodbye.

The minute they were out the door she gave Dave a hug too.

"What was that for?" he asked.

"For being wonderful. I can do you pancakes with maple syrup if you want a second breakfast."

7.

It was Zoë who got me through to the actual wedding. She made sure I ate my breakfast and told me exactly how she wanted me to do my makeup. She checked my little purse to make sure I had everything I needed for the day.

The wedding was simple and rather nice.

Two people temporarily darkened the niceness of

the wedding. Two little morsels of my past. Across the room I spied him. Very romantic. Except he was ogling my legs. His gaze was, as ever, limpid and almost innocent, and the ogle was out of the corner of the eye — you have to admit, Rudolph is a master of his art. No wonder people invite him to all sorts of social events. Including weddings, dammit.

Nick Senior caught my gaze and turned his own limpid gaze on Rudy. Eventually Rudy noticed, caught my eye, gave a wink, and turned his attentions away. I think the whole ogle was with intent to annoy. I wonder what stories he's telling about me, and what bitchy comments he makes. I bet my bitchy comments are better.

The other blast from the past was more expected, and more depressing. Peter was there. He'd not had the common sense to turn down the invitation. I nodded to him in a casual manner from across the room. At least, I hope it looked casual. As soon as I could, after seeing him, I found an excuse to go to the bathroom and give in to the shakes. Once that was over I felt almost myself. Sort of.

When I came out of the bathroom, I was able to look at him. I gleefully catalogued the grey hair and the hairpiece and yes, he had indeed gone to fat. He might have the whole world at his feet and a big house and a luxury car and a charming wife and a gorgeous family but I had an even more gorgeous family. And I was wearing a miniskirt.

When he turned to talk to someone, I saw his back. On it, in the handwriting of the Dark Side of the Lin, was a sign that said, "This man is a bastard." I have no idea how she got it there without his knowing. I wondered, too, why no one had told him it was there. I smiled.

I was able to look suitably rejoiced when the ceremony was over and we went over to the newlyweds to tell them how wonderful it all was and they all were. I'm not sure I like my father, but I managed to look happy for him on that day.

My Nick shook Dad's hand too. Zoë outshone us all and gave everyone long and happy cuddles. She likes weddings and she likes people. I like the way Dad's eyes followed her for hours, proud and a bit surprised.

Zoë caught him looking and walked right back to him. She looked up and smiled and then reached out and hugged him half to death. I swear there were tears in his eyes. I found myself looking for Belinda to project my *That is it — he's lost* thought at her. Dad was a doting grandfather without any time to become used to the idea.

There were other minutes of lucidity. When everyone was dancing, I found myself with Rudolph. He didn't say a word, just held me gently and danced as if I were special. I looked up at him and he looked down and me, and he didn't smile. He just held me, and we danced slowly. At the end of the dance he disappeared and I realised how very wrong I had been. I was in love with him.

Too late, he was gone. Or was he? Rudolph was a master at keeping me off-balance.

8.

Two days, two articles. That was all the time Rhonda was willing to give herself. Rhonda wanted to get it all out of the way. She hated hiding from Dave, and she hated hiding from herself.

Before Rhonda wrote, however, she sat down and planned the whole process of writing and emailing the article and coming down with the prophecy-illness.

She planned it like a campaign, from the first word

she would type until the final article would be sent. She chose an internet café computer for the first article and following frenzy, and a different internet café — in the middle of the biggest shopping centre she could find — for the second. She worried a bit about the cost, then realised that she could do all the work at home for both articles, and just do the final write-up and emailing and then the chat room garbage on the alien machines.

Rhonda sat back, pleased with herself. She was so pleased with herself that she allowed herself two full dollops of rich cream in her coffee, and licked the sweet spoon afterwards. Her drafting was shadowed by the taste of richness and the fragrance of coffee. Life was as it should have been years ago.

Her first article was about relics. "The last chapter of Charles Mackay, LL.D.'s Extraordinary Popular Delusions and the Madness of Crowds," wrote Rhonda to get herself going, "is simply entitled 'Relics'. It is shorter than most of the other chapters, and has less substance on show. Instead of ten lines of sub-headings, it lists just over two lines. The True Cross. Tears of our Saviour. The Santa Scala, or Holy Stairs. The mad Knight of Malta. Shakespeare's Mulberry-tree. This is all he talks about in the seven pages he devotes to the subject. Why?"

Rhonda pointed out that it was not because Mackay scoffed at relics, because his first words on the subject were, "The love for relics is one which will never be eradicated as long as feeling and affection are denizens of the heart."

For the rest of it, he talked about how emotions were important in establishing relics and that miracles were not something modern. Rhonda laughed. If anyone were to believe in relics and miracles, it should be her, with her obnoxious gift. But she didn't. And so she was perfectly happy to deal with relics the way Mackay dealt with them, as proof of veneration.

The only way she could reach the right word length was by padding it with cynical descriptions of modern relics. She found herself becoming more and more purple in her prose and judgemental in her opinions. She was rude about the thorn of Glastonbury and even more impolite about the Turin shroud.

I'm going to be rent life from limb if anyone really religious reads this article, she thought. *But then, they would either damn me or venerate me because of the grumblings inside, and I am neither saint nor sinner. Besides, I use a pseudonym,* and with that decidedly unclear thought, she finished the draft of her first article.

She packed her deathless prose onto a disk and went to the café. *Web mail,* Rhonda reminded herself, as she set it up for emailing. *You need to use an email client on the web so as you won't show where you are.* And so she did. The article went to her editor. Rhonda was able to log into a chat room and wait for prophecy or illumination or madness to strike.

She tried not to notice the people round her. None of them would walk past and look at what she was doing, surely? Rhonda was boring and middle-aged and of no consequence.

Then her insides blurted themselves onto the screen by way of the keyboard and she was relieved of any capacity to worry about the moods of passers-by. When she read back what she had written, she was relieved to find that it was nothing too impossible. It wasn't even prophecy. It was a revelation of wrongdoing.

Someone had come up with all sorts of results proving, through DNA analysis, that various relics were real. She had declared they weren't and had typed strings of babblecode to prove it. In an entirely lazy and self-indulgent mood, Rhonda didn't copy the babblecode. She keyed in the main part of the blurt, saved it to disk, erased her whole session, checked that she'd paid using cash, and faded. Her fade took her into a computer shop and she spent a very joyous hour working out what she was going to buy when next she got her hands on some dosh. Rhonda was a very happy geek indeed.

When she got home, she found a message on her answering machine. "Sorry, hon, can't come round tonight. Think I might have a lead. I'll ring you when I can."

"Hate myself, hate myself, hatemyself, HATE." Rhonda refused to cry herself to sleep. Only wimps did that. Instead, she stayed up all night watching bad movies. The next day she was shadowed and felt as if her whole carcass had been salted by her unshed tears.

At least, she thought, I'm still alive. And I may dislike myself intensely and think I'm a lonely old bitch, but I don't actually hate myself anymore. Well, not much.

Her fit of depression was entirely perfect for the article she was supposed to write. Except now Rhonda didn't want to write anything. She wanted to walk slowly around the shops and pity herself.

"If I take Mackay with me," she reasoned, "and am prepared to pay a bit more for longer on a computer, then there's no reason not to do both." An hour later she was sipping the chocolaty drink she always ordered when she felt as if her world was coming to an end. Coffee was too clean. It presupposed a future.

As she read the opening words of Mackay's chapter, she wondered who had been poisoning her and why. Because those words made it obvious what was happening. They said, "The atrocious system of poisoning by poisons so slow in their operation as to make the victim appear, to ordinary observers, as if dying from a gradual decay of nature, has been practised in all ages."

Except the poisoner was Rhonda herself. Slow poisoning by acceptance of misery.

"Mackay talks about secret poisons," Rhonda wrote,

but the interesting thing from a modern perspective is secret hatred. Most of the famous secret poisoners in history are women with no way out. Imagine being so burdened with unhappiness and having no other escape. For many people, they can't kill someone else, so they kill themselves. For a few, they think the solution to their problems is murdering the cause of their secret hatred or the object of their despite. And of all the types of murder, slow poison must be the most tempting, because, until recently, it was almost impossible to prove.

Sexy. Her fit of depression was producing a sexy article.

Secret poison is the ultimate in revenge for a blighted life. Imagine a poison that cannot be tasted. No almond-scented coffee showing an unhealthy dose of cyanide. No buzz on the tip of the tongue to show an allergic reaction. No sense of something foul. Nothing. Only slow and unremitting failure of life.

This is why Mackay cannot forgive the slow poisoners. And this is why it is so important for us to look at them and wonder why they did what they did.

Her special talent could be considered a slow poison, Rhonda decided, if she allowed it to be. She had a choice though: she could learn to live with it, or she could let it cause the slow and unremitting failure of her life.

She looked up from the computer and round at the café. This was life and she was in it. Somehow. Somehow. And she was going to keep hold of it. Somehow. Somehow.

She ordered another mocha and paid for an extra hour on the computer. However much time she needed, she would take. That was the trick. Be as slow as she needed to be, to match the slowness of the poison in her system. And she would beat it. She wasn't going to let it drive her to suicide, or to living her life silently in an asylum.

Rhonda smiled. She took the melodrama from her soul and poured it into her article. She tried to balance the furore of Mackay with the furore of her heart. Slow poison as high treason; slow poison as a way out of impossible situations; what it meant to live with slow poison. Nightmares of life that would never get better.

Rhonda ignored much of Mackay on this subject. She was weighed down inwardly, and her inner weights shaped the article. She had to do a sidebar though, so she did one on misdiagnosis. "How can we be sure that it was slow poison," she asked, "when it could well have been illness misdiagnosed? Or a cure that was borne of a poor diagnosis?"

Rhonda read back the first half of the article and pronounced herself well satisfied. If she wrote quickly, it would all be over in an hour. Maybe less. She felt as if she had escaped from an emotional death, but was still frail. The world was very big and noisy around her.

Rhonda plunged into the second half of the article. She realised that she had been writing the article all wrong. Mackay hadn't been picking on women in dead-end circumstances; he'd been talking politics. Too bad: she wanted to write about the despair a soul could feel when there was no end to the misery.

Rhonda selected carefully from Mackay's case studies and talked about the young widows of Rome and their use of a clear and tasteless poison to relieve themselves of the torment of married life. She pointed out that divorces were not possible in early modern and eighteenth century Rome, and that women of station were increasingly bound by expectation and

hedged in by restrictions. Rhonda fell short of con-
doning murder, but only just.

She wondered about the 'hag named Tophania' who
had supposedly murdered more than six hundred people. How would that have been possible? She and her
predecessor, La Spara, were worth further investigation, Rhonda wrote near the conclusion of her article.

Were they murderers or frauds? Did they provide
the wherewithal for others to murder, and if so, why
wasn't the blame shared? And was there really a mania
for poisoning? Or had there been a mania for finding
poisoners?

Two of Mackay's poisoners (both women, both
living in Paris) deserved the dignity of the second sidebar, because they raised all the questions Rhonda
wanted raised. Lavoisin and Lavigoreux apparently
sold poison mainly to women who wanted to get rid of
husbands, and they told fortunes on the side. Both of
them were burned alive in 1680, after torture.

This is a case that needs to be re-opened. Were they
mass-murderers? Or is the society that killed them
guilty?

Rhonda read through, corrected errors, left every
ounce of melodrama, and then emailed it. And she was
caught up. All the anger and fear and woe left her with
a rush. She had nothing inside but an emptiness.

For a few minutes she sat at the keyboard, letting
the clanking and clicking and talking surround and fill
her. Then the grumbling started to emerge, and she
hurriedly logged into a chat room. And then it was
later. Considerably later. Her prophetic self had taken
over entirely this time. She wasn't certain she cared.

When Rhonda read back what she had keyed in, she
was a bit surprised. Her brain analysed her text and her
own astonishment at it as she retyped it and saved to
disk to take home. She had listed six murderers who

used poison. Rhonda also found she had listed their victims, the poisons they used and the reasons they'd not yet been discovered.

She looked at the careful sequencing her inner self had done and thought, *What a beautiful TV documentary this would make, revealing these people one by one, with their methods and what each poison does and then going in for their faces as they find out that there is no escape.* Not a nice thought, but a fabulous TV documentary.

Rhonda saved everything to disk and moved her mouse to leave the chat room. Time to go.

"Hi, Rhonda, what are you doing at an internet café?" It was Dave. Standing over her shoulder. Nemesis revealed.

Of all the people in the world, why did it have to be Dave? And why now? She logged out of the chat room while her mouth made polite conversation. She thought he had come round to where he could see the screen too late to see what she was up to, but she wasn't sure. Damn. Damn. Damn. Damn. Damn.

"You hang out here?" Stupid question, but it gave her those moments she needed.

"Just part of my work."

"Oh," Rhonda felt blank. She prevaricated. "Let me stand up so I don't get neck ache looking at you. I was just finishing, anyhow."

"Don't you have a computer at home?"

"Yes, but the connection was dicey and I had to get something out in a hurry."

"You have more deadlines than a—"

"Make a clever simile, I dare you."

"I can't think of anything. How about I buy you coffee?"

"I can never say 'no' to coffee," Rhonda found just enough life in her to put on a mournful tone.

As she drank the coffee she wondered what Dave

had been doing in the internet café. He wasn't pursuing every detail of her activity as he usually did: she would lay a bet he was hiding something. As was she. What a well-suited couple. Rhonda looked across at Dave and gave him her best and most loving smile.

9.

We pretended to be tourists for the rest of Easter. I re-encountered lots more of my past. Some of it was better undiscovered, I must admit. Like Belinda dragging us to a suburban park and telling my kids that this was where I had my first kiss. It wasn't even the right park.

When the squabble over the right park did not abate, Linnie's Nick produced a notepad from his pocket and asked if we wanted to know what Ada's note had said, in her scrapbook. Of course we did, but we managed to get one last rudeness in apiece before he read it out loud.

It didn't say much, that note, I mean in terms of ideas. In terms of length, the anticipation was far longer than the event itself: *I am writing down my recipes and placing them in a box for my granddaughter, for my daughter will not cook. This is the index to them.*

CHAPTER FIFTEEN

1.

RHONDA WONDERED WHAT SHE'D DONE TO DESERVE SUCH a fraught week.

She also wondered what she had done to deserve TVwhore as a friend. When she logged on that night, she found a series of messages on her blog, all from TVwhore, saying, "Please, I need to talk. Don't ignore me. Please."

Rhonda replied saying, "What's wrong?"

TVwhore must have been online, watching, because there was an instant answer. "I need to talk. Live. Real. I mean, telephone. I tried to ring you, but they said your number was not listed."

Maybe today was the day Rhonda's secrets were all revealed? Maybe. But Rhonda was damned if she was going down without a fight. And she would be damned if she went down without a bit of grace. Her personal Titanic would sink with Rhonda's personal style.

"You wouldn't have got me," Rhonda said, "I haven't been home most of the day. Give me your phone number and I'll ring you," she promised. "If you delete the message straight after I get it then no one else'll see it."

"Okay," was the instant answer, along with a UK phone number. Rhonda sighed melodramatically and miserably, got offline, and made herself a coffee before she dialled.

"I'll ring you," she'd said, and she had to. Rhonda wasn't happy about it, but she couldn't just walk away from TVwhore. This was a problem. An increasingly irksome problem. She should never have made friends. Acquaintances you can dump when the need arises. Friends have problems and need help and get closer and closer and you're trapped. There's no running.

As long as TVwhore was hurting, she wouldn't find out Rhonda's secrets. Rhonda felt exceptionally guilty when she realised she was saying this to herself over and over, as if it would protect her. Not good. Rhonda quickly went back online to tell TVwhore, "Something has come up. Can't ring you till tomorrow. Is tomorrow afternoon your time okay?"

"It'll have to be, won't it," and Rhonda could see bitterness oozing off the screen. She hoped that the delay wouldn't cause TVwhore to do anything unforgivable, but balancing friendship and possible betrayal and taking precautions just in case was surprisingly tricky.

By the time Rhonda collected enough cash for an untrackable payphone call the next day, and found a payphone that took money, she had talked herself into a thoroughly oppressed mood.

The conversation with TVwhore left her feeling even more oppressed. She had no idea what her friend wanted. The high voice at the far end of the phone was not TVwhore, but a total stranger with an educated London accent hiding some faintly regional vowels. Although they talked for a full half hour Rhonda wasn't at all certain she knew why TVwhore wanted to talk. She didn't want to think about it. She didn't want minor deadening mysteries cluttering up her already confusing life. She just wanted to get off the phone and collapse in a heap.

When she got home, Rhonda realised that what she needed was sleep. Forty-eight hours of sleep. She skipped the rest of the day. She unplugged her telephone. She slept.

2.

This was what happened to me, emotionally, in the land of my childhood. It was like finding the person I had once been. Memories. Memories I could share with my children.

I loved the feeling of catching a tram. Even though the trams have changed and the tickets have changed. I remembered counting all the digits on our numbered tickets and adding them together to predict what our school day would be like or what mood Dad would be in when he got home. We caught a tram to St Kilda Beach on the Tuesday and hunted family remnants. The old house had been pulled down, so we kicked sand along the beach and fed the seagulls instead.

I remember it was the Tuesday because Belinda and her Nick took us all to dinner on the Tuesday night. It was Zoë's first restaurant dinner ever, and we dressed up in the wedding clothes all over again. Zoë was overexcited because it was her second proper late night in a week. There was nothing I could do about that one — Linnie had been trading looks with Cow Eyes (making eyes at Cow Eyes?) ever since we hit Melbourne and so the dinner was inevitable. Well, they would learn, on the morrow, when Zoë became fretful and tired, that late nights are not a choice to be made lightly.

Originally I assumed that Lin brought Dr Nick

along to help shut Dad up and to draw attention away from me. Belinda is clever about these things and must've known? I didn't know anything anymore. I am Judith the fallible, Judith the silent. Judith the alone. And that night I was Judith the failure.

Belinda announced her engagement, and I ordered champagne and we toasted her in style. There is a feeling of contentment in the place of my heart that's devoted to Belinda. But dammit, I am lonely. Not lonely in the sense of company. The other kind of lonely. I may just have to put up with that. I'm not good at relationships.

Zoë has her moments. She had just a little puddle of champagne in the bottom of the glass, and thought it made her drunk. She was acting the way she thought drunks acted. Which was cute. Well, it was cute until she let out my nicknames for Dr Nick. He raised an eyebrow and toasted me. And this is going to be my brother-in-law? Damn all relatives and their big toes, is all I can say.

At least I managed to shut Linnie up — while she was sipping plonk, no less — by saying that we just needed to find 2.35 children for her and she would be exactly average. Sad waste of champagne, that mouthful. Zoë and Nick offered half of themselves each, which meant the newly affianced couple only had 1.35 children to find outside. It was Zoë doing the maths out loud that lost that second sip. Lin's Nick was mean and said that they might just give up on children and invest in goldfish.

First thing we did when we got home, Nick and Zoë and I, was dump our bags just inside the front door. Then we walked right out again and went to Paddy's. Three of us to do the carrying of market vegetables, plus a bus back, would solve a myriad of catering issues for the next few days.

Zoë insisted on us buying an inordinate number of carrots. My blonde-haired carrot-skinned daughter. I asked who was going to carry them, and she said, "Me!" indignantly. They were her carrots, and belonged to no one else.

I made my mind up at Paddy's. Nick could become an honorary woman. He'd done so much and been there for us all throughout such a trying year, that he deserved it.

Naturally Nick didn't believe a word of what we were saying about magic (we may have babbled a trifle), but he humoured us. The three of us planned and planned and planned until, one Sunday, we were totally ready. We trooped down to the Queen Vic Building.

It was as early as we could actually get into the building on a Sunday morning and, thank goodness, there was no one there. Only the cafés were open, and the top floor was entirely empty, except for us and our papers and our warped minds.

Nick helped me read the first charm. His enthusiasm quickly lapsed into astonished silence.

A sad feature of the Great Australian Clock is this Indigenous guy, always excluded, always on walkabout, passing by supposedly great scenes of Australian history. My decision on this momentous day was to let him do what he wanted to do.

The first scene he passed was an Indigenous group, before European settlement. He gave the group a thumbs-up and a "G'day, mates," and then turned round and gave us a great grin.

The scene after that our gentleman also made a gesture at the tableau, but it was very impolite one. Two fingers instead of one thumb — and I admit, Captain Cook deserved it. He'd pretended he was a god in the Pacific, after all, and opened the way to Great British Settlement. I can't really complain about the Great

British Settlement, since my family was a part of it. But I still enjoyed the rude gesture.

The third scene he wandered past was horrid and brutish, a convict being whipped at the triangle. Our friend shook his head in sad wonderment. He stuck his tongue out and turned round to give us that grin and point at the following group — explorers crossing the Blue Mountains.

He trudged along as he did all this, moving from one scene to the next, marking the seconds on the big clock. The next place he passed was the tableau representing the stolen children. The whole clock started weeping, and our friend looked to us, his face wrung with tears. All the sorrow of all those bereft families emerged in that one moment. Zoë started whimpering and so we moved her along to the next attraction. It was not supposed to be an unhappy morning.

I held her hand and marched her to the bridal cart. This was Nick's first piece of magic. This was the moment of truth. Nick's voice was steady. Zoë stopped fretting as she listened to her brother with the ear of the expert. Every time he paused you could see her mouthing the words, helping him along.

He'd decided on a dream from his childhood. He wanted the attendant and bride to tell stories to him and to Zoë. And so they did. The attendant left the cart and knelt down so he could look Zoë in the eyes, and he entertained her with a fairy story.

I was half listening to that and the other half of me was listening to Nick flirt with the beautiful maiden in the cart. No fairy stories. They exchanged solutions for computer games. It was one of those very rare and special moments, nearly spoiled by me biting my hand to stop laughing.

Next, since this was the Queen Victoria Building and the hour was about to strike, was the old clock. It was Zoë's turn. She wanted the figures to come to life the same way as the Indigenous bloke, but she refused to tell us any details. Nick and I exchanged long, worried looks as we watched the little one mutter her spells. I swear I heard her cackle somewhere in her incantation. My child the carrot-faced, blonde-haired witch.

Elizabeth I lopped off Drake's head, then marched boldly into Charles I's scene and lopped off his head as well. Henry VIII was tickled into submission by his various spouses, and ink splattered the glass enclosing the scene when King John lost his temper, refused to sign the Magna Carta, and threw the inkwell at us.

Those were our individual spells.

The group spell was rather rushed, as the clock's music had attracted some attention. I had to do my bit of muttering very quickly so that we could have the satisfaction of seeing the various elements of the Crown Jewels lose all their fur. We then beat a very hasty retreat. Very, very hasty.

Over our morning milkshakes and coffee, I made a mental note to thank God fasting that we had put limits on the magic, and that everything would've returned to normal as soon as we were on the staircase. It was a shame. We'd caused such a glorious havoc.

We turned home for our Jewish Christmas pudding. The truth is, we had made it and moistened it with brandy, and then completely forgotten about it.

So we were all looking forward to a pudding lunch, and Zoë was trying to talk me into letting her put extra brandy on hers as we walked our shopping to the back gate.

3.

Rhonda regretted not having toughed it out. TVwhore must've been hanging out in that particular chat room. She should go online and fix it up. She should. She didn't want to. But she should. Her mind went round and round and round in useless little circles.

It was precisely seventeen minutes before Rhonda opened the door to Dave, who just stood there and said, "Em forty four fucking Em. I have been looking for you for two fucking years."

"If I faint, will it help?" Rhonda didn't know what else to say.

Dave strode in, dominating the room. "You are Revelator," he stated, leaving no room for argument.

"How could I be? I'm me." He swivelled and faced her. "Stop doing that," she complained. "It's intimidating."

"Damn right it's intimidating. You need to be intimidated to all hell, girl."

"I'm not a girl. I'm an adult." Why was she stuck on saying the obvious, Rhonda wondered. Why was it so hard to deal with the situation? Maybe because the situation was so impossibly impossible?

Dave glowered.

Rhonda gave up and made coffee.

Patently she was busted. How much of Rhonda would remain after Dave the journalist exposed her; that was the question. She was his big story and he had come across the world to get it. She doubted he would let her privacy get in the way. Rhonda wondered if arsenic in the coffee would solve anything. Dave must have seen the look on her face because he asked, "What was that face for?"

"I was wondering if putting arsenic in your coffee

would solve anything. But I haven't got any arsenic, so the question is moot."

"I think I might make the coffee," and Dave gently shouldered her out of the way.

Rhonda could do nothing except wait and get more and more nervous. Dave had hated it when he had sniffed out secrets before, and this was the secret to end all secrets.

The doorbell rang. Rhonda answered it with a kind of relief. Her execution was going to be delayed. At her front door was a long slender girl, not more than twenty. Very pretty, in a very pale and Gothic way.

"Can I help you?" Rhonda asked, politely.

"Um, yes. I think so. I'm Barbara." The accent was British and the voice familiar.

"Yes?" Rhonda made it very clear she wasn't trying to be impolite, but that she had no idea who Barbara was and why she was standing at her door. Rhonda was very impressed with how much information could be encoded into a single syllable. Even if she did half-recognise the voice.

"TVwhore?" Barbara said, tentatively. "I had to come."

"You're TVwhore," Rhonda was astonished. "I imagined you all big and strapping and acerbic-looking and about ten years older. Come in."

She came. Very elegantly, too, Rhonda noticed, but diffidently, like a shadow.

"I thought you were in the UK," Rhonda said, to fill in the empty space. "If I'd known you were a local, I would've met you for coffee." Then she damned herself for an idiot. The phone call she had made the other day was to the UK.

"I . . . I . . ." TVwhore's diffidence faded her right into the floor.

"Come and sit down. Dave is just making coffee." At least, she hoped he was making coffee.

"I'm here," and Dave appeared, looking big and genial, and held out his hand for a shake. Where had he found that geniality?

"Dave?" Barbara looked entirely bewildered.

"The boyfiend, remember?" and Dave smiled as if he and Rhonda were united on all things. Under the circumstances, she felt justified in being bewildered. She hid behind pouring coffee and let Mr Geniality make polite conversation and find out what the hell TVwhore was doing in her lounge room. After all, Dave was the bloody detective. Or journalist. Or whatever.

Barbara looked from one to the other in bewilderment.

"TVwhore, I mean, Barbara, what's wrong?"

"I came because I thought . . ."

"You thought I was a pretence," Dave's voice was soft, but his eyes were focussed and tough. "You thought Rhonda was trying to run from you because she was scared of her own sexuality."

"Oh no," said Rhonda to Dave, "Don't be silly." Both Dave and TVwhore looked across at her, in silence. "Dammit." Dave looked faintly amused. "Barbara, you really thought I invented Dave? And you really thought I was gay?"

"It was all those jokes about being in denial. And you never talked about anyone close to you until I started to show I was interested. Even your husband faded after those early conversations — either he had gone from your life or he never existed. Then suddenly you had a boyfriend and the timing was too clever. So I thought I would come here and prove that you didn't have to be scared." All these words came out in a rush.

Rhonda looked across at Dave, accusingly. "Don't laugh. Don't even think of laughing."

He opened his hands and held them out, and he kept his face sober. "I wouldn't dream of it, honey."

"Why did you think I was gay?" she asked. "I mean, what signals did I give? They weren't intentional, I can assure you."

"And I can assure you that she's with me." Dave leaned forward, making it very clear. "I'm real."

Rhonda looked across at him in surprise. Somehow, she had thought he might disown her. But no, there he was, leaning forward and looking more possessive than anyone had a right to look. And she found herself smiling in his direction. Even though she knew, by the way his hand was gripping her shoulder, that this was a story they were telling TVwhore.

"You acted as if you had secrets. And you never talked about your love life until I showed an interest."

"She didn't know you were interested," Dave said softly.

"Dave said you were, but I didn't believe him. I thought you were lonely."

TVwhore laughed. It was a very tinny laugh. "I'm alone by choice. Then I met you."

"Oh, God." Rhonda pulled her hands through her hair. "What a mess. I didn't mean to lead you on. And I certainly didn't intend for you to come all the way to Australia to discover I wasn't leading you on. Why didn't you just ask?"

"Because you would've run away if she'd asked," Dave said, still soft and still intent.

"How did you manage it?" TVwhore was asking Dave. "She runs from everything — why didn't she run from you?"

Dave's stillness rippled through the room, bringing silence with it. Finally, he broke the silence. "She couldn't run from me," he said reluctantly, "I didn't give

her a chance. And she isn't going to run from me now."
There was a finality about that statement.

"So that's it then."

Rhonda felt helpless about TVwhore, but she also found herself moving close to Dave. The story had to be completed, otherwise this young girl was going to hurt even more.

"I don't know what to do about you, TVwhore. You came all this way. And I don't think you want to hear that I just wanted to be friends."

"You were so lonely," TVwhore sounded accusing.

"Well, sure I was. I was alone and miserable and had made a total mess of my life. And then I met Dave and I wasn't lonely or miserable anymore, but you and Phased and Starchild are my friends. I don't believe in losing my friends, just because I fall in love." Dave looked across at her steadily, giving nothing away.

"I thought I was more than a friend."

"I'm beginning to realise this." Rhonda couldn't stop the irony in her voice. TVwhore was so very central to her own universe. Such a child. And the question followed the thought, as sure as night follows day, "Just how old are you?"

"Seventeen."

"You mean I've known you since you were, what, fourteen?"

"Yes."

"I never knew. I'm thirty-five. I didn't realise that the worlds we lived in were so very different."

"Nor did I."

Rhonda looked and saw the sulk beginning to fade. "When did you come out?"

"When I was fourteen."

"Oh hell," said Dave.

"That was brave," said Rhonda.

"Don't condescend."

"I could swear your lip curled then," Rhonda said admiringly.

And TVwhore giggled. Suddenly she looked her age. Suddenly she looked as if life wouldn't blow her away.

"I'm not giving up Dave for you, you know," Rhonda added, just to make things clear. Dave's arm snaked round her and tightened possessively. God, he was a good actor. "But that's because I don't want to give up Dave for anyone."

"But I love you," and TVwhore's face had that almost despairing look.

"You love the computer-version of me," Rhonda said. "Someone once said to me that I have many voices. You don't know most of them. And you don't know most of me. I'm old enough to be your mother. And I love Dave. That's three big reasons for us just to be friends."

"I don't know if I want to be friends."

"For me, friendship comes first. For me, I made sure I was friends with Dave before I let him too far into my life. He didn't know my secrets until I trusted him completely and utterly. I didn't do that with my ex-husband. I fell in love with him and thought that friendship wasn't important. We only became friends after we divorced. And he's not speaking to me at all at the moment. Damn. Sorry, both of you. This has been too much for me. The last few days have had about a life's-worth of emotions."

"Tony isn't talking to you?" Dave sounded perturbed.

Rhonda shook her head. "And not letting the kids see me either. But Lana says he is getting counselling about the alcohol."

"I suppose that's something," and Dave's tone was acerbic. He turned his face back to TVwhore. "Look, I understand your problem. I'm sorry you came all this way. All I can do is suggest you take advantage of being in Oz and have a holiday. I'm happy to help you out financially, or find folks you can stay with, but if you stay here, then Rhonda will hurt. And I don't accept Rhonda being hurt."

Rhonda took a deep breath. She wished she could take that last statement as the truth. She also hoped TVwhore would take Dave's advice, but it didn't matter. What mattered was getting through the mess. Then . . . nothing. Maybe there was nothing left. But she had to get through the mess. Helping her friend through.

"MissTRie?" TVwhore's voice was small.

"I'm sorry, Barbara, but Dave's right. I can't even imagine how it must have felt to come all the way here and find this out. But it's not going to go away or get better if we spend time together. All it will do is make both of us unhappy. If you take a holiday, then you'll at least save face with friends back home."

"I don't want blood money."

"If you don't want Dave to help you take a holiday, then don't let him. That's your choice. But it's my choice not to complicate your life unduly."

"I don't have anywhere to stay," and TVwhore's voice was a whisper.

Rhonda couldn't believe how vulnerable her acid-tongue friend was. And then she found she could believe it. Such a young lady to have such big emotions. And Rhonda sighed. "My cousin Belinda just got back from Melbourne. She's got a spare room. We could ask her."

Dave whipped out his trusty mobile phone and dialled.

"He's up to phoning a friend," joked Rhonda. Barbara just sat, silent as smog.

"Hi, this is Dave. Rhonda's friend, Dave. Your new

cousin, Rhonda?" Both the women sat and listened as Dave explained that he had a young girl from the UK who had landed on his girlfriend's doorstep and needed a hand. "Done," he said to Barbara. "You can stay with Belinda as long as you want, and she'll make sure you get where you want to go afterwards. The only thing I'm asking is that you email Rhonda when you get home, because she'll worry."

"I don't care if she worries. This whole thing is humiliating."

"You should've thought of that before you landed on her doorstep," and Dave stood up, picked her bag up and walked out the door with it, not even looking to see if he was being followed. His whole posture suggested he was holding a vast anger in, tightly.

He would let that anger loose when he returned. Rhonda knew this. She didn't know what it would mean. She didn't want to know. She wanted to reel back her life an hour and then stop it dead at that point, when she was still happy. When she still had a future.

"Take care, TVwhore, please?"

TVwhore looked undecided, as if she had no idea if she should stay and win her woman, or follow Dave to dubious safety. In the end she just walked out the door.

Rhonda closed the front door then went back to the couch. It was still warm from Dave, so she curled up where he had sat, and then she cried herself to sleep.

When she woke up, it was to the tap-tap of a keyboard. She uncurled and wandered over to her computer to investigate. Her mind was not in a state where she could comprehend what was happening.

"Are you all right, hon?" asked Dave, his eyes fixed on the screen.

"As okay as anyone can be, after a day straight from melodrama. Is Barbara okay?"

"Sure she is." Dave sounded as if he meant it, "She

was fifty per cent putting on an act. My daughter did it at the same age."

"Your daughter?"

"Hey, I have secrets too. By the time we had driven two miles, that child was chatting to me as if we were best friends."

"It was just me she was shy of, then?"

"Sorry, hon."

Rhonda listened. She heard the 'hon' and looked at Dave's body language and she felt the warmth from a small spark of hope. She couldn't let it catch fire. She couldn't handle more false happiness. "And the rest of it?" she asked.

"What do you mean?"

"Are you going to write an exposé and tell my secrets to the world?" Rhonda could hear the dullness in her voice.

"Don't be stupid."

"Why is it stupid? I mean, you're a journalist. This is your big story. And I'm getting in the way of it."

Dave looked across at her and he smiled, cautiously. "I had time to think, while you were asleep." He reached out and pulled her onto his lap. He swivelled them both round to look at the screen. On the screen was a chat room. Dave was signed in as M44M. His last few words had been, "And that's the truth of it. I'm sorry to have led you all astray, but I'm a journalist writing an article about reactions to the Revelator."

"Oh," said Rhonda.

"I'm going to write that article, too."

"And then what?"

"And then what?" he laughed. "Dammit, Rhonda, I have the Revelator in my arms. I'm going to torture you until you promise you will give me every word of every damn prophecy you make. My paper is going to worship the ground I tread on. And I'm going to protect my sources."

"You're going to protect your sources." Rhonda said this reverently.

"Damn right. I always protect my sources. Now quit distracting me, woman, I have some more protecting of sources to do."

Rhonda watched and helped as he methodically went to every place she'd been during the last year, and logged on using her aliases, and admitting to being a fraud.

"But what about the Revelator?"

"I'm a damn good journalist, you know," he typed.

"Part of the gift-thing I have is that I have to announce things in public fora, you know," Rhonda whispered shyly.

"Is that so?" asked Dave, and typed an addendum to his comment:

"Don't think I'll give up posting the fruits of my labour here. I like the reactions. I'm going to write regular articles as well. Consider yourselves in the know — you get the surprise first and the interpretation after."

"So it was just a publicity stunt," someone said.

"Sure it was. And didn't it make all the spooks go bananas?"

When he logged off, Dave said, "I don't want to go home tonight."

"I don't see why you should go home tonight."

He smiled lazily. "I have to write an article before anything else."

"An article?"

"The one I just talked about online."

"For real?'

"For real. I'm going to cover for you, and you're going to let me use the information you find."

"I don't know where it comes from," confessed Rhonda. "It's like automatic writing. I read things back afterwards and it seems all new."

"Is it just you, or can anyone else in your family do this?"

"Maybe others. One of my great-uncles committed suicide. I don't know about the new branch. I'm scared of asking."

"So that's why you're so alone."

"That's why." Rhonda said it as defiantly as she could.

"Oh, hon," Dave said, and gathered her in his arms. "Shame your information can't be sourced," he said after a while. "I'll have to find a way of proving it. One piece at a time. It'll be a challenge."

"How can you even believe all this?" She had spent all her life fighting, it just didn't seem right that Dave could give her a hug and say it was all fine and boy, what a useful talent his girlfriend had.

"I've seen you prove yourself too often to disbelieve," Dave replied quietly. "At first it looked . . . not credible. That's why I started to investigate. It was a great story, I thought, revealing the truth behind the greatest faker of all.

"The thing is," and Dave's logic was remorseless, "Now that I've thought it through, I want to be there for you. I can't believe how alone you've been for so long, honey. Your ex is a fine man when he is sober, but the water was too hot for him."

The next day, things looked less clear. For one thing, she was alone again. Dave had an interview to do and a meeting to attend. He wouldn't be back until after midnight. She'd sworn faithfully to stay awake for him. He'd sworn faithfully he would bring chocolate mud cake. All should have been perfect.

Except Rhonda felt caged. For the first time since

forever, she'd been honest with someone. There were no lies creating a secret chasm between her and Dave. He knew her secrets. And she felt caged. How stupid was she? The man she loved understood her, and she instantly wanted a bit of space? She sighed. Then she laughed. This was as good as it got. And gilded cages were the best variety.

Rhonda walked restlessly round the bookshelves, looking for something to read. It was one of those nights where anchors and reading and letting the brain work a little all sounded very, very good. Her gaze rested on a battered volume of Shakespeare. The complete works. Very nice. Except . . .

Rhonda took it from the shelf and pretended to read Hamlet. Her favourite play. She wasn't reading, though. Tear after tear fell onto the open page.

She had discovered an awful truth about herself. She could solve her own life. She could live with her own talent. She'd sorted out one of her inheritances and found some happiness. Her own happiness.

Auntie Jane was still silent in an asylum. There was no simple solution for her because Rhonda had found out a terrible truth. She had inherited that other part of her family culture: she found she couldn't face the thought of helping her aunt. She found that taking care of herself was the most she could do.

Rhonda found herself looking for a pen and paper. She found herself writing a letter. At least she had come through this, she thought savagely; at least she could see what her secret self was telling her normal self.

Dear My Self,

It is too late to help your aunt. She will die tomorrow at 3.07 p.m.. Grieve for her. Grieve for our family. Then face reality.

Sam's teenage daughter will need a great deal of help very, very soon. Sam will ring you three days before Christmas. Make up the spare bed. Christmas presents would help. I have written a wish list over the page.

Love,
Your other self.

Rhonda watched as her right hand flipped the paper over and started writing teenage Christmas dreams. Whatever her future held, it appeared it would not be boring. And if she ever felt alone, she could write notes to her Other Self.

Rhonda laughed and started calculating where she was going to get money for her niece's presents. Temp work over the holiday period, perhaps, since writing brought in too little too late. She watched in fascination as her Other Self took up a second piece of paper and wrote down a list of women who would testify against Mr Ick in court. Names, phone numbers and what he'd done to each of them.

No, her life was not going to be boring.

She wondered if Dave liked covering minor court cases. She wondered if he could deal with distressed teenagers. She guessed she'd find out soon. Very soon.

JUDITH'S EPILOGUE

I FOUND A PARCEL IN THE LETTERBOX. I DIDN'T WANT TO
wait to open it, since parcels and packages had been
very strange this last year. It was gourmet chocolate,
from Rudolph, with a note saying, "Counting down the
months." I quickly stuffed it into my bag.

There was a commotion just inside the gate.

'Twiddles!" cried Zoë, joyously. She dumped her
backpack and wrapped her arms around a solid white
neck. "I brought you lots of carrots."

"Twiddles?" Nick asked, sceptically. I stood there
and stared.

Twiddles was about the size of a Shetland pony. He
had a very nice horn in the middle of his forehead. I
looked. His feet were fully cloven. If we took him to a
kosher butcher to get him killed, we could eat him for
dinner, I thought, irrelevantly.

"I called him," Zoë boasted proudly to her brother.

Twiddles just stood squarely in our backyard and
waited for a carrot. A very placid, dull kind of a unicorn. His presence explained why neither of my children had turned bright orange by eating so very many
carrots. And maybe not all the devastation in the yard
had been by the weirdo who hated our lemon tree.

Maybe some of it was the charming churning from the hooves of one miniature bloody unicorn called Twiddles.

Then it registered. Zoë had called him. My daughter had done a spell and had not so much as asked me if she might. It may have been before our little heart-to-heart, but she'd done the spell. Called a bloody mythical beast from Great-Grandma's bloody bestiary into our garden. My garden. Without permission.

"Zoë," I said, ominously. "Unwrap your arms from around that creature's neck. We need to talk. NOW."

Dear reader,

We hope you enjoyed reading *The Wizardry of Jewish Women*. Please take a moment to leave a review, even if it's a short one. Your opinion is important to us.

Discover more books by Gillian Polack at https://www.nextchapter.pub/authors/gillian-polack

Want to know when one of our books is free or discounted? Join the newsletter at http://eepurl.com/bqqB3H

Best regards,

Gillian Polack and the Next Chapter Team

ACKNOWLEDGMENTS

Satalyte Publishing first released this work in Australia in 2016. Thanks to Stephen Ormsby, Marieke Ormsby and the rest of the team for all their work and support.

The second edition was through the amazing people from Book View Café. Special thanks to Judith Tarr, Vonda N. McIntyre, Maya Kaathryn Bohnhoff, Chaz Brenchley, Deborah Ross and Marissa Doyle.

This novel was written very companionably over quite a long period of time. My family helped ensure the background was realistic, talking and walking me through things ranging from floor layouts for various houses to the cemeteries in Ballarat. My cousin Anna and my mother Sonya were especially wonderful, with my stepfather Les, my sister Suzie and her daughters Miriam and Johanna giving a hand. Eliya Cohen helped me understand pre-teen girls, and Fiona Formiatti gave me much-needed moral support. Domestic violence expert Anne Morris checked my draft to make sure that I was not seriously off about the subject (luckily for me) I knew least about, and Jewish Studies expert Jennifer Dowling made sure I didn't lead readers too far astray on the magic side. Tamara Mazzei was always there for me as a friend.

When I faltered, some new friends appeared. The Canberra Speculative Fiction Guild did their share of reading. Of them Elizabeth Fitzpatrick, Donna Maree Hanson, Trevor Stafford and Stu Barrow deserve special thanks for this novel. Jen Mason advised on some critical subjects and made a vast difference to my plot choices.

Elizabeth Chadwick and Wendy Zollo gave me tons of email support — especially with swapping word counts and maintaining sanity. Milena Benini checked the near-final draft, when I had married the strands together, and offered some wonderful insights into what could be done better. Several of my students donated their experiences of the Canberra bushfires to enrich Belinda's journey through them.

Special thanks to Emma Pallett, Spinster, whose scrapbook I own. She inspired the scrapbook in the novel and I used her poem (in her handwriting, though I don't know if she was the author) and some of her jokes. Despite the poem, she's not Ada, nor anything like Ada.

You need to know two more things.

First, most of the external events in the book actually happened (despite my warped time-lines), even though the characters in the book are entirely fictitious. We all still live with the legacies of fire and hate.

Second, readers often come to me and say, "You are this character." I'm not. I'm especially not Rhonda. A couple of Judith's life experiences, however, are drawn from mine. None of my beta-readers and friends have successfully guessed which unless they were actually involved in those experiences. Consider the whole novel fiction, therefore. Because it is. If I were all the characters that readers tell me I am, I would need psychiatric help.

ABOUT THE AUTHOR

Gillian Polack is an award-winning Australian novelist, editor and historian. Her hobbies include reading, cooking and making bad jokes.

The Wizardry Of Jewish Women
ISBN: 978-4-86745-620-0
Mass Market

Published by
Next Chapter
1-60-20 Minami-Otsuka
170-0005 Toshima-Ku, Tokyo
+818035793528

30th April 2021